For Faith

part one

MASHA (*she takes off her hat*): I'm staying to lunch.

(Tchekov, *The Three Sisters*, Act I)

chapter 1

It was not usual on a dark Monday morning in January for the approaches of St Mark's Church, Kennington, to witness so much bustle and excitement. From about nine-fifteen onwards, at diminishing intervals, first a trickle then a flow of people arrived. They came by car, by bus, on foot from the tube station. One intrepid spirit turned up on her bicycle, in spite of the brisk wind and heavy skies.

The earlier batches disappeared at once into the low building beside the church; those who came later seemed in less of a hurry. The manner of their greeting ranged from warm – embraces, hugs, cries of delighted recognition – to reserved, with enthusiastic handshakes upon more formal presentation. They made up little shifting groups and hung about in the open air, talking excitedly, until at last the icy temperature caused even the most fervent chatterers to come to their senses and retreat indoors.

On the other side of the road a 159 bus set down two passengers. The first, a man in a dark blue donkey jacket, strode off at once towards a small parade of shops, while the second, a young woman in a long woollen coat and muffler, stepped quickly back from the kerb to avoid the spray of dirt thrown up as the bus shuddered away towards Brixton.

Another bus. Another beginning. Bella Provan stared across the road to where St Mark's loomed up, a large, ugly pile with a blackened steeple, and a more modest construction squatting at its feet. Another church hall – though this one looked quite modern, less dispiriting than most.

As Bella watched, the last stragglers of the group in the forecourt filed through the door of the church hall, leaving the scene bereft. The traffic too had melted away and for a moment even the road lacked animation. A few thick flakes of snow floated into the air and landed on an eyelash and a cheek, and on to her mass of blonde hair. She stopped where she was and looked up, dropped her head back and stuck out her tongue to catch more. Then she straightened up. Not much point in putting things off. Her destination lay before her. Having no further use for the little folding umbrella clutched in her hand, she thrust it into her basket and crossed the road.

A large sign had been taped inside the glass door of the church hall, crayonned in elaborate blue lettering:

THE NEW COMPANY
UNCLE VANYA
WELCOME!

Before Bella reached the door she heard someone calling her name. She turned round.

'Miss Provan?'

Bella had seen only the retreating back of the man in the donkey jacket, as he preceded her off the bus. She recognized him now that he stood in front of her, and it gave her a small, unaccountable shock to find herself face to face with him. He held out his hand.

'Donald Ballader. I'm so sorry there hasn't been time for us to meet properly before this.'

'Oh. Well. That's my fault. I'm sorry for taking so long to make up my mind . . .'

He waved her attempted apology aside. 'Just as long as you're here, that's what matters. Yelena is an impossibly difficult part. I think you were born to play her. We couldn't think of anyone else, frankly.'

'This must be a big day for you.' Bella in her turn cut him short, in a mixture of awkwardness and impatience.

Smiling, he shook his head. 'I am simply beside myself. I think I may just pop,' he laughed. 'Terrified, but thrilled to the core!' He tapped his pocket. 'Haven't smoked for two months and I've just been to buy myself a packet of fags.'

Bella shivered in the cold and at once he reached across to open the door of the hall. 'I just wanted to say that I'm overjoyed that you're with us. Thank you.'

There could be no doubting the sincerity of his welcome. Bella murmured something suitably gracious in return but, unable to match his sincerity or his warmth, turned her head away as she passed in front of him, and did not meet his eye.

The room they entered presented a friendly, even cheerful aspect – a change from the usual run of dusty, run-down rehearsal spaces hired out to acting companies. There was a polished wood floor, and a red-curtained stage at the far end; above, a band of windows set high up along the length of two sides of the room allowed a surprising amount of light to fall on the throng gathering below. Someone claimed Donald's attention as he came through the door, and other arrivals forced Bella to move further into the hall.

Panic clutched her for a moment – more than the usual first-day butterflies.

Eighteen months ago, at short notice – practically overnight, in fact – she had joined the Royal Theatre Company, a company so illustrious and so well-provided that it luxuriated in rehearsal rooms of its very own; but these were austere, giant spaces, with towering walls of black-painted breeze-blocks that dwarfed any collection of human beings. Then, Bella had walked into a room filled with strangers, whereas more than a dozen of those here today she had worked closely with, at the Royal, for over a year. But then all her hopes (and her idiot heart) had been high and, she reflected, her naïvety great. At least she had wanted to be there. Now, she no longer cared much where she was.

Someone waved at her and blew a kiss from across the room. She smiled and waved back, forcing herself to move, keeping the smile up as she hurried across to the side of the hall to deposit her coat. She changed her boots for some softer shoes, and was pulling a foolscap envelope out of her basket when someone touched her lightly on the back. As she stood up a big man with a thick dark beard grasped both her hands in his. This was the director, Victor Todmorden, one of the New Company's three founders, with Ted Danniman and Donald Ballader. He had taken her to lunch the previous day.

He kept hold of her hands, bowing over slightly in his eagerness. Then he let go, to put an arm lightly round her shoulder. 'Who don't you know? Ah! Come and meet Hilary, our stage manager – the power behind the thrones.'

Bella allowed herself to be led forward into the hall, supplied with a mug of coffee, reunited with friends and introduced to strangers – a multitude of actors, stage staff, administrators and publicists, whose names fled from her memory almost as soon as they were uttered. She smiled and played her part, trying to respond in kind to the friendliness and affection she met at every turn; but it was a relief when, after about fifteen minutes, people began to move towards the three long trestle tables that had been set up in the middle of the room.

She felt relieved, too, to find herself seated between Nancy Bailey and Dolly Caesar, both former Royal Theatre colleagues. Eighty-year-old Dolly, Dublin-born, had been one of the outstanding actresses of her day, a noted Hedda; she was playing the old nurse. Nancy was playing Sonya, so they would have several scenes together. In Bella's first weeks at the Royal she had been one of the first to befriend her. Nancy had left the company six months ago to do a television series and they had not met since. Bella wondered how much Nancy knew.

'This is a bit different, isn't it?' Nancy remarked, surveying the table; and indeed the occasion bore no resemblance to any first read-through that Bella had ever attended. Even the hush that fell as Ted Danniman, the administrator, rose to speak, did not diminish the sense of elation and anticipation that gripped the room. This was no ordinary read-through. The gathering today embodied years of dreaming and months of planning, negotiating, cajoling, fighting. Today, as everyone present knew, was the first day of the first rehearsals of the first play of the first season of a dazzling new theatre company: the New, Donald Ballader's brainchild. His shockingly simple notion was to form a repertoire company where actors would have as much of a say as directors – combining the repertory system with the old actor-manager style.

Early promises that speech-making would be kept to a minimum quickly fell apart, as speaker after speaker rose to express their exhilaration at having got so far. Though her own involvement in the venture had been tardy and less than wholehearted, little by little, in spite of herself, the good humour, the triumphant hope, the sheer happiness that filled the room could not help but seize Bella.

By the time Donald got to his feet, to hearty cheers and clapping, she found that she too was smiling and applauding. Around her, the company at the table relaxed visibly, leaning back in their chairs and smiling more broadly, stretching their legs out underneath the table.

Donald took his time, looking around slowly, registering each separate presence as if he were savouring a rare delicacy. When he reached Nancy, Bella found herself dropping her eyes as if to forego her turn. Several minutes passed before she looked up again. He had folded his arms by this time and stood considering the entire group.

'What a wonderful sight,' he said at last, 'each and every one of you. I can't tell you how grateful I am to you all for being here.'

He spoke for some time, offering tribute and thanks, it seemed, to almost every individual in the room; reporting on the refurbishment of the theatre off Charlotte Street that was to be the company's home, and outlining the artistic plan. The idea was to start out on the safer side with one or two old favourites and a few better-known contemporary plays and then strike out down less charted paths, find new writers, perhaps rediscover one or two lost and abandoned ones.

Bella, observing Donald, could not deny that he was an attractive figure, though it was hard to define why, or to explain at a glance the wearisome lady-slaying legend that had attached itself to him. No single arresting feature distinguished his face, except perhaps his eyes, which were blue and at this moment full of humour. His light brown hair, cut in what Bella always thought of as schoolboy style, with a side-parting, had a tendency to fall across his eyes. He was fairly tall and of medium build, dressed in dark blue corduroys and a dark blue, hand-knitted Guernsey polo neck. She saw, when he raised his hand to push his hair out of the way, that one sleeve had started to unravel.

What he did generate, even when, as at this moment, he took a long pause, was the quality that distinguished him on stage: an electric clarity that made other people seem almost out of focus.

'The great thing will be to get away once and for all from the ghastly hide-bound, director-bound, boring bureaucracy of certain places that shall be nameless! Let's at least give the old Royal a run for their money! And incidentally it's a huge thrill to see here so many faces from the old barn.' He nodded towards Dolly Caesar. 'Dear Dolly, we're grateful especially to have you with us . . . Most of you I've worked with, some I haven't,' he said, looking at Bella and one or two of the younger actors. He paused and said more quietly, 'How tremendous, to be getting down to the work at last, after so much planning and anticipating . . .' And here he suddenly interrupted himself, throwing back his head and shouting, 'AT LAST!' He paused again, then said, 'Victor?' and sat down.

Victor, with a broad grin, looked up without rising to his feet, and invited everyone around the table to say who they were. That done, he added simply: 'You'll all be hearing more than enough from me over the next four weeks. So let's read.' As they opened their scripts someone pointed at the windows and said: 'Look – Dr Tchekov's blessing.'

Outside, the thick white flakes had multiplied and were whirling and dancing in the wind. The read-through began in a mood of holiday intoxication. By the time they left that evening, the snow lay an inch thick on the ground.

chapter 2

From the first day of rehearsals Bella's bleak mood eased and, as the days went on, began to lift. Her curiosity revived, and with it her appetite for work. Relief overwhelmed her. She had forgotten that it was possible to look forward to rehearsals. Was it the simple fact of having made a decision and removed herself from a source of hurt? The hurt was not gone, but gradually it ceased to be an incessant exhausting bludgeoning. Was it the work, the change of scene and rhythm, the yielding atmosphere; the feeling of being in at the beginning? Every member of the company experienced the powerful charm of total commitment. They were all in it together. It was up to them.

As well as Dolly and Nancy, there were others of the company whom Bella knew from her time at the Royal; but she had never worked with this director. Victor's tall form towered over everyone, clad, whatever the weather, in a dark shirt and leather waistcoat. From the very beginning a concentrated but breathable atmosphere prevailed, centred round Victor's calm presence.

As for Donald Ballader, Bella decided that in all fairness she must reserve her judgement: it is almost impossible to meet with an open mind someone about whom so many tales are told. Though Donald had been gone a month at least when she had joined the Royal, neither he nor his rakish habits had been forgotten. For a start, he had caused consternation by leaving the Royal when his contract came to an end. He was playing

Vershinin in *The Three Sisters* and the production was such a hit that the management extended the run. Their astonishment knew no bounds when Donald refused to renew, announcing simply that he'd had enough of kow-towing to their whims and fancies. It was time to keep faith with himself, he said. Long after Donald had gone, this revolutionary act, and his dream of starting a company for actors, formed the chief topic of conversation at the Royal; but so did talk of his life, his loves and his marriage. For Donald's departure had precipitated a further crisis.

After only a few weeks little Amy Dee, who was playing Masha (and with whom Donald was having one of his famous flings), found she couldn't bear his being gone and upped and followed him. The embattled Royal, left Masha-less, had hastily called in Bella Provan; at which point Claire Ballader, Donald's long-suffering wife, who had been understudying Masha, finding herself doubly passed over, had taken double leave – of her husband and of the Royal, both. Bella had come to perceive that one way or another, however indirectly, it was to Donald Ballader and his indiscretions that she owed her job with the Royal. Added to the many awkwardnesses of taking over a part and trying to blend in with an established team, it was a perception she had found curiously uncongenial. The reigning artistic director of the Royal, who had acted with more haste than tact in his lightning recruitment of Bella, did not lack shrewdness or an eye for what would serve his company well. He had thought to counteract the negative with the positive – to offset dubious publicity with something that offered bloom and appeal – and his prompt action had saved the day; but the saloon-door comings and goings at the Royal could not help but present an unedifying spectacle.

On the first day of the *Vanya* rehearsals, the New Company had laid on a buffet lunch by way of celebration, but after that most of the company had taken their midday break in the nearest pub, the Stag at Bay. Bella, preferring to be on her own and quiet for an hour, had confessed that she was not mad about pubs and found a small café nearby; but today, the last day of the first week of rehearsals, she felt like being with the others, and Dolly easily persuaded her. Dolly's particular affection for Bella dated back to those first days at the Royal, when Bella was being rehearsed into *The Three Sisters*. One afternoon, exasperated, Bella had rounded on the young assistant director and berated him for not showing Dolly a proper respect, and ever since that day Dolly had dubbed her her 'saviour'. At the drop of a hat she would relate to all and sundry how Bella's castigations had 'reduced the little squirt to smithereens'.

Though Dolly and others had assured Bella that the Stag was usually half-empty, they had broken late for lunch and today the place was noisy, smoky and full to bursting, everything she most hated.

'Over here, Bella!'

Across the saloon bar, over the thicket of shuffling swaying bodies, she saw Dolly and Nancy signalling to her: they had grabbed a booth, just vacated, and, having caught her eye, had sunk abruptly from view. Bella held her plate and glass up in the air and started to thread a path through the crowd. At her halting passage the men who made way for her would stop talking, and as she progressed between them they would nudge one another, raising their eyebrows and pushing out their lower lip. 'Steady as you go, sweetheart!' Then they winked at each other and took reinforcing swills of beer.

'Here you are, my darling,' Dolly said, her pale watery eyes beaming up at Bella.

Nancy slid along the settle to make room as Bella set her tomato juice and a generous ploughman's platter on the table opposite Michael Brodie. Michael, who was playing Vanya, was an old friend and compatriot of Dolly's, a short, stockily built man with a cap of close-cut, white-blond hair and the face of an ageing cherub. Bella had taken to him at once.

'I've been hearing from these two about your horrible

beginnings at the Royal,' he said to Bella. 'This is a bit more like it, eh?'

Dolly answered for her, cutting off a piece of Stilton. 'I should say so! Now Victor's what I call a director – he's in there with you, not like that little runt of an assistant, sitting back with a sneer on his face, saying, "Show me"!'

'The dreaded Luke,' put in Nancy. 'He used to sigh a lot,' she explained to Michael. 'He seemed to think rehearsals were a waste of his time.'

Michael raised his eyebrows. 'I know the type!' He turned back to Bella. 'It does sound as if you were thrown in the deep end there,' he remarked. 'Did this Masha girl leave just like that, in mid-contract?'

'Yes, she did!' Dolly replied, not without admiration. 'Bold as you like. She didn't give a damn, my dear. She was far gone. Oh, she got a note from her doctor – "severe nervous strain . . ." I'll say!'

'What's happened to her, by the way?' Nancy asked. 'I'm completely out of touch.'

'Well – apparently the whole Donald thing is off already! Or so I heard. It didn't take long!'

Bella got up. 'I forgot to get a napkin. Does anyone want anything? Any more drinks?'

If they were going to start on one of their endless rounds of gossip she would leave them to it for a bit. She wondered sometimes whether she had some essential gene missing from her make-up. How else explain her aversion to the tittle-tattle that seemed to make up the very spice of life for most of the people she worked with? She had been enjoying the conversation up to now – putting the Royal experience firmly in the past, seeing the good and bad in it; but this kind of idle chat was her cue to quit the scene.

Bella's aversion to gossip had not prevented her from becoming herself an object of abiding curiosity among her peers at the Royal. As they prepared to receive her in their midst, speculation concerning Claire's usurper had become feverish.

The company radar had scanned every possible source without finding great reassurance. The interviews Bella gave to the press suggested an articulate presence, verging on the arrogant. She projected clarity and confidence to a degree that both unnerved and excited the journalists who encountered her: the thrilling paradox of a woman who possessed both strong views and lips that could be called kissable.

This latter description gave rise to a topic beloved of journalists: who were Bella's boyfriends, and where were they? It was scarcely credible, given the way she looked and having attained her late twenties, that Bella had no suitors, that she was not kissed and kissed a lot. None of their business, came her angry retort. (To judge by her interviews, Bella never failed to rise to this bait: she would sound off with engaging ferocity about the press's preoccupation with sex, and the way they always dwelt on the mating habits of her fellow professionals. She used words like 'mores' and 'prurience'. It was perfectly possible, she maintained, to be an actress and to be faithful and chaste, to be a good actress and a 'good' woman. Nobody believed her, but it provided splendid copy.)

An entire feature devoted to Bella in the March issue of *Vogue* magazine launched another career as well as advancing hers. The young photographer's black and white portrait was to become famous: the perfect oval face around which billowed a cloud of pale, unchecked hair; light, grave eyes fixing the lens with a candid stare, head tilted, full mouth – a little lop-sided – lips glistening slightly. ('Just moisten your lips for me, sweetheart, would you?' he had said. 'That's *beautiful* . . .')

The article that accompanied it had taken enchantment for its theme (and the enchantment of the writer with his subject blazed from the page). His descriptions of Bella were, in acting terms, over the top. As well as offering a dual incarnation of intelligence and sex appeal, she gloried in 'a warm, fragile beauty' and was presumed to be about to lead 'the charmed life of a fairy-tale princess'. No rags-to-riches stuff here, but dazzling cosmopolitan origins: father in the Diplomatic service, mother a

New England heiress, schools in Switzerland, holidays in embassies all over the world. 'But where was the prince?' Clearly the poor fellow's head had been turned, and it was not hard to see why.

Backstage at the Royal, the copy of *Vogue* circulated till it fell apart, providing the first seeds of information about Bella, which quickly swelled and sprouted, watered with rumour and nourished by gristy titbits from actors, or friends of actors who had known Bella Provan at drama school, or at Bristol or Birmingham, where she had been in rep after her first starring role in a BBC series. These casual reporters boasted a more down-to-earth style than that of the besotted journalist, and she emerged less a fairy-tale figure than a teething and slightly snotty student with a tendency to put people's backs up. She was not brilliant, one informant said, but a hard worker; and something of an enigma, too: was she standoffish or just dedicated? She had a reputation for being frightfully proper – much pursued but always out of reach (promised forth to some diplomat chap, so the story went).

To add to the charges of classiness and outspokenness there came the potent indictment that she was a 'difficult' actress.

'Oh, Lord – Heaven preserve us! Not another one!' Someone – most likely Aubrey Morris, bringing to bear the weight of his years and experience – pointed out that 'being difficult' might mean merely that she liked to get things right: that she had standards and was prepared to fight for them. (Like Bella, Aubrey Morris did not hold with gossip. If it could not be avoided he simply pretended he had not heard it, perhaps in the hope that it would avoid him.)

Into these eddying surges of speculation, antagonism, goodwill and, indeed, prurience, Bella Provan had been plunged.

During the initial breakneck rehearsals for *The Three Sisters*, Bella had been working too hard to take much else in. There were those in the company who did not successfully disguise their resentment that the management should have brought in an outsider just because she was a 'star' – or being tipped here and there, more and more frequently, for some sort of stardom; but for the most part she was welcomed; congratulated even, by Aubrey Morris, for standing up for Dolly. 'Fighting the good fight,' he had called it.

She was not, in theory, coming to the Royal as an understudy, but she quickly understood that if she wanted to play the part, rather than simply replicate the moves and moods of her predecessor, she must fend for herself. Her own intuitions about Masha fed on the work and already by the end of the third day it was more and more frustrating to find herself expected to mope or smoulder where she wanted to storm; to take things literally lying down – on a red plush chaise-longue that slanted across the centre of the stage – whereas her Masha would have paced out her frustrated rage. She had felt like an Ugly Sister trying to cram not just one foot but her whole being into an unyielding slipper; but she refused to let herself be put off. She kept her eyes fixed forward and dedicated herself to mastering the rudiments of the work, step by step. It had not taken her long to realize that she would not get much help from her reluctant director.

After crossing swords with him a few times and finding him both crass and condescending she had shut up and got on, and vowed to stay shut up; not to lose energy and concentration by fighting. Clearly her real work would have to be done once she was on stage, in front of an audience.

When at last *The Three Sisters* came back into the repertoire, Bella's angry, sardonic Masha had found favour with the critics but Bella had no time to bask in any kind of glory. On the following Monday she joined the cast of *The Changeling* for the start of rehearsals and settled at last into the same routines as her colleagues.

chapter 3

Bella found some paper napkins among the cutlery and condiments at the end of the Stag's long curved bar and moved round a little way to order Michael's 'other half' of Guinness. Across the room a group of men, just leaving, held the door to let others in and Bella saw Ted, Donald and Victor come in with the designer and the production manager – they had stayed behind for a snatched production meeting. Donald detached himself and approached the far side of the bar, while the others moved along into the other part of the L-shaped room. Seeing Bella, Donald made no move to join her but grinned and raised his hand in salute. She smiled back at him, nodded and looked away.

Surprised as she was at her own present – relative – contentment, it still struck her as one of life's barmy ironies that she should have ended up, after all, with the New Company. From the very first her resistance to the idea had been strong. When her agent, Bill Forster, had taken her to dinner one night after a performance of *Rosmersholm*, she had known that something was up. Bill's large eyes had seemed rounder than ever and he had stammered slightly – a sure sign that he had something of moment to impart. Bella, glass in hand, gave him her full attention. He announced with gravity that the New Company wanted her, very badly. 'Oh. Do they?' Bella had said and finished her wine.

At this time – about halfway through Bella's second season with the Royal – the ripples of anticipation that had attended every step of the forming of the New Company were beginning to swell to tidal proportions, and no doubt the flatness of her response had amazed him. She never ceased to amaze him, as he frequently told her. Bill was almost old enough to be her father. Bella had been with him since she left drama school and he expected great things of her; but sometimes, thinking of her, Bill sighed. It was not Bella's fault. She was ambitious enough, and she was impatient too; she wanted to work. The trouble was that she had had a charmed career, snapped up to star in a big classic serial almost before she had got her diploma; and she had not stopped working since. Charmed. She had no idea. He wondered to himself how it would have been if she had had to wait more or fight more, settle sometimes for less as, over seventeen years as an agent, he had seen so many have to do.

He outlined the New Company's proposition as forcefully as he could. He was prepared for counter-arguments – Bella was not one to go leaping after glamorous packages – and, as if not to disappoint him, she had pointed out at once that she was still a relative newcomer to the Royal.

'It seems a bit flighty, Bill. Not to say disloyal. It feels as if I've hardly been there two minutes.'

Bill saw this as a plus. She had got them out of a hole, remember; she didn't owe them anything. Still she protested. He seemed to be urging her into fickleness, to change for change's sake.

Bill redoubled his efforts, warming to his theme. Her impact at the Royal had been fantastic, and the Royal had been good for her, yes; but the new team promised to be the most exciting set-up in town.

'Bella, you know I never push you; but I think that for you this has to be the right move at the right time. You've had a wonderful season at the Royal, but the line of parts the New is offering is, if anything, better. The buzz is amazing. Think about it, please. Apart from anything else it's a tremendous compliment to you.' Then, casting about for still more enticing arguments, he remarked, 'I could give you a list this long of actresses who would kill for this offer, believe me, to play opposite Donald Ballader.'

'Donald Ballader!' she had exclaimed.

In his enthusiasm Bill missed Bella's note of sarcasm. Sensing, however, that he had made an impression at last, he could not resist embellishing, and began to conjure up for her benefit a glorious array of soon-to-be depleted actresses, all joyously prepared to sacrifice right arms and eye-teeth for this chance to play opposite Donald Ballader. He would have done better not to remind Bella of Donald Ballader and his ladies. When, eventually, Bella relented, the thought of becoming Donald Ballader's leading lady could scarcely have held fewer charms.

Donald Ballader's professional pedigree was akin to Bella's own. After a rapid rise through the larger reps, he had made a name for himself in a West End revival of Albert Camus's *Caligula*, playing the role created by Gérard Philipe. He had travelled with the production to Broadway and Broadway had gone mad for him: 'Ballader triumphs as demented emperor!', 'Sweet, sad, superior sadist' . . .

Bella had caught the play five years ago, before it transferred, at the Phoenix on Charing Cross Road – and here was an actor she could admire. He made the audience aware of his presence without hogging the stage; he conveyed ruthlessness and slyness and all the cruel logic of the character, but at the same time he had the ability to suggest delicacy, and the depths of grief and disappointment, so that the portrait of a terrible, perverse nobility emerged. Bella had been very moved.

But, however much respect he might command as an actor, Donald's extra-curricular life offered nothing that could excite admiration. He represented a prime example of that kind of behaviour among her colleagues that pained and puzzled her. Scrupulous in performance of the roles they assumed in order to earn a living, their conduct of their own lives made no sense. It was as if they were moral imbeciles. They paid nightly lip-service to decency, but they were inconstant, deceitful, pleasure-seeking, treacherous. This one went off with that one's partner; friend betrayed friend; loyalty, self-sacrifice, were themes from speeches, soon forgotten. Sometimes there might be the faintest of faint excuses: that the players were actually seduced by the play, so that, for example, commanded by the godlike playwright to love, love they did. If the love did not last beyond the run of the production, it was too late, it was too bad. The heart, the family, was broken, the damage was done. But just as often, in Bella's view, there was no real excuse.

This peculiarly old-fashioned moral stance, with its element of crusade, did not put her companions off. They were as broad as they were loose, inclined to live and let live. Bella was cool, sharp-witted, armoured; she seemed to know her mind. Some found her intimidating, some devastating, desirable but unattainable. But she was not cold; and she was not a bitch; even though, to defend herself, she might speak sometimes with a bitch's tongue. Bella and her antique attitudes were tolerated.

Bella carried the glasses carefully in front of her, alternately anticipating and apologizing as she made her slow return to the table. As she drew near she heard Dolly's voice. Years of training had wrought havoc with Dolly's power to curb her audibility – she was incapable of whispering successfully. So although, no doubt, she was doing her best not to be heard above the crowd, her words reached Bella quite distinctly, tinged with the hushed enthusiasm of the born storyteller: '. . . one of those distressing relationships. You could scarcely recognize her. She seemed to go into a state of shock. Such a lovely girl, so talented. And nothing at all you could do or say—'

'Ah, Bella!' Michael interrupted Dolly feverishly. 'Speaking of lovely ladies. What kept you so long, girl? We were going to send out a search party, and me dying of thirst here.'

Bella had just had time, before the subject was changed, to catch a sight of each face – Dolly's full of sweet concern, Nancy's frowning, disturbed and a little disapproving, Michael's wearing the intent, concentrated look of the eternally curious. Clearly she herself had been the subject of the conversation.

A powerful fatigue swept over her for a moment, undoing all her strength to hold off the thousand things she had to hold off in order to go on. Why bother? But anger and pride, much maligned of the seven vices, succeeded where her will might have failed.

'Sorry,' she said. 'There was a bit of a queue.'

She handed over the two glasses, sat down in front of her plate of bread and cheese and pickle and forced herself to eat.

chapter 4

'How's it going? Tell me all! My aunt sent me a frightfully glamorous photo of you from the *Telegraph* of all places! I want to hear everything!'

Bella's oldest friend, Helena, had called from Geneva – a terrible extravagance; but Bella's remonstrances were by now half-hearted. She had so often blessed Helena in the past for her familiar friendly ear, and especially during the first months at the Royal. Sometimes she thought she had only struggled on because of Helena's phone calls. When somebody else voiced her own worst fears, it became possible for Bella to sweep them aside.

'The photo must have been from the press launch,' Bella said. 'I suppose it was "frightfully glamorous", if you like that sort of thing.' Flashbulbs flashing, cameras clicking, cast and directors posing in every permutation. Eager journalists with notepads or little tape machines siphoned off the actors one by one or in pairs. There were even TV cameras. No one seemed in the least surprised that Bella should have decided to throw in her lot with Donald Ballader's company. 'But I find it all incredibly nerve-racking, having to talk about things before you've done them. It's bad enough afterwards.'

Helena laughed. 'You always say that, and you're always wonderful. Anyway, they looked very nice, I thought. Who's the big man with the beard?'

'That's Victor, he's directing *Vanya*.'

'And what's Donald Ballader like? I didn't think it was a very good photo of him.'

'He seems okay. He is a marvellous actor. I think I'm really going to like working with him.' This was only week two.

'He's married, isn't he?'

Bella recalled how, seated beside Donald as they faced the press, she had admired his evident skill at side stepping every reference to his own marriage.

'Yes. To somebody called Claire.'

'Hmm.' Helena paused and then said in a particular casual tone of voice that Bella recognized only too well, 'So. Is there anyone . . . you know – nice?', and it was Bella's turn to laugh.

'Don't start, Helena! I know you're never going to rest until you get me married off.'

Helena assured her that marriage was really very enjoyable. If Bella were to come to Geneva she guaranteed that she and her husband would introduce Bella to someone in no time.

'I do wish you would come.'

Bella smiled and urged Helena to give up – she was useless as a matchmaker. 'Apart from anything else, you know that is absolutely the worst way to go about things with me. Besides which, your dear husband is going to divorce you when he sees the bill for this call. I'm truly grateful for your concern but I'm much too busy just now to give that sort of thing a thought. Thank God. I simply haven't got time.'

The press launch had rounded off the first week of rehearsals with a swing. Now they had five weeks left, as they kept reminding one another.

'Still four weeks more than you'd get in weekly rep!' one of the older actors observed gruffly, and set Dolly off remembering bygone horrors; though she had known some of the glories too, and in break times the others would urge her to tell stories about the legendary actors she had worked with.

The first read-through had been followed by a further reading and then blocking, just rough moves to get a shape; then they began a gentle working through, scene by scene, Act by Act; then working through again in greater detail, revising, reconsidering. Victor did not claim to know all the answers – though he made it clear that he felt the responsibility for finding them lay ultimately with him – but set out to find the play with the cast. He worked steadily, without pressure and with a lot of laughter, allowing the actors to get to know each other, as if time would surely expand to meet their needs.

He started the day seated behind the director's table; but when rehearsals began in earnest a moment always came when Victor could no longer sit, but jumped to his feet to make a point, and stayed there, almost inside the action, arms wrapped round his torso as if he might make himself invisible while he watched and listened to the scene, to the exclusion of everything about him.

During the teabreak each day, Victor and Hilary, the SM, would go into a huddle to discuss the next day's work, and shortly afterwards Hilary's trim little form would be seen posting up the calls for the next day, calls Victor rarely kept to; but most of the cast turned up whether they were needed or not, to watch on and join in if they could.

One morning, doing Act I, Bella sat in a rocking-chair with a cup and saucer on her knee, her mind half engaged with the scene to come between Yelena and Astrov; but something about the bitterness unleashed by the preceding exchange between Vanya and his mother caught Bella's imagination. The kind of acute, intimate relationships that cause only pain. It threw her suddenly back to her grim last months at the Royal, everybody acting for the best and only misery coming of it. She went on rocking, feeling chilled and sad. Then: 'Oh my God! It's me!' she cried, and began hastily, '*What a lovely day! . . . Not too hot either . . .*'

The room broke into hilarity, not just because Bella had dried – Tchekov had written a pause there anyway – but because her preoccupation had been so intense that for a very long time no one had realized that she had dried.

When Victor recovered he said: 'Seriously, Bella, I think that's marvellous. If you dare, I think we should keep it. Perhaps just a fraction shorter!'

It intrigued Bella to discover that, unlike Victor, Donald was far from relaxed. On stage his relaxation had impressed her. Beneath a certain amount of bluster and bonhomie, he arrived each morning quite keyed up, full of zeal and energy that seemed exactly right for the visionary doctor Astrov.

Occasionally Victor would want to work with one actor only, or two, and he would send the others away for an early lunch or a long teabreak, and this he did one day to work with Bella on Yelena's monologue in Act III. The speech was a tricky one, during which Yelena, having offered to find out for her stepdaughter Sonya whether Astrov could ever consider marrying her, realizes with growing agitation that she is half in love with him herself. Victor asked Donald and Michael to hang around a bit for the scene that followed on.

They worked through the speech a few times. Then halfway through Bella stopped. At the start of the scene, she had tried moving towards the piano as if she might sit down and play while she waited for Astrov. Then, instead, she picked up some prop music from the piano rest and moved away again, more and more absorbed in her thoughts. Suddenly she looked down at her hands, then at Victor. 'I hope this isn't valuable?' she murmured. She found she had rolled the music up and practically twisted it in two.

'I don't think so,' he smiled. 'Hilary?'

Hilary looked over her specs and shook her head.

'It's lovely what you're doing, Bella,' Victor said. 'You've never fallen into the trap of doing a kind of abstract of boredom, of getting listless – especially in Act I. All this energy is terrific.'

Pleased, Bella sighed. 'It's such a marvellous mixture, this speech, of being honest with yourself, or thinking you are, but then when it comes to it, not being able to live with the logic that that throws up.'

At this point Hilary reminded Victor that he had planned to run the act before the end of the afternoon and he cried: 'Break! Sorry, Michael, sorry, Donald, for keeping you hanging round. We'll get to your part of the scene later, or first thing tomorrow. If I don't do this run Hilary will throttle me.'

'Ten minutes, while I set up from the top of the Act,' Hilary announced.

The rest of the cast had begun to drift back for the run. Bella crossed over to a table in a corner of the hall where she had put her basket with her script, and took it out to have a quick look at it; really just to collect herself for a moment before they started again. She put it away and stood with one arm round her waist, the other at her mouth, gently rubbing her lips with her forefinger.

Donald, passing, gave her an encouraging smile which she returned in a distracted way. He had a trick of coming up to her and making odd disconnected remarks for no particular reason, whatever came into his head – just to be pleasant, she supposed. She did not want to get into a conversation at that moment. But now he came closer and rested his arm lightly on her shoulder.

'You okay?'

She rewarded him with a stiff little smile.

'Whatever are you so uptight about?' he asked gazing down at her. 'Why are you so tense?' He took her arm and shook it as if it were a banner.

'Ow!' She snatched it away, angry, but not wanting to show it. 'I'm supposed to be "uptight" in this scene, I think! Or don't you agree?'

'*She's* supposed to be tense. You'd better not be or we won't get past the first dress. What's the matter?'

Bella eyed him without answering.

'Do you think you're not beautiful enough to play Yelena, is that the problem?' His voice was teasing, his eyes were not. 'There isn't an actress alive who is, my sweet, so don't let that worry you – with the possible exception of that Italian woman,

Silvana what's-her-name, and she's a film actress, *esclusivo*, useless on stage.'

No doubt, he went on, he wasn't up to it either, and there were plenty of other actors who were, but she'd have to put up with that and use her imagination, close her eyes and think of someone else.

Bella and Donald were standing on their own in the corner of the big hall, but Donald's remarks, neither shy nor sly, rang out in his clear friendly baritone. 'You'd be far more attractive – you'd really be very sexy – if you relaxed. You've got a nice body, good breasts.'

Bella blushed scarlet. How she loathed this sort of chat: boorish and juvenile; degrading to both parties. She refused to engage in these lewd verbal skirmishes – she could not rise to a bait that was so far beneath her. She turned her head and moved away. Now, with the rogue Ballader at her elbow, practically breathing down her neck, she felt a pang of longing and regret for Aubrey Morris and what had already become for her the old days, the old team, the pain she knew.

chapter 5

When Bella had turned down the New Company's first offer, her motives had been far less high and pure than Bill Forster had happily supposed, perhaps even than she had supposed herself. Whether or not the Royal inspired feelings of loyalty was not the question. Other feelings had taken hold, which made the thought of leaving the Royal or going anywhere else on earth peculiarly lustreless.

At their very first encounter Aubrey Morris's air of old-world decency, his courtesy, the slightly archaic, conscious way he spoke, had made a strong impression on Bella.

When she had arrived on that first day, full of trepidation, to rehearse for *The Three Sisters*, Aubrey had gone out of his way to make her welcome. He alone of the company seemed to have any inkling of how strange she might be feeling.

The big rehearsal room at the Royal had two sets of double doors to keep out noise. She remembered going through the first set, and standing in the tiny chamber listening to the murmur of voices on the other side before pulling open a second door and going through. For a brief moment she had longed for flight. Then a tall man with a greying beard had come towards her, dressed like a country gentleman, in cavalry twills and a tweed jacket. She recognized the long narrow face at once from her visit two nights before to the Royal's production of *Twelfth Night*. Malvolio. Aubrey Morris. He had introduced himself, fetched the director, brought her coffee and announced his intention of keeping an 'avuncular' eye on her, as befitted his role as Chebutykin.

As the season went on the two had been thrown together a good deal, though at first without having many scenes in common. Rehearsals for *Three Sisters* had scarcely allowed time for more than an occasional greeting. During Bella's dress rehearsal for the Tchekov, Aubrey had watched from the auditorium whenever he was not on stage. Nancy Bailey, playing Olga, reported that he had waxed lyrical about Bella's performance, singling out in particular the farewell scene between Masha and Vershinin – the one Bella found most elusive. Bella admired Aubrey. He had a passion and a reverence for acting and, where he found an audience – which he did in Bella more and more – spoke about it articulately and incisively. His attention gratified her. After she had stood up for Dolly, he had made a point of thanking her, waiting behind instead of dashing off with the others to prepare for the evening's performance.

'Well done!' he said. 'You put us to shame. That boy's in danger of turning into a prize bully.'

Because of all this, when they met for the read-through of *The Changeling* she had shown more warmth towards him, less reserve, than was her wont. The warmth was mutual; temperatures rose in a sharp curve. In the new season they both appeared in *The School for Scandal* and Schiller's *Don Carlos*; but they had done little more than exchange pleasantries, swap newspapers and supply one another with the occasional solution to a crossword clue. Then they were cast opposite one another again in *Rosmersholm*, Aubrey as John Rosmer, Bella as the strong-willed Rebekka West. Aubrey, who admitted to having passed his half-century, touched Bella by confessing to her that he was worried that he was too old to play Rosmer, a former priest released by his wife's tragic death to the possibility of a new life. The word was that, quite apart from his age, as a man with long experience of unhappy marriage Aubrey had been well cast.

Rosmersholm was rehearsing in a dusty church hall in a derelict limbo-land near Ladbroke Grove. One day, after devoting the morning to the Act II scenes with only Rosmer and Rebekka, the director and the stage managers were obliged to break early for a production meeting at the Royal. The director decided they should call it a day: 'Give you a chance to get the lines under your belt.'

Outside the church Aubrey and Bella looked at each other, uncertain how to use their freedom. Aubrey's manner became tentative, but – if Bella were not planning to rush off home to study – 'What about a spot of lunch?' When she agreed he proposed an alternative to the usual pub lunch – 'Not essentially a pub man myself' – and led the way to a small restaurant, furnished with old plush sofas and easy chairs with squashy velvet cushions. The manageress and the waiters welcomed Aubrey with delighted cries and settled the two of them at a table opposite each other, in soft armchairs. Would Bella like to take some wine? He didn't want anything himself: 'Never at lunch.' He did not eat very much either. His tastes were frugal, but he encouraged Bella to consume and 'build up her strength', insisting that the meal was on him: his belated welcome to the 'madding crowd'.

'And may I say what a great pleasure and honour it is to be working with you, my dear. I could not be more delighted.' Bella was not quite sure if she liked being called 'my dear', yet how could she mind it? It sorted so well with his grave, considered style, which made him seem older than he surely was, with his cavalry twills and yellow waistcoat, and his perfect manners. He had a way of screwing up his eyes as if he were trying to recall something that troubled him, or to forget it. Bella felt an urge to pass her fingers across his forehead and smooth his brow.

Lunch prolonged itself and it seemed sensible to walk it off in the park, where mauve and white crocuses were just giving way to daffodils; and walking produced a thirst that, Aubrey declared, only tea at the Rembrandt Hotel could quench. To assuage their consciences for having played hookey all afternoon, they decided to run the lines of their scenes in Act II. Murmured to each other here, in the subdued intimacy dictated by the discreet hotel lounge and the half-dozen other guests, the words they had been speaking that very morning took on fresh nuances.

'I always feared that sooner or later our pure and beautiful friendship might be misinterpreted and reviled . . . Oh yes, Rebekka – I was right to keep our relationship so jealously to ourselves . . .'

'Oh, what does it matter what other people think? We *know that we are guiltless.'*

'I? Guiltless? Yes, I used to think that – until today. But now – now, Rebekka . . .'

The intensity they achieved over the tea tray surprised them. They chose to attribute it to the surroundings. In weeks of rehearsing at Ladbroke Grove they would never have stumbled on such an authentic note.

'We should come here more often!' they declared, laughing, without meeting each other's eyes. Bella sought refuge in her teacup, only to find it empty. Aubrey ordered fresh tea.

The conversation over lunch had been more personal than any they had had before. Aubrey had spoken very briefly of his marriage and the two boys he was so proud of. He had asked Bella about her career, about where she hoped it might lead her – he knew she would attain great heights, he said. Now, 'without wishing to pry', he expressed surprise that no young swain had, as yet, swept Bella off her feet. Bella had told him of her brief engagement to a young attaché in Oslo.

'We were both terribly young. He and my father got on very well. I think I thought my father wanted me to marry him, but when I told him we were engaged Pa looked simply astonished first of all, and then really rather put out. I came back to drama school in London and somehow it fell apart after that.'

'Poor chap,' Aubrey said.

Bella laughed. 'No! I think he was rather relieved. He wasn't very keen on my becoming an actress. I think he would have put a stop to that first chance he got!'

While they waited for more tea Aubrey smiled sadly. Their eyes met. When Bella looked away Aubrey continued to study her face. 'Bella,' he said, but to himself, not to her. 'It's such a remarkably lovely face.' After a moment he gave a sniff and straightened his shoulders. 'Tell me – at the risk of sounding as if I have strayed from the set of a B-movie – tell me about yourself. What has made you what you are? Who are your parents? Which of them do you resemble?'

Bella laughed, a little relieved: where to begin with so many questions? 'I'm supposed to look like my mother.'

Aubrey observed that she made a little grimace. 'Do the two of you not get on?'

'Oh, I haven't seen her for years. I don't know really. She lives in Buenos Aires.'

'Oh.' He waited.

'She came from Boston, and she and Pa met in Washington – his first posting, I think. After they married he was posted to Moscow and, I don't know, she must have been expecting it all to be so exciting. Perhaps it is, for the men – well, for some of the men. Not for the women. My mother certainly didn't appreciate it. She found it unbearably claustrophobic. A sense of impermanence combined with monotony. It's not so bad if you can dip in and out. A very tight-knit world within a world. She and I went back to Boston for a time, so I could go to school. I think she was probably very spoiled – she was an only child like me. I suppose they didn't really stand much chance. Eventually, when I was about ten, she met an Argentinian beef baron and went off to live with him. We didn't see much of her after that. She writes occasionally. I think it must have broken Pa's heart. I find it very hard to forgive her for leaving him like that.'

Bella had not talked about her mother for a long time, or attempted to consider things from her mother's point of view.

Aubrey's eyes had not left Bella's face. She looked at him. 'I'm rather a stuffy person, I'm afraid. I think marriage should mean something, or you shouldn't get married. I don't mean because of children.'

Aubrey nodded slowly, his eyes fastened on her face, almost as if he could hardly believe what she said. 'Yes, yes, yes,' he murmured, 'I so agree. I so agree. Marriage is for life. It must be so. However harsh, however final a sentence that may come to seem.' He looked at her intently for a moment and when he looked away his eyes were glistening. 'You poor girl. Poor child.' He paused. 'I am married – as you know. I believe, like you, that the marriage vows are sacred.' His smile lifted only one corner of his mouth. 'It is very simple. It can be very cruel.'

From this time forward Aubrey made no secret of Bella's attraction for him, any more than he did of his marriage and family life and ethical principles. In the moral wilderness they inhabited, the respect which they had discovered they shared, that day over lunch, for the sanctity of the marriage vows became one of their most powerful bonds. Aubrey never spoke a word of criticism against his wife or betrayed so much as the germ of a negative thought about her – he often praised her virtues as a mother and cook and gardener – but Bella construed his silences, and understood that this was an unhappy couple growing steadily further apart. Tales of Martha's ferocious drinking and wildness reached her from other sources.

Bella could only speculate on the deep distress all this must cause to her new friend. But Aubrey was a man of principle. He had shouldered this burden and would endure his growing sorrow with humility; just as he was about to endure the pain and the guilt of his love for Bella – a requited love, it was true, but hopeless for all that.

Because they preferred not to acknowledge their association to themselves, Bella and Aubrey indulged in a joint fantasy: that no one but themselves was aware of it. The reality was that not only had it been spotted in its infancy, noted, accepted and woven into the general fabric; but that the company, which inclined to judge others by its own example, assumed the union to have advanced already far beyond such tremulous mutual tenders, curbs and self-denials as had in fact occurred. In the corporate imagination Bella and Aubrey, this pair of paragons, had long since progressed from companionable twosome to couple: a palpable, culpable affair.

And yet. Still something about the two of them placed the thing above the raised eyebrow of simple sex gossip. Both were notorious for the loftiness of their moral viewpoint and for having conducted themselves in accordance with it, till now, without deflexion. So that in those who observed them there had been – as well as neat curiosity – a sitting back, a distancing, which accepted that this was out of the normal run of love-affairs that blow up and blow away, full of sound and fury. People looked on and registered; but though the air was thick with expectancy – of something, something momentous and painful that was likely to happen – hardly anyone had cared to hazard a prediction as to what or how.

The relationship limped along for several months, a poor platonic specimen. It had its high spots – afternoon visits to the cinema, a trip to the Chelsea Physic Garden – and its poignancies, and might simply have gone on, had there not come a turning-point for both of them.

The sequence was begun innocuously enough, when Bella moved from a shared flat on Clapham Common to a large converted studio-flat near Primrose Hill. The previous tenant, thoughtlessly – without a word to Bella – had not only changed his address but taken the telephone with him. Had the young man known how much heartache this simple selfishness would cause perhaps he would have been more generous. Or perhaps he knew only too well what he was doing: when Bella appealed to the GPO she discovered that a new number might take up to six months to install. She must begin life in her new flat without a telephone. She was desolate. She pleaded and cajoled: she needed a phone for her work, for jobs, for rehearsals. She wrote letters, persuaded the theatre and her agent to write letters on her behalf. Finally the GPO had relented and the new telephone was promised 'any day'. And today at last that day had dawned, a bright sunshiny day, full of warm breezes. The engineer had arrived, finally, breezy himself and jovial, offering her a choice of 'a black or a black apparatus'. He had installed, tested, departed. She could breathe again.

She could hardly have believed what a deprivation it was to be without a telephone even for a week. On those days when they were not both called at the theatre, her growing feeling for Aubrey left her in the grip of a terrible isolation. There was never any question of her telephoning him at home, and now he could not reach her either. Aubrey's birthday, just past, which he had spent in the bosom of his family, had pointed up the pain of separation. In a few weeks, when *Rosmersholm* came out of the repertoire, Aubrey was due to go away for a month's tour, staying in digs, still more difficult to reach. A telephone, so Bella imagined, would ease the pain. At least he would be able to call her.

But on this very day of its arrival her new support system had almost destroyed her. Her immediate, joyous impulse had been to try to reach Aubrey to tell him the good news. She had rung the theatre and a studio where he had said he might be, doing a voice-over; but she had had no luck. She did not like to leave messages for him.

Against her better judgement – not wanting to tempt fate – she had given Aubrey the number the GPO had sent to her in advance. Now she hoped he might just try it out during the day.

It so happened that in the afternoon she had to stay in for a coaching session – Lindon Grant, a young composer who worked often with the Royal as musical director, writing incidental music and songs as required, was coming to teach her a song she had to sing in the next production. Lindon had already coached Bella for some odd moments of dance and song during *The Three Sisters*, and she had enjoyed these sessions and the release, at the end of a hard day, of finding herself dancing. The choreographer had gone on to another job, so Lindon not only sang the music that they danced to, but stood in for Vershinin, who had evening performances.

Lindon had appealed to her sense of humour as well as to her eye. Far from being an absent-minded composer with his head in the clouds, he was down-to-earth and a stickler for accuracy. He had a slight, elegant frame, which he showed to advantage, dressing stylishly in tasselled moccasins and a blue suit and waistcoat of a finely woven tweed. He viewed most of the theatre establishment, and almost all actors and directors, with ironical detachment. Music mattered more than any of their shenanigans. It obsessed him; but at least his obsessions differed from those on Bella's current diet – he breathed another air. He had a sharp eye and he made Bella laugh. After their brief session he always insisted on rewarding her with a drink or coffee, and even offered to take her through her lines.

On this occasion Lindon duly admired Bella's new abode, an ingenious one-room arrangement which managed to squeeze a small bathroom and tiny kitchenette into a huge high-ceilinged bed-sitting room that looked over a double row of leafy back gardens. He especially approved Bella's window-box, full of geraniums. His wife, he informed her, was an authority on geraniums and Lindon promised that he would make her take some cuttings for Bella.

He had not been there many minutes and they had just settled with cups of tea and a tape machine when, to Bella's excitement, the telephone rang – the first time since the engineer had taken himself off. It could only be Aubrey. She had given the number to no one else. She had been superstitious even about giving it to him, in case it turned out in the end to be a different one after all. She excused herself to Lindon, and answered the phone breathlessly. 'How wonderful!' she cried. 'You're the first!'

She became self-conscious, lowering her voice, and avoided using Aubrey's name in front of Lindon. 'It's so ridiculous, having a phone again. It makes me feel like a real person!' She laughed like a child, and Aubrey was thrilled on her behalf. He took full advantage of her new circumstance and began to describe his own day with very few questions asked of Bella, and almost nothing needed in the way of response. Saying so little made her even more self-conscious. She did not turn her back on Lindon, but turned half away, stooping over the phone as if to shield it. She had tied her hair straight back, to give an impression of seriousness – having to sing made her nervous – but one strand escaped over her ear, which she kept pushing back with her free hand.

The telephone, though it oppresses some people, liberates others. As Aubrey went on he became eloquent. Suddenly he could speak to Bella, essence to essence for the first time: of his love, his need, his guilt. And these intimacies did require something more from Bella – assurances and reassurances, denials, protestations, reaffirmations. She should have spoken at once, 'Aubrey, there's someone here . . .', or simply, 'Can I call you back?' But by now he had talked well past the moment at which that was possible. She had been afraid to say anything, for when would she be able to speak to Aubrey again? To hang up seemed like a little death. So she said nothing in the first crucial minute; and, as the minutes wore on and some response from her now became essential, it began to be obvious that she was in some way constrained, that she was not speaking freely and affectionately and without inhibition. She answered for the most part in monosyllables which she tried to make as warm as she could; but very soon Aubrey smelled a rat.

He broke off. 'Bella? Is there someone there with you?'

Bella was relieved at first that he had at last caught on, but alarmed in the next second, at the change of tone she now detected down the wire.

'Oh! Well then! Goodness! I'm so sorry to be taking up your time! Do forgive me. I had no idea.'

She bumbled an apology, though without quite understanding why there need be one.

'Not at all. You're a free agent. I'm so sorry to have interrupted you. Humble apologies. Shan't let it happen again.'

'I'll call you back,' Bella said in great distress.

'No, no. No need. I won't be get-at-able. Goodbye then.'

'Aubrey!' Bella called, heedless now, after so many pains taken to avoid speaking Aubrey's name in front of Lindon. 'Will you call me? Please?'

There was no answer. She could not be sure whether he was still there.

'Aubrey? Will you call me later?'

Still silence. Then he said merely, 'I don't know,' and hung up.

After a moment of paralysis Bella hung up too. Then she began to shake. Lindon studied her with alarm. 'Are you all right, Bella?'

She said that she was, but it was clearly impossible for them to continue their session. She had turned very white.

'What about some more tea, love,' Lindon suggested, and she agreed, busying herself at the gas stove with kettle, teapot and cups. But once she had poured the boiling water on to the tea leaves, she stood staring down at them with glazed eyes. She turned to Lindon and said: 'Lindon. Do you have your car? Could you possibly take me into town?'

chapter 6

Bella urged Lindon to drop her somewhere in the centre, but her state of high agitation disturbed him. She looked haunted. He refused to abandon her without seeing her into safe hands and a calmer frame of mind. He did not voice his concern. On the contrary, he took care to adopt a very casual air, as if time and traffic meant nothing to him – which was far from the truth. He lived in deep country, protected and waited on by a wife whose respect for his genius and its many needs – silence, stillness – was as all-encompassing as his own.

Bella at this moment was neither silent nor still. She would not stop talking, filling the air, apologizing, saying, without saying, what was going on, while pretending that nothing was.

Rehearsals for Aubrey's play were being conducted in a British Legion hall in Kentish Town. Lindon parked outside. Bella seemed to remember that Aubrey had not been called for rehearsal that day – which was why he had been free to fit in his voice-over, but Bella wanted to check every possibility. She could never have brought herself to ask it of him, and felt all the more grateful that Lindon had stuck by her. On the pretext of keeping an eye out for traffic wardens, she could sit in the car while Lindon went looking for Aubrey. But there was no one who knew. Debbie, the brisk, plump ASM, who knew everything, had gone to buy milk. Somebody, trying to be helpful, suggested Aubrey might have gone for a costume fitting, but couldn't really be sure. Bella and Lindon drove on to the Royal. Yes, Aubrey had been in, collected his mail, the stage-door keeper had seen him. He had not seen him go out, but that of course did not necessarily mean that he was still there. They tried wardrobe, or rather Lindon did. Bella tried Aubrey's dressing room. She tried the green room, a quick, guilty glance round, dodging out again before anyone there could engage her in conversation – not many there at this hour of high-tea turning to supper or post-rehearsal pints. She met Lindon outside the stage-door and hesitated by the car as he went round to the driver's seat.

'What is it?' he asked.

'It's just, oh—' she sighed. 'I've just thought – there was someone in the green room reading the paper. I didn't look. It might have been him, perhaps.'

Lindon nodded, without any trace of impatience, and went back into the theatre. He returned in a few moments shaking his head. 'No paper. No Aubrey,' he said. 'Where now?'

Bella opened her mouth but had nothing to suggest.

'What about the pub?' Lindon asked.

'He doesn't like pubs.'

'I've seen him in the Bear.'

Bella tugged at a hangnail with her teeth. 'I doubt it. But I can't think where. He has to be here for the half, and he won't go all the way home between times' – not if he can avoid it – 'It's not worth it.'

The horrid thought hit her that Aubrey might even now be telephoning her to make amends for his painful behaviour; and a new thought followed that perhaps he had even gone to the flat to find her. She said: 'I think I'd better go back. You've been awfully sweet, Lindon. I can't thank you enough.'

'Why don't you hang on here for a bit?' Lindon suggested. 'He's got to turn up sooner or later, hasn't he?'

'I don't think that's fair on him. I'll be seeing him anyway tomorrow, for goodness' sake! You must think I'm barmy.' She was trying to be brave – at that moment tomorrow was a euphemism for eternity. She passed both her hands over her face pushing back her hair, now looking decidedly less severe.

'Come and have a quick drink before you go. You need one, I'd say.'

Bella frowned and said she really must get back.

'One drink and I'll take you back,' Lindon urged her. 'How's that? If we go now we'll hit the worst of the rush hour anyway. Come on.'

She gave in. He took her by the elbow with one hand, fished a coin from his pocket with the other and fed the meter. Then he led her round the corner to the Bear and Ragged Staff.

'What'll you have?' he said, as they pushed through to the bar.

'Oh no, Lindon – you must let me! Don't be ridiculous.' She squeezed past him and found herself staring across the curve of the cluttered counter at Aubrey. He was standing, drink in hand, with Victor Todmorden amid a knot of actors, not all from the Royal. Bella recognized Sir Paul Stern and Michael Brodie among them, deep in heated, boisterous discussion. Aubrey, seeing Bella, gave a faint sweet smile which could have been part of their old vocabulary of discretion – or of a new one of death and disaffection. She smiled back and continued to stare at him, paralysed again. Again Lindon stepped in, ordering two white wines, paid for them, nodded vigorously at Victor Todmorden, who was a buddy of his, and moved in his direction, steering Bella, who was clutching her unwanted glass, before him.

Victor Todmorden introduced Sir Paul, who was cordial, and very soon Lindon engaged all their attention, launching into a diatribe about the use, or misuse, of music in the theatre; but not before he had managed to mutter at Aubrey what a thankless afternoon he had spent, having gone all the way to Chalk Farm to teach Bella a song, under the misapprehension that she owned a piano. Lindon was unable to expunge from his tone a note of reprimand. Though he had only heard, literally, half the story – Bella's half of the unfortunate baptismal telephone conversation – he judged Aubrey's behaviour to have been harsh, absurd. And of course he knew for certain that with regard to himself, at least, Bella was innocent. For all her porcelain looks and amazing honey-coloured hair, he did not even find her all that attractive. He liked his women more robust. She was certainly not very gifted musically. If he had stuck by her it was because she had not pushed her anguish down his throat. On the contrary, she had tried repeatedly to let him off, to get rid of him in fact. Of Aubrey he knew nothing, except that he was married to some loony foreigner. Lindon was definitely on Bella's side. Before transferring his entire attention to Victor and Sir Paul, he gave Aubrey a long withering look, which caused Aubrey to raise his eyebrows at Bella, in an attempt to get her to share the joke.

He caught her just as she was glancing away from them, her face frozen in an expression he had never seen, the blank fear of someone confronting total darkness. It was Aubrey's turn to be afraid. As she looked up, her eyes focused and met his; but her expression did not change, so that now he seemed himself to be the darkness which locked her gaze. He murmured, 'Hey! Bella!', desperate to get her to smile, holding out his hand to her. She tried to smile, but her eyes filled with tears that she blinked away. She began again to shiver. He took her hand and squeezed it so hard that it hurt her.

'It's all right,' he said. 'We're all right. I was jealous. I'm sorry. Forgive me. Please.' She was afraid to look at him, but she nodded, pressing her lips together to stop more tears. 'Excuse me,' she said, and left them all where they stood. She reached the Ladies in time to be violently sick.

Thus it was that some five and a half hours later, and several months after her supper with Bill Forster, at which she had turned down the chance to become Donald Ballader's leading lady, Aubrey Morris was to be found sitting on the wide bed in Bella's new flat looking across at Bella.

Both understood that their friendship had reached a critical stage. Now, if it were to flourish, great measures of delicacy would be required. Although compounded of trivia, the train of events that had brought Aubrey here tonight with such an abandon of proprieties, still packed the full punch of a lovers' tiff – more powerful, because they themselves had not yet dared to admit that lovers was what they were, and that they had just dragged each other through hell. Having failed to acknowledge that they were walking a tightrope, they had proceeded on their way with confidence. It had come as a shock to fall off.

Aubrey had never been in this room before. They had never been alone together before in circumstances that were not to some extent public. They had been for quick meals in coffee bars, walks in the park, visits to galleries; they had shared a stage nightly in front of a thousand people.

Among its many charms the flat offered solitude and privacy, both of which Bella had craved; but privacy gave rise to a paradox. Ever since their tea together at the Rembrandt Hotel circumstance and temperament had been nudging Aubrey and Bella towards a mutual, if unspoken, tenderness; but circumstance and temperament had also protected the happy unhappy pair from any illicit consummation of their bond, for without conscious and shameful contriving there was nowhere for them to go. In removing that difficulty Bella's new home inevitably presented them with another: the absence of difficulty. Opportunity might prove the mightier test.

Aubrey had come in a taxi without telephoning, straight from the theatre. In the normal way of things he would take his time removing his make-up – the full slap. A fingerful of Cremine, scooped from a battered blue tin, rubbed well in, swept away with a tissue; then he would attack again with soap and water and towel and go home at last on the tube to Richmond, to his wife. Tonight his ablutions had been less thorough. Bella could see traces of white still, on the inside rim of his lower lids and the remains of the red dots he persisted in painting in the inner corners of his eyes. Younger actors teased him for sticking in such ancient ruts – half of them had never seen a stick of greasepaint in their lives, let alone have any clue what '5 & 9' was; but he dismissed the young with jibes of his own: at least he made sure he could be seen, *and* heard too! He refused to change for change's sake or simply to keep up with the young. Yes, he admitted it: he was a creature of habit: not, however, out of mindless laziness, but because his habits were useful. They saved time. Bella admired him for sticking to his guns. It was one of the qualities that set him apart.

Now he was subdued. A warm breeze shifted her new white curtains, but Bella found herself shivering. Had she brought him to this? Since three o'clock that afternoon she had been racked by almost unbearable apprehension, longing to see him and be with him, just like this, the two of them alone; but now her own feelings lost all importance. Aubrey looked so unlike himself. He was sitting a little slumped on the pink printed Indian counterpane, as if someone had struck him a blow in the chest; and the remnants of smeared make-up were at odds with the bright head of white hair, and with the neat half-belted linen jacket that had put in its appearance with the arrival of the first days of spring. He looked drained, but spoke with near-ferocity.

'My dear, dear Bella – it would be so easy for me,' he said, 'so easy, to stay here with you. As I long to do.' He repeated the phrase. 'As I long to do.' The words came out slowly, haltingly, he repeating and qualifying them, as if he himself could only just make out their meaning. He drew a deep silent breath. 'I think I wrong Martha if I stay and perhaps – I cannot be sure – perhaps I wrong you by not staying . . . No!'

He held up his hand to prevent her interrupting as she wanted to do, to contradict and reassure him. His face creased with pain and the attempt at honesty.

'Please, my dear . . . my dearest Bella,' he murmured, half to himself, his voice caressing. 'I behaved unforgivably this afternoon. I could not help myself. It swept over me – such a feeling . . . But it was – unforgivable, to hurt you as I did. I think perhaps, obscurely, I wanted to. Some kind of revenge I was taking on you for having gained this power to hurt me. I don't know. Bella . . .' He gazed at her intently, where she sat perched on the arm of an easy chair. 'Bella,' he murmured.

He caught his breath and could not speak for a moment.

'I have nothing to offer you, Bella. Nothing.'

He dropped his eyes from her face and bowed his head. After a moment Bella rose and crossed the room to sit beside him. She put her arms around him and touched her lips very lightly to the back of his neck; then she turned her head so that it was bowed beside his and they sat like this together for a long time, without moving.

Aubrey left on his brief tour with some dozen of the company. Bella's eyes became darker overnight, her face paler, her mouth – and tongue – sharper, as if she were under a great strain. Her work suffered. She lost weight and lacked energy; she caught cold. Leah Waters, a former dancer who had been sharing a dressing room with Bella since Nancy had gone, worried about her. She tried, without success, to reach Nancy and alert her to Bella's sorry state; but Nancy was on location and in the end Leah grew tired of being held so firmly at arm's length, and withdrew her metaphorical shoulder. She assumed that when Aubrey came back, after the weeks away, the clouds would pass and Bella would return to her old self again, still distant but perhaps less damning, and whole.

If anything, things got worse. With Aubrey back in the building and liable to be bumped into round any corridor, or in the green room – not to mention the rehearsal room, once rehearsals for *Anna Christie* began – Bella's colour turned from white to grey, and there were black circles under her eyes. She was not yet thirty; she looked forty. The lines of Aubrey's face deepened and a permanent furrow creased his brow. It became apparent that they were avoiding each other: whatever it was – and Bella had confided in no one – had been. It was over.

This state of affairs, or non-affairs, went on for some months. During this period not one but several members of the company, of both sexes, attempted to offer solace to Bella, to no avail. Her unhappiness did not make her more accessible but seemed to act as fortification, not foothold: the moat was full and tar was boiling on the battlements. In her grief – she was like one bereaved – Bella, who had always remained a little removed, kept to herself more than ever.

If Bella was virtuous she was not happy, not even content. Virtue was not its own reward – she had nothing to reproach herself with, that was all. She was admired, she was respected. She had everything to look forward to. It was not enough. During this time, as existence became a matter of indifference to her, Bella had found herself surveying her life as if from a great height, through the wrong end of a telescope. She noted with dispassionate interest that the phenomenon of her life crazing, like a windscreen struck at speed by a pebble, did not affect her career. The structure still held. You punched away enough of the little squares of glass till you could just see through to what lay ahead, and on you drove, even if there were a force-eight gale blowing in your face.

From that time Bella sustained life in a time capsule, a place of almost but not quite total sensory deprivation. On some Sundays, she spent the day with her father in Stockbridge. Occasionally, when he was in town, she had lunch with Lindon Grant, who continued to have a protective feeling towards her after the time of the telephone; or with Nancy Bailey, who had left the Royal to be in a television sitcom.

Then one evening Bill Forster, her agent, took her out to supper again. Bill did not give up easily, and he had not changed his mind about where Bella's best move lay. The New Company had renewed its offer, but time was running out. This evening Bill put the proposition to Bella one more time and took a different tack, which he hoped might prove to be psychologically more apt. Psychology interested him. Bella was movable, he knew that; but, though after seven years he knew better than to shove, he reproached himself because he had not yet located the little switch that would set her gliding forth. It was hard for him. Bill was a man who liked to speak the truth and his clients so often made that difficult to do.

On this occasion he kept very calm, offered information and

guidance, without pressure. He brought up the New Company offer almost as if by the way. Bella registered astonishment that the new management had still not finalized its company, with barely a month to off. Oh, someone had withdrawn, he said, a wrangle over contracts. When Bella supposed that in any case it would not have been all that easy for her to withdraw from her own contract with the Royal, he lightly supposed back that, although – naturally – they would not have liked it, if that had been what she had wanted, it would never have been a problem.

'It can still be done,' he said, and went on to mention again the fact that, unbelievably, the Royal (unlike the New) had still not come up with that third play for her in the next season. He didn't know what they were playing at. 'A lot could hang on that for you, darling, don't forget. I appreciate your loyalty to them – it's marvellous in fact. But it has to cut both ways.'

part two

(*MASHA gets up, takes a cushion and leaves angrily.*)

(Tchekov, *The Three Sisters*, Act III)

chapter 7

Bella did not regret the move. Bill and Lindon had been right: she was better off here in the warm and the light, with no ghost behind every battlement. No battlement.

Rehearsals for *Uncle Vanya* continued smoothly as the New Company entered its third week. Spirits were high. Most of the cast were already absorbing their lines and coming off the book. People were getting used to props, appearing in odd bits of costume, shoes, hats, to wear them in. Now, Michael Brodie as Vanya wore an ancient frayed linen waistcoat and caught back the sleeves of his shirt with an old-fashioned expanding steel armband as he took Nancy's face between his hands and stared down at her:

'*My child, there's such a weight on my heart! Oh, if only you knew how my heart aches!*'

And Nancy, enveloped in a strange voluminous smock, spoke Sonya's lines with tears in her eyes, '*Well, what can we do? We must go on living. We shall go on living, Uncle Vanya.*'

When Bella and Aubrey had come to their decision to go their ways, there had been no doubt at all of the pain, which was sudden and severe. Images of amputation had flashed into her mind, of heads crushed under buses; a shining steel fist pounding into the solar plexus, sharp and agonizing, arresting her breathing. Then she went numb. She had listened to her agent and her friend, and had made her choice: she had dragged herself away from the scene where no crime had been committed. Worse lay in store, she knew. When the numbness wore off, what would happen? What would she be exposed to then? But there was to be no time for such a complete cycle – for nerves to tickle back to life again, or scabs to harden and flake away from the newly formed, reddened, toughened skin. For what happened was Donald. Perhaps he happened too soon. He certainly happened fast.

If Donald had noticed that his little attempt at getting Bella to 'relax' had been a signal failure, he certainly did not let it discourage him. He continued, like a picador, to launch little darts her way, almost as if he feared that she might otherwise lapse into a deep sleep.

'Do you jog?' Donald asked her one morning. 'You ought to. It would do you the world of good. Loosen you up. Release you.'

'I don't know whether he jogs,' Bella remarked to Dolly, 'he certainly jars!' Donald laughed and when she turned back to him and murmured, 'Thank you. Actually I prefer yoga,' he shook his head.

'No, no, far too inward. You should take up running, you know. It would help you to stop thinking about yourself.'

'I must say,' Bella pronounced at large, feeling cross and absurdly self-conscious, aware as she spoke of how arch she sounded, 'I'm beginning to feel as if I *have* entered a marathon – or, no, an obstacle race! I wish it could make me lose track of you!' She smiled brightly at Donald. 'Why didn't someone tell me?' she mocked. 'Is he a man or merely a stumbling block?'

Donald laughed even more and bowed his head at Bella. 'Just stumble over here, duchess, and let's do the scene, shall we? Try to call to mind, if you still can, the last man you found irresistibly attractive. Your father perhaps?'

Eyes fastened on Bella, whose face, after months of moon-paleness, was now showing colour for the second time in as many days, and some, in the know, thought of Aubrey. She said nothing, but gave Donald a curious look as she crossed towards him with long slow strides, pushing her rough rehearsal skirt out in front of her with each step. He returned an equally curious glance, sidelong, and said in a loud whisper, 'Don't be fright! I promise I won't let you melt! Though I confess I am awfully curious about the other nine-tenths . . .'

Many men noted Donald's enviable success with women, and could not quite fathom it. He might be a little larger than life, a little bold, but basically he had not that much more to offer than others. His secret would always elude them, for its simplicity lay beyond their comprehension, in the plain fact that Donald liked women, really liked them; and it was this genuine liking that accounted for the good fortune that attended his unremitting essays at loving them. For there are many men who need women and court them but whose proclamations are threadbare. Resentment and dislike peep through their urgency; they feel unsafe; sooner or later they lash out to avert the threat. For Donald, on the contrary, women were like air and water, the essential elements. More: their very existence was for him a cause for huge and continual celebration and thanksgiving. They made life worth living. He needed them and rejoiced in his need. He hated to see a woman unhappy.

And the waste of Bella shocked him. He knew her work, he admired and respected her quality, her actorly gifts. But when he looked at the woman he saw a fruit in bud about to wither and die on the branch for lack of sunlight; and underneath his nagging and his banter and his crude, coarse cheek, she heard affection and concern (the voice of the agronomist) and thought she discerned strength. She was in a bad way, and – though she could never acknowledge it – was grateful to him for knowing it; for knowing how bad and for persevering. In the mind's womb, where thoughts shift and breed in amniotic darkness before they take form in word or gesture, she understood that Donald of all people could do something about it. He would save her.

And did it faintly, fatally, cross her thoughts, that she would save him?

He did save her. He told her that she was too thin.

'I don't mind for myself,' he said; 'but I've based this chap's whole character on his relationship with his mother – you see my difficulty. His mother's a real Russian babushka, substantial. He could never go for a woman with no flesh on her – that's why poor little Sonya doesn't get a look in. Perhaps you and Nancy ought to swap.' A guffaw from Nancy's corner. 'Or I'll have to feed you up. Yes. Dine with me tonight, duchess. I brook no refusal!'

Bella shrugged and shook her head. She treated Donald's frequent exhortations to lunch or dine with him as a joke – she was never sure whether he meant them.

It was another break, for members of the cast to examine props that had been brought in and, while the stage-management set out an assortment of objects, samovars, birdcages, a travelling medicine-chest with many drawers, two guitars, a set of scales, besoms, some knitting, and an ancient wicker bathchair, Victor took the opportunity to play a record of some possible music. A lilting waltz by Glazunov floated out. Suddenly Donald caught Bella by the waist, tight to him, and spun her once around the room, her heavy rehearsal skirt billowing out until they came to a halt by the trestle table laden with coffee mugs.

'Tea or coffee, duchess?'

He made her a cup of coffee, paying particular attention to the proportions of coffee and milk, determined to get it right, and insisted that she eat at least two biscuits.

Over the next days, as Donald addressed himself to Bella, and kept on in spite of her disdain and chilliness, she found herself drawn to the spar, against her custom and her judgement. Little by little, during this period, she abandoned judgement of every kind.

Bella had never met anyone like Donald Ballader, though she thought she had and thought she knew the type: the *homme fatal*; and thought herself a match for him – whereas her very sense of being armed to the teeth left her most vulnerable. The steel cladding of reflexes and responses that had defended Bella for so long could be unbuckled, or simply lifted off with a magnet. When Donald applied himself, to the pursuit either of women or of his craft, he drew upon an almost unerring intuition, an instinct for what would work. His approach to Bella was direct. (In life he never lied, at least not about things he considered to be important.)

Until she encountered Donald, Bella had never really been at home to anyone. Others had waited politely for her reserve to fall, but no one had come close enough to tell whether it had fallen or not, let alone be invited in. And yet for Donald, after only the most fleeting of sieges, and almost without parley, she let fall the drawbridge and saw him prance in to her, plumes and banners flying, the breath and virtue of him lifting her up, bearing her forth, towards a new life undreamt of.

chapter 8

One evening, about two and a half weeks into rehearsals, after Bella and Donald had been working late with Victor on the map scene in Act III, and on Astrov and Yelena's farewell, the two men insisted that Bella join them for a meal, and she was happy to do that. She was enjoying the work. As long as she was working she was at least less unhappy. To find fulfilment in playing an unfulfilled character offered a little knot of irony that Tchekov himself would have appreciated.

She had come to love working with Donald. Even his sideswipes were delivered with affection, and when it really mattered he was always encouraging, always observant, noting and building on whatever was on offer. What he offered himself was unforeseeable and at the same time had such an inevitability about it that she found herself released into a curious hypothetical world: they were not themselves any longer, they were not real; but they embodied real possibilities. Throughout the work there was the excitement of feeling always on the brink of discovery, on the verge of finding the clue to the scene. They might find it and lose it or discard it, but if they did it was in favour of a new possibility, a new direction uncovered.

She came back from the loo to find Donald and Victor deep in discussion. She settled herself on the edge of the table where the big prop map was spread out and listened across the rehearsal room as they explored how complex or simple Astrov's responses should be at any given moment. Here was another view of Donald; not the womanizer, his attention wholly absorbed elsewhere. He was inventive and thoughtful, exhilarating in full flow, pacing the floor, expatiating on the possible responses of a man confronted by '*a woman like that*: attractive as well as beautiful – not always the same thing at all . . . Aloof, remote and yet – amazingly – apparently – beckoning! And to me! Are my senses deceiving me? Is she like the others, really flesh and blood?' Donald's analysis became more specific to the play – how at first Astrov assumed the pose of a cynic: all women are the same underneath. 'He *was* a doctor, after all! So he amuses himself speculating about her: what would it be like with her? He starts thinking about her just like that, to amuse himself, pass the time – he has those vast distances to cover.'

'Permanent physical exhaustion,' Victor put in.

'Right,' Donald agreed. 'Except now he can't stop. It's got his juices going. That's a gift in itself – when you're that whacked, and suddenly, out of nowhere, out of nothing there's Something, some stimulus powerful enough to get you going.'

Victor nodded: 'He *is* a man of the world, of course. Experienced. Not short of opportunities either, all the houses he goes into—'

'Oh, yes! He certainly sees right through her, of course he does. But it's a wilderness – there's no one like her for miles around. She is something else. He's hoist with his own "What if?" He feels himself becoming obsessed. He's fascinated by his own fascination. Deeply romantic, yet he watches himself the whole time. And her.'

Donald had come to rest in front of Victor. Now he leaned forward, resting his arms on the back of a chair. 'You know that thing, Victor, when there's this woman you really fancy . . . and it throws you back years and years. You don't ever want to be that vulnerable again. Well, you do – but at the same time you try like mad to protect yourself.' He laughed like a boy.

Bella watched on, still, it seemed, invisible – they were so absorbed in their talk. She saw none of the deliberate coarseness that she associated with Donald's daily Don Juan persona, the user and waster of women. In his eyes as well as appetite there was awe, and he moved her. For an instant she was on her mettle, nose out of joint that he should be able to direct himself so completely to something or someone – an idea, an image, an ideal of woman – that was not her. Or was it not an ideal but a reality? A woman he had known or still knew. His wife, Claire?

Victor looked up. 'Aha – the woman herself!'

'Talk of the devil,' Donald said. 'Bella *sans merci*.'

Victor was reaching for his coat. It was time to call it a day. 'Let's hit the road.'

As they left the rehearsal room the two men continued to labour at laying loud male jollity over the mood Bella had broken, but failed. The result was an absurd parody, a complete lie, that Bella found touching.

In the restaurant Bella was subdued. Respect mingled with admiration, an unaccustomed contentment and quiescence, began to take possession of her.

'Get me a vodka and tonic, would you, Donald?' Victor was on his feet again almost as soon as the three of them had settled at a corner table. 'I must ring Viv.' He made for the public telephone at the back of the restaurant.

Bella was disconcerted to find herself awkward and ill at ease. It was the first time she had been alone with Donald. She could think of nothing to say.

'What about you?'

'Me? What?' She stared at him.

'What would you like to drink?'

'Oh. Nothing to drink, thanks. Oh, a juice perhaps. Something cold.'

Donald ordered two Kirs, and when she said she'd rather not have a drink drink, he said it was mostly blackcurrant juice. 'If you don't like it we'll get you something else.' He added, 'Stop worrying! Wipe away that frown.'

His gaze was kindly, objective, almost sad, as a man might gaze at a painting. She told herself that he was right, it would be foolish to make a fuss. What's more, under his eyes the grip upon her of the terrible powerful peace was growing stronger. Useless to struggle, she was doomed, chosen; if confession had been forced from her she could not have pretended otherwise. She looked the same but she was not the same. She was moving forward in mind, though not in time. She even congratulated herself on having gained time, by her own innate wisdom in having resisted Donald's earlier invitations. Tonight at least, she thought, thank God, sipping her drink, there is Victor. But Victor's call apparently was a long one.

She had refused a second Kir but had not protested in time to stop Donald pouring wine. She did not intend to drink it. She had just asked for some water when Victor returned. He looked ruffled, chewing his cheek, beard askew. He raised a despairing hand, lifting his coat from the rack with the other, and shook his head: 'I have to go, folks! Sorry! Infuriating.'

A message had not been passed on. Heads would roll. Someone had been waiting in the office to see him, all the way from Hull, for two hours. He cursed, picked up the roll from his plate, swallowed his vodka and tonic in one magnificent swill, and deserted Bella.

Donald's mercies could not have been more tender. At first he laughed at her a little. 'Don't look like that,' he said.

'Like what?' Bella reached for her glass; her throat was dry.

'Well – like some creature out of one of Disney's forests. Your eyes have gone very wide, and your ears have gone flat.'

'You can't see my ears!' Involuntarily Bella put her hand up to the side of her head.

'I'm imagining them,' he said.

She found herself boasting that her ears were naturally very flat, and indeed like little shells, but she refused to reveal them for his benefit.

All at once, like a skilful interrogator, he changed his tack and dropped his barrage of jocularity. He became grave, almost withdrawn, turned to generalities, though to generalities which affected him deeply. He spoke about the Russian tradition, about the play, about Tchekov, and the difficulty of reaching him; the danger that actors enjoyed playing him too much and left the audience out.

'Have you done much Tchekov?' he asked.

'*Three Sisters* was the first. Not the ideal way to begin.' Bella suddenly stopped herself. She had been about to describe how and why she had taken over Masha, but Donald, no doubt, knew at least as much about it as she did.

Donald grinned. 'You were a vast improvement. Amy never really got the hang of it. Did you enjoy it? Yes? It is amazing stuff, isn't it?'

Bella nodded, but said nothing, more interested in hearing what Donald had to say.

'It's a good exercise to play Tchekov entirely without irony. English actors tend to resort to irony at the drop of a hat. Especially when they're faced with Tchekov's great leaps back and forth. They can't really believe in all that. They're terrified of unvarnished emotion. That's what was so wonderful about your Masha – because you can do both: sit on your emotion, and then it just poured out like a volcano. Wonderful!'

He had said some of this before, but with no intention to flatter – always, as now, detached, analytical. Bit by bit Donald established a respectful distance between himself and Bella that he had not allowed to exist before, that he had busily prevented. Bella calmed down as she listened to him. The back of her mind grew aware, as time moved on, that he had stopped his teasing. As she allowed her defences to fall away, she had barely time to note just how high and tight they had been, against him, and men at all. The muscles of her mind relaxing left in their wake a pleasant sense of exhaustion, that affected her body as well as her spirit, as if she had undergone some strenuous exercise.

He spoke a little of himself, and began to ask about Bella. Was there greasepaint in her blood?

'Heaven forfend!' she laughed. 'Unless you count the masks of the Diplomatic Corps.'

He wanted to know all about the Diplomatic Corps, which he imagined must be full of glamour and excitement. For the second time in the last six months, Bella found herself telling the story of her parents' ill-fated marriage; the unsettling reality, once the marriage had failed, of having no single place central to her life. 'Not so frightfully glamorous at all,' Bella concluded; but Donald begged to disagree.

Bella's childhood rhythms, alternating boarding school in Switzerland and holidays in a succession of countries, following her father's postings, sounded both secure and exotic compared with his.

'Tell me about yours.'

'Mine? Well.' For a moment his eyes looked into hers, their blue intensified by the dim light of the restaurant; he seemed to have forgotten the question. Then he went on. 'Raised in "humdrum Hereford", chiefly by my mother.'

His father, a country doctor, had been killed in a motor accident, skidding out of control one frosty Sunday after a visit, delivering a baby.

'It sounds peculiarly romantic when you tell it, but it wasn't. There was no money. A sort of genteel poverty. Mum working at whatever jobs she could, to support us – me and two older sisters. All the plans – grammar school and university for me, and possibly careers in medicine for at least one of the girls – well, all that went straight out the window. Not a great loss to me, but a real shame for Janet and Sukey.' He had joined the village choir, the local school choir, got a scholarship to the big school, a part in the end-of-term play. His English teacher had encouraged him to try for drama school. A hard decision, to go in for something so precarious when they were so short of money. But it had become what he wanted to do, his mother and sisters had backed him. He had applied to three schools, been accepted by all three and got a grant to go to RADA. 'Boring stuff. I'd far rather hear some more tales of girls' boarding schools and the Diplomatic Corps. Did you have midnight feasts?'

Donald poured more wine for them both and put the bottle aside. Then he said, 'Do you mind?' and taking off his jacket hung it over the back of his chair. His face was gleaming; he loosened his tie and undid the top button of his shirt. Meanwhile, as they drank the bottle down, so the wine went about its work of soothing and confusing Bella, undoing her resistance to its own properties. With a hazy sense that he was treating her like a new person, anybody, a stranger, she looked on unprotesting as Donald topped up her glass. She understood, if she could only any longer care, that this new deference, which put such space between them, though less threatening, was far more dangerous than all his little darts and jibes. Her thoughts failed quite to keep up with him. They did not present themselves to her as sentences any longer, but as sensations.

She too had begun to feel warm, and attempted to slip off the knitted patchwork jacket she was wearing. He half rose and leaned forward and with his help she succeeded in freeing one sleeve that was caught.

'This is lovely,' he said. 'It suits you. Did you knit it?'

'A friend of mine, in Switzerland. Helena.'

'Lovely.'

And now, all of a sudden, Donald fell into silence.

Bella had taken to wearing her hair up for rehearsals – she felt it loosen and he watched as she skilfully reset her hairpins to hold it in place. For some reason, as she sat adjusting the pins, a French locution from her Geneva schooldays, that had stayed with her long after more useful phrases had faded, strayed across her mind: *Reculer pour mieux sauter*. Bella had an overpowering, helpless sense of Donald, like an athlete, drawing back to create some distance before the huge effort of the jump. He had introduced a space between them which he prepared now, with a wary, tender confidence, to abolish. Under cover of his silence, while appearing to concentrate all his attentions on the home-made apple pie he had just ordered, he was inching towards Bella; he invaded her thoughts until he overran them completely. Now that she had no words to attend to, no answers to make (she was past initiating any remarks of her own), her efforts to ward him off were futile, like batting air.

He poured a blanket of thick cream over his pie and tucked in. Bella watched. She was reduced to disparaging Donald by enlisting thoughts of Aubrey, whom she made it her daily discipline not to think of; abstemious Aubrey, who eschewed puddings and sweets of any kind. She took note of her own stratagem and laughed at herself. Donald did at least relinquish the crust and pushed the plate away, rucking the red-check tablecloth, disrupting the pattern. He pushed his hair out of his eyes and leaned one elbow on the table, his large square hand supporting his chin and masking the lower part of his face, his eyes fixed downward. He was to all intents and purposes alone, lost in thought. What or whom was he thinking about? Bella needed to know. She could not tolerate this neglect. He looked up at her briefly and away again. With his free hand he began to tilt his glass, not quite empty, and turn it very slowly by its stem. He considered the glass with an oblique, resentful gaze, as if it in some way offended him. His jacket, hanging on the back of his chair, had leather patches at the elbows. Now she too was staring down at the table, seeing the slowly revolving glass out of the corner of her eye and a ruby red star reflected through it among the squares of cloth. She felt him looking at her. Paralysis. At last she willed herself to look up and meet his eyes.

He was not looking at her at all – until he felt her eyes on him and awoke from out of his dream. He cleared his throat and asked if she wanted coffee. She nodded. She never drank coffee. He ordered coffee and a brandy. 'Bella, would you like a brandy?' Then suddenly he leaned forward, saying, 'Excuse me,' and stroked his finger very delicately under her left eye. She was as shocked as if he had struck her. He was examining a tiny creature he had lifted from her cheek. 'Must be off those chrysanths,' he muttered. He flicked it from his fingers.

'Yes,' Bella said, 'Thank you. I think I would like a brandy. Please.'

chapter 9

After a long time during which nothing was said and only the sound of Bella's quiet weeping disturbed the stillness of her room, Donald, who had been sitting motionless and at a loss at the end of her large bed, slid across to where she huddled, head in hands.

Bella, without thinking, had kicked off her shoes as soon as they came through the door of her flat and moved across the room to turn on a lamp at the head of the bed. She had begun to unbutton her long coat, then hesitated, and Donald, going to her aid, had kissed her. When they drew breath they were seated together on the edge of the bed. She looked at him, eyes brimming, confessed her terrible secret, then sidled away from him like a crab and subsided into tearfulness – almost an orgy of sobbing, in which Donald sensed a kind of relief, the end of something. Donald still had on his raincoat, which had hampered his movement along the bed, dragging him down; when he reached her he managed to free his left arm so that he could put both arms around her, and now he held her, much as she had once held Aubrey. But Donald swayed with her a little, to and fro, and hushed her like a child that has had a fall, until at last she became calm, or was cried out. She even stopped straining away from him and let him take her weight; her breathing became deeper and more regular.

'You looked so sad that day on the bus,' Donald said suddenly.

'When?'

'The first day of rehearsals. I saw you up in front. I was going to come and sit beside you when the person next to you left, but I got a glimpse of your face. You looked so desperately sad. I thought you'd be better let alone.' Light as a butterfly his hand stroked her hair until, with a sigh, she pulled apart from him – though he would not release her altogether.

'I'm sorry!' she said; but he forbade her to apologize again.

He could not see her face. The only light, on the bedside table, was behind them and they sat in their own shadow.

'I feel such a fool,' she sighed.

Donald scratched his temple. 'Well,' he said, 'it's not for me to say. You probably are. But a very lovely one. You don't know what you've been missing.' And how on earth, he asked, could she have been allowed to reach such a ripe old age in such resplendent chastity? 'How old?'

This line of questioning caused Bella to recover some of her spirit: 'Twenty-nine and a half . . .'

'Good God!' The men she had known must have been even greater fools than she. (He was thinking of Aubrey in particular.) She shook her head. She met his eye with a look of wry defiance.

Donald, so very alive now to the incongruousness of Bella's revelation, had some trouble not to laugh out loud. That the worldly, much pursued Bella should unfold this tale, of innocence maintained at such lengths and cruel cost, and against such mighty odds; that he should be sitting there in his raincoat, looking into grey eyes, reddened and swollen in the blotched face of a child, made him feel incredibly merry. He was moved in spite of himself that she should have stayed afloat for so long with such a set of bygone virtues, insisting on paddling on alone in the life-raft and ignoring the helicopters overhead. Hearing her weep, proclaiming in daft confusion that she was a virgin, made him want to weep with her and protect her; it exhilarated him also, to feel such a shock of tenderness for her.

He touched her cheek. 'Do you think you can manage without your coat?' he enquired gently.

Had Donald been a lesser man, or had he been any less

wholehearted in his own feeling, he might have been checked by the flood of emotion he unstopped in Bella; but Donald was a man who lived by feeling, and thought that the most natural thing in the world. To experience – as he now did, belatedly – the most dense and vital concentration of affections he had ever known, transported him beyond reason, and beyond caution or control. To be requited – the object of feeling equal to his own – was a great thing; but to be, libertine that he was, the liberator, perhaps even the animator, of such a conflagration in the mind and body of another being, was intoxicating. He felt promethean, godlike.

And Bella, released to the wild, was drunk too, without having any head for it – unlike Donald. What was for him a difference (a mighty difference) of degree, which he had all the means to measure, was for her a difference in kind, a plunge into another element. After the first terrifying immersion, a blind threshing, she came up spluttering but shouting her triumph, as if no one had ever swum before. Together they were colossal, their vigour irresistible.

The next day was a Saturday. Bella and Donald arrived at St Mark's separately; but later on Victor Todmorden swore that after one look at them he had understood that his defection from the restaurant on the previous evening had had momentous consequences. It took the rest of the company a little longer to catch on, for this morning they had their first 'stagger-through' to cope with, and each and every person needed to direct all available energy and attention to what came next, where to be and why.

'Very good work for a first time through. Well done. A bit spacy but there were some moments that were tremendously vivid.'

Victor had taken heart from the run-through; but, as Dolly pointed out, the better he was pleased the more notes he gave. He mentioned, among others, Vanya's entrance in Act III with roses for Yelena, where he catches Astrov embracing her.

'Perfect today, Michael. You weren't doing anything at all that I could see, but you made me feel that somehow you'd just walked into the wrong world.'

Michael looked uncertain, as if he thought his leg were being pulled. 'Yes,' he said. He mussed his short blond hair in a vigorous movement. 'Well. I don't know. I had.' He was about to go on but stopped himself. 'Yes. Well, maybe. Thanks.' He looked briefly at Donald, then at Bella. 'They were very convincing,' he said.

By the middle of the following week no further doubt existed as to the state of affairs. Donald and Bella both, but in differing degrees, sent forth a dazed and dazzling beam of exhilaration; Donald softened, almost subdued, into a state of greater relaxation; Bella, previously hard-working, conscientious but not the sunniest member of the cast, burning now; and others were illuminated by the blaze, or caught fire themselves.

People who are in love, so successfully in love, become immortal, if only for a little while. And yet, in spite of their immortality, they are impatient. They behold the world transformed by the light of their new true belief, and they cannot wait for the world to see itself as it really is: through their eyes. The sharp focus of loving triggers a crucial ability in the new lovers to usurp their own egos and subordinate everything to the beloved. Every blemish is – unconsciously but systematically – smothered, in the struggle to present to the – equally deceiving – loved one a picture of perfection worthy of the being that is beheld.

Bella's inexperience was great. She saw no distinction between loving and being in love. For her there was none. None yet. And meanwhile Donald's eyes would light up at the thought or sight of Bella and she basked in her own reflected light: two gilded beings learning each other glimpse by glimpse into each other's soul, which each one bared by tentative degrees. They made confession of the weaknesses they knew about (counting this courage as a strength); but there were other weaknesses which they did not declare, and could not:

most obviously, those they did not know – and, among these, some they did not know because they thought of them as strengths.

Donald's greater realism prevented him from even thinking of changing for Bella's sake. And when she bravely detailed to him her faults – intolerance, narrowness, meanness of spirit, snobbery, ignorance; fear of failing as an actress; fear of not being loved, which made her possessive – he had no trouble dismissing them, or gathering them up into one single quality, hardly a fault, which he could adore if not love: she was a perfectionist.

'You're the one who suffers, you know, angel. It's yourself you're hardest on.'

Bella had always been hypercritical, she admitted that. She took after her father, the diplomat. From him, no doubt, she had inherited her high standards.

'Though he's not a great one for passing judgement – I've never heard him say a word against Ma, in spite of everything. He believes that everyone has to work things out for themselves.'

A shrewd man, a good judge of character. Donald was that too, yet he – only too aware of his own failings – was never censorious. Bella felt humbled by his greater gift of generosity, and resolved to change her model, be more like him.

On this Saturday afternoon they had the top of the bus to themselves and were sitting at the front. For once Donald had no production or planning meeting to attend, so that they could enjoy the luxury of going home from rehearsals together – the last time for the time being from St Mark's Church Hall. The following Monday would see them all in the theatre at last for the final week of rehearsals.

Talking of her father, with the bus rolling over the Thames at Lambeth Bridge, prompted Bella to tell Donald the story of how she had learned to swim. How, when she was little, she had been tossed without ceremony (though with much trepidation on the part of her mother, who was not reassured by Walter Provan's presence in the water, dog-paddling with great energy) from the back of a rowing-boat into icy Lake Geneva, there – in the old phrase – to sink or swim.

' "We only have one daughter, Walter! What are you trying to do? What if she drowns?" Ma got quite distraught.' Bella laughed.

Walter Provan had insisted. It was how he had learned to swim.

'It is positively medieval, Walter!' his unhappy wife had moaned. 'It's like ducking witches.'

But Walter Provan knew best.

Bella had swallowed a fair amount of pure Swiss water but had, at the last, surfaced and come through with flying, floating colours, confounding her mother's fears and vindicating her father's harshness. She had been rewarded in addition with a breakfast of hot chocolate from a thermos, and her favourite crisp Semmel rolls, bound with butter and dark cherry preserve. Well-being had invaded her every sense as she crouched in the swaying, bobbing boat, wrapped in a thick towel, munching and sipping, her teeth clattering between mouthfuls. From that time forward sink or swim had been her sounding-rod, the measure she applied to herself and to all others.

Donald remarked that he had yet to have the pleasure of seeing Bella in a bathing suit. 'Roll on the summer!' he exclaimed loudly. 'The future is full of wonderful possibilities.'

And when the bus reached Piccadilly he suddenly decided they must get off and go straight to Simpson's, where they both bought swimsuits, and then to the restaurant upstairs at Fortnum's for a late lunch, so that she could show him her favourite painting: an unfortunate lady without a swimsuit (without anything at all, for that matter), wife of a French sea-captain, defeated at the Battle of Trafalgar, gazing from her raft in the foreground upon the remains of the French fleet. Though she had not a stitch on, her hair, from behind at least, was immaculate.

*

The opening of *Uncle Vanya* took the town by storm. The dailies, the weeklies, the Sundays, all vied with one another to find sufficient superlatives for this 'triumphant' production and prophesied a brilliant future for the New Company, were the rest of the season to prove even half as accomplished, half as fresh, half as authoritative as the Tchekov. Critics seized on the opportunity for enthusiasm and waxed lyrical about the cast, the company, the direction, the designs. At some point every aspect was singled out for special mention; but, above all, Bella and Donald, whose dual stage presence, 'magnetized and hypnotized together', emerged as new spheres circling in the ether.

'*Go away, then. Finita la commedia!*' Donald said one night, as Astrov, taking leave of Yelena in their Act IV farewell. Bella, following Tchekov's stage direction, took a pencil from Astrov's tall desk and thrust it into the pocket of her elegant fur-trimmed coat. '*I'm taking this pencil to remember you by,*' she said, looking briefly in his eyes, then at the ground, anywhere. Suddenly, just after a pause, as Donald was about to speak Astrov's lines ('*How strange it is . . .*') a loud gasp broke from the stalls and almost stopped them in their tracks. A desperate subdued sobbing followed. Donald hesitated, and then spoke his lines at last: '*. . . Here we've known each other, and all at once, for some reason, we shall never see each other again. That's the way with everything in this world . . .*' and as he leaned forward to give Bella a chaste kiss at the end of the speech, he murmured, 'So much for scenes from country life.'

One critic likened them to linked kites, 'soaring and swooping through the upper air in a dizzy, dazzling unison', which made Donald almost nostalgic for bad notices. 'Just an odd one here and there. The only thing worse than a really bad notice is a really good one.'

But bad notices, for the time being, were few and very far between.

chapter 10

The New Company was embarked. The troupe that had assembled six weeks before to read a new translation of a dead doctor's classic now regrouped to give voice to the first play by a new, living author – her first. Six weeks on, with the new play mounted, they would reassemble to read and block a Tennessee Williams piece; after that *As You Like It* would follow, the last of the plays in the New Company's first season.

Donald and Bella rehearsed together and apart, a syncopated order of read-throughs and rehearsals, costume fittings, wig-fittings, stagger-throughs, run-throughs, dress parades, techs, dress rehearsals, previews, press nights, speed-runs, matinées, evening performances, read-throughs, rehearsals, costume fittings . . . In the eye of this hurricane the complex business of knitting two lives together carried on breakneck.

One night, about a week into performances of the new play, before rehearsals started for *The Glass Menagerie*, they took Hilary, the stage manager, out to dinner with her boyfriend, down from Manchester, and Nancy with a friend. No sooner had they sat down than Donald had to go back to the theatre. He had forgotten something and could not be persuaded to leave it until next day. He came back with a paper carrier bag, and then, when they left, forgot that, so that they had to turn the taxi back at the top of Charlotte Street.

'We can pick it up tomorrow,' Bella urged. 'They know it's ours. They'll hang on to it. What is it?'

Nothing important, he maintained; but insisted all the same

that it had to be retrieved that night. Bella assumed that it contained stuff Donald had picked up from his room at Victor and Viv's house, where he spent less and less time. Slowly his belongings were finding their way to Primrose Hill.

Bella had not shared a room since her schooldays in Geneva with her friend Helena, but the first flickers of apprehension she had felt had been unfounded. On the contrary, as she cleared drawers in her cupboard, found spare hangers, tried to make space in the tiny wardrobe, she had found herself smiling, as if she were engaged in some untoward and daring enterprise. She could not get used to the pleasure of finding Donald's things about – even ashtrays with half-smoked Gitanes.

Tonight she came out of the bathroom in her robe to find Donald in the easy chair by the bay window, studying his script, with his feet up on the low table. By the side of the bed lay the carrier bag he had been nursing, and another beside that, an altogether smarter one from Knightsbridge. On the bed she saw a strange creature with a small trilby-topped cushion for a head, a woollen scarf at the neck; the body, where socks and scarves and rolled-up tights filled out a shapely form, consisted of a three-quarter-length dress in ink-blue silk jersey and dark patent boots, carefully crossed at the ankles. One sleeve of the dress reached across the bedside table towards a tumbler of whisky and soda.

'You took so long in there, you've gone and lost your place,' Donald observed.

'Donald. It's beautiful.' She caught up the dress and held it against herself. She looked at him, and he grinned and said, at exactly the same time as she did, 'You shouldn't have!'

'Well,' she admonished him, 'you shouldn't!'

'I can't help it, I like it!'

She opened the cupboard door, to try the dress on in front of the mirror. Donald came to fasten the five little covered buttons that held the high neck in place. He had made a good choice. The dress moulded itself to her figure, falling in full, graceful folds from the hip. Donald crossed his arms around her, holding her to him.

'Oh, those breasts,' he said, rolling his eyes.

In the weeks they had been together the collection of garments, books, earrings, shoes, hats Donald had bought for Bella had grown apace. She constantly forbade him to buy another thing – there was no room for anything more, she complained, and he couldn't afford it.

Neither of them could afford it. But with the little money he had Donald took pleasure in spoiling her; adorning her, paving the way for her to lavish more love on herself – slowly at first, always having to overcome her system of checks and self-restraints, of constant justification, of scrupulous application of the spiritual to the material.

But tonight, Bella maintained, he had overstepped the mark. The boots, perfect as they were, were, so to speak, the last straw. Although neither she nor Donald had vast wardrobes the little hanging cupboard had filled up quickly. The dress could just be squeezed on to the rack – nothing more! – but the boots could not be accommodated and keep their shape.

'We'll have to find a place with a bigger cupboard,' Donald said.

On the whole the two of them had so little time together in the flat, just their Sunday, and much of that spent in bed – it had hardly seemed to matter. But they decided now that they must look for another place, a little more room, set up house. When they could find a moment.

Who is Riley, who has such an enviable life, who has appropriated all the gravy, with jam on it; whose existence is a mouthful of silver spoons, a bowlful of cherries, an ongoing picnic? Whatever his lost ancestry, the spirit of this patron saint of winners hovered over Donald and Bella, and for an enchanted period their lives in every sphere partook of his genius, and threatened to give the lie to all those cynics and realists who cannot help but question the happy ever after.

The very next day, as if by magic, a flat practically found them. Bella remembered Nancy at supper mentioning that one of her cleaning lady's other ladies was moving on. The lady had not yet put her flat on the market. So, on the following Sunday, after lunch, Donald and Bella went to see Mrs Barrow.

Within a week they moved into the little flat off the Fulham Road, into a precocious summer of scented air and amber light, late drinks and supper after the performance, on a balcony flooded with early geraniums; evenings melting into darkness, suspended over other people's gardens. On stage they played together as two long-established virtuosi come together to create a shimmering chamber duo. Audiences held their breaths and leaned in to them, clamouring for more; they themselves could feel a kind of electricity when they were on stage together. In part no doubt it came from expectation that had been magnified by publicity and success. Expectation caused their audiences to pay attention and so create the ideal condition for performance, eliminating all distraction for spectators and actors alike.

In fairy-tales, though there are stepmothers aplenty, ex-wives are most often conveniently dead. The fortunate princesses never have to deal with them; whereas Bella, high-minded Bella, had to begin her new life by living with her prince in adulterous sin. Her expanded feelings, like a new lung pumping oxygen and energy to her whole undernourished being, were shadowed only by this fact of Claire Ballader's existence, of not being able to be married to Donald. But Donald promised to meet with Claire, a 'reasonable' woman. He could see no reason why she should oppose a divorce. There were thankfully no children to complicate things – they were as good as divorced already. And so happy and so busy was Bella that, at first, sinning hardly hurt at all.

For love trebled Bella's energy. She worked harder and longer, exercised, went to class, slept less, ate hugely or forgot to eat, forgot time, forgot almost everything except those things which were linked with Donald. Her happiness rolled over everything. She became impatient for their friends and colleagues to be as happy as she and Donald were. She could not remember what it was like to be anxious, depressed, despairing.

From the same world Bella and Donald had chosen very different friends and sooner or later most of these friends came to the theatre and found their way backstage. There followed a period of reckoning and adjusting as each led the select and special few forward for presentation. Their likes and dislikes could only be applied in theory – for when did they have time to spend with even the boonest companions of days gone by? But now, for a while at least, they looked through each other's eyes with borrowed generosity and saw what the other saw, beyond flaws and beyond façades. Together they were strong, their tolerance amplified.

But chiefly during this period it was the company that was family and friends together. Apart from precious Sundays, they had only the brief extra-curricular spaces between curtain-down and bed-time; and, especially now that Donald and Bella, launched on to the choppy waters of fame, were the toast of the town, there was hardly time to spare for history.

Not all their friends lived within striking distance of London. Donald's sister Sukey could not easily get away from Lincoln. Janet and her husband had settled in Inverness and rarely undertook the trip south. They followed Donald's career from afar. And Donald had yet to meet Bella's father. He knew that plans were afoot for Walter Provan to drive up from Stockbridge one weekend and the idea of the meeting intrigued him; he was looking forward to it. He wanted to hear more about Bella from someone who had known her always. He wanted to find out whatever he could about the ingredients that had gone into her making.

One Thursday night after *Vanya*, having refused to be lured away to dinner with Bill Forster, they came straight home instead. They had a first run-through the next day of *As You Like It*. Donald had proposed cooking Bella a light quiet supper of her favourite pasta. All the way in the taxi Bella had been agitated about her performance that evening. She felt she had pitched her monologue wrong and put out the rhythm of their scene together. Certainly it had been different – she had been oddly abstracted – but Donald had thought, and tried to convince her, that there had been some interesting new elements, a different quality of tension.

He had already dressed the salad and put it on the balcony table. He went out to set the steaming plates of penne alongside it, then stepped back into the kitchen to fetch his glass of wine and called to Bella, who had been bathing.

'*Madame est* . . . served,' he said, lighting the candle, as she appeared. 'I suppose it should be *la Signora*. Some more wine, darling?'

'*Signorina,*' she said, holding out her glass. She sat down. 'Mmm. Smells wonderful.'

Donald pushed the little bowl of grated cheese towards her. She took it, sprinkled some over her pasta and pushed it back in his direction, still abstracted.

Something made him ask Bella if she knew any more about when her father was coming up from Stockbridge.

'Oh.' She looked a little put out and said, to his surprise, 'On Monday.'

'What, Monday as ever is? Really? When did you hear?'

'Yes.' She paused. 'He's going to drive up on Sunday evening and do some bits of business on Monday, see friends, and come to the play in the evening. I told him Monday's never a very good day to come, after the weekend and everything, but he says I mustn't fuss. Anyway, that's when he's coming.'

'Well. That's very nice. Isn't it? What shall we do?'

'What do you mean?'

'Well,' Donald said, 'shall we take him out for dinner on Sunday night? Or after the show? Both, if you like. Where's he staying?'

'Oh, I think Sunday's out. I think he's made arrangements. I might join him, perhaps.'

'Monday then? What is it? Bella? You're looking decidedly shifty, my girl.' The possibility began to dawn on Donald that Bella had no intention of introducing him to her father. 'Don't you want me to meet him?'

Now Bella looked troubled. 'Of course I want you to meet him. Some time.' She helped herself to some more cheese. 'I don't really know what to do,' she admitted.

'Don't you think he thinks you have boyfriends? He must do.'

'Well, I haven't had. Many.' She gave him a little pert stare.

'He must think you do. It's only natural. Well – not in your case, of course!' Donald tried to lighten the atmosphere.

'I don't know,' Bella replied, as if the conversation had begun to weary her. 'We don't talk about it.' Now she looked away from Donald. 'Anyway, there's no point just now.'

Donald understood. The man Bella introduced to her father would be the man she intended to marry. Bella changed the subject. 'Do you want some fruit?' She got up to clear the plates. 'Are there any raspberries left?'

Donald said, hoping to assuage Bella, 'Why don't I try and see Claire, then, on Sunday? If you *are* seeing your father.'

Donald knew that it had come as a shock to Bella that Claire did not intend to give Donald up easily. So it had to Donald, too, and he could not quite fathom it. While he and Claire were still at the Royal, before he had left to start the New Company, Claire, long-suffering, had finally been driven to issue an ultimatum. She had had enough of his philandering, and Vershinin's very public fling with Masha had ended the marriage. Yet somehow through all the wrenches and disappointments they had managed to remain friends. Their dealings were without bitterness, which made it still harder for him to understand why Claire should want to stand in his way. When he spoke to her on the telephone she always said: 'I'm sorry, Donald, I can't talk about this sort of thing on the telephone. It's too grisly.'

But when they met, at odd times, for tea, or coffee on a Sunday morning, they barely talked about the matter in hand;

not because there was any awkwardness between them, but because Claire would brush aside the whole idea of divorce, treating it as a tiresome distraction. 'Oh not just now, darling. I want to hear about . . .' and she would ask about one of their friends or tell him a piece of gossip. It was a bit like old times, in the early days of their marriage, meeting between rehearsals, between towns, when and where they could, in Soho teashops and suburban shopping parades.

On occasion he did not even touch on the reason for their meeting and would justify this lapse to himself and to Bella by saying that he was building up goodwill: sooner or later Claire would come round and the whole thing could be accomplished without hard feelings. If ever he did manage to pin Claire down she looked at him fondly and a little sadly and said, 'But do you *want* a divorce, really? You see, the trouble is I don't want a divorce.' He might have been able to counteract arguments, had she put any up, but she could not, or would not explain further. She only said: 'I just don't.'

When Donald reported these conversations to her, Bella pointed out rather tartly that Claire's resistance might well be down to the fact that she was seeing more of Donald now than she had done for years.

Donald did not know what to make of Bella's avowed feelings in the matter either, though he had understood that she needed him to divorce Claire. It was not that she was longing to have a child. (They both wanted to wait at least a year before they even thought about a family, though if Claire continued to hold out it would take several years before a divorce would become possible.) Donald's married state made Bella miserable in a way that he could not grasp; yet if ever he raised the subject she swore that it was not marriage that was the issue for her. It had nothing to do with wanting to marry him or not. What did matter to her was that he was not free. He belonged to someone else.

'People don't "belong" to other people,' he had declared,

regretting it at once when he saw the look on Bella's face, and adding, 'You know that if I "belong" to anyone I belong to you.'

chapter 11

From the list of those whom Donald grappled to his soul, Bella knew that there was one person she had still to get to know: Tony Tell, Donald's agent and one of his oldest friends. For the last year a new office in Los Angeles had begun making heavy demands on Tony's time, though he had flown back for each of the New Company's first nights. He and Bella had been introduced, but they could not really be said to have met. They planned a dinner as soon as Tony came back for long enough to draw breath.

At last Tony announced, towards the end of August, that he had done with transatlantic trips, at least until the weather cooled off in California.

'I've invited him to dinner,' Donald told Bella.

'Good. Where?'

'Here.'

'Here?'

'He said no more eating out for at least a year. If he has to see the inside of one more restaurant he'll faint.'

So far they had done no entertaining. They had talked about it, but it remained always in some distant future, and probably awaited some other flat. As he had known she would, Bella looked alarmed.

Donald derived great pleasure from the number of Bella's eccentric non-accomplishments. What if she could type and ski and speak fluent French and German? She couldn't spell English or drive or ride a bike or knit; but her dazzling ineptitude in the kitchen ranked highest on his list. Belcastel, the school she had attended in Switzerland, had attached importance to deportment and the social graces, but had evidently assumed that its graduates would be employing their own chefs.

'I'll cook,' Donald reassured her. 'Just a few people. It'll be fun.' Still Bella took some persuading.

The size of the Fulham flat and the hecticness of their life made entertaining on almost any scale a logistical challenge; but for Donald, if not for Bella, the sheer silliness added zest to the enterprise. They opted for a Sunday night when neither had a rehearsal the next morning. They could shop on Saturday before the matinée, cook on Sunday morning – all day if need be – sleep in on Monday and do the washing up before they left for work.

When the day dawned Bella rose early, as if for a workday, and scurried round the flat in her dressing-gown, dusting and hoovering. Donald turned over in bed and refused to budge, muttering, 'Sunday morning for God's sake, two shows yesterday.' As a special concession she brought him coffee and toast and marmalade in bed, with the *Sunday Times* and the *Observer*.

'You should see *The Times* review of *Winter's Tale*,' she said. 'That will wake you up, if nothing else does.'

'Come back to bed at once,' he said, 'and be quiet.'

Bella complied. They read the papers for a while. Bella drank most of Donald's coffee.

'My God, is that the time!' Donald shouted suddenly. He leaped out of bed. 'The beef should have gone in an hour ago.' At the sight of Bella's face he looked contrite and fell back on to the bed.

'Sorry, couldn't resist. Come on, give us a kiss. It's only a few friends for supper.'

'Why am I in such a state?' Bella sighed, and gave him his kiss. 'It's worse than a first night. I think I'm nervous about meeting Tony.'

'Tony! Good God. You'll love him. He's a great charmer, old

Tone. And not a bad agent either, all things considered. He'll probably try to seduce you away from Bill Forster.'

Once she had set the table and rearranged the flowers Bella ran out of things to do. Donald took pity on her and allowed her to assist him in the kitchen. She might learn something. He set her to peeling onions and potatoes, and they worked side by side at the narrow wooden worktop.

'Tell me about Tony again,' Bella said, like a child asking for a favourite story.

Donald picked up a crust of bread and stuck it in Bella's mouth. 'That's to stop you crying over the onions,' he said, 'and interrupting me all the time.'

Donald's friendship with Tony Tell went back a long way, and talk of Tony implied talk of Claire, Donald's wife – a subject Donald increasingly tried to avoid, but Bella increasingly did not. The three of them – Claire Craig, as she then was, Donald Ballader, Anthony Tell – had met at Oldham Rep, straight out of drama school, all three in the first job: a little stage-managing, a little walking on, a lot of carrying spears. Even Claire had carried a spear, and brandished a sword – to make up the ranks in *Antony and Cleopatra*. Tony maintained that it was her lightning transitions from warrior to houri, from yashmak to cuirass, that had done for Donald. Donald and he were already friends and rivals, from the same year at RADA, whereas Claire had trained in Manchester, in the University Drama Department. They would take her to task for her cerebral approach. She took them to task for only ever thinking about sex. Donald told Bella that Tony had been very anti Donald and Claire marrying.

'Was he keen on her, do you think?' Now that she had moved on to the potatoes, Bella had dispensed with the crust of bread.

'I don't think so. He was fond of her. Of course he was right in the end.'

Donald fell silent and busied himself slicing up strips of bacon rind. He remembered that particular conversation very clearly. He had asked Tony to be his best man and Tony had agreed, but reluctantly and only, he said, because someone had to be.

'You realize, Donald,' he had said, 'that this is a job for life.'

'Marriage? Naturally.'

Tony shook his head, 'Best man, old boy. You never get rid of your best man. Remember that. You especially.'

Donald knew that Tony had once – before the marriage – had a brief affair with Claire; but over their long acquaintance the two friends had had too many girlfriends in common for Donald to imagine that Tony's objections had been in any way related to specifics. Tony's oracular announcement had puzzled Donald but he had never forgotten it. Tony offered no explanation, merely repeated what he had said many times: all marriage was a mistake, but for Donald (and presumably for himself) it was worse than a mistake.

As long as Donald had known him, Tony Tell had been a law unto himself. The two were very different. Tony had always made it his proud claim that he did not hold with happiness. He did not expect it himself, and in his view those who looked for it got what was coming to them. The secret of his constant bonhomie, his cheer, his affability, lay in his having laid aside very early in his life the pursuit of the unattainable. What he went for was pleasure – transient, but simple, immediate and renewable. Once he had understood that as an actor he was good but not superlative, he abandoned ambition and set about carving another path. He made himself agreeable and reliable. He was never out of work, he never took himself too seriously, never ate his heart out.

When it came to his many amours he applied the same principles but followed a slightly altered logic. As a lover, he made himself agreeable but unreliable; he was never without a woman, he never took her too seriously, he never ate his heart out. He blessed the girl next door who, long, long ago, had nearly married him, but didn't.

His announcement that he intended to quit acting for agenting struck first as a surprise then as the obvious course. He acquired an office and clients, Donald and Claire among them. Producers found him plausible – he didn't waste their time;

actors were treated to a blend of sympathy and realism. He was astute and diplomatic; he prospered. He came to an arrangement with an agent in New York and very soon became a partner in the firm. They opened the office in Los Angeles. He became affluent and influential and, as Donald observed, 'more arrogant than ever'.

'Impossible!' came Tony's reply.

Donald swept a heap of diced bacon rinds from the chopping board into the casserole. If, crudely put, each had in his time had more girls than hot dinners, each had supped very differently – even at the same table. For one was a compulsive snacker, a fast-food man (and fast-food can have its glamour and preciousness: nothing simpler than caviare on toast with a scatter of hard-boiled egg, nor quicker than an oyster); the other a natural-born banqueter, for whom a plateful of baked beans with a touch of butter and garlic and Worcester sauce or sausages and black pudding with fried eggs and tomatoes could be a feast. Seduction can be concocted with a wild variety of ingredients. Tony and Donald between them rifled many orchards but even they, even in their gusty youth, were limited by the restraints of time, stamina and rehearsals.

'Give us the wine, darling.' He poured rather more than half a bottle of red wine over the simmering beef and put the lid on, then carefully adjusted the heat. 'Anyway, angel,' he kissed the tip of Bella's nose, 'Tony will love you.'

Viv and Victor Todmorden were the first to arrive. Tony coincided with Nancy Bailey and a young director friend. Tony had brought a giant bunch of rosy peonies for Bella – having first found out from Donald her favourites – and a bottle of pink champagne, 'in celebration for having escaped from Hollywood in one piece'.

Tony was taller and heavier than Donald, with wavy dark-gold hair and a long pale face, which coloured up when he became expansive. This he did increasingly as the evening progressed. Tony clearly liked to be at the centre of things, 'stirring' as Donald called it. The liveliness of the evening owed much to Tony's evident fondness for adopting an opposite view. He weighed in almost immediately, over the vichyssoise, when Victor asked Donald if he'd seen the *Sunday Times* review of the Royal's *Winter's Tale*. Nancy, who had seen the production, pronounced it ponderous.

'Way too heavy. It isn't a tragedy after all.'

Tony seized his cue. 'Oh no?' he demanded. 'Of course it is.' And he launched into a discussion of the universal misreading of what is tragedy and what is comedy – rather a one-sided discussion, as he hardly allowed anyone else at the table to get a word in.

'Think about it – all those so-called comedies. *Much Ado, Measure for Measure, Merchant*, they only *just* turn out okay, and then only by the unlikeliest of chances – grown women spirited away and kept out of sight for years on end! Of course it's a tragedy. It's not Hermione he gets back, it's a ghost, and too late.'

'They do have a child,' someone objected.

Tony gave a snort and shrugged, 'Yes, but it's only a daughter,' at which the women bombarded him with bread pellets and the odd sprig of parsley. He put his hands up to shield himself and cried, 'I'm on your side, I'm on your side! Children aren't everything. Don't make yourselves into slaves!'

'I think that's my cue, isn't it?' Bella said wryly and cleared away the soup-plates. They had managed to devise a way of seating seven people, just, on the balcony, which made for slight congestion at the table, but great convenience for the cook.

As Bella stepped from the balcony into the kitchen she heard Tony say: 'Oh, by the way, Ballader, Claire gave me this to give you. I nearly forgot.'

Bella peered through the small half-window, set a little high in the wall beside the sink, and saw that Tony had drawn a postcard out of his inside jacket pocket.

Donald glanced towards the kitchen. 'I'll have a look in a minute,' he said, in the midst of pouring wine.

But instead Tony took it upon himself to read the message out loud. 'It's from Naomi, another new address (she's the only person I know who communicates chiefly by change-of-address card. I've got a whole page in my address book devoted just to Gerd and Naomi): "Special love, a big kiss and a kick up the bum each," ' he read. 'Something – her writing hasn't improved any – oh, "presumably": "(presumably still much needed) to those two monster louts. No chance either one of them has grown up yet I suppose?" ' Tony gave a little bark of amusement.

He passed the card to Donald and touched his napkin to his mouth – a delicate, almost feminine gesture, dabbing only at the corners, like a woman trying to avoid smudging her lipstick. Donald took the card briefly and handed it back to Tony.

'She certainly seems to have got your measure, Tony darling. Who is she?' Nancy asked.

'Naomi's someone we worked with in our very first job.'

'Which is where Donald and Claire and I met,' Tony added.

'No mention of Gerd,' Donald said.

'Perhaps they've split up. I never could understand what she saw in him.'

'Sour grapes, Tony! You always had a terrific thing about her.'

Tony pulled a face, as if the idea were too absurd to be worth denying.

'You did! He did!' Donald assured the table.

'The one that got away, perhaps?' Nancy suggested.

'Too Jewish for me,' Tony said.

'That's rich,' Victor said.

'No no. Jewish women have no mystery for me. It's too much like incest. It's not that they turn into their mothers, it's that they turn into mine. That's the problem.'

'Naomi was very attractive,' Donald said.

'She was very attractive.' Then: 'Why does she write to Claire? Why doesn't she write to *me*?' Tony demanded.

'Do you ever write to her?' someone asked.

'That's exactly what Claire said.' Tony studied the card a

moment and then slid it back into his jacket pocket. 'But Claire *is* an exception. Claire is a marvel for keeping in touch with people. She makes the effort, even if it's just the odd card. I'm always waiting for the right moment to write a nice long letter, so of course it never happens.'

Viv Todmorden commented that it was hard enough to keep track of people when you all lived in the same city, let alone when they moved to the ends of the earth, and Donald, taking the empty bottle and a soup-plate that she had missed, went to the kitchen to help Bella. As he went he heard Tony saying: 'I wish Naomi could see Donald now. Look at him – turned completely domestic all of a sudden. I never thought I'd see the day.'

By the time Donald returned bearing the mighty casserole and followed by Bella, resolutely bright, carrying a dish of mashed potatoes and a bowl of peas, Tony had reverted to his original theme and proceeded now to madden the company by expounding the thesis that comedy and tragedy are interchangeable.

'Didn't someone say that comedy is, somewhere, usually about theft and tragedy is about murder,' Bella suggested, giving the peas to Nancy to pass on.

'Oh Lord, that's very boring,' Tony said. 'I think "someone's" been reading Bentley. Tragedies tend to be bloodier, that's all. There's very often just as much blood in comedy, and certainly as many deaths (especially of incompetent actors), except it's all in the mind – offstage, the way the Greeks do it.'

A strange sensation had begun to take hold of Bella. She had been disposed at first to find Tony's superior manner amusing; then the studied offhandedness began to wear her down. Did he treat everyone in the same way? He seemed to let slip no opportunity, however slight, of dismissing her. If two people are making an effort to establish common ground, however awkward, however reluctant the attempt, their eyes must sometimes meet; but, that night round the table, Bella began to notice that, exactly at the point of meeting, Tony's glance, with quite heady timing, would slide away from hers. It was like a game; a sophisticated version of playing peek-a-boo with a baby. Just once she had caught his eyes resting on her, as she stood at the end of the table occupied in serving Donald's *pièce de résistance*, Baked Alaska, amid great applause and excitement. Large, light, almost amber eyes, the colour of his hair. When she held his gaze, about to make some smile or flicker of acknowledgement, he did not smile or avert his gaze or respond to her in any way, just went on looking for some seconds, his eyes slightly narrowed, as if he were appraising a colour scheme. It was she who looked away – looked away, and puzzled over the extraordinary, bruising insult, out of all proportion, that was conveyed in this sleight of looking without seeing.

Was she being paranoid? She knew that Tony mattered a great deal to Donald. She had so much wanted him to like her. Perhaps she was trying too hard; but, even if that were so, surely he was not trying enough, if at all. She wondered whether Donald had been sensitive to this manner of Tony's, the way in which Tony had simply not dealt with her, had directed no remark to her. The only time he had picked up any remark of hers had been indirectly to disparage it, and her too. When the guests expressed pleasure or offered compliments (however undeserved) to the hostess, Tony had sat like a waxwork, as if some total irrelevance were holding up the evening. He remained oblivious to any but the most frontal question. Oh, when he was offered more vichyssoise – delicious – or more coffee, he had responded; but having once said yes, or no, and passed down his plate or cup, his attention had instantly fastened elsewhere.

'So tell us then, Tony,' Victor asked when they had reached the coffee stage, offering Bella a box of Turkish Delight that Nancy had brought, 'as a matter of interest, where does farce fit in, in your scheme?'

'Ah well now.' Tony tilted his chair back on its hind legs brushing perilously against the geraniums on the wall behind him, and picked at one of his teeth with his little fingernail.

'Farce is very special. Your tragedy and your comedy are about people with what you might call incompatible moralities.' By this, he explained, he meant people who didn't fit in, who went against the prevailing morality because they had ceased – for whatever reason – to accept it. 'So people mess each other about. Kill each other and betray each other and so on.'

He took a slow sip of his port and put his head back and studied the night air. 'Farce is much more straightforward. In farce, as in life, people try to have their cake and eat it, to subscribe to the system and cheat it at the same time. Most of us are engaged in farce most of the time: we're just not very honest when it comes down to it. With ourselves or anyone else. Tragic, really. Or comic. Depends how you look at it. Bella, my dear, what a delicious meal!' It was the first time he had addressed her directly.

By the time everyone left it was after two in the morning. Bella and Donald, far from being exhausted, felt high, as if they had just been through a first night, and took advantage of their mood: washing up piles of plates together had enough novelty about it to seem almost glamorous. Donald tackled the wine-glasses while Bella scraped gravy and cold mashed potatoes and peas on to an old newspaper and stacked plates on the draining board.

'I don't think he likes me, you know,' Bella remarked, picking up a dishtowel.

'What on earth makes you think that?' Donald asked, and then added with a laugh that Tony didn't like any woman he couldn't sleep with.

Bella, in her turn, swept his dismissal aside. 'Perhaps it's because of Claire,' she went on.

'Claire?' Donald considered briefly. 'Could be, but I don't think so.'

'Who is Naomi?' Bella asked suddenly.

'Naomi?' Donald looked up from the sink. 'Naomi. Oh! Naomi Richard.' He repeated what Bella had already heard him say, that Naomi Richard had been stage manager at Oldham in their first season there.

'I think if Tony was ever really in love with anyone it was with Naomi. Truth to tell we both were. I think it's the only time we ever fell for the same girl at the same time. Not that it mattered. We met with equal and resounding failure. She treated us with total contempt. She always insisted on calling Tony Anthony, which annoyed him extremely, for no reason. Probably the way she said it.' What he had told Bella had been true, he reflected. Tony had never been in love with Claire.

'What was Naomi like?' Bella asked.

'Quite a character. Very flamboyant, very tough, but quite beautiful and very funny, too. She was a few years older than us. We'd neither of us met anyone like her – fearfully exotic and elusive. She didn't reckon actors much – she maintained that they were off balance.'

'What happened to her?'

'Well.' Donald yanked up the plug to let the dirty water drain away and reached for more washing-up liquid. 'It caused quite a minor sensation at the time. The company manager had a motorbike accident on his way to the theatre. It was the dress rehearsal of *Midsummer Night's Dream*. Naomi just stepped straight into the breach and carried on as if everything were normal. But then – and this was the surprise – Naomi spent every single second she could at Gerd's bedside, whenever she was not needed at the theatre.'

Donald picked up a pile of side-plates and sank them in the bowl of suds, remembering how utterly flabbergasted everyone had been. 'No one had the remotest idea there was anything between them, other than purely professional. Gerd was very much the strong silent type. Perhaps they didn't know themselves. Anyway, by the time the next season came round they'd got married, sold up and gone off to Israel – on another motorbike. I've pretty much lost touch with her, except for the odd postcard.'

Mention of the postcard brought back yet again the scene on

the balcony earlier. Donald had put Tony's inept timing – to say nothing of his dragging Claire into it – down to sheer social obtuseness, but Bella had obviously been upset by it.

'I really think you're imagining it, darling,' he said, trying to reassure her. 'If it is because of Claire, whatever "it" is – this thing of Tony's – then maybe it's a terrific compliment to you. Tony's nose is a bit out of joint, that's all. He realizes that you've changed the old order for good and all. It's Falstaff losing his boon companion because Hal's suddenly gone legitimate on him. It won't last. Nothing does with Tony.'

Bella still looked doubtful, standing teatowel in hand, the other hand suspended halfway to the dishrack, not quite sure what Donald understood by 'legitimate'. She stood there so long, studying Donald, that he looked up from the sink.

'I think you're exaggerating, angel,' he insisted. 'He was only saying to me what a fabulous actress he thinks you are. I told you what he said after *Menagerie*. He thinks you have the most amazing range. I know he's going to try to tempt you away from old Bill.'

Bella said she thought that very unlikely.

'Oh yes,' Donald went on. 'I said I didn't think he stood much chance, but that I'd mention it. He thinks he could do amazing things for us if he were handling us both. So what you're saying seems hardly likely. Quite the opposite.' He shook his head. Her observations made no sense. 'Even if it were remotely true, he'll come round. He couldn't help it. But it's not.'

Bella was less certain. 'Anyway – it doesn't *matter*. It's just unnerved me. I want your friends to like me. I feel a bit threatened I suppose.'

'We won't ask him again.'

'Oh we must!' She put the dry plate on the kitchen table. 'But he won't come.' After a moment's debate with herself she added, 'Perhaps he's like me. Perhaps he doesn't hold with living in sin. Perhaps it will be better once the divorce happens.'

Bella took care to ration such references. She did not want to seem a nag. She knew by now, from the air of breezy confidence

Donald adopted whenever it arose, that this was not comfortable territory, and she let the subject drop.

Tony did come again, he came often, whenever they asked him. He took them out to dinner. And sometimes Bella thought, yes, she had been paranoid. This Tony was affable, amusing, gallant and even affectionate. Sure enough, as Donald had predicted, he took Bella out to lunch on her own and attempted to woo her away from Bill. He did not confine his observations on her work to compliments or simple flattery, but spoke objectively and very much to the point. He urged her to go to a voice coach – and recommended one – saying that she was neglecting half her vocal range. Her voice had the potential to be remarkable, an incredible asset. On another occasion, at supper with Bella and Donald, he paid tribute to Bill Forster: one of the old school, but no longer entirely with it. Bella was wasted on him, Tony said. Bella could be a great actress, a great star as well, if she wanted to be.

'I'm not saying that that won't happen anyway. But if you decide to come to me it might happen sooner.' He parted his palms in a sharp abrupt movement as if throwing the matter to the gods, and closed the subject. 'Think about it.'

Donald caught her eye and lowered his chin, as if to say, what did I tell you? Bella, at this moment very much her father's daughter, said meekly that it was a wonderful idea, that she would indeed think about it.

But still Bella could not shake off the apprehensive feeling that she always had around Tony, or the memory of his behaviour at that first supper. The impression remained of a calculated rudeness, designed both to be invisible to Donald and to demonstrate to Bella that as far as Tony was concerned she did not exist. Very two-faced. Very Jacobean. Perhaps Tony did feel threatened by her. Or perhaps – the thought waylaid her – Tony's eyes had been seeing through her to Donald's wife Claire, making unfavourable comparisons.

At this period, to Bella's unease, thoughts of Claire broke

through more and more often. The other woman soon displaced the enigmatic Tony in her thoughts – previous, legitimate history. Bella did not go out of her way to gather information about Claire but she had no need: it found its way to her. Via her own supersensitized antennae. Via the kindness of friends. What she learned disturbed her because it was almost all favourable.

Donald and Claire, she learned, had first parted just before Donald's career had ski-lifted into another ether. Since then they had come together again and parted again, several times. In spite of his growing fame and success Claire had always refused to accept any money from Donald, on the ground that children were the only possible justification for accepting help. While they were married they had moved from town to town and flat to flat following the work, never dreaming of investing in somewhere permanent. When Donald had moved out of the last flat, Claire had stayed on, taking work as a receptionist or waitress to pay the rent. Their last attempt at making a go of it had been undone in the very same season in which Amy Dee and then Bella had played Masha in *The Three Sisters*. Claire had hardly worked since the day she had resigned from the Royal – a small and futile protest.

Instead she worked unpaid for various charities to fill her time. She became a Samaritan; she taught reading to illiterate middle-aged men and English as a foreign language to a succession of Gujerati-speakers at her local library. To Bella, the picture that emerged became almost heroic. It inspired her admiration. Had that same admiration not instilled fear also, Bella imagined that she might have liked to meet Claire, whom Donald had loved and married, and still liked, still had so much in common with. If they had had so many tries at making the marriage work, it suggested that Donald had formed a habit of going back to Claire between affairs, and that she was willing to have him back.

Bella had no need to dislike Claire, but it would have been easier to discount her if reports had conjured up a more flawed human being. Even the negative areas, uncovered for Bella's sake in an effort to be obliging – on the assumption that Bella wanted to hear Claire disparaged – betrayed no real rot, but only faults of omission or inaction. Claire was 'lazy' or 'too choosy'. She let herself be pushed into the background too easily (by Donald, it was implied; or, alternatively, was not that good an actress and had only got as far as she had because of Donald). Bella, conditioned since drama school to be awake to the importance of the Point of View, could easily read 'laziness' as lack of ambition or lack of ruthlessness; 'choosiness' as singleness of purpose, an attachment to her own values, a certain standard, an unwillingness to do any old rubbish, a wish to develop. Claire, Bella deduced, was neither ruthless nor ambitious; she just wanted to do good work.

Bella was choosy herself, for that matter. She might have attracted the same label, except that she had been lucky from the start and her choices had always been between two or three or even (once) five jobs – good jobs; not between one lousy or depressing job and her own sense of why she had become an actress at all. Now, as it happened, Opinion might have awarded Claire higher marks for commitment, for after a year and a half of having had not even a smell of work, she was at last prepared to take any acting job, no matter how awful, that would allow her to keep body and soul together.

With Bella's agreement, if not blessing, Donald continued to meet with Claire from time to time to discuss a divorce. Claire remained immovable.

'Why?' Bella asked Donald; but he could offer no explanation. 'She's not a Catholic or anything, is she?' she asked.

Bella never imagined that Claire's resistance might be of the same order as her own insistence: a belief in marriage. Claire's pointless hanging on tried Bella's temper – she stopped short of anger because she was baffled; she had no means of understanding such tenacity. It was aggravating, it made difficulties, it obscured the horizon. But it was more than that, it unsettled Bella because she could not follow the logic of it. To Bella, if you loved someone you wanted their happiness. You put their happiness before your own, that was the only way. So it had been between her and Aubrey. She had colluded with Aubrey to put his happiness before hers; in the most paradoxical of situations, since his ultimate happiness could only lie where his duty did, in misery. He, by the light of his duty, had put her happiness first by breaking with her, though it had caused them both so much suffering. He had turned off the path; Bella had found the strength to walk on, and the path had led her to Donald. Bella understood sacrifice. What she could not comprehend was clinging on, come what may. Claire's stolid hoping unnerved Bella. Hope was weakness and Claire seemed so strong.

But other people had other ideas. What if Claire's logic differed from her own? The notion haunted Bella that such persisting hope might be a symptom not of Claire's weakness, but of Donald's. Did Claire, who knew Donald so well, hang on because she knew that sooner or later, in some circumstance, he must come back to her? Surely Bella, brave Bella, had changed all that. Hadn't she?

chapter 12

For the most part during this time, Bella and Donald and the New Company floated together on a golden cloud of success that blotted out the few awkward elements of Bella's personal life. Donald and Bella found themselves fêted by familiar-looking strangers as much as by their friends. Illustrious admirers, artists and aristocrats begged to be admitted to their dressing rooms to sing praise, and to be allowed to wine and dine them as well, and offer them luxurious relaxations for the precious Sunday of rest, and introduce them to more of their kind. The supper scene moved across Charlotte Street, from Bertorelli's to the Étoile and the White House. Intoxication dissipated exhaustion, fame toned the muscles, giddiness generated its own energy. They had become a celebrated pair.

The New Company extended the season, and then extended it a second time, continuing the four plays in the repertory and adding an old-fashioned melodrama to take them through Christmas. At that point – when they would have been going for a year – it had been decided to take a break for a period to allow further refurbishments to the Scala: more seats to be added, as well as improvements to be made backstage. Expenses that could now be more than justified. It came as a shock when Michael Brodie announced one evening that when the company reconvened he would not be of their number. He had been asked to go to Manchester at the end of February to do a drama series for Granada. 'What can you do?' He cast his eyes upwards. 'Some can't afford to leave and some can't afford to stay. I have a wife and three children to support.'

Most of the company hoped to be invited back; but though the New Company now paid more than the average provincial rep its salaries did not match those of the West End or television. Those who could do so offset necessity against pride and pleasure in their work, and tried to supplement their pay packets with voice-overs, radio, the odd day's filming.

Bill Forster had passed on some 'interesting' offers to Bella, including a good part in the series Michael had accepted – not, Bella thought, as good a part as his. She could even go back to the Royal for a season, if she wanted. But these offers seemed tame beside the tempting morsels that Tony had been dangling before Donald to boost his income.

'It's no good you looking like that, angel,' Donald reproached her, his own face reflecting her crestfallen expression. He had just told her of Tony's latest titbit, thrown into the pool for him to nibble on – a job that would mean that Donald would be away for two months, filming in Africa. 'We've told you what you have to do. It's one thing to be loyal to Bill – and I know you've been with him for yonks. But, good and decent as he is, he is a bit of a one-man band. Plus, he doesn't have an office in LA. Not only does everything – everything – cross Tony's desk, but these days things are beginning to get to his desk very early indeed. He knows everyone. He's not lazy, that's one thing I'll say for old Tone.'

Bella could not deny that Tony was assiduous. She had lost count of his visits to the Scala. The New Company's budget might not stretch to understudies, but they need have no worries about that, Tony declared; he had seen so many performances he could play the king – and the queen too for that matter. He had every part by heart, he could go on for the entire company. He came often and never alone. He brought producers, directors, transatlantic film stars and the cream of casting directors on both sides of the pond.

It was a casting director, a voluptuous and forthright

brunette whom Tony brought along to see *As You Like It*, whose casual comments over supper clinched the argument. She remarked how lucky Bella was to be with Tony. 'He's becoming a real force.'

When Bella replied that she was not with Tony but with Bill Forster, the lady's eyebrows arched in surprise. 'Bill? Oh. Yes, well, he's very solid. I like Bill. Depends what you're after. If you want a quiet life, perhaps.'

It happened at this moment that the casting lady's eye fell on Donald, seated at the other end of the table, and rested there awhile, as she smiled with evident pleasure at the sight of him, a little raucously berating Tony for wearing a jacket that was loud enough to wake the dead.

'You have to move with the times, my boy,' Tony returned loftily. 'You've never known how to do anything with style, let alone dress.'

The lady returned to her scampi and to Bella. 'Has Bill put you up for Denny Denman's new film? I'm not doing it, alas, I was already up to my eyes, but there's a part in it you could be very right for. I know they're seriously thinking about Donald.'

The next day Bella telephoned Bill. He couldn't do lunch that day but as it sounded urgent he suggested she come to his office for a drink on the way to the theatre. He welcomed her with his usual warmth, coming out from behind the outsized, old-fashioned pedestal desk so that they could sit together on the big blue sofa. He bustled about, insisting on finding a bottle of sherry that was not too dry, asked after Donald, told her about his daughter's school play. Then he stopped talking. 'It's lovely to see you but I mustn't take up your time, Bella dear. You have a show to do,' and he waited, owl-like, looking at her with his large dark eyes.

When at last she brought the words out, for this time it was she who stammered, he betrayed no surprise at all, or hurt.

'That's okay, Bella my dear,' he replied. 'When a client suddenly has to take me out to lunch that very day – or sometimes it's dinner, but of course you're working – it's usually the one thing. I'm more than sorry to lose you, of course. If I don't try to persuade you otherwise it's because I know you, and I can see that you've made your mind up. Tony Tell. Well, he's very good, very hard-working. I think he'll do well for you.'

'It's really Donald,' Bella apologized. 'I think Tony's in a position – well, he might be able to get us more work together.'

Bill laughed, rather sharply. 'Very possibly! Of course that can become a mixed blessing,' he added. 'Don't look sad, Bella dear. Drink up. It's not a tragedy. When you've been in the business as long as I have, it's more like a merry-go-round.' He leaned forward and touched her glass with his. 'I wish you well. I really do. I'm only sorry to be offering you sherry and not champagne.'

Bella left Bill's office feeling more mangled than she could have imagined. She did not wait for the lift, or look back when she heard Bill call after her, 'Keep in touch,' before he closed the door.

Tony, when she told him of her decision – she made an appointment to see him in his office the next morning – rubbed his hands together and jumped up from his seat. 'My dear Bella, that is excellent. Excellent news! Great wisdom in one so young.'

She had half expected him, in his enthusiasm, to come round his desk and kiss her, and found herself better pleased that he did not do that, but instead remained where he stood, mouth open, eyes narrowed, considering her. Up and down. The cool objectivity in his look reminded her of the evening of the supper party; but in this context she found his gaze less unsettling. Now he clapped his hands together. 'Excellent!' he said again. 'Now we can really get cracking.'

He was as good as his word. In between his visits to the Scala Tony continued to criss-cross the Atlantic. His trips to Los Angeles were not wasted and soon his busyness began to bear fruit. Well before the season at the Scala was finally due to end, Donald and Bella were being prised away from the theatre to be in a film, Bella's first. It would slot neatly into the break before rehearsals started for the second season. Provisionally entitled *Love Catches Cold*, the film was a lighthearted Hollywood story of sex, death and espionage behind the Iron Curtain. The producers adored the idea of poaching two British classical heavies to be in their avant-garde romance. The film was shooting on location in Budapest and Geneva. Bella and Donald (though 'heavy') were not yet 'big enough' in the States to play the leads, but the parts were good and the money was dazzling. Sadly they had no scenes together: Donald was to play a Russian, Bella, to her delight, a Swiss, and the twain only met once, towards the end of the script.

Their new wealth allowed them to be each other's groupies. Though she was not needed until Switzerland, they decided that Bella should fly to Hungary with Donald.

'I might pick up a few tips.'

'Tips on what?'

'Acting for the big screen of course. I wonder if Pa knows anyone at the embassy there.'

'There's only one tip. Don't act. Be like Bogey. Do nothing.'

Bella looked dubious. 'It can't be that easy.'

'Easy? Certainly not. You try it.'

'I can't wait.'

She was very excited. This would also be their first time in an aeroplane together.

It was not until they were at the airport, handing over passports and visas and being subjected to the cold scrutiny of strangers, that she found herself thinking ahead. When they got to the hotel what would they do? Pretend to be married or pretend to be single? She had forgotten how much she minded not being married. Suddenly it hit her hard again. It had got worse, not better, though she could hardly express why. Some fundamental nerve that nagged at her. In part her own rootedness in sheer convention, in part a horror of taking what was not hers. Lately, in London, she had been too occupied to give it much thought. Within their circle they were a couple, though she had still not been able to bring herself to admit Donald's existence to her father, let alone introduce them. The bustle of their lives had lulled her senses, and other people's values had blunted her own. How easy it was for other people to accept second best on your behalf and for you to be drawn into their compromises. The flight she had been looking forward to so much was spoiled for her.

Donald took her silence for nerves, though she had never mentioned that flying bothered her. The stewardesses had recognized them and made a discreet fuss, smiling special smiles as they poured champagne. Donald and Bella clinked glasses. Donald smacked his lips in appreciation.

'Mmm. I think it really does taste better out of a glass.'

'As opposed to what?'

'As opposed to Economy plastic.'

'Donald,' Bella said. 'Do you think they'll have booked us into one room, or . . . ?'

'Or what? Two?' Donald leaned over and peered at her. 'Is that what you've been brooding about, you old daftie? If they have we'll ask for another. Preferably next door – unless you object.'

The stewardess passing heard 'ask for another' and looked abashed. 'I *was* just coming back, Mr Ballader!' she assured him, and she went to fetch more champagne.

The production team and most of the actors were at the Budapest Hilton, a modern tower of brown glass, incorporated into the ruins of an ancient monastery in the old town. It was disappointingly unHungarian in spite of some attempts to supply a Magyar touch: display cases of linen worked in cross-stitch, and painted pokerworked cooking utensils in wood and enamel. Their rooms adjoined – a suite, with sweeping views over the Danube.

They settled into the cloistered routine of filming, rising early and bedding early. Bella stayed away from the location until midday, when the first assistant would send one of the unit cars to bring her out for lunch. She enjoyed having the mornings free, all for herself. She woke up with Donald's alarm call and watched him, through half-open eyes, go about the room preparing himself for the day. He went on tiptoe as if she were fast asleep, but also out of respect for the muffled hour – still pitchdark outside – and his own need to collect himself for the work. Once he was dressed and had strapped on his wristwatch, patted his back trouser pocket to make sure of his wallet, taken a clean handkerchief from the drawer, he would stand before the mirror just for a moment. There he would square up to himself, lifting his head as if receiving instruction; then scoop up his script and his sheepskin jacket, come round to her side of the bed, drop script and jacket on the floor, to fold her in a long hug, a kiss, then back again to pluck script and jacket up again. The door clicked open and closed, and he was gone.

She tried on the first day to be luxurious and have breakfast in bed (moving back to her own room for the purpose). But the move woke her up too much and defeated its purpose; and she was too impatient and excited. While she waited for room service she got up and stood by the window to look out over the river across to the other half of the city. The coffee, when it came, was grey and cold and the rolls dingy. The little rectangles of butter were wrapped in foil and the jam was in plastic packets. She wanted curls of fresh butter and bowls of thick apricot or cherry preserves. After that she preferred to go downstairs for breakfast, then out into the square, to idle for a few hours until the car came.

She wandered into the cavernous Matthias Church and then up to the Fisherman's Bastion. This quickly became her favourite spot. She would sit there for hours at a time looking at the water traffic and the bridges far below, until the cold froze her toes and finger ends. One morning she took one of the orange single-decker trams as far as it would go; past dowdy women in headscarves, shopping in outdoor markets, to the beginnings of woods on the hillside, where pine trees grew in sandy red soil. Through the trees she glimpsed large, grand houses, with big gates, part of a distant, bygone life. She did not want to do too much without Donald. She was content to wait and cram in what they could on his days off, explore the new town, take the trip down the Danube to the island of Balaton.

The driver who came to pick her up each day – a local man – never failed to express astonishment that she should pass up the chance to eat lunch at the Hilton. She tried to explain to him that she found the location stews and roasts and rough bread far preferable to the hotel fare. His English was good, but it was a concept he could not take in. Bella could not explain to him that for her the true luxury was this new freedom, the sensation of being alone without being alone, because Donald was always imminent. She would sit on her stone bench in the Bastion, gazing through the arches which framed the river until she felt that she was the river, flowing between two strong banks, which gave her strength. The river created the banks, the banks held the river. The few days off, all day long together, were different from any time they had spent with one another before, self-contained with the two of them isolated to each other. This was what a honeymoon should be, Bella thought, and sighed.

Evenings, once filming was over, were more social. They dined once or twice with the two producers, once with the American star, together with his new wife and new baby and a teenage daughter. The circuit of restaurants was small and word went round quickly. If they went out they were bound to run into others from the unit. From her visits to the location Bella was beginning to be able to identify individuals: the script-girl, the cameraman, the make-up team. She watched Donald when he was working but he told her there was no way for her to judge anything much from the outside. It was all in the cutting.

'You can't even tell a lot from rushes. Though they can give you a bit of a clue: whether the director's a madman. Or a genius. Or both.'

The director was suffering from the failure of the rushes, or 'dailies', to make any appearance at all so far. For some reason they were being processed in a laboratory somewhere in Paris; it was taking too long; there were hitches.

'I don't know what the hell I'm doing. I need my dailies, my dailies fix! I'm in withdrawal here!' he screamed at the producer, only half in jest.

'Soon, Jerry, soon. I trust you. I trust you,' the producer promised.

'You trust me – but do I trust you?' the director returned. Everybody agreed 'it'll be okay once we get to Switzerland', where the laboratories could be relied on.

Ten days later the unit relocated to Geneva.

Going back to her old school town a double nervousness excited Bella. Her pleasure would be magnified by the delight of showing everything to Donald. In the sudden switch of roles she became the one who knew her way around and spoke the language. She would show him all her favourite haunts. Her old schoolfriend Helena had offered to put them up, but they had opted for the hotel. The other cause of Bella's nerves, this time laced with fright, was the prospect of her first filming. Donald assured her that she would take to it like a duck to water.

'The first day is always the hardest. But you know everyone by now and that's the worst part.'

The work in Geneva started with a night shoot. In her first scene Bella had to walk to a mysterious assignation along a narrow back street and meet a dark stranger underneath an archway. There were no lines and there was very little light.

'I can't believe the camera can see anything at all,' she commented to Donald, while they hung about in the floodlight by the catering van and waited for the next set-up. The second assistant called her away.

'We're ready for you now, Miss Provan.'

'It's like the dentist!' she groaned. Her stand-in came to take the coat she had over her shoulders, on top of her costume coat. The make-up girl came to have a look at her. 'There's no point looking, Jill,' Bella said, 'they won't be able to see a thing, it's so dark.'

'You'll do fine.'

Donald blew Bella a kiss as the second assistant led her away.

Slowly, after a few days' shooting, Bella began to get used to the strange new medium, though not yet to get anything like the hang of it, she thought. But she did grow accustomed to the absurd, startling surge of adrenalin triggered by the words 'turn over', and the shock of speaking her lines, unrehearsed, on camera. Most of her scenes were with Sir Paul Stern, who had arrived to play the English spy chief. He was an old hand, and put her at her ease by professing to be still totally at sea and as nervous as a cow. They arranged to have a meal together one evening, just the three of them.

'I prefer to dine early, if that's all right with you and Donald,' said Sir Paul. 'Shall we say seven-thirty? Unless you're going to rushes?'

'Rushes?' Bella said. 'I didn't know there were any rushes.'

'Oh yes, yes, yes. My goodness me, yes. At the end of the day. Or sometimes at lunchtime, of course. I don't know how they have the stomach for it, let alone the stamina. That's where they all disappear to when we wrap. Take my advice. Don't go!'

But Bella, like Pandora, could not resist. Jill's glowing reports boosted her confidence. Why feel so insecure? At the very worst she would learn from what she saw. The screening-room had been rigged up next door to the director's suite and the next day, full of nervous curiosity, and a little self-conscious, Bella made her way there, with Jill and Fred from make-up. The lighting cameraman, the designer, the leading man and others were already there chatting. The director arrived with the producers and the script-girl and first assistant. The lights were switched off and the first of the previous day's rushes flickered on to the screen.

Bella watched herself with disbelief. Waiting behind the clapperboard while the shot was being identified, looking startled, blinking as the director called 'Turn over!', and again as the sound operator registered 'Speed!' On 'Action!' she moved forward (she remembered being terribly uncertain where her mark was and wondering whether she had managed to hit it or not. In fact she had not, the first time. This must be take three or four). She said her lines. Okay. Then she looked startled again at 'Cut!' Then it all happened again, almost exactly the same. This time the cameraman called out, 'Cut it, cut it! Sorry!' – something wrong with the timing of the tracking, but they had printed the take anyway. The next time she got her lines the wrong way round but ploughed on regardless until the reprieving 'Cut!', when she pulled an agonized face. Her profuse apologies could be heard briefly amid much laughter. It was a relief when they showed the reverses on Sir Paul, shot over her shoulder. She had been almost more nervous of fluffing her lines in his takes than in her own; she gave him the lines all right but not much else. This was not much to show for a long day's work, she thought, so few takes out of dozens – and these were supposed to be the best. Murmured observations concerning 'the stock' and 'the framing' floated up in the darkness. The script-girl uttered a squeal of relief: 'There! The umbrella *was* in his left hand!' Everyone laughed. After fifteen minutes Bella slipped out of the room unnoticed.

'You shouldn't have gone. You should have listened to Paul. He knows whereof he speaks.'

Donald had been having a drink in the bar with some of the crew and came into Bella's room to find her sitting in front of the mirror looking stricken, staring at herself.

'Is that what I really look like?'

'You'll get used to it. I promise. I like it, the way you look. That should be enough for you.' Donald tried to sound sympathetic, but the sceptical expression Bella threw at him made him laugh out loud. 'You never wanted to be a film star, anyway. You told me so. Now's your chance not to. Never again.'

'But, darling, it was *so awful*. It was grotesque. Not just the way I look – which is gross, awful—'

'Everyone keeps telling me how stunning you look.'

'—it's what I am thinking. I can see, every second, what I was thinking, every doubt – terror – should I have come in there, did I overlap, did I pick the paper up there? It's too frightening.'

'Don't go again. You don't have to go. No one expects you to.'

'Talk about your life flashing before your eyes. It really is like have your nose rubbed in your own mess.'

'You're not being fair, Bella. You can hardly compare yourself to a naughty puppy.'

'What do you mean?'

'Well, think about it. A dog's mess is a biological necessity – a dog is doing the right thing, just doing it in the wrong place, a social error. You're doing the wrong thing in the right place – a professional disaster.'

Bella hit him, hard.

'Thanks a lot! Fat lot of sympathy I get from you!'

He fended her off. 'Well, angelbum, some people think they can learn from it. You must do whatever you want to do. Don't go to rushes.'

But of course she did go, in case she could learn from it; and by the following week her bruised feelings had healed sufficiently for her to turn the whole horrible experience into a lively entertainment for half a dozen friends of Helena's, at a picnic Helena and her husband gave for Bella and Donald. They had shrieked with laughter at her exaggerations, how absurd, not believing a word. They could not wait to see the film.

chapter 13

Bella got back to the hotel at the end of the day's shooting to find a packet waiting for her, delivered by hand. She opened it in the lift on the way up and found a thick wad of photographs and a scrawled note from Helena: 'WHEN am I going to SEE you? – Hope you and Donald enjoy these mementos of our little picnic on the ice!'

By the time she had had a wash, Donald, having made her a drink, had settled back on the sofa again to finish reading a new script that Tony's office had sent. Bella decided to treat herself to a sneak preview of the photographs and curled herself up at the opposite end. The photos had been taken at the picnic. A series of squeaks and sighs, followed by a burst of gleeful recognition, caused Donald to look up.

'What are those?'

'Photos of the picnic,' Bella murmured, engrossed.

'You don't mind photos, then, only rushes?' Donald observed.

Bella shook her head. Photos did not seem to trespass upon her in the same way. Then she gave a snort of particular pleasure and looked up at him with a grin.

Donald put his script down. 'Come on. Enough of that. No secrets. We'll look at them together!'

He came and sat down beside her. The snap that Bella was studying with such satisfaction displayed Donald sprawled on the ice, with his own bruised feelings almost visible.

'A sight too handy with the bloody Leica, your friend Helena,' he said.

The photo Helena had taken just two seconds before was even better, the face of a man who feels the ground sliding away from under him.

'Serves you right,' Bella said, 'for being so pally with that ghastly girl.'

'Which girl?'

'Well, there weren't that many. The Italian with the legs. What was her name?'

'Her? Pally? I couldn't get away from her. You should have saved me. I was probably trying to get away from her when I fell over. Yes, look, that's her in the background. Is that the one? They are very long legs, you're quite right.'

They went through the whole pack of photos together, starting again from the beginning. Eventually Donald went back to his end of the sofa. Bella, for a while, continued to study the photos.

They showed a group of nine: Helena's husband Harald and their two little girls, Donald, the girl with long legs, Bella, the girl's husband and another couple. Bella tried to work out what it was about the girl that had put her back up so. She was no beauty but she glittered with confidence and sex. She had made a great unashamed play for Donald; but women did pay him attention, that happened all the time. This one, however, had acted as if Bella did not exist. That did not happen all the time, or Bella had never felt it if it had. The girl looked nothing in the photos. Bella wondered what she would look like on film.

Several of the photos caught Bella and Donald, dancing on the ice or attempting to dance, Donald clinging to Bella for dear life, his expression that of a man being tickled on the edge of a high clifftop. It had been ages since Bella had been skating, but it had come back very quickly, a great joy, only her ankles ached a lot afterwards. Donald, who had never been on skates in his life, had been game to have a go and everyone had rallied to the task of keeping him vertical. The Italian in particular had taken it on herself to be his instructor. She was a champion skater. As well as her long legs, she had big teeth in a big full mouth ('All the better to eat you with') and she kept flashing these in a wide smile and grabbing hold of Donald saying, 'I teach, I teach.' She gave a nod at Bella and said, 'I teach your husband.'

'It's all right, thank you,' Bella had said. Not her husband, of course. 'I think *I* teach him. Thanks all the same.'

'*You* teach?'

'Yes. Why not?'

At this the girl had thrown back her head and indicated with a ripple of laughter her delighted admiration of Bella's sublime British sense of humour. 'Oh, yes, yes, yes! You teach! But I have diploma!'

The camera had not immortalized the look on Donald's face as the Italian then proceeded, crossing one arm behind him and the other in front of herself, to clasp him by each of his hands, to slide him slowly and purposefully away across the frozen water. Nor had it captured the look on Bella's face. The Italian husband was as redoubtable as his wife, though subtler and less peremptory. His wife's high-handedness seemed to amuse him. He lavished attention on Bella, skating at her side and paying her many compliments, on her skating, her Italian, her flawless skin, her hair, her eyes, her modesty. It was when they were all reconvening to partake of Helena's exquisite picnic that Donald, attempting the Olympian feat of pushing his blades across the twenty yards to Bella to demonstrate his prowess, lost his footing and went flying.

Bella smiled to herself. 'Served him jolly well right!' she thought.

At last, after about two weeks, Bella found herself with a free day, though Donald remained on stand-by at the hotel. Bella and Helena seized this first real opportunity to spend some time alone together, to catch up. Helena collected Bella from the hotel after breakfast.

'A little outing, I think,' Helena suggested, looking sly.

'Belcastel!' Bella guessed at once. 'What a horrible, perfect idea!'; and the two climbed into Helena's tiny blue Fiat and set out with gleeful anticipation, like a pair of schoolgirl conspirators.

They said very little at first, while Helena negotiated the busy central streets and headed towards the outskirts of the city. But as soon as they were clear of the worst traffic she attacked at once.

'Now! How did it all come to pass? It's so wonderful to see you so happy. You must tell all. I think he's gorgeous, by the way. So do all my friends.'

'I noticed,' retorted Bella.

'Oh – you mean Carla and Alberto?' Helena laughed. 'Yes. They are a bit predatory. Quite nice, really. Don't evade the issue.'

Helena wanted to know everything from the very beginning, with all the trimmings, and Bella obliged, savouring the luxury of talking to someone who knew her so well, and the comfort of being able to recount past nightmares that had resolved towards a happy ending. Even to Helena, Bella had never talked about Aubrey. Now she described the passage from the painful months at the Royal to the first weeks with the New.

'If it hadn't been for all the business with Aubrey, I suppose I'd still be with the Royal now.'

'You mean if you weren't such a prune.'

'It wasn't just me,' Bella objected.

'No,' said Helena. 'He sounds a bit of prune, too, I must admit.'

'I mean his wife.'

'They don't sound very happy.'

'He has children. I didn't want to get into one of those sordid affairs, Helena. Neither of us did.'

'Well, you're having one now, aren't you?'

Bella did not answer. In any matter that concerned Bella, Helena never fussed or tried to spare her feelings. She had known Bella too long, they knew each other too well to get away with half-truths. Once, Helena had pointed out that a time would come when Bella would be so rich and famous that she,

Helena, might be the only person left in the world who could be honest with her. 'So you'd better learn to enjoy my little homilies! You've never lived in the real world, as it is. It will get worse.' Bella set too much store by behaving 'well', Helena had said – an impossible thing to do, unless you were a saint.

Bella did not think of herself as a saint; but no more did she think of herself as a person who had affairs. Being with Donald did not seem to be just an affair. Did Donald think of it as 'an affair', Bella wondered?

They had reached a cluster of white houses at the foot of a wooded hill. Helena pulled into the side and parked the car. 'Well, I must say, affair or not, it suits you.'

They got out. Ahead of them two white turrets rose among the trees. Their first glimpse of Belcastel.

'Oh, look at it.' Helena clasped her hands to her bosom. 'My heart sinks. So romantic without . . .'

'. . . and so without, within.' Bella finished off the school's well-worn joke. They laughed.

'It still looks like something out of Walt Disney.'

Another, smaller square tower came into view, rising among a mass of steeply pitched tiled roofs.

'We mustn't be rude about our old Alma Mater,' said Bella. 'She did introduce us.'

They decided for old times' sake to leave Helena's little blue Fiat at the foot of the hill, and toiled together up the cobbled street. An older woman was walking ahead of them. Though she was moving at a slower pace they drew nearer without overtaking her. She passed the iron gates of the school before they had reached them.

'Did you ever notice something sinister about this street?' Bella asked. 'There's never anyone coming down the hill. The women are always going uphill, into the distance, like all those Utrillo paintings. The women always have their backs to you.'

'That's only because you were going back to dreaded BC. Whenever we were going down the hill into town we were in such a state of ecstatic anticipation we never noticed anyone or anything. I was, anyway. Come on, let's have a photo of you in front of the gates. Famous escapees.'

The new headmistress – so unlike their own formidable Madame Talbot – offered them coffee in her study, which looked out over a deep valley towards distant mountains. How odd, in this building, to be treated like grown-ups and have doors opened for them. Helena, who had been a rebellious pupil, observed how amazing it was that such a beautiful view could ever have taken on such unpleasant associations. She explained that she and Madame Talbot had never really hit it off.

'I'm sure things are very different now,' she added. She had pretended, as pretext for arranging the visit, that she and her husband were thinking of the school for their daughters, in a few years' time.

The headmistress smiled. It was often the most reprobate girls, the lively ones, who got the most out of the school. She invited them to wander at will, though naturally, because of the vacation, the building lacked its customary animation. They would find some changes but much that remained the same. 'We are always happy for former pupils to come back and visit us.'

'To prove that there is life after Belcastel,' Helena muttered, as they set off.

The narrow corridors had not changed – muffled with dark-green carpets and veiled by a perpetual underwater dimness, in spite of high arched windows and whitewashed walls. They climbed a staircase to an upper floor where a confusing succession of identical heavy-panelled oak doors confronted them. They had bets on what they would find behind each door. But one room they were unanimous about. They knocked and waited, then entered. It was roomy but a little chilly, white, high-ceilinged, with carved wooden furniture painted almond green. There were two desks, with curved legs, two armchairs, two brass bedsteads at either side of a large window. This was the room, and this was the view the two of them had shared for two years, fourteen years before. It showed the other side of the same valley, a postcard view of scattered dwellings on green slopes, and distant snow-capped mountains, beyond which – the world. They looked upon it with a certain amount of wonder, thinking of what they had hoped for and what they had become. Helena considered her life and housebound times and sighed.

'You know, I always thought it would be completely the opposite. You very married and settled down with babies, being terribly efficient with nappies and feeds; and me bumming the world with pencil and notebook. And here's me locked into Harald and two infants, and still in *Geneva* of all places, can you beat that!'

She walked across to the window.

'Not that I would change it, mind you. I adore the girls. I'm sometimes afraid I'm in danger of eating them up I think they're so gorgeous. Harald's the same. But it does come as a bit of a surprise being so domestic. Well, not all that domestic, I suppose.' She giggled. 'I'm sorry, I do go on a bit. It's just that I get overexcited when I see a grown-up. Harald says I should get a nanny, but I simply won't. I had enough of that myself – well – you know . . .' She glanced at Bella and stopped speaking.

'It's not just living in sin, you know, Helena.' Bella looked at her forlornly. 'It's living with someone else's husband. It's wrong. *I* think. Donald thinks I'm daft.'

'You're afraid of turning into your mother, that's all. Do you still hear from her?'

'On my birthday. I think my father writes to her, oddly enough. He never talks about her. Do you remember that letter she wrote on my fifteenth birthday: one day I would understand . . . by now my father would have told me the whole story and I mustn't judge too harshly. All that stuff.'

'Dimly,' Helena said. 'What did your father say? Did you ever show him the letter?'

'He wouldn't read it in front of me. He didn't want to talk about it. I don't blame him. I let it drop. *He* said I shouldn't be too hard on her. They both say the same things.'

'*Are* you afraid of turning into your mother?' Helena asked.

'No! Good heavens!' Bella protested. 'What do you mean? I could never do what she did.'

'Didn't she run off with someone else's husband?'

'Donald's marriage was already over.'

'Then why don't you get married?'

Bella explained about Claire.

'Good heavens, girl,' Helena exclaimed, 'is that all! How perfectly feeble. You can deal with that, can't you? Surely? Do they have children? No? No children? Well, what's all the fuss about then? Where's your resources? What would Madame Talbot have said? This girl Claire, she's only an actress, for heaven's sake, isn't she? Sorry! But you know what I mean. No match for you, I'll bet.'

No match for her? Bella sighed. She had felt helpless, confronted by the image of Claire, in all her exemplary niceness; but Helena sometimes acted upon Bella like an energetic gardener, wading into her mind and yanking out the weeds to clear the terrain, so that productive thoughts that had been choked and overgrown could reach up for light and air. Braced by distance, both the real distance and the distance lent by Helena's view of her case, Bella began to feel a little more optimistic. There must surely be arguments that could sway Claire.

They had lunch on the way home and Bella telephoned Donald from the restaurant. He had been released for the day after all and they arranged to meet at the great monument to the Reformers, Calvin, Knox, Cromwell, Coligny and William of Orange, and then wander through to the flower market. Helena had to get back to pick the children up from school.

'When are you back off to London, you lucky sausage?'

Bella had one more week of filming in Geneva.

'And then what?'

So far filming had not supplanted the theatre in Bella's affection, and appetite turned to real hunger as she outlined their plans for Helena. The next season promised to build on the company's growing reputation, with Ibsen and Webster in prospect, and a rarely performed Russian play. As soon as they got back Bella and Donald would begin rehearsals for *The Rivals*, and that would be followed by a modern play which did not involve them; but the centrepiece of the season was to be their *Macbeth*. They had not worked with the director before but had heard great things about him. Bella began to feel excited at the thought – of the plays and of getting back to a familiar world, familiar work. 'It does all sound so incredibly glam,' Helena exclaimed.

On the drive back they arranged to have one last dinner, before Bella and Donald took off. Helena, at the wheel, chattered on, in joyful complaint about family life, until they were back in the middle of the town.

'Don't have children, whatever you do,' she advised Bella, leaning across to open the car door for her, 'they simply devour you. But do something about that Claire woman, Bella. You must!'

As Bella waved goodbye and watched the little Fiat dart into the stream of traffic with an energy and aggression that belied its size, Donald came up behind and put his arms around her.

chapter 14

'The witches are always a problem. Solve the witches and you're ninety-three and a third per cent there, believe me. The witches are key.'

Laurence Goddard was addressing the assembled cast of the New Company's *Macbeth*, gathered on the first day of rehearsals. The success of the second season had so far equalled the first. Now, the prospect of tackling a difficult and bloody play with a new director boosted the company and helped to banish fatigue; Goddard's growing reputation for a fresh, liberating approach, influenced by some time spent in Eastern Europe, generated keen anticipation. If for no other reason, a director who could insist upon, and obtain, a fourteen-week rehearsal period had to command respect. He stood before them now, an elegant understated figure in caramel cashmere over a faded blue plaid shirt, caramel cords.

He had started his introductory talk sitting tidily in his chair within the wide circle of chairs, but it had amused Bella at first to note that, like Victor Todmorden, he did not remain there long. Sheer enthusiasm, or possibly a need to dominate, had compelled him before long to rise to his feet, and now – one suede boot planted on the seat of the chair, his clasped hands working in unison to help him make his points – he leaned forward to persuade them.

After two hours their studied expressions of interest were beginning here and there to leak traces of some personal subtexts. Donald's was ambiguous: fascination but with a frown; his eyes were cast down and elusive, his creased brow might equally portend concentration or consternation. Bella's wide-open eyes, on the other hand, could have been registering either edge-of-the-seat enthralment or a stare of disbelief, but whether at so much genius or so much garbage, who could say? Perhaps two conflicting emotions merged as she tried to absorb the idea that she was to play one of the witches, along with the Porter and the Doctor, as well as wife to the thane.

Goddard asked for forbearance: 'just in case you are all hearing the sound of alarums ringing!' Nothing was fixed at this point, he promised. He leaned forward still further and seemed to engage each person directly. 'No. It just might be useful to kick it around for a bit, see what emerges from the woodwork. You never know. Especially with this piece. Don't worry,' he laughed, 'if it doesn't work we throw it out!' Several people shifted in their chairs. He smiled a broad smile, sweeping his eyes round the group. 'Any questions?' There was silence. 'Then let's have a read of it, shall we?'

At this there was a ripple of undisguised alarum. Julie, the company manager, spoke out. 'We ought to break pretty soon, Laurence. It's five to one.'

'Good God!' Laurence was as amazed as the next person at how long he had managed to go on for. They broke for an early lunch.

'Back at one-thirty everybody,' Julie called. 'Everyone to be here, please, for a read-through, then we'll look at the sets, discuss costume, wigs and so on. Oh and we'll be making appointments through the afternoon for each of you to go to wardrobe over the next few days, and for wig calls as necessary. Thank you.'

Waiting rooms always looked to Bella like bad sets, got up by a rep designer on a very low budget. There were a great number of components, but they didn't add up to anything. This one, with its long polished table in the centre, set among regency chairs with seats in striped red and cream satin, looked as if, in real life, it masqueraded as a dining room; but there was nothing that suggested hospitality or good cheer. The dull gold brocade curtains, drawn full length across the windows, excluded the world and dulled the sound-effects of traffic outside, a motorbike roaring, the juddering of a taxi engine, voices and the hollow slam of a door as the passenger got in, before the engine picked up and the taxi drove off.

The central candelabra was a crude modern fitting whose fluorescent glare obliterated the mellower light of two standard lamps that stood in opposite corners. The little display light over the oil-painting above the mantelpiece – a ship foundering in heavy seas watched from the shore by a huddle of people – was unlit. Though far more sombre, it reminded Bella of the painting at Fortnum's of the French captain's wife clinging to her piece of wreckage. In the middle of the mantelpiece, in between two small baskets arranged with dried flowers, stood a golden clock under a glass dome. When Bella hurried in straight from rehearsal, she was relieved that it said only ten to six.

Bella had not visited Dr Beale before. She looked round the room for somewhere to sit. In the middle of the table and on the sideboard, there were more dried flowers, a larger bunch, flanked by piles of magazines, mainly out-of-date monthlies, *Country Life*, *House and Garden*, *Harpers* and one or two colour supplements thrown in. Along the wall, at right angles to the door, the only note of welcome was struck by a deep sofa in reddish leather, but the thought of succumbing to this lure and sinking into it made Bella nervous. She chose instead the hard highbacked chair between the sideboard and a small aquarium, which remained hidden until the door was closed.

She felt worn out. She leaned back and tried to absorb some of the calm and quiet of the room and recover from the scramble of getting to Harley Street. The rush-hour traffic had jangled her nerves still further after an aggravating rehearsal. Why did Laurence always have to make everything as difficult as possible? Yes, he had agreed to release her fifteen minutes early so that she could get to her appointment, but so reluctantly!

Then, when the time came to leave, he had managed to make her feel like a criminal, by the subtle technique of ignoring her as if she were some naughty schoolgirl. She had been forced into an elaborate pantomime, tapping her watch and pulling faces at Julie to indicate that she had to go; all the more annoying since, although Laurence had scheduled the Letter scene for that afternoon, there was clearly no chance that they were going to get to it. They probably would not get to it tomorrow morning either, but now Bella would have to be there first thing, and how she longed to sleep in just a little, just one morning.

Nor could Donald and Laurence be said to be hitting it off. More than once that afternoon Bella had thought that Donald was about to lay Laurence out flat, 'If I can summon up the energy from somewhere.' With each succeeding day of rehearsals the feeling had grown, that instead of contributing to the dynamics of the work Laurence sucked all the energy from it. That morning he had been expounding his theories on free will and posing searching metaphysical questions about whether the presence in the play of the supernatural robbed Macbeth of any choice in his actions. Macbeth had only half understood the prophecy, he argued. Had he known the meaning of 'a man to woman born' he would have acted differently. He droned on about how in effect this passed the power in the play back to God (and to the powers of darkness) and made Macbeth less a tragic than a pathetic hero.

'All the Greeks did it of course, with the oracles. They never give you all the information. You wouldn't have a play if they did.'

Donald gnashed his teeth. He knew now from experience that these meditations of Laurence's rarely solved the immediate problem of how to get characters on and off stage, let alone how to keep the audience interested.

At night, at home, Donald would rage.

'He talks in bloody programme notes. I don't mind a little healthy discussion! Of course things have to be sorted – but the *time* that man wastes in sheer gab! No wonder he needed fourteen weeks! We don't get any work done! I'm the one who has to go out there!'

She had not dared to tell Donald how Laurence had reacted to her request. How much longer would Donald hang on to his temper, she wondered? He was having a hard enough time hanging on for his own sake; something like this, concerning her, might easily have him – as he was fond of saying – 'flying off the handle and hitting the fan'. Asked in an interview on the BBC why *Macbeth* was such a notoriously unlucky play to perform, Donald had replied, 'Because of Laurence Goddard, I imagine,' and then had apologized profusely and pretended he had misheard the question.

So far Bella had suffered less than Donald under the hammer of Laurence's loquacity. She sensed that Laurence preferred not to deal with women. He merely observed that her scenes were 'pretty straightforward really', and, though he offered little help, he did not interfere either, and that suited Bella fine.

The spell of filming had increased Bella's enjoyment of work and the routine of their days: leaving with Donald in the morning, or meeting him at the theatre if he had left early to work out at the gym; staying on at the rehearsal to watch his scenes and give him moral support (and try to avert impending explosions). She thought of Helena, whose life was easy and pleasant enough; but Helena hardly saw Harald except in the early mornings and the evenings and at weekends.

Bella longed for a cup of tea. That might revive her a little. The doctor did not seem to be in too much of a hurry. She leaned back in the chair and glanced into the aquarium beside her. Its light, like the light above the painting over the mantelpiece, was not on, so that at first she assumed it was derelict. But after a moment, having rejected the heap of magazines by her right shoulder, she looked to her left into the glass box and became aware of movement in the gloom, small disturbances, little flicks and flurries. Aquariums are supposed to have a soothing effect on human beings, but after she had stared into the lugubrious shadows of this one for a few moments Bella wondered why. All the same, she found it easier to fix her eyes on these dark little sliding shapes – it really was a very small tank – than on the synthetized décor. Even the clock, whose face she had been so relieved to see when she came in, was clearly not 'practical' but a prop, since it was still telling the same story, ten to six. This small asphyxiation of time gave Bella a shock that she could not explain.

She turned back to the aquarium. Inside the box the tiny dark forms were still performing their inconsolable digressions, aiming hard and then, without coquetry, making sudden abrupt turns; two small striped fish and two others, smaller still. In the corner, where some light pierced through from one of the standard lamps, she noticed one slightly larger, gaudier fish, red and orange with a strange false tail, a long black queue tacked on to a fluffy burnished fan, just where you would have assumed the fish ended. It was a touch of pure elegance.

This fish had different patterns of behaviour as well as of design. It did not swim along the water following horizontal planes, but moved against the currents, up and down, confining itself to one corner only; up and down, back up and down again, always facing the glass, a compulsive, obsessive rhythm. A neurotic fish. Perhaps, it occurred to Bella, it was able to make out its reflection in the glass and was frantic to get its own attention, driven wild by its apparent imperviousness to its own splendour, incapable of comprehending its own mystifying unpiscean responses. It was a relief when at last it broke its own gaze and swam away from the glass with unblinking eyes and sorrowing expression; but soon it flipped back on itself and returned again to meet its own expressionless stare. Up and down.

'Miss Provan?' The receptionist, short, bright and blonde, dressed unexpectedly in a cornflower-blue suit, had thought at first that the room was empty; but, popping her head further round the door, she had spotted Bella beside the fish tank. 'Oh, there you are! Dr Beale is ready for you now.'

Bella got up, a little dazed.

'Aren't they fascinating?' the girl said brightly. 'I must remember to feed them. We lost a few last month.'

She held the door open and stood aside to let Bella through into the hallway. 'You know the way, do you? First landing, the door on your left.'

Bella knew that she would never forget Donald's face when she told him that she was pregnant – looking first as if he must not have heard properly, then falling into bewilderment as he took the meaning in. For a moment she thought he might cry; then somehow, slowly, his face reconstructed itself with wonder and pride and solicitude and he came over to her and held her. Why had she said nothing till now?

'Well, I do sometimes miss a period if I'm tired or under a lot of pressure, so I didn't think too much about it.' She hardly needed to tell Donald about the pressure, which had been growing steadily throughout the season, building towards *Macbeth*. Great expectation surrounded this production in particular. Bella and Donald, when Donald could be spared, were continually being hauled out of rehearsals to give interviews; but the enthusiasm and optimism they felt obliged to express in public reflected less and less the discouraged atmosphere of rehearsals.

'At first I thought: give it just a few more weeks until we get stuck into rehearsals.' She had half believed that her body would adjust itself, once *Macbeth* opened. Even when she missed a second period she had been inclined to attribute it to nerves, aggravated by the mood of Laurence's rehearsals. Tension mounted daily within her. As time went on her tiredness and low spirits dragged her down and made it so hard to work – she could not shake them off. Such feelings had plagued her earlier life, and some of her time at the Royal, but since she and Donald had been together she had almost forgotten them. At this rate, she had begun to doubt whether she would manage the long haul to the first night. 'Finally I thought I should be a good girl and go and see someone, just to be on the safe side.'

Dr Beale had simply confirmed the strong, growing suspicion that Bella had been keeping to herself.

Donald's evident emotion at the prospect of parenthood displaced her own confused feelings. To her amazement he began almost at once to behave like a stock character, and to treat her like some exquisite and fragile plant. He demonstrated a powerful need to join in, to pay homage to the event-to-be, to associate himself with it, in a series of endearing, classic gestures. Only half in jest, he instantly urged her to put up her feet and offered to make her cocoa. Was it all right for her still to drink alcohol? She had to wrest her celebratory glass out of his hand. 'I'm allowed a glass of wine!' she declared. 'Or two!'

He kept shielding her from draughts. 'What about Lady M, my darling? Isn't it a bit risky? What did the doctor say?'

Bella reassured him. Some women worked on almost to term these days. 'Dr Beale didn't seem in the least bit worried – just said I should be careful not to overdo things. Anyway, with luck *Macbeth* will be practically over before I'm even beginning to bulge. Ma said when she was carrying me she barely showed, even after five months. Otherwise wardrobe will just have to make a few cunning adjustments!'

'What about the new season though?'

The new season was another matter. Of course Bella would have to drop out. The baby, everyone assured her, would more than make up for *The White Devil* and *The Queen and the Rebels* and *Hedda Gabler*. Bella felt less sanguine. Donald's simple delight helped her to struggle with her disappointment. He treated her as if she had been touched by the philosopher's stone.

But out of it all there did come one compensation, over which Bella could only rejoice. In the face of this powerful fact of Bella's pregnancy, Claire Ballader capitulated. The marriage was dead: long live the marriage.

chapter 15

At the thought of giving up a day's rehearsal for the wedding Laurence Goddard's teeth had clenched tight, rippling his jaw – a familiar sign of his displeasure. Christmas would already interfere quite sufficiently with his rehearsal plans. Now he was being asked for another sacrifice, a precious Saturday morning.

Donald's enragement crossed new bounds. 'One morning out of fourteen suppurating weeks! I nearly hit him.'

'It will be getting a bit close to opening,' Bella said. She was feeling a little shaky, unnerved as much by Donald's fury as by Laurence's reluctance.

'We have a whole damn week of dress rehearsals, for Chrissake! Two public dress rehearsals! Well, I'm going to put my foot down, otherwise he's not going to have a show worth spitting at.'

Laurence, when tackled a second time by a grim-faced Donald, clasped his hands, reversed the clasp, palms down, and examined the floor directly in front of him. (This was his habitual response to any remotely difficult question, which one of the cast had labelled 'Looking for the show!') He got as far as muttering, 'I wish . . .' and then, fortunately perhaps for him, stopped himself. He gave his consent.

'I think he was actually going to say "I wish you'd thought of it before." I think he was going to suggest we get married on a Sunday,' Donald reported afterwards to Bella. 'Register offices don't open on Sundays.'

'Laurence doesn't know that,' Bella said. 'He thinks it's all very irresponsible. Bad planning.'

'No planning at all!'

'He can't imagine that I would choose to play Lady M heavily pregnant.'

'He probably does. "Oh. I see, Bella? Yes. Well? Quite an interesting character choice, Bella dear, just a touch inconvenient at present . . ." '

'He may well get his wish. If the divorce doesn't come through in time there won't be any wedding.'

'Well, that won't be the end of the world. There's still a few months before the little bastard's due.'

Bella sighed. 'I was thinking of Pa. I just think he'll take it better about the baby if we are actually married when it arrives.'

On the following Sunday Donald and Bella drove to Hampshire for lunch with Walter Provan. Now that Bella was going to make a respectable man of Donald, she had seen fit to allow him to meet her father. Walter Provan had suggested that, as Mrs Hunter, his housekeeper, did not come in on Sundays, it might be more agreeable if he did not attempt to cook for them (Donald had chuckled. 'Like Father, like daughter!'). He proposed instead that Donald and Bella join him round the fire at home for a pre-prandial glass of sherry, before repairing to the Grosvenor Hotel in the High Street.

The Drover's House turned out to be a modest red-brick cottage, surrounded on all sides by a garden and white picket fence. The garden, now swept and bare, was composed chiefly of lawns and fruit trees, with deep borders along the front of the house, where in this season only a few shrubs survived. Evidently Walter Provan had been keeping a look-out for them, for as soon as the car turned into the lane he appeared at the open door and moved briskly forward to greet them, a slightly built, fit-looking man of medium height, with white hair that seemed to make his face still more youthful.

'Welcome, welcome!' Walter Provan hugged his daughter

briefly before turning to Donald, smiling and gripping his hand firmly, eyes scrutinizing his face. 'How do you do, Ballader. Good journey down?'

Donald's immediate sense of Bella's father, which an afternoon in his company reinforced, was of a man of the world whose extremely attractive surface, his social ease, cultivation and charm, made it difficult to determine where his true nature, his passions, might lie. Except where his daughter was concerned. Although he teased Bella at every point, and laughed aloud when she repeated Donald's suggestion that she must have inherited her culinary skills from him, every time his eyes fell on her the lines of his face softened.

Bella commented on how splendid the house was looking, and indeed not only did it present a well-cared-for aspect, but it had nothing about it to suggest the house of a bachelor. It was tidy but not austere, there were chrysanthemums and cyclamens in shining planters. 'Mrs Hunter takes good care of you, Pa, from the look of it,' Bella said, coming back from the kitchen with salted almonds.

As she joined them by the fire Walter Provan declared that he had not yet got used to finding himself with an actress for a daughter. He confessed to feeling some alarm at the notion of actors as a breed. 'Don't get me wrong, Ballader. It's a breed for which I have the warmest respect. I studied Greats at Oxford and I think my ideas have never budged much beyond the ancient origins of the drama – actors as a kind of religious scapegoat, do you know? Priests almost, partakers of life on our behalf. Fanciful, I daresay.'

'Well, sir, who knows? If I may say so, yours seems altogether a very charitable view,' Donald said. 'I have to admit to having a similar sense of the mystery of your own profession. I may have slighted Bella's kitchen know-how earlier, but I must say I've always put her histrionic abilities down to heredity. Don't you think the Diplomatic service might equally adopt a mask, or masks, as the emblem of its trade?'

'Touché!' Walter Provan had laughed again and refilled Donald's glass.

'Mine, too, Pa.' Bella held out her glass, encouraged to see that Donald seemed to be meeting with her father's approval, and pulling a face at Donald's reproving frown.

She had prepared her father for their news only by telling him that she wanted him to meet someone very special. Donald had objected. Surely it would be kinder all round not to spring it on him at this first meeting? But Bella said she could not tell him just like that, over the phone.

Now, as her father leaned down to top up her sherry, she said simply, 'Pa, I have something to tell you. Donald and I are going to be married.'

Walter Provan straightened up, looked at Bella, looked at Donald, almost frowning, and then said quite crossly, 'Bella, I wish you'd told me that when you came in. We could have been drinking champagne. I put a bottle in the refrigerator.' He turned to Donald. 'I thought something must be up. She doesn't bring her young men to meet me as a rule.'

Only now did he embrace Bella, and turn to shake Donald's hand, patting his shoulder at the same time, his face a little flushed. He fetched the champagne and crystal flutes and they toasted each other. He toasted them, they toasted him; all trying, under cover of small rituals, to gauge the sincerity of each other's reactions.

Bella left them together for a moment to fetch her coat, and Walter Provan raised his glass once more. 'Useless to try to stop my Bella once she's got an idea into her head; even were I to wish it, even if you were the most out-and-out bounder!' (Did Donald detect a fleeting anxiety in the older man's eyes?) He went on: 'I must say she seems very happy. At last. Thank you. Take care of her.'

By the time the three of them settled round a table by the window in the panelled dining room of the Grosvenor Hotel and had had another bottle of champagne, they were behaving more like old friends, or the family parties that surrounded them. Donald studied the former diplomat as he sat holding the heavy synthetic-leather folder away from the table, looking down his nose through half-glasses to peruse the wine list.

In her father's features Donald could trace pale resemblances to his beloved, translated into the masculine form, the grey eyes set closer and deeper; the same hooded lids, fine straight nose, the positive line of the jaw – Walter Provan's was more square. But he too had an intent yet abstracted way of listening, with a slight frown, as if waiting for the polite moment to leap in and disagree, and then, on the contrary, agreeing with fervour, and a frown even more marked.

As for Walter Provan, he seemed to welcome Donald almost with relief – a man to talk to, perhaps the son he had never had, who could reassure him that Bella would have someone to look after her. He did look a little put out when they began to talk about the arrangements for the wedding.

'I had a suspicion that something was impending,' he confessed. 'I had not foreseen such imminence.' He looked thoughtful but said nothing more. Instead he expressed his approval in a roundabout way, pressing Donald to have some Stilton as well as pudding, and issuing jocular warnings over a glass of armagnac. 'I just hope you know what you're taking on, young man. She has a mind of her own. Be warned!'

He and Donald combined forces to tease Bella. The elder man took delight in regaling Donald with tales to illustrate the wayward side of her nature. Ignoring Bella's groans of protest, he produced a stream of reminiscences – fondly logging the characteristic acts and small disobediences of her childhood.

One story he relished in particular concerned Bella, aged about twelve, going with him into the village store of the small seaside town where they were staying for a few days, to buy some gloves. But before they got to the gloves Bella's eye had been caught by a notice advertising some small handmirrors 'guaranteed unbreakable'.

'She gave me no peace. I had to let her try to see whether it was true, so, with the owner's permission, try she did!'

The mirror had not broken but it had, however, bounced. It had bounced up at a sharp angle hard against the large central display case and smashed its front to pieces. Shards of glass had fallen on to the neat rows of scarves and gloves and socks. Walter Provan shook with laughter at the memory. 'I shall never forget the poor man's face! I warn you, Donald – she'll put you to the test!'

Bella decided the time had come to put a stop to these slanders, and forbade her father to tell any more tales. It hadn't been at all like that, she protested; but her annoyance was transparently feigned. A mixture of deep contentment and excitement stole over Donald as he observed Bella's glowing face, basking in the affection of the two men she loved. It could be the fabled effects of pregnancy or simply the effect of being perfectly happy that made her at that moment more beautiful than he had seen her.

'I think he's a bit lonely,' Bella said afterwards.

Donald doubted it. 'He is a *terrific* charmer – *and* I'd say he's got quite an eye for the ladies.'

'Pa?' The outrageousness of the idea appealed to Bella. 'Never! He can be awfully charming, but he's actually very shy.'

She had not told her father that she was expecting a child, but Donald had an idea that the older man had guessed. Certainly, Donald thought, he was not the man to have illusions that his daughter was living chastely in London, nor to pass any judgement on her if she were not. The illusions were more likely to be on Bella's side, fancying she needed to shield him from reality. He seemed a person who attached importance to appearances, to 'form' – it may well have been through him that Bella had acquired her fondness for the more conventional moral structures. Yet Bella's portrait of the stern puritanical parent, deserted in his most need by a shallow wife, did not seem to square with this worldly, reflective man.

The three of them had discussed the most likely date and the arrangements for the wedding, which must not only be truncated but could not be entirely relied on, since they depended on the expedition of the lawyers dealing with Donald's divorce: the ceremony to be followed by lunch for a very few friends, Walter Provan, and Donald's two sisters and their families, if they could make it. Walter Provan insisted that it was his prerogative to pay for the wedding lunch: 'You're letting me off easy. I was prepared for something far more lavish.' He even proposed staying on for a week or so in London and coming to see *Macbeth*. 'I'll put up at a hotel. No need to give me a thought. You won't even know I'm there.'

When they were leaving and Donald brought the car round from the car park, Walter refused a lift and insisted on walking home.

'You've given me a lot to digest – quite apart from the Grosvenor's efforts.' And he patted his stomach.

He saw Bella into the car, making sure that his daughter's skirt was well clear of the door frame and that her safety belt was fastened. He leaned forward so that he could see both their faces.

'Well then. You know your way. Drive safely.'

Donald started the car, but Bella's father had something more to say. He hesitated. Perhaps it was from stooping down that his face had reddened.

'Em . . . I ought to say . . . There is . . .'

Bella and Donald waited, looking at him.

'There is someone I should very much like to bring to the wedding, if that's in order. Someone I should like you both to meet.'

Donald said, 'Certainly, sir. With great pleasure. That will be simply wonderful. Terrific.'

'Good. Splendid.' He slammed the door and Bella wound down the window. 'Safe journey, then,' he said, and added, slapping the roof of the car, 'Precious cargo.'

chapter 16

Bella did not dwell on the difference between the wedding she had and any wedding she might ever have imagined having. For one thing, it had never occurred to her that when she repeated her marriage vows she would be with child. Nor did she imagine that the number of guests at the wedding buffet would be swelled by the entire cast of *Macbeth*; or that instead of a honeymoon she would be looking forward to an arduous week of technical and dress rehearsals.

Probably the words 'marriage' and 'wedding', which once were clear and sharp and embraced images of blue skies and frothy whiteness, had begun to fray when her first ill-fated engagement had fallen apart. Her subsequent trespass, with Aubrey, into another woman's marriage had further shredded the edges. Now Donald's existence invested the words with a new meaning and urgency. Need, necessity: the need to know that she would not lose him. Beyond his words and her certainty, she needed rights. Essentially, she needed to dispose of Claire. She could do without church aisles and red carpets and orange blossom; a low-budget production could be equally effective.

The Times printed a photograph of Donald and Bella above the legend 'Mr and Mrs Macbeth – a quiet wedding', and gave details of the forthcoming production, as well as an account of the wedding celebrations. This time Victor Todmorden, not Tony Tell, played the part of best man (and wore a jacket to mark the occasion); but Tony also featured, looking out to left of frame, next to an attractive dark-haired woman (not identified in the caption) on whose other side stood the father of the bride, looking distinguished and beaming. In the background Nancy Bailey and Lindon Grant, Dolly, Michael Brodie, in fact the New Company in full force, could be made out. The wedding guests all had their mouths open, frozen in mid-phrase as if they were shouting abuse or jeering at someone offstage, while Donald and Bella smiled into each other's eyes, standing behind a three-tiered wedding cake and sharing a knife.

And the world looked upon the union and said, on the whole, 'Yes!' Approval was widespread, if not universal. Of course there was a handful, a good handful, of dissidents and denigrators, nauseated by the sight of so much success. Otherwise, those who were happy themselves were among the more optimistic. Those who had once been happy wished them well – a few good years at least – but otherwise reserved judgement; because you never know.

The world experienced a second, unlooked-for frisson on the first night of *Macbeth*, for one or two enterprising photographers managed to get a shot of Tony Tell arriving at the theatre with his companion for the evening: none other than Claire Craig (formerly Claire Ballader). To some folk this choice seemed decidedly odd; but others suggested that it only went to show the cordiality, the sophistication of the relations between Donald and Claire and Bella – otherwise how could Tony Tell have contemplated, let alone brought about, such an unlikely event?

The fact was that it was Tony who continued to spin the thin thread that linked Claire to the world. Tony was not given to having women as friends; Claire was the exception. Once a week without fail he burst in on her down the phone and blasted her ears to buck her up, bullying her into a sense of shame, and seeing to it that, in this time of famine, even if she had no work she did at least go to class from time to time, however irrelevant and juvenile it seemed to her.

In this way, he frequently invited Claire to the theatre and managed to make her feel that when it came to evenings at the theatre she was his favourite date: she always looked a million dollars, always had a good time, always liked the same shows as him and – on those occasions when duty obliged him to sit through a client's play to the bitter end – if she did go to sleep she slept quietly. What more could an agent ask? He acquired a decorative companion for the evening, and – by rescuing her, however briefly, from the humdrum spiritual grind of an out-of-work actress and allowing her to be seen out and about and still in active circulation – he performed the kind office of a friend as well as an agent.

Was she free to go to a show on the 19th? Of course she was. It had not even occurred to her to ask what show they were going to see. It had taken her several days to make the connection. When at last she did, she telephoned, pronto, to extricate herself, crying: 'Tony, no! *No*. I've just realized. The 19th is the Scottish Play. It's out of the question, Tony. No.'

'Claire, yes!' he had returned and proceeded to scold her for a host of shortcomings, childishness, cowardice, self-indulgence, oversensitivity, arrogance, rating herself too high and rating herself too low.

'No,' she said. 'Sorry. But no. Really. I don't see the point. Why should I drag myself through all that? I mean, it's one thing to go out a bit and be seen to be a going concern, quite another to be stripped naked and publicly burned at the stake.'

Tony had roared first with laughter and then with outrage and warned her that she was in danger of becoming crazy and boring. He refused to stand by and let her do this to her life. What after all could be more natural than to go to the theatre with one's agent? In the end Claire had pursued the easier course and given in. Tony had taken the decision from her hands. The responsibility, if not the pain, would be his. So Claire went to the ball; not for any of Tony's excellent psychological or professional reasons, but because even the possible hurt would hoist up some kind of landmark in the plateau of her days.

And, certainly, Claire's consuming aimlessness vanished during the ten days that ran up to the 19th. She made herself a dress for one thing, out of an old silk taffeta evening gown she'd been meaning to do something with. She went back to her neglected hairdresser as a 'Student's Night' model and had some highlights to put in to 'lift' the hair, and herself.

'Stunning,' Tony breathed into her ear, kissing her just above the blusher on her cheek, when he collected her that evening on the dot of five o'clock.

An hour and a half later, by the time they were sliding away from the Ritz, where Tony had taken her for champagne and a 'pre-emptive' smoked-salmon sandwich, and were enjoying once again the cosy grandeur of the chauffeur-driven limousine, with the rain fretting the windscreen, Claire, though not drunk, was ever so slightly afloat, slightly above it all.

At the theatre Tony deposited their coats and umbrella. Claire greeted and was greeted by friends, kisses and exclamations in abundance. The surprise – seeing her of all people, here of all places – was real but so was the affection. She began to feel glad she had come.

'You see?' Tony said, pleased with himself, as they filed in to take their seats. The play began in silence. The lights went down, the curtains hissed upwards, there was no music, no fanfare. It was only normal for Claire, along with most of the actors in the audience, to feel her heart lurch and her stomach contract. She said an involuntary prayer.

The interval seemed to arrive within minutes. Tony guided Claire through the milling critics, strangers and acquaintances to find their drinks on a window-shelf. Across the foyer friends, unable to make themselves heard, caught each other's eyes with a query and nodded their answer. Their faces signalled approval.

'Yes? No?' Tony asked her.

Claire laughed and shrugged. 'Yes and no. Donald's in voice. He's terrific, don't you think?'

Tony narrowed his eyes. 'Yes . . . when he's not trying too hard to be soft. He doesn't have to play irresolution, for God's sake, it's ingrained.'

Claire said, 'That's not fair. You'd never think that to meet him.'

Tony said, 'What about Bella?'

At first she thought he was referring to Donald's relationship with Bella. In mid-breath she changed tack and remarked, 'I'm not the best judge perhaps.'

'Even so.'

But at that moment Victor and Viv Todmorden and Ted Danniman came up, with Sir Paul Stern, and each gave Claire a big hug. They exchanged views, praising Donald especially.

'What about my other client?' Tony asked. He had a way of conveying interest and disinterest at the same time. His view of Bella's performance appeared unaffected by whatever he thought of her as a person.

'It's interesting to make her so vain, I suppose,' Claire offered, 'and so rapacious.'

'Yes. A touch of the spoilt brat about it,' Tony mused. 'She's not afraid of being unsympathetic, I'll give her that. But a bit refined, isn't she? All that "unsex me" and taking milk for gall and so on. I wasn't really convinced. Were you?'

'I thought that was rather good,' said Ted Danniman.

Viv confessed that at first she had not believed it either, as she watched, but now she found it had made her think again; perhaps the thane's wife, as well as the thane, had had to wind herself up, screw up her own courage to make it stick, so that she could urge her husband on. Perhaps it was by measuring it against her own that she was able to recognize the extent of her husband's trepidation.

'It is interesting,' Victor mused, 'though I'm not altogether sure that it's a reading that's entirely supported by the text. Call me pedantic!' he added, laughing at himself.

Sir Paul agreed. 'I've never seen it done in quite this way, but how excellent to be made to see something that has never struck one before. It's quite another side to Lady M. Bella always manages to lead one to something new.'

'The famous vulnerability,' Tony murmured, downing his whisky as the interval bell rang for the third time. The others headed off to the far side of the foyer and Tony held his arm out in the direction of the stalls, inviting Claire to precede him. 'They're good together though,' he said as she passed in front of him, 'very sexy.'

Which was the verdict of the audience too; and certainly no dissenting voices were to be heard in the backstage corridors, when the play was done.

chapter 17

The applause was punctuated by shouts of 'Bravo!', tentative at first but gathering confidence with each curtain call and achieving an almost Continental assurance when Bella and Donald came on to take a separate call. Laurence Goddard allowed the cast to coax him on stage, the designer too. The calls prolonged themselves – 'They'll be calling for the author next,' Tony commented, but he had been one of the first on his feet, whether in genuine tribute or from professional canniness it was hard to tell. A standing ovation could do his clients no harm.

Once it became the less conspicuous position, Claire stood too and applauded with the rest, but her mind was pushing on through to the next scene, backstage.

'Tony,' she said, trying to catch his attention. 'Tony?'

'Mmm?' His eyes continued to scan the auditorium.

'Listen. I don't think I'm up for the backstage performance too. I've had a lovely time, but now I'd really just as soon go off home.'

Tony barely heard her. The evening was beginning to turn untidy. Half the audience was still applauding and calling, and looked like settling in; the other half, in a dogged frenzy, were weaving in and out among the half-empty rows, trying to beat the rush to the cloakrooms and to taxis. The stage manager took matters into his own hands by bringing up the house lights.

'Tony? Why don't you just put me in a cab?'

'What? Nonsense. Don't be an idiot.'

Tony's usual practice was to wait until the auditorium emptied and take the short cut backstage, bullying his way through the pass door if need be; but here Claire asserted herself.

The thought of blundering backstage like a duck on to dry land held a familiar terror: out of this half-world into that other half-world, the two far from complementary; along corridors where preoccupied, unfamiliar actors with not much on jostled against overdressed first-nighters; friends and agents and administrators, dressers running from room to room with laundry and props and bits of costume, dressing-room doors ajar revealing bright lights and mirrors where more actors were reflected, in underpants and body make-up, grabbing towels and peeling off facial hair. 'Can you tell me which dressing room . . . ?'

'The entire cast will be in the shower for at least twenty minutes, Tony, washing blood off themselves.' There had been a lot of blood, even for the Scottish Play. 'If we must go,' Claire continued, and she doubted her strength to resist Tony if his mind were made up – though why should she feel under any obligation to Tony for heaven's sake? – 'I definitely don't want to be the first there. I don't actually want to be there at all. But if I have to go you must give me a drink first.'

On this point she prevailed. They had a drink in the stalls bar; and afterwards took the legitimate route, through the foyer, out the front and round to the stage-door, stepping out of the theatre into the damp street as into some brutal decompression chamber – a shock of icy oxygen – then quickly back inside the theatre again, past a clutch of fans at the stage-door, where they entered to breathe a clamorous third air, backstage.

Bella had been finding it difficult to breathe at all, before, during, afterwards. Donald had been way up all evening, his form of nerves not at all fearful, working for him. She was glad. Still more because her own nerves had been of a new order such as she had never experienced before, something extreme. She had said nothing to Donald – he had enough on his plate – but it had been an effort. She had had to expend precious energy to hide her state from him, so that concern for her did not distract him. For herself just now everything seemed to go by extremes, including sudden and disconcerting swings of mood. Not for one second had she anticipated the terrible plunge of her spirits that had followed the wedding. She put it down to tiredness and to pregnancy. She was not sleeping and of course that made all things worse. So tonight's manifestation did not surprise her – an exaggerated form of the first-night excruciation she usually suffered; but she had never known it take such a physical toll. So – even towards the end of the play, before her last entrance, the sleepwalking scene, so far in – she stood shaking behind the black masking at the top of the stairs. Her dress was a heavy velvet, shot red and green, manageable on the ground; but going up the narrow plank stairs to get to the upper level of the scenery she needed both hands to lift it, and had only a scaffolding rail to one side of her and the weight of the long train dragging her backwards. Craziness.

Of course it should have been a nightdress, or some undergarment. Laurence had quoted some batty historical notions about Elizabeth I being afraid to go to bed towards the end of her life and sleeping sitting up, fully clothed. What was historical about denying the text where everyone goes on about a nightgown? And the high wired collar obscured her vision left and right, hemming her in. Never again would she try to oblige a director just because he was having a few problems during the dress. (After the wedding he had managed to imply that every problem he had – and there were many – arose from having allowed Donald and Bella half a day off.) Margaret, who was dressing her, could have helped take some of the weight, but Bella had let her go off to help with somebody else's quick change. Bella needed Margaret now. Wardrobe would have to find someone else tomorrow to see to that. There was no sense in this. Literally bending over backwards.

She had got to the top at last but only by leaning forward to counter the dead weight of the costume, almost kissing the steps as she crept up them one by one, skirts lifted, so that she took the weight with her shoulders. All the while as she climbed she was aware of a low dragging sensation raking her body. The pain under her right collar-bone was still there too, making it difficult to take proper breaths. 'This is wonderful!' she thought, trying not to panic. Slow deep breaths usually helped to control her panic, but tonight each breath was like a knifing. At the top her eyes darted to and fro. Where was the cue light? Not where it was supposed to be. She peered into the blackness for a little red warning glow. It had not been there at the dress and she had meant to mention it during notes. Why hadn't she? So many things had needed attention. Hers were not the only problems.

At least the actors were audible from up here. On the stage below, Michael and Terry had just begun projecting their hushed dialogue. Of course! During notes she had been sorting out about the taper. As soon as she had set eyes on them it had been obvious that those stairs made a nonsense of the taper. It was one thing to mime descending a staircase in a rehearsal skirt in broad daylight, quite another to manage all this and a naked candle too, however terrific it looked from out front. The fireman would probably have objected in any case. A lantern had been substituted. But where was that? The lantern was not there either. It was supposed to be set at the top of the stairs. Where? She shifted the inky folds of the blacks beside her and peered about in the darkness. No lantern. It probably was there somewhere, but unlit she could never spot it.

Now she became aware of a silence. Her cue? Had she missed it? She strained to hear. Nothing. If it was just a pause it was a long one. Her heart had begun to pound, so hard that her body began to oscillate, rapidly, back and forth in rhythm. Still nothing. Not a sound. Nothing for it. She pushed open the door and moved on to the platform at the top of the staircase.

'That, sir, which I will not report after her . . .'

Too soon! She was on too soon. She steadied herself. It was all right – not so bad – only a fraction too soon. It would give Michael and Terry a chance to register that she had no light. She held her downstage arm high, and crooked it, cupping her hand as if she were shielding a light in the other, empty hand, which her long, hanging (totally unperiod) sleeve concealed. This of course meant that her face was partly obscured too. Then, crossing along the upper shelf high above them, she reached the platform on the other side of the stage. Here she found a pool of light on the floor and mimed setting the non-existent light down. Then she spread out her right palm before her, slowly pushed back the heavy sleeve.

'*Yet here's a spot.*'

'Never seen it better done! And we've seen a few, haven't we, Tilly?' Sir Leslie Berwick, explorer and keen theatregoer, raised his voice above the din so that his wife could hear and corroborate. 'How do you do it? How do you people do it? The sleepwalking scene,' Sir Leslie added.

'Oh, superb!' cried Lady Tilly. 'Breathtaking!'

'Heartbreaking, too, in many ways.'

Bella smiled and was gracious and modest and did not roll her eyes or mutter 'if you did but know' as she had a few moments before, when Michael Brodie and Nancy Bailey had intercepted her slow progress through the throng of party guests. They had congratulated each other and exchanged notes about the performance, which for them had gone well. She had described her own backstage horrors in full.

'The vomitorium was never so aptly named! I haven't had it out yet with Laurence but tomorrow night it's a nightgown or—'

'Or nothing!' hooted Michael.

'Or nothing!' Bella hooted back, holding out her glass while a waiter topped it up. Michael lowered his great voice, which just about reduced it to the level of an ordinary mortal shouting.

'That *would* be a new reading! And the *blood*, my dear, the daggers,' he enthused. 'Even from the wings. It all worked wonderfully. It was *so* sexy! And very, very disturbing.'

Another waiter presented a tray of tiny diamond-shaped

sandwiches. Bella hesitated. She was too high to feel hungry but took one to mop up some of the champagne. 'Well, at least he knows how to throw a party. This is very nice.' At which point someone had pulled her away, saying, 'You must come and meet Jacques de Santis. You know, the French film director. He's a tremendous fan!'

In this way, tugged off-course by well-meaning admirers she proceeded across the room, a gentle odyssey whose object was Donald. She was full of a pleasant hysteria. The buzz was good. This select, prejudiced portion of the audience seemed happy, and genuine in its rush to eulogy; feeling, like all first-night audiences, as much on the spot as ever the actors were; as nervous, as much afraid of foolishness and failure; and now equally flooded with relief, light of head and heart.

Bella excused herself from one group and stepped apart, pausing for a moment. She took two deep breaths from the stomach, exhaling through rounded lips as if she were cooling porridge. Her own relief was mighty, great enough to dull the pain under her collar-bone, though not to send it packing. A woman in tight green satin, with a tiny cocktail hat to match, stared at her and said, 'My God – it is all your own hair!' Then apologized, started to gush praise and apologized again. Bella smiled and nodded and moved on. In the midst of all this hubbub she felt lonely.

Backstage, immediately after the show, there had been a different kind of hubbub, a greater confusion, double toil and double trouble; but those comings and goings had been cosier, the out-of-context faces she was too tired to put a name to had all been benign. Donald's dressing room and hers were adjacent but not communicating ('Just as well,' declared Donald, who claimed that her voice exercises drove him potty). At one moment, when she was leading Sir Paul through to Donald to pay his 'humble respects', she fancied that she had seen Aubrey in the corridor. She must have been wrong. Surely he would have said hallo at least. She did see Tony, reflected in the long mirror beside the day-bed. He had put in a perfunctory appearance in her room earlier on, kissed her, pronounced a few cryptic sentences of congratulation and then made himself scarce. Now he spotted her reflection, smiled and nodded, raising his glass. Any first-year drama student would have disqualified his performance as far too generalized. He turned to pour champagne for a woman in a red dress of some shot fabric, whose face she could not see. As Bella turned to go back to her own room a man came up and took her face in both hands. Lindon. 'Magnificent!' He fixed her eyes to impress on her the degree of his sincerity. 'Utterly magnificent!'

Once the two dressing rooms had cleared of guests, Bella and Donald had snatched a few dizzy moments, drunk a toast and then retired to finish cleaning up and dressing. They had left backstage together, making for the circle bar, where the party was; but once there she had got separated from Donald almost immediately. From time to time she could hear his laugh, somewhere at the other side of the room by the gilded swing doors. She pushed forward a little in that direction; but people *would* grab hold of her, grasp her by the elbow and hug her, cluster round to congratulate her. Large as it was the bar was crammed and very hot. She extricated herself yet again.

'I must find Donald a minute.'

She found Donald, his back to her, with one arm propped on Tony's shoulder, balancing a glass on Tony's velvet smoking jacket. Donald's other arm curved round the waist of the woman in the red dress whom she had noticed with Tony earlier, who raised her head to say something to him, which made him laugh. Bella recognized Claire Ballader. She was just like her photo in *Spotlight*: Bella had sneaked a look at it in someone's office. Not beautiful, but Claire's quality might be preferable – she held the eye. And did she hold the heart too?

Happy ever after. That should have been it. Marriage had fulfilled Bella's objective: Claire's wifely rights expired and Claire duly became ex-Mrs Ballader, a ghost. It should have been enough; but of course Claire Craig lived on and to her Bella attributed both malevolence and power. If *she* had been Claire

Ballader, Bella felt sure, she would have refused to go to the first night of *Macbeth*. What an incredible thing to do. What did it require, courage or an excess of bile, to sit for two and a quarter hours in a darkened room watching your former rival, worse, your successor? Could you be objective? Could you admire, or only belittle?

Bella realized she had broken out into a sweat and she felt again the twisting pain in her lower abdomen. Donald threw back his head and laughed, a huge liberated laugh. He removed his arm from Tony's shoulder and caught Claire with it, hugging her to him for a brief moment. They all three laughed. Bella looked on as if she were Macbeth watching the apparitions. She became invisible, enveloped by silence and stillness, and terrible cold. This, she knew, was the moment when she should move forward, join them, be introduced to Claire, behave like a human, or superhuman, being. She must somehow break the spell – or curse, was it? – that held her back. Still she hesitated, and in that moment the green satin woman was led up to the three of them and introduced and all three at once damped down their mood to proffer a degree of polite attention. The show was over. Now she could step forward.

But now Aubrey stood in front of her, smiling, a little unsure. His eyes were moist. He took her hand. She had forgotten how soft his hands were. He murmured superlatives and told her how proud of her he was, how happy to see her happy. They had done the right thing, he implied. Just now he was playing an old-fashioned army officer in a French play in the West End and had grown a moustache. It made him look older. He seemed unreal. A total stranger. Out of the corner of her eye she could see a tender little scene of departure being enacted. Tony helped Claire on with her coat. There was an awkwardness, then Tony gave Donald a bear-hug goodbye, even kissed him. Claire did not. All the while, as Aubrey spoke and she answered him, she was watching them at it. Not very accomplished performances for such experienced actors. Over the top – a touch too demonstrated.

chapter 18

In the end Bella never made it to the post-party supper, or rather she only got as far as the French Club, which had stayed open especially. Had Tony and Claire been invited she would not have got even that far, and either Donald or Tony must have known it. She had regretted at once not joining them, but it was too late, she had missed the moment. She ought to have coped, she told herself. Magnanimous in victory. Meet Claire, be gracious, kill the king. But she had stood rooted to the spot. Someone else had joined Aubrey and her; Aubrey had left. This time the well-meaning intrusions had been a relief, until finally Donald had come to the rescue, enclosing her with one arm proudly round her, kissed her cheek and whispered in her ear, 'Okay to move on?'

When they got to the club she had gone to the loo and found some blood. Not very much. A show of blood. 'Show!'

(*Show his eyes and grieve his heart*
Come like shadows, so depart!)

She came out of the cubicle and washed her hands, noting that even in the dim pink light of the Ladies she looked ghastly. She had to sit down for a moment on the little gilt upholstery chair trying, for the second time that night, not to panic. It might be nothing. Nothing to worry about. She had had a hell of a day. A hell of a few months. Maybe this was a warning to take it a bit easier, which now she could begin to do.

When she was calmer she got up to go on downstairs, but

then had to go back into the cubicle to take one more look – the lighting in the room was totally inadequate. Afterwards she washed her hands again, slowly and carefully, making a lot of lather with the rose-coloured soap. She dried her hands on the tiny pink napkin and went downstairs. Donald saved her the fuss of having to seek him out; he had come looking for her.

'What is it?'

Her pallor alarmed him but she managed to reassure him. She was flaking out, that was all. In the circumstances she'd better not overdo it, even though it was still early days. He was reluctant to let her go, but agreed that it would be rude for both of them to disappear. He would stay for one course and then come home. He found a taxi and put her into it. She turned to wave through the rear window and saw him, on the pavement, anxiously watch the cab to the end of the street. Now that the end of effort was in sight, exhaustion swept over her in a great wave.

There was no more bleeding; but the next day she had gone to see Dr Beale all the same. He commended her prompt action; it was better not to take any chances. He showed due concern but no alarm, only advised her to rest as much as possible, take it easy, take a few weeks off; and it might be as well to make an appointment to come for an extra check-up in two weeks' time. Hearing his recommendations Bella had laughed out loud. Then he had looked stern. 'You lead a strenuous and exacting life, Mrs Ballader. As I warned you, if you want to keep this baby, you may have to make sacrifices.'

Bella noted the use of the word 'warn'. Had he? She did not remember any warning. She went home and rested until it was time to go to the theatre. The fact that there was no more bleeding reassured her; and a few days later, to her relief, the pain in her shoulder went away. She woke up one morning and it had vanished. The morning nausea disappeared too – even better. Her breasts eased, the soreness left them and she began to feel unexpectedly lighter – all was well. She had not lost the baby. So much for Dr Beale!

Lighter in body; but her spirit was not entirely weightless. Certainly it had been terrible to learn that she might lose the baby. In their fright both she and Donald had had to dig deep for comfort. He had brought himself to say to her, but without much conviction, that really, awful as it would be – should the worst happen, too awful to think about – this was perhaps not the perfect time for them to concentrate on a baby. There was time ahead, all the time in the world. They would choose their moment, do the thing properly. As long as Bella was all right . . . the main thing . . .

Now, thank goodness, these black thoughts could be discounted. But they could not be unthought. And there was one thought, exclusive to Bella, that lingered on, a thought that had barely risen to the surface before being submerged again in the deepest depths. Gone but not forgotten. For Bella was such a careful soul, so fastidiously counting the days and taking her pills. And all the more careful since she was such a novice at the business. How could she have made such a mistake, to have become pregnant just now? To become an unmarried mother? She had joked about it: 'Just as well we're not doing *Measure* – at least it's better to play Lady M pregnant than Isabella!'

Now they fell asleep thinking of names for the baby. They called names out to each other from the bathroom, or telephoned from the other end of town.

A week later the bleeding returned, heavy.

'It's like a period.'

Dr Beale's secretary promised to relay the information at once. Her tone angered Bella. She said, 'Don't worry, Mrs Ballader, I'm sure you'll find it will turn out to be nothing to worry about,' and made an immediate appointment.

It was a period. The baby was dead inside her.

'An abortive abortion,' said Dr Beale.

Bella didn't understand.

'Your body was trying to abort the baby, but failed. What a tragedy for you,' he added. His very professional expression of sympathy failed to reach his eyes.

'What does it mean?' Bella asked.

He articulated in words of few syllables that it was the body's safety valve. Her body was protecting itself and her (as if they were two entities!) by rejecting a foetus which was in some way and for some reason unsuitable. 'There is a miscarriage. Perfectly natural and healthy procedure. It goes on all the time. Menstruation itself has been called the weeping of a disappointed womb.'

The complication in this case, Bella's case, was that the foetus had not been expelled. The question was whether to wait for a spontaneous expulsion or to intervene.

'To intervene or not to intervene!' Dr Beale exclaimed, and was disappointed that his little joke, intended as a compliment, met with no response.

'Intervene,' said Bella. She could not bear to be neither one thing nor the other. It would be a question of a few days off. Charmian, who was playing Lady Macduff, would have to go on for her – the chance of a lifetime. The sooner Bella put this behind her the better.

It was not so easy to do. The intervention passed off smoothly: the womb was scraped clean, there were no outward or visible complications. But a full recovery was less simple; Bella's thoughts could not be scraped out and dropped in an incinerator.

Dr Beale had to be banned from Bella's bedside, so loathsome had the sight of him become. She began to tremble as soon as he tutted his way into the room, but the same insensitivity which provoked her rage protected him from it. He remained immune.

'He drives all his patients mad and then assumes that that's their natural state and ignores it. He must have a pretty distorted view of the world!'

On the pretext of needing a private word out of Bella's earshot Donald, trying to keep calm for Bella's sake, would get Beale outside the room. Donald became fascinated with the man's odd professional skill of being able to smile and frown at the same time, an expression intended both to demonstrate concern and to reassure.

'Don't you worry yourself unduly, Ballader,' he counselled Donald. 'Women are funny creatures. She'll be as right as rain in next to no time. Above all, don't whatever you do let her see that you're anxious – that's going the right way to put the wind up her good and proper. Hormones. That's all it is. Her body's just a little confused at the moment, that's all. Right as rain, you'll see.'

Donald tried to make light of things, as the doctor had ordered. He submerged the terrible ache he felt at the loss of the baby – a continuous but curiously stunted pain, like an incomplete breath, starving the lungs; and alongside it an unfocused pity for the baby, that would catch at him unawares. If he had these feelings, what must Bella be going through? So as far as he could he hid his anxiety, following Beale's prescription. But the doctor's advice had its good and its bad points. He might equally have said, 'Be sure you let her see that you mind too, that you are not untouched, that you need help and comfort. It will help her to be needed by you. Your need will help her to cope with hers. Otherwise she may feel that you blame her.'

Dr Beale's prescription for Bella had been two weeks' complete rest – 'minimum' – before she could contemplate going back to work, and Bella had poured scorn on Dr Beale's notions. She was accustomed to throw illness off with a will, and she anticipated at most three or four days away from the theatre. But even Dr Beale's cautious prognosis proved a wild underestimate. A week had already gone by before she was allowed home from the hospital. She had put up a fight when they kept her in, but it had lacked conviction. Yet coming home had failed to produce the expected boost to her spirits; once there she lacked even the stimulus of irritation that Dr Beale and one or two of the more patronizing nurses had provided. She needed company but could not summon up the enthusiasm to get herself out of the flat, and she shunned the thought of visitors.

'They'll all want to talk shop. I couldn't face it just now.'

Sometimes Donald, returning late and tired from the theatre, found himself at a loss for something to talk about that would not depress or aggravate her. So often the news he had to tell concerned the theatre, their friends, goings-on at the Royal, the things they had in common; but in her present state of mind these topics seemed only to bruise Bella. The discovery of her pregnancy had been made just before the coming season needed to be made final, and at once Victor and Ted had determined that they would have to think again. *Hedda* and *The White Devil*, in particular, had in large part been chosen with Bella and Donald in mind, as well as an unblinking eye on the box office. Robbed of Bella they had retained the Russian piece, *He Who Gets Slapped*, and substituted a nineteenth-century melodrama, *The Bells*, and *Coriolanus*.

Now, with Bella so sadly and unexpectedly free, they had little to offer her. *He Who Gets Slapped* would start the season off, but its circus setting created problems. Bella declared that she would be perfectly fit by the time she had to start 'circus school' and rehearsals; but the company's insurers, after referring to Bella's physician, took a different view. Their rejection shook Bella and cast her into darker gloom.

'It's Beale!' Donald shouted. 'It's that bloody man!'

'Don't shout, Donald. Please.' Bella closed her eyes. The noise was too loud, too live. 'Anyway, he's probably right. The way I feel.'

At last after a meeting at the theatre, Donald came back one morning to have lunch with Bella, pleased that he had some relatively cheering news. Charmian was to continue as Lady Macbeth 'for as long as necessary'. The company had decided not to bring someone in to replace Bella.

'So we can dispense with doctors and insurers, do you see, darling. It's entirely up to you. As soon as you feel up to it you can come right back in. The great thing is that you can do it at your own pace – just a few performances a week until you find your feet again.'

'Oh, Donald,' her sad eyes met his and they regarded one another for a moment. 'What's the use? Frankly, I don't believe I'll ever feel up to it again.'

'Oh, what nonsense, angel. Of course you will.'

He stepped across and kissed her and stroked her hair. He had to leave to meet his tutor, who would be coaching him later on, to play the part of He – the gentleman/clown. He could see that the good news had only deepened Bella's depression. She had reached a stage where no light was to be found anywhere.

'I do wish you'd just take off for a few days, my darling,' Donald pleaded. 'Or a few weeks. You need some sunshine, and complete rest. Mallorca or somewhere. Or even one of these health farm places. Or why don't you go to Switzerland? Helena keeps phoning. You know how thrilled she would be. She'd simply love to spoil you. It's just what you need. Go for my sake. Please.'

Bella was tempted. Her sadness set a barrier between them. She knew it, and made an effort to hide her mood. 'All right, I will!' she smiled.

But when Donald set about arranging flights and booking tickets she could not face it. She could not face anything. The loss of the baby had jeopardized everything. She began to feel that she would never work again.

chapter 19

A week later, between the matinée and the evening performance of *Macbeth*, Donald arrived home and let himself into the flat with as little sound as possible. If Bella had done as she had promised on the phone she might just be fast asleep already. He had called her after the performance to find out how her morning had gone.

Today had marked a semi-return to work. Bella had gone to her first post-synching session to dub some of the outdoor scenes from *Love Catches Cold*. He had hoped – they both had – that this little taste of work would rekindle her appetite, but he had not liked the sound of her at all. Terribly bright and breezy. A brave show, he told himself grimly.

He jumped into a taxi and came straight home. Too bad if she were cross with him. He was not much good at naps between shows anyway. He hummed a little as he hung up his coat, and made characteristic domestic noises, so that she would know it was not some marauder. She called out 'Donald?', and as he went into the sitting room he caught her sliding a tumblerful of whisky under her chair. She could not slide her weepy red eyes out of sight so easily. Unmasked, she broke into hiccuping sobs, her misery mingled with relief at the sight of him. He held her until she became a little calmer. They were both relieved to be able to stop pretending that everything was fine.

'It was the post-synching that started me off,' she said, almost whispering and trying to smile. 'Isn't it the weirdest thing in the world though?'

At first she tried to make a good story out of this new experience of dubbing, seeing the short section of film cut together, hearing the crackly guide track and trying to resay and synchronize long-forgotten lines.

'It's almost more horrendous than watching rushes,' she said. 'It seemed so long ago. Light years ago. All those shots of Geneva in the background. It seemed unreal enough then. But it was so weird watching that scene on the pavement – you know, the row with Paul.'

She had stood at the mike in the viewing cinema off Wardour Street, with its deep velour seats stretching behind her in the darkness. She put on headphones and faced the screen with a panel of red neon digits below, running numbers up to the shot, and watched as a thick brown line passed from left to right across the screen. At the precise moment the band hit the right hand side Bella had to speak her lines and try to fit them to the movement of her lips on screen, while her own voice sounded in her ear to remind her how she had spoken them on the take.

'I kept missing the timing at first, but gradually I sort of got the hang of it and the whole process began to fascinate me.' Sometimes the director asked her to say the line a different way, to be more upbeat, or more aggressive than she had been on the take.

'It's possible – well, *you* know – you can change the intention of some lines entirely. We even substituted entirely new lines in one scene, to tie in with a new thought Jerry had had.' The revoiced version altered her character's attitude. 'It makes her far more equivocal. Less sympathetic.'

She had enjoyed the session, seeing Jerry, the director, again in this new context, and meeting the editor; but as soon as she left the little cinema her spirits had dived. She had measured the distance between her feelings then, in Switzerland, and her present state of wretchedness. The afternoon had taken on a different aspect. She had responded to the technical challenge, getting the words to fit exactly, either as she had said them, or with subtly altered inflections; but now something about it disturbed her: 'It's so totally false to begin with. But it was like applying falseness on falseness, layer after layer. I began to feel frightened that nothing would ever be real again.'

'What you need is to get back to work. You'll feel better as soon as you get back to work,' he said; but she said that work had not done her much good that afternoon. 'You know what I mean. This was something entirely new to you. I mean back to the theatre. It's time Tony came up with something. He's only got to speak to Mark at the Royal, suggest a play, Mark'd jump at it, darling, you know he would. I'll speak to him.'

'Tony already has.'

'You didn't tell me.'

'Because I turned it down.'

'What was it?'

Even if she felt a million times better, Bella said, she would have said no; she didn't like a single one of the parts they were offering. She had adopted a haughty, belligerent tone.

'I told Tony to turn them down. He agreed with me, they were really crap parts.'

Donald looked at her sadly. She swore because he always said it didn't suit her. She was reduced to antagonizing him in an attempt to draw him into her own frustration.

'I don't think I ever want to work again. I simply cannot imagine any play, any part that could tempt me.'

'All it takes is one phone call, as you know perfectly well. Then we'll have to hold you down, strap you to the bed.'

She tried to change the subject and insist he have something to eat before the evening performance.

'Not until you talk to me. Properly. It's no use carrying on like this and making yourself miserable. I can't help if I don't know what's wrong.'

She saw his face full of concern for her. He didn't speak of his own needs. She knew that she was being selfish. He too suffered loss and guilt at the baby's death. She saw him push them aside to attend to her. And he had a performance that evening.

'Just talk to me. Tell me what's on your mind.'

What was on her mind? It would be easy enough to tell him – she had had plenty of time to think during the last few weeks – but she had also had time to persuade herself that, however it might soothe her to tell it, the truth was not necessarily indicated here. She persuaded herself that Donald must be put first. Donald had to be reassured; and, since she must tell him something, she decided to take a leaf from her bogey-man Dr Beale's book, and tell him as much as she thought he might be able to accept, enough to calm him, selected thoughts.

She admitted that she had been lying – to reassure him. Things were not all right, of course. 'I'm sorry. It's been daft of me, trying to pretend.' Donald's sigh told her that this was the right way to go. It told her more – that admitting this lie gave greater weight to the lie she was about to tell and moved her further away from having to admit the truth.

She had heard Dr Beale warn Donald one day, in his unskilled *sotto voce*, 'She may well become a tad depressed. Nothing to worry about unduly. She may fear that she could be doomed to a series of these ill-fated pregnancies. That sort of thing. Not to worry. Keep your eyes peeled and reassure her if need be. If the depression goes on too long we'll give her a little something for it.'

'I suppose,' Bella began, 'the thing is—' She sensed that reluctance made her confession more believable. 'I suppose I have this awful fear that I could go on having a series of miscarriages, one after another.' She hesitated. 'The worst is – I really can't get rid of this thought – that I might not be able to bear you children at all, ever.'

Donald's face cleared at once, for these secondary lies superseded the first and set his mind at rest. These, to him, were reasonable worries, and medical expertise could be brought to bear on them.

'My God, there must be other medics than Beale!' he cried. It was an inexpressible relief to share Bella's laughter at the mention of the dreaded Dr Beale. From here they could progress to normality again.

As if to reinforce this possibility, the phone rang while Donald was in the kitchen making them both scrambled eggs. He carried the tray in and balanced on one foot while he closed the door behind him with the other. Bella was already off the phone.

'Who was that?'

'Sue from Tony's office.'

Donald put the tray down beside Bella. 'What did she want?'

'She's sending round a script for me,' Bella said. 'A play.'

'Who by?'

'No one anyone's ever heard of. But apparently it's good, and there's a wonderful part. It's from Robert Rayner's office.'

Donald was impressed. 'Bob Rayner? That can't be all bad.'

'According to Sue, Rayner thinks I'm the only actress who can do it justice.'

Donald took a taxi back to the theatre in good time for the half. The clouds had lifted. He had left Bella looking brighter than he had seen her for weeks. It was an infinite relief that this spectre had been dragged from the cupboard, so that they could both look it straight in the sockets and see it for what it was. He bounded into the theatre and threw himself into the company warm-up. He even did some voice exercises.

What Donald did not know was that the skeleton in Bella's cupboard had a cupboard (and a skeleton) of its own. Bella had not told him everything because she understood that her thoughts, if she expressed them, might constitute a form of blackmail. She did, as Dr Beale had hinted, have grim fantasies: that she might become, like Martha in Aubrey's life, a permanent invalid, breaking Donald's spirit; an incubus that forced him to tear himself away from first-night celebrations and from winding down with the company in the pub after the show. Or not tear himself away. (How Donald had raced home today!) But she had no fear of another miscarriage, because she did not mean to become pregnant. She did not want a child. She doubted now whether she had ever wanted a child. The loss of the baby had revealed unexpected things.

What should she tell him? Should she tell him that she believed he might never have married her if she hadn't got pregnant? And should she tell him that she wondered if perhaps – she would never know for sure – she had got pregnant so that he would marry her?

When Donald got home Bella was curled in the chair in front of the gas fire, absorbed in the script, with half a mug of cold tea on the table beside her. He bent down and kissed her.

'I'll make you some more tea,' he said. 'How is it?'

She looked up. 'I think it's going to be great! I think.'

'Great? Terrific!' He laughed, kissed her again, then picked up her mug and made for the kitchen. 'And is there a part for me?'

chapter 20

There was a part for Donald. It was a sizeable part, and Bob Rayner was more than keen that Donald should play it. Except that Donald didn't like it.

All the same he went to see Rayner a few days later, in the antique office above the Princess Theatre: through the foyer as if making for the stalls, turn right instead of left, up to the fourth floor in the creaking secret lift, of which it was said that if it ever carried more than one passenger at a time it would constitute automatic grounds for divorce.

A grey-haired salt-of-the-earth secretary received Donald with enthusiasm and ushered him into Rayner's bright office without delay. The office was situated in the bulge of the building which lower down formed the grand theatre foyer, and was almost circular in shape. It was nicknamed the Round Office, after the Oval Office in the White House. In the territory of West End theatre Robert Rayner's powers were presidential.

Rayner rose and came round his desk as Donald entered, extending his hand. He was a slight, dapper man, with rosy cheeks, a sharp nose and a courteous and deferential manner. He offered coffee, sherry, whisky, while his secretary stood by, awaiting their order. Donald had pleaded a prior engagement to avoid lunching. He was there out of politeness. His mind was made up.

In fact Rayner would have been surprised as well as delighted if Donald had wanted the part, but on principle he never pretended to know any mind other than his own; so he tried to persuade Donald nonetheless, pointing out that the character, who was on stage almost the entire time, was not like anything Donald had ever done before. Perhaps it was time for a change? Donald leaned forward, resting his elbow on his knee, in an attitude suggesting that he had just heard an unexpected and novel idea; he passed his hand across his forehead and cupped his jaw, so that Rayner could not see the expression on his face. Rayner said: 'It's a wonderful part, Donald. Of course you could play him standing on your head.'

'It might be the only way I could make him interesting. To myself, I mean!' he added.

He had no wish to seem rude. He explained that it was not what he wanted just now. The timing of Rayner's offer was unfortunate. Donald's line of parts in the New's next season included several that were outside his obvious range.

Rayner tried harder. There would be time for Bella and Donald to have a good long holiday before they had to get down to work, which would get Bella nicely back on her feet again and be just the thing for Donald, too. A good rehearsal period, a chance to get the show nicely run in on tour – Bath, Brighton, Bristol, Bury St Edmunds, the 'B' tour! etc., plus a few more – all very nice dates. And then, all being well, Donald and Bella could settle down to a nice long run in the West End – there was already tremendous interest.

'I know that you would want to be sure you're in safe hands. What would you say to . . . Ben Strick?' He named a director currently hot in the commercial theatre, whose last three productions in succession had been smash hits; two had transferred to Broadway. Here was the unknown element, the juicy mystery factor, hitherto withheld, which was evidently intended to tip any balance. 'Well?' Rayner leaned back in his chair and tweaked his trouser before crossing his leg. But he had taken the wrong tack. The West End and its perks were not of much interest to Donald at that moment; he still shook his head. Yes, he said, the play would run and run, and it was a marvellous part for Bella. It was what she needed just now; and of course she was very much what the play needed.

'But it's not for me, Bob. Sorry.'

'Won't you perhaps think it over? Let me know in a week.'

'No point, Bob. Really. Wasting your time. Sorry.'

Rayner raised his eyebrows and gazed at the carpet for a moment with his large melancholy eyes. He clicked his tongue. 'Well! I can't say how sorry I am,' he said. He picked a tiny thread of cotton from his exposed sock and rolled it between his fingers. 'Bella will be very disappointed. She wanted it to be your decision, but I know she had set her heart on the idea.'

And, in acknowledging defeat, he touched on the one argument which might have swayed Donald.

On the way down from Rayner's office Donald considered yet again whether he was doing the right thing for Bella. He had no doubts about what was right for himself, or for Bella, as actors. Before her miscarriage they had both been excited by the invitation to go back to the Royal, though the Royal had dragged their feet about finding the right parts for Bella. Then her illness had thrown things into question and now time was getting on. It was late but perhaps not too late for something to be found for her at the Royal, if that was what she wanted. Rayner's play, arriving out of the blue, seemed like the answer to a prayer. The real problem was that Bella was not fit enough yet to undertake a full repertory season. Eight West End performances weekly could be gruelling, but had a steadiness which, if it did not suffocate you, was at least manageable. You could live a life around it. Whereas up to eight performances a week in repertory, of different plays, with rehearsals for other plays during the daytime, was something else. It kept you either on your toes or on your knees, sometimes both at the same time. This new play would drive him round the bend at full tilt, but it was ideal for Bella in her present state. It would provide one focus, it would let her get her strength back in easy stages, as Rayner had suggested. It was easy to see what was best for Bella to do. Donald was not so confident of his best course of action as a husband.

For Bella would indeed be disappointed. She was waiting near-by at their favourite restaurant, on the corner of Old Compton and Dean Street; and now he must break the news to her. She surely expected it, and in her heart of hearts she agreed with him, but she would be disappointed. She would frown and purse up her mouth, breathe one brisk exorcizing sigh, give his hand a squeeze and say, 'Okay!'; and then look at the menu and take the other path without a second glance at the place where the road forked.

Baldly, the choice was between being together in circumstances that were adverse, with only one of them at full stretch, and being apart in conditions that were favourable to ideal, with both of them working flat out. Not to be sharing the same work, or even the same building, would be a wrench, but it might bring compensations of detachment and freshness, for each to offer the other. Whatever his intentions, Donald knew too well what his temper would be, after even a few days working on a role which, in his view, was tedious as well as overstretched, and with a director moreover whom Bella liked and he did not. Another long-winded intellectual. Donald believed that the way to act was to get up and do it; with this man they would be sitting round a table talking and theorizing for two weeks before they ever got on their feet. But even this he would have undertaken like a shot, if he had felt that his presence would benefit Bella; and he was convinced otherwise.

At the moment her courage was undermined, though his for her was not. He would be too much present at rehearsals, too easy to consult, and too tempted, most likely, to criticize out of sheer frustration. Bella, to make up for his sacrifice, would be drawn – unlike herself – to defer to his instinct instead of fighting for her own which, if she held firm, was so often her best resource. Just now, he knew, she needed his approval. More – she was, for perhaps the first time, prepared to lean on someone, and that he was determined she should not do. Into the lake with her! She would be grateful in the long run.

Plump Mrs Price, the proprietress of the Colombina d'Oro, whose surname belied her Tuscan origins, bustled forward from behind her tall desk and greeted Donald effusively, waving her plump hand towards 'their' table in the corner. '*La signora è già qui.*' Donald kissed Bella, tracing her cheek with the palm of his hand as he sat down; and the waiter, with an effusive greeting, mimed pushing Donald's chair in behind him and handed him a small hand-written menu.

'Well?'

The waiter flicked open a napkin and floated it on to Donald's knees, then poured him some red wine and refilled Bella's glass. Donald waited until all this was done before looking up at Bella. They looked at each other a moment.

Bella shook her head. 'Never mind,' she said, and smiled, looking away.

While she had been waiting she had broken the roll on her side-plate in half, and now she began to press her finger on to fragments of crust and transfer them one by one to her mouth. Then she pulled some of the crumb out of the roll and squeezed it between the tips of her fingers.

'He took it very well – Rayner,' Donald said, being as offhand as he could, applying his concentration to another activity as he spoke the text – screwing up his eyes and peering at the menu (a corny but effective stab at the abstract of Indifference).

Bella frowned and picked up her glass. 'You're absolutely right, of course.' She took a sip of wine, gave a sharp sigh.

The waiter returned, full of cheerful anticipation, pencil poised. '*Sono pronti, i signori?*'

'Oh, yes, thank you. Bella?'

'Minestrone for me, please, and then – oh, I'll have the *penne alla putanesca*, and some spinach. Lunch is on me by the way,' she added to Donald.

'*Signore?*'

'Minestrone too, Mario, please, and I'll have the *osso bucco* and a green salad.'

The waiter thanked them, putting his pencil away, collected their menus and replenished their glasses for good measure. They watched him in silence.

'Rayner's very chuffed with himself, I must say. He's like the cat that swallowed the cream – you being the cream. But I'm afraid I shall be *persona non grata* for a long time.'

'Oh. I think he hoped Ben Strick's name would do the trick. He swore me to secrecy. I did warn him that it would probably have the opposite effect. Oh' – she signalled to a passing waiter – 'could we possibly have some of your lovely gri-sticks?'

Donald had bargained for disappointment, had thought she might become cross or even tearful – she had been given lately to little bouts of weeping which she quickly controlled. In fact she preserved a drastic calm and her performance rivalled his, presenting the abstract of Imperviousness – a performance he failed to penetrate, much as it puzzled him. It could be read as disappointment or anger, or hurt pride. Donald was on the point of elaborating, explaining himself, when the waiter placed two large plates of minestrone in front of them.

'It's all right.' She glanced up at him. 'Don't look like that. We both know it would be a complete and utter waste to give those parts up for this one. There's no point. It would make no sense.' And she took his hand across the table.

What they sacrificed to sense was romance. And that was odd. The two of them had undergone something akin to the phenomenon which scientists have named a heat exchange: a temporary transference of opposite qualities. Donald, the dreamer, had turned hard-headed to rescue practical Bella, and clear-sighted Bella had turned misty-eyed. Of course a new dynamic had entered the equation: Bella's miscarriage had swept her out of her depth, too far out to recognize that Donald was behaving out of character, let alone that she was herself; and Bella was still floundering in a dream of romance in which

Donald's love for her proved stronger even than his fear of being bored.

'What about Ted and Victor? You'd better put them out of their misery,' Bella said.

'I'll phone Ted straight after lunch. And Tony.'

Rehearsals for the new season were due to start in just over six weeks. The company was chafing at the bit and breathing fire, finding itself so close to going into a new season without having one of its leading actors under contract; but it stretched patience out against the odds, treading with delicacy because of the recent domestic tragedy.

'I know at least half a dozen actors who will be even sorrier than me when they hear the news. They are wonderful parts,' Bella remarked, in a little brittle voice. She tried to sound detached, aware by now that if she were to pass her growing despair off as something tiny and trivial she needed to take up a more active mask than imperviousness. But her tones were those of a thwarted heiress.

For the first time she felt separate from Donald. When she had lost the baby she had perceived a possibility that had frozen her with terror: that somehow she would lose Donald too; that he not only would no longer love her, but would like her less. Her fears had been proved wrong. Instead they had become closer. Now this decision of his, perfectly reasonable, threw everything into question. She faced him across the table as if she were facing a stranger. Not a complete stranger, either, but the man she had known before she knew him. The man she knew by sight and by reputation.

It seemed, in the event, that it was her own feeling that had fallen off, she who liked him less. Every response that he had first inspired in her (as man, not actor) of wariness and mistrust, of shocked disapproval of his whole being – his lightness, his unworthiness, everything he appeared to stand for – rushed in upon her now. Two years of intimacy had augmented these feelings instead of wiping them out. He didn't want to be with her. He was lying to her, thinking only of himself. Now she knew what made him tick. Now she was right not to trust him. What if he liked her or didn't like her – she did not like him. Now she only hated and adored him.

This was Bella's dark lunchtime of the soul, and in due course the darkness gave way to a kind of twilight. She saw Donald preoccupied with her as much as ever, attentive, and dependent, as she was on him, and she laughed at her own foolishness. But she laughed alone. She remembered reading a newspaper item, about a man brought to trial for the attempted poisoning of his wife one breakfast-time. The jury acquitted him and, according to the report, the couple resumed their life together. Bella had tried to picture their homecoming, after the trial: the celebratory supper, champagne perhaps. Then, hot-water bottles made and 'Would you like a cup of tea to take up, darling?' 'Oh yes, darling, I'd love one, but don't you do it, let me!' 'No, let me!'

She never told Donald that she had doubted him, for what could he have said? What answer could he have made after all? To voice her doubts was to describe a battlefield and prepare the ground for war. Donald would surely tell her that she was being silly, that he had taken his decision (in some indecipherable way) for her sake, so that she should not become too dependent on him, to toughen her up. It was even possible, Bella thought, that he believed as much. She toughened up. But she wished that Donald had not been so tough already that he could stand being so much apart from her.

After lunch, they bought pasta and salami and cheese for supper in Old Compton Street, and fruit and vegetables from the stalls in Rupert Street, then took a taxi back to the flat. Donald called Ted and then Tony, to say that it was all on. Tony said, 'About time' – he didn't know why the company put up with him and his shillyshallying. He reminded Donald that his rehearsals for *Play for Today* began in five days. Or had he forgotten about that? And would he please sign the contract and send it back as of yesterday – or was he planning to back out of that now, at this notice? He went on to suggest that as Bella's rehearsals were a luxurious uninterrupted eight weeks away she would do well to take a proper holiday, that is to say, a holiday from Donald. Donald put down the phone.

'Bella!'

She had left the room as he started dialling. He found her in the kitchen putting the lettuce and celery and carrots she had just washed into the fridge, and waiting for the kettle to boil.

'Cup of tea, darling?' she asked.

'No time for tea!' He caught her by the waist and whirled her around. 'Pack a bag. I'm a free man for four days. We're going away from all this.'

They had their tea on the train to Glasgow.

chapter 21

'Feast your eyes and fill your lungs!'

The grey sea in front of them mirrored a grey sky only a few shades lighter. They could not imagine why they had not come before, why they would not, in the future, come often.

They had spent the night at a hotel in George Square, next door to the station, so that they could take the six o'clock train up to Mallaig. There they had hired a car for the short drive to Arisaig. Their wedding present from the bride's father had been a tiny house close to the sea. Walter Provan called it his *folie écossaise*. He had bought it on his honeymoon when he and Bella's mother, still in love with each other, had fallen in love with Scotland. When his wife had left him Walter Provan had kept the house on out of inertia, and in the hope that his affection for the place might one day allow him to put sad associations behind him and spend time there after he retired. Now that he was retired he never visited it because Marion Hunter, the dark-haired friend who had been Walter's surprise guest at the wedding, found Arisaig too remote and spartan. She preferred to stay in Hampshire, and Walter preferred to stay with her. ('I told you so!' Donald had crowed, reminding Bella that he had been the one to spot that Walter Provan was not the lonely divorcé his daughter fondly imagined. 'He's obviously been living in sin too all the while – just like his daughter!')

Someone had kept an eye on the house for him over the years, opening the windows and occasionally lighting a fire, but the place had stood empty a long time. Walter wished Bella and Donald greater luck and more fortitude than he had shown. For them it might not prove such a folly. They might be grateful for a place where they could escape their hectic lives. This was the first opportunity they had had since the wedding. Bella had always avoided the place. The idea of it, its complex association with her mother, with disappointed hopes, disturbed her. But now, seeing it with Donald, she fell in love with it, as he did.

From Mallaig they had driven out past an estate of ugly bungalows on a coast road that became less and less well maintained. The houses became fewer, the dark rock more prominent. Just before the road in front of them looked as if it must run out altogether and come into collision with a great face of black granite looming ahead, they rounded a slight bend and saw a flash of white and blue. There it was: a modest house on two floors, whitewashed, with low-silled windows jutting from the dark slate roof. The window frames were painted cream, the lintels a deep blue. White pickets around the little garden defined its limits, separating it from a surrounding field, which itself was separated by a wire fence from rough terrain that sloped up behind to the mountain. From all the windows at the front you could see across the edge of the low cliff to the sea. Donald had proposed a tour of inspection only, because their time was brief. The plan: to make plans, assess what needed to be done, so that their next visit – though Lord knew when that might be – could be in earnest, armed with fuel, provisions and the names of the local electrician, plumber and joiner.

It was in better order than they had expected. Dusty, full of spiders and cobwebs and tiny beasts preying on one another, generally in need of care and attention, but it was not damp. The windows opened with little protest. Donald tore up the morning's paper, found a remnant of coal, gathered a bundle of kindling from the rocky shore, and lit fires in each room. Bella drove back to the local shop to buy lunch and returned to find the house crackling and blazing with life. They feasted by fire and by candlelight on ham and tomatoes and buttered morning rolls, with a bottle of Blayberry wine. The morning sky had started fine and blue, but a hard cold wind that blew all before it soon covered the clear horizons with heavy cloud, and towards five o'clock white flakes began to float in against the darkness. Donald stood on the path while Bella locked up the house, watching the light fade fast over the sea. He heard an urgent whisper behind him.

'Quick darling, look!'

He turned to see Bella staring towards the great hill that rose up from the rough field behind the house. In the middle of the field, blended almost to invisibility amid the moss and bracken, stood a stag. Head towards them, its mighty antlers raised up, he was so still that he might have been carved from stone. For a long time he stood motionless, then without warning set off at a gentle trot, almost ungainly, lolloping away across the field until he became part of the failing light.

That evening Bella described the adventure to the landlord of their hotel in tones of one who had been vouchsafed a rare vision; but he was not impressed. Yes, from time to time the beasts did indeed come down quite close to the dwellings. A sign that the weather was thickening higher up on the moorland. 'It's a pity ye'd no taken your gun,' he remarked.

Two days later the train back from Mallaig to Glasgow carried them through a sunny landscape that had been transformed by the late snow. Where before the mountains had presented contours of rust and brown, white peaks now glistened in the sunlight. The shifting perspective offered an unending series of majestic impressions. Bella and Donald attributed this freak enchantment to a magic of their own, not to chance. Having survived a great misfortune together and been strengthened by it, they still believed in their own special deserving. They had been singled out, again. They were excited and grateful, each for the other's sake; but not, at heart, surprised. Donald was pleased with himself. He watched Bella as much as he watched the passing scene. He had not seen her so vivacious for months, full of plans: for the house in Scotland, a house in London – time to escape from the flat, it was getting her down – and she must take herself in hand for the play, do her homework, prepare. She considered coming back to Scotland on her own in the weeks before her rehearsals, to set about putting the cottage into more habitable order; she could do that and get herself concentrated as well. But she checked herself: the best would be to do it together, if they could find that sort of time. She looked at him for a moment, suddenly blank and still, then as suddenly returned to the idea of the house. She was keen for it to be put in proper order, and very soon: it would be a wonderful place to retreat to, to work, or just to be. She said, 'We need somewhere where we can be together away from everything.'

Now and then, as the train pressed homewards, clouds passed across the sun, and then followed thicker and faster until the sky was covered and the day dark before its time. The brief, intoxicating dispensation from foul weather, that they had enjoyed for four days, began to lapse. At Euston the appeal of a cosy supper of scrambled eggs on toast at home in the flat was strong, but Bella doubted whether there were enough eggs, and they had picnicked on the last of the bread and cheese and fruit on the journey up to Scotland. 'Well then, let's sup in style – we're still on holiday!'

They took a taxi, left their bags in the cloakroom and were soon seated once again at their favourite table at the Colombina d'Oro. As Bella sat down a girl with her parents at the next table asked her for her autograph, her young face flushed with excitement and embarrassment, while Donald was claimed by a tawny-headed playwright who urged him and Bella to join her and her friends. They thanked her and stayed where they were; but their brief holiday dissolved as though it had never been.

Donald's *Play for Today* was a naval play, referred to by him as 'Seven ill-assorted sailors in a submarine'. He had agreed to do it six months before and wished now that he had turned it down. The part had intrigued him, a very unheroic role, and the chance to work again with Victor – 'I've earned it,' he exclaimed, 'after working with Laurence Goddard!' – as well as with Sir Paul. But he had been harrowed enough over the past few months, and the thought of spending the next weeks immersed in the claustrophobic atmosphere of the piece no longer held much attraction.

'I get enough of all that at home,' he joked. He wished now that he had time free to be with Bella during the day. As always she took Donald through his lines when asked, but the play did not appeal to her at all. She was far less interested in how the rehearsal had gone than in who had been in the canteen at lunchtime, whom he had seen, what other productions the BBC had going in the big rehearsal rooms at the 'Acton Hilton'.

'I feel as if I've been away from everything for a thousand years.'

He wondered if she were nervous about going back to work, but she denied it utterly.

She had set herself two goals for the next weeks, while Donald was at the BBC: she would find them a house and she would learn to cook. Donald was still doing most of the cooking. He was better at it and he enjoyed doing it – mostly just for the two of them, but now and then they would invite a few friends for unambitious suppers, or for Sunday lunch. Bella decided that the time had come to extend her narrow range of domestic skills. Since Donald was so busy, she would conquer this new world and pamper him, so that he could devote all his energies to rehearsing. She bought a subscription to a weekly magazine of gourmet cooking. Now, in every house that she inspected, attended by assorted hopeful estate agents, the kitchen and dining room received especial scrutiny.

This sudden interest bemused Donald and made for a different order of life. He had been a carefree cook. Cooking improved his temper. It was one of his happiest, most reliable relaxations, but he ceded his role gladly to Bella. Bella had to work at cooking, but wrestling with the chemical mysteries of applying heat to matter might one day lead her to spend times as happy as his own, engrossed over a hot stove. If she were appointing herself *chef de cuisine*, he would appoint himself official taster, a role that required courage and deserved reward.

His responsibilities in his new office turned out to be more onerous than expected. Donald quickly discovered that relaxation was not to be the keynote of Bella's regime. She set about her self-chosen tasks with a determination that started out dogged and became fierce. Something driven in her approach, even to such a simple domestic challenge as making a soufflé, precluded any relieving, necessary lightness. When he closed the front door behind him on arriving home, he now had to submit to a rigorous timetable drawn up for him by Bella according to the evening's menu. A bath, one Bloody Mary (permitted but frowned on by the new cook because of its effects on the taste buds – he nonetheless sneaked another); an hour to relax, return phone calls, watch the news, even sometimes chat with the staff, if she were in exceptional control; then they would sit down to an ordered and sometimes challenging meal. At first he gave himself up to the new schedule with happy abandon. However disconcerting the rigid order of things, the sheer galvanizing intensity of Bella's involvement fascinated him and in the end never failed to make him and – sooner or later – Bella laugh.

Arriving home early one evening, he caught her, to her fury, measuring Pernod into a jug, for a fish sauce. The Pernod, a 'mystery ingredient', was supposed to defy detection, 'mystifying and delighting' sophisticated dinner guests with its aromatic and elegant savour, especially when combined with 'the Prince of Fishes, the succulent Dover sole (or more economically with its humble cousin – the Lemon sole)'. Bella had wanted to confound Donald's boast that he could guess every ingredient in any dish. She had better success in that direction with an old recipe of Helena's, for prune mousse.

After dinner came study time, allotted to the play, but Donald found himself beginning to prefer the early hours of the day, and often rose at daybreak to spend time alone with his script.

By now Bella was seeing three or four houses a week, but so

far she had dismissed each one with a shrug or a groan. It did not bother her that none of them was right. She would know, she said. And then he would know. Each fresh example of what was wrong strengthened her feeling for her ideal. She knew now that she liked high ceilings, but not high window-sills; she wanted a kitchen that you could eat in, but with a cooking area slightly apart; she wanted to see trees; she had no objection to a railway running along the bottom of the garden – there absolutely had to be a garden. The act of looking defined the difference between possible, perfect and imperative.

'And what if "imperative" turns up just before you start work?'

'That's okay!' she declared. 'It'll be fine. These things take ages to complete. Months and months. Rehearsals, the tour, the West End – we could still be waiting to exchange contracts in a year's time.'

After the panic of a threatened electricians' strike at the studio, the television recording went without a hitch, leaving Donald glad to be shot of it and thrilled by the delicious novelty of having the daytimes free for a whole week. He and Bella went to the pictures on a few afternoons, after having lunch out; they caught up on a few plays. Then the time came to plunge in again. Donald's rehearsals started for *He Who Gets Slapped.*

'Your face!' Donald said, kissing Bella as he set out for Charlotte Street. 'You look just like my sister Sukey, when I went off to the big school in town and she had to stay behind.'

'It feels so odd not to be going off with you,' Bella said mournfully.

Now that he was back at the theatre, working every day with people she knew, he noticed that she began to take an interest in his rehearsals again. More than an interest – her appetite for news became all-consuming.

The action of the play concerned a young aristocrat, a writer and philosopher, who, when his friend steals not only his ideas but his wife, quits society in disgust to become a clown. Since, because of the setting, almost every member of the cast had to master at least the rudiments of some circus skill, there were plenty of stories to tell. The entire company spent an afternoon watching a performance and meeting their circus counterparts afterwards. But Bella wanted to know everything, even beyond the daily sessions with circus folk, in acrobatics and juggling and tightrope walking, and wanted to know in exhaustive detail: who had said what, what reefs had been struck, who was on the book, how Rina Marshall, the most recent company recruit, playing the bareback rider Consuelo, was tackling playing the personification of beauty and innocence – 'I hope she's not making her too milksoppy.' How was Nancy (playing Zinida, the lion-tamer) coping with her old flame George Farr, taking the part of the handsome bareback rider? How were the designs? How was Lindon's music? Donald began to be grateful for any little thing that went awry, so that he would have something to report.

'Interesting flavour, this soup,' he remarked one evening.

'Do you like it?'

'It's interesting.'

'Why ever didn't you tell me that Aubrey Morris is going to take over Mancini from John Lomax? How is John by the way?'

'Give us a chance, darling. I've barely sat down. I was saving it for the pudding. There is going to be a pudding I hope?'

'Of course! When was it decided?'

'John's going to be fine, by the way, but out of action for a few months, poor sod.' Donald picked two small round objects out of his soup. 'What are these?'

'Oh! Sorry. They're not supposed to be there.' Bella ran round the table with her spoon and fished about until she had removed three more, muttering, 'I don't know how those got through.'

'What are they?' Donald asked.

'Juniper berries. You're not supposed to eat them. They're just there for the flavour.'

She served him grilled mackerel with gooseberry sauce and asked, 'How is Aubrey?'

'He sent you his fond love. He's fine. We're lucky. In some

ways he couldn't be better casting for Mancini. He has that loftiness, and this morning he was already making him wonderfully slithery – I wasn't sure he'd be able to get that side. How did you hear?'

'Lindon telephoned after he'd done his session this morning. He said Mark's having a little trouble getting the hang of his pipes.'

'Poor Mark, everyone keeps telling him how easy it is – he'll get there. But Lindon's come up with terrific stuff – some of it has that really tacky blaring sound, but then turns into lovely tunes, quite haunting.'

'He's very enthusiastic about it. He said some of the rehearsals are really looking good. He says Nancy's going to be wonderful. I still think Zenida's a better part than Consuelo. How is Rina Marshall doing?'

'It would be wonderful if she could just play herself.'

'She is awfully pretty.'

Bella had bought every paper that covered the *He Who Gets Slapped* press launch and had pored over the photographs.

'She *is* very pretty,' said Donald, 'and she's very innocent, the trouble is she keeps trying to act innocent and it comes out as silly. She doesn't need to do anything.'

'Perhaps she should play it like a child, you know, with that bossiness children have, trying to be helpful. She needs to be very focused. Why don't you get her one day – in your scene in Act III – to try treating you like a foreigner, or a pet, or a child – someone stupider than her, who makes her feel clever? Just as an exercise. It might give her that hardness children sometimes have – that will play against the soppiness.'

'I'm not sure that's quite what's needed.'

'Why not?'

Donald sighed. 'I wish you'd come and tell her all this yourself.'

'Well. Perhaps I will.' Bella smiled at him across the table. 'Rhubarb crumble?'

The kind of rehearsal Donald preferred left little residue. What was not thrown off was absorbed and fed the next day's work. Bella's enthusiasm was boundless, her appetite vast. She studied the play herself, knew it almost as well as he did by now, and seemed to want to experience every moment of the work with him. He began to wish that Bella were at the rehearsals so that there need not be this painstaking raking of every detail at the end of the day. The rehearsal always continued for him anyway; he went on 'cooking' as he called it. But he found it a chore to have to put his thoughts into words 'after hours', to account for them and crystallize every single one.

As time went on he became grateful for the respite that meals afforded, more as topic than event, since once the food was on the table and the inquest performed, Bella returned at once to her themes, and his rehearsals. Her expertise in this subject, which should have thrown light into dark corners and made their talk helpful – had done, always, in the old days (the old days!) – now began to produce a silent screaming in Donald's head. Panic, or worse – dullness. He did not understand it, and the built-in urgency of the rehearsal state prevented him from stepping far enough back or to one side, to view the situation with clarity. All he could suppose, which seemed ungenerous, was that something in him rejected the sense that she – someone, anyone else at all – and not he himself was the generator in their discussions. He could not remember ever having had such feelings. But the conversations unnerved him. They were so set up. They lacked any spontaneity. He felt he was in a workshop learning how to play insincere.

But according to received theory you were supposed never to play adjectives, always to find an 'action'. What on earth was his action? To lie to Bella? He felt as if his head were being clamped.

He took to watching television, a thing he rarely did when he was working – he found it too passive and too draining at the same time. Now he pretended that there was a particular programme he needed to see, or an actor or director whose work interested him. He sat with his eyes fastened on the screen, but not watching, taking refuge in silent staring, interrupted by laconic comments from Bella. Television made her very impatient. Left to herself when watching she hopped channels non-stop, which drove Donald mad.

'How you would hate people to watch you the way you watch,' he told her.

She agreed. 'Oh I know! That's why I hate doing television.'

'Well, do something useful, then. Hear my lines for Act III.'

Brief reprieve was to be found in getting her to take him through his lines, which she would now do with the smallest encouragement. With Bella, this occupation was fruitful and rigorous – almost as draining as watching TV, though far from passive.

'You're paraphrasing!' she would reprimand him, refusing to accept so much as an 'a' for a 'the'. (An interviewer asked Donald and Bella to describe a day in their working lives. 'My good wife doesn't "take" you through your lines, she puts you through them,' Donald told the man, 'rather as you put washing through a mangle.')

In the weeks that followed he found himself, without conscious decision, inventing ways to prolong the day – wig and costume fittings, planning meetings with Victor and Ted about the New Company. It became essential – for the sake of 'company feeling' – that he join the others in the pub after rehearsal. Instead of having his PR appointments at lunchtime or during breaks, he got the publicity girl to arrange any interviews or photo sessions after work. If ever he was let off early he hung on and watched the rehearsal, or took his script to a café and consumed quantities of tea. He could scarcely bring himself to admit how hard he put off going home.

The interrogations continued. Donald tried all ways to block her questions (except the obvious, direct way). He evaded her with teasing or vague answers, changed the subject. He did try to be direct, but some undertow of guilt made directness difficult.

'Why the hell aren't you working on *your* play?' he burst out on one occasion.

'What on earth do you think I do all day?' Bella replied, and gave him a cocky little smile.

chapter 22

One evening Donald came home at about half-past six to find the flat dark and empty; no sign of Bella; total silence. Order in the kitchen; a pie and a dish of chicory waiting to go in the oven, a saucepan of broccoli on the stove. Donald found himself swinging between the sneaky pleasure of having the flat, and his head, to himself for half an hour, and anxiety that it might be for more than half an hour; what if something had happened to Bella?

He decided not to get into a sweat. He made himself a mug of tea and took it through to the sitting room. Everything was peaceful. He could watch the news and return Tony's call. On second thoughts he had better put off calling Tony in case Bella were trying to get through. (Or the police? What if she'd had an accident?) He finished his tea, sipping it slowly and deliberately. He couldn't concentrate on the television. Obviously she had not just nipped down to the corner shop. He went into the kitchen and washed up his mug. Bella had left a colander full of a mess of strained vegetables and a couple of odd bowls and wooden spoons in the sink. It was unlike her not to have washed everything up as she went along and put it away. The vegetables didn't look like much, but he put them to one side just in case they were destined for a grand future, and rinsed out the other things.

He fetched his script from the pocket of his leather jacket and went back to the sitting room, poured himself a vodka and tonic and tried to look over the scene they had been working on that afternoon, which he had gone on studying for an hour in the café after the rehearsal, before he caught the bus home. Every now and then he started up from the sofa, thinking he had heard the front door. In the end, when it did open, he did not hear it because he was pouring himself another vodka and opening and shutting the door of the drinks cupboard. When Bella came in they both spoke at the same time.

'Where on earth have you been?'

'I'm sorry I'm so late. I got caught in the traffic.'

'But what have you been doing?'

'Just some research.'

Donald's anxiety burst out as anger and he barely noticed Bella's curiously muted response. She made no attempt to explain where she had been and he did not ask. She gave him a quick kiss and disappeared, promising that dinner would not be long, as if that were the cause of his irritation. He heard her in the kitchen moving about, opening and closing the door of the oven; then a loud cry. He ran into the kitchen.

'What is it?'

'My stock! Honestly, Donald!'

'What stock, for Christ's sake?'

'In the bowl. In the sink.'

'What do you mean?'

'You've poured it away. Have you?' She pointed to the big bowl upended on the draining board. 'It was for the potatoes *à la hongroise*.'

'How the hell was I supposed to know?'

'Well, didn't you even look?'

'I thought it was the vegetables you were saving.'

She stared down into the sink. She seemed in need of an apology.

'I'm very sorry,' he said, and added on his way out, 'Why can't you use a bloody stock cube like everyone else?'

Now that Donald knew she was not lying somewhere in a pool of blood, he became furious, like a mother whose child, eager to tell her some school news, has dashed across the road in front of a car to be greeted with a sharp smack that astonishes both parent and child. Now that he knew Bella had been safe all along he wished he had had time to enjoy having the flat to himself for a few hours longer.

He took his half-empty glass to the drinks cupboard to top it up. Bella came in, to apologize for making such a fuss, and said, 'Oh Donald, don't have another drink just now, we'll be eating quite soon.'

Donald banged the bottle down on the side table. The glass top cracked from side to side.

'For God's sake, woman, I'm not a child. Can you not shut up and leave me in peace for five minutes? Five minutes, that's all I ask!'

They were stunned. Bella went very pale. She became anxious, then hurt, then irritable. They talked it over, made it up. But the air was not cleared.

Bella could hardly tell Donald the reason why she was late. When she had implied that, in addition to cooking and house-hunting, she spent a large part of her days working on her new role, she had been less than candid. In the beginning it had been precisely so. Then she decided one morning, as part of her researches, to pay a visit to the National Gallery. Her role in *Catalan* spanned several centuries, and often she found paintings offered a useful, oblique path towards a role. If she were lucky, one particular artist or work might set a mood, or offer an insight into an age, that coloured her whole approach.

She couldn't remember the details of Donald's day, except that he said he had some meeting with Ted Danniman and the PR people after rehearsals, but would be back in time for supper. It struck her that he might be free for a quick snack at lunchtime. By mistake, instead of putting her through to the rehearsal room the switchboard rang the offices, and she got Ted himself. They spoke at cross-purposes for a time, as Ted kept insisting that he had no meeting with Donald that evening – their meeting with Daphne Brent, the PR girl, had happened two days before, during Donald's lunch-break.

'I was just down in rehearsals a minute ago. I think Donald's got the afternoon off, as it happens. Except for a costume fitting.' Ted's voice was cheery. 'Perhaps he got mixed up with something else.'

When Donald had got home Bella asked how the meeting had gone. 'Oh, fine. Ted's got everything very much in control. We may be doing a tour, abroad, early next year. He's very excited about it.'

'What was it about?' She handed him his Bloody Mary.

'Oh, general – publicity, strategy, you know the sort of thing.'

'She's very good, Daphne Brent, isn't she? She got wonderful coverage for the press launch. What's she like?'

'Yes. She is, very good. Doesn't nag. Gets a lot done.'

Donald's face had betrayed nothing, and Bella had not doubted that he spoke with a clear conscience, telling part of the truth, for he had indeed met with Ted and with Daphne. Two days ago. But what had he been doing all that afternoon until now?

Bella felt surprised by how calm she felt. Her head began to spin a little, but the feeling passed once they started supper. Something inevitable had happened; she would deal with it methodically. She must not accuse Donald, or alarm him. She surprised him by saying that she wanted an early night. Could he manage his lines without her this time?

Donald's guilty relief at the prospect of an uncharted evening mingled with concern. He could see that his preoccupation with rehearsals made him neglect Bella. Perhaps, now he knew she had work to look forward to, he had assumed too glibly that her recovery was complete – because he needed it to be. He promised himself that he would make it up to her once the play opened.

On that evening, beyond enquiring about his rehearsals the next day, Bella had asked no more questions. She yielded to his insistence that she let him do the dishes, and went up to bed.

The next morning she had found a pretext to telephone Harry at the stage-door, and ask him to check the week's calls that were posted up on the board. Harry had been only too delighted to hear Bella's voice and to be of use to her. He supplied the schedule in laborious detail, including production meetings and fittings, some from the previous week, and the week to come. Aubrey's coming into the cast complicated an already complex timetable because he was still working at the Royal and had two matinées. It seemed that there were quite a few days where Donald's rehearsals finished early. Donald had never mentioned it.

So tonight Bella could not tell Donald the reason why she was late, for although she had indeed been occupied in her researches, none of them had any bearing on her work. Today, as on quite a few days over the last week, she had been in town stalking him. Since three-thirty that afternoon Bella had waited like a private detective in an alley across the street from the theatre, wearing an old raincoat of Donald's. He was due to finish at four, at which time, according to him, he had a costume fitting. At ten-past four Bella had seen him come out of the stage-door with Michael Brodie and Victor. He had stood chatting to them for a while, then they had gone their separate ways. Donald had thrust his tattered script into the pocket of his jacket and turned down Charlotte Street, then cut through Rathbone Place into Oxford Street, down Soho Street, through the square, down as far as Old Compton Street. He had gone into the Amalfi and stayed there for almost an hour. He left alone.

Bella waited until he had walked through to Charing Cross Road, presumably to catch the bus, before going into the café herself. She looked about her. There were no single women at any of the tables. No single woman had come out while Donald was there. She did not know what Daphne Brent looked like, but she would have recognized Rina Marshall. Bella had then taken a taxi, intending to get home before Donald, but an accident – a car running the lights and clipping the back of the cab – had delayed her. A jangling experience but nothing serious – voices raised, red faces. It had taken some time to find another cab.

And Bella had not found answers to any of her questions.

How did he spend these hours? Whom had he gone to meet? Why did he bother to lie?

Her anxiety increased. Donald's own rage over the incident disturbed him and left him feeling more anxious than ever.

Towards the end of the second week of Donald's rehearsals Bella made an announcement. Donald, she declared, had outlived his usefulness as a guinea-pig. ('Miraculously!' he groaned.) Now she wanted to practise her culinary arts on a wider audience. Donald was in no mood to be sociable, but he did want to make her happy and her desire seemed innocuous enough. She threw herself with such a mixture of delight and trepidation into planning her menus that he had not the heart to protest. He could hardly guess that the point and effect of all this immense amount of work was to create a smokescreen which would allow her to examine his colleagues at close quarters and assess the opposition. Nor did Bella acknowledge it to herself.

'You won't have to do a thing,' she promised. 'I'll do it all. I'll do, I'll do and I'll do!' she laughed, a little shrill. 'I want to!' She set about organizing.

The guest-list baffled him: drawn entirely from the cast. True, quite a number of her old colleagues were still there, including Aubrey, now cast to play the Polish Jew in *The Bells* as well as Mancini, but these were not necessarily the ones she invited. Bella was limiting herself to the cast of *He Who Gets Slapped*. He had supposed the whole purpose of these social dos was to give him a break, to provide distraction and new invigorating stimuli. But Bella seemed to be pursuing some ideal of company feeling: the company was like family and would therefore be no strain. Donald's experience of the familiar and of the familial was very different. He refrained from pointing out to Bella that you can have too much of a good thing. Fond as he was of the rest of the cast, he would have liked one day's break from them. On the other hand, he might have enjoyed catching up with a few old friends or even family. They had not seen Walter and

Marion for a long time, or either of his sisters and their offspring. He and Bella had been keeping to themselves a lot lately.

Bella produced a sumptuous spread. Leek and artichoke soup, chicken teriyaki and Helena's famous prune mousse with special almond biscuits, salads, cheeses, fruit. 'Everything must go!' Bella declared, and the danger that they would be spending the following week eating left-overs rapidly receded.

Nancy, who had blossomed with the success of her television series and could now afford to drape her increasing curves in silk jersey, shook her head sadly, unable to resist a second helping of the mousse. 'If you could see the uniform I have to get into for *Major Barbara*, Bella, you wouldn't let me do this to myself!'

Donald found some escape in playing host, topping up glasses, clearing plates, opening bottles. He watched Bella out of the corner of his eye. She looked radiant and content as she gossiped with Victor, commiserated with Nancy over her complex love-life. Rina Marshall confessed herself a longtime fan of Bella's work, and now of her cooking, and they exchanged recipes and telephone numbers. Donald looked on, punch-drunk. He had nothing to say to anyone, but said it in a loud voice with a bright smile. Every now and then he took refuge at the kitchen sink. Bella, breathless, running in for the biscuits to go with the mousse, kissed him and cried, 'Donald! We can't have this! We'll have a dishwasher in the new house, whatever else!' and dragged him back to the throng, silencing his protests. 'I've got all tomorrow to do the dishes, while you're running Act I.'

When the guests had gone Bella sank into a chair and reclined at her ease with a glass of wine.

'A triumph!' she declared. 'It beats acting any day!'

Donald, who had settled to a glass of cognac, agreed that it certainly made a change from watching television. His assent was a continuation of his own, as he thought, triumphant – even heroic – performance.

From where she was sitting Bella suddenly spotted a large

patch of spilt red wine. 'Oh Lord, look at that! I wish people would say.'

'People are probably too pissed to notice.'

Bella put her glass down and bounded out of her chair, returning from the kitchen with a blue plastic pail, a sponge and a bottle of carpet cleaner. 'The quicker you do it the more chance of getting it out.'

She began to rub the carpet energetically. She looked like a cartoon of Lady Macbeth and he hoped that the connection would not strike her and perhaps upset her, but suddenly she gave him a grin and said, 'A touch of the Lady Mackers!'

She went on working, following the instructions with great care, working from the outside of the stain towards the inside. 'It's just as well we've decided to move eventually. This carpet is beginning to look like a disaster area. A few more parties and we'd have to get a new one anyway.' Then she began to talk about the following weekend – another party: so that the rest of the cast and stage-management would not feel left out, and anyone who had not been able to come this time, could. 'And what about that PR girl you said was so nice – Daphne?'

Donald could not believe his ears. 'And what about the front of the house and box office? And wigs and wardrobe?'

Bella took him at his word. 'Wait, wait!' she cried. 'I must get a pencil,' and she rushed out into the hall, knocking over the pail as she did so. 'It's only water,' she said, coming back with pencil and pad.

By the following evening the wine stain was almost gone, but over a much wider circumference, Donald noticed, the water had left a perceptible mark.

Instead of two parties on successive weekends, they compromised and had one huge Open House, the Sunday after the play opened. By this exhausting means Bella got to know just about everyone in the company that she did not already know, and – which concerned her more closely, though she did not formulate the idea to herself – made sure that they were more than aware of her existence. This was the mysterious sustaining purpose that had eluded Donald. She made herself material and she made herself vivid. She expended all her energies to eliminate any chance that she might become shadowy and dismissible, like Aubrey's Martha.

It was hard for her, for she loved to be private, but she placed a primitive faith in the laws of hospitality. These people had been in her house. They were, in the gentlest way, under obligation to her as well as to Donald. She was too frightened to rely solely on Donald to protect her. By this means she acted for both their sakes, though she acted alone. Each day, she weighed his words and probed his every utterance, like a dentist trying to identify those little trouble spots that could signal future decay. Her medicine was preventive: brush after every meal and a lot of flossing – a hygiene of the heart. However much Donald might yearn to come home to Bella after a hard day – or think he did – she no longer trusted herself to offer him the ease and intimacy he sought, or him to be satisfied with such domestic simples for long. She protected herself by offering an alternative, and, seeking in this way to disarm the enemy, she stripped herself of her own weapons.

Hard to pin down, the moment when two people cease to look inward at one another and, having endured all manner of stresses and tugs and life-threatening struggles (threatening the life of their partnership), draw strength to turn outward again, in unison, to confront the rest of humankind. It can happen soon or late, it may not happen at all. From society's point of view it may not even be desirable, but if the two are to stop being two people and become truly a couple – a multiplication of strengths far greater than the sum – it is essential. Timing is crucial.

Bella's miscarriage and Donald's decision – the attempt to allow her to mine her own strengths – had arrested them at a crucial moment, just as they were about to shift their weight and look out beyond themselves, well-nigh invincible. Unity, invincibility: this was the impression they still gave, but it was false. They did look out towards the world, but now, at the same time, out of the corners of their eyes, they watched each other: Donald, to discover what it was in Bella that gave him the strange sense that he had lost her, and Bella, to discover the moment when Donald should give himself away.

chapter 23

He Who Gets Slapped opened to more varied reviews than the New Company had earned hitherto: ranging in tone from ecstasy to bewilderment or sneering dismissal; from 'New Company flies through the air with the greatest of ease' to 'High-falutin' high-wire act!' to 'Big Top Big Flop'.

Some audiences enjoyed the production on a purely visual level, marvelling at the acquired skills of the cast, juggling and balancing and performing cartwheels and handstands behind the action of the play. Donald's ugly awkward clown and Aubrey's particular brand of seedy decay met with general favour, and critics found in Nancy's sad, haughty lion-tamer a 'fierce sexiness' that was a 'revelation'. Rina Marshall fared less well.

Donald began rehearsing *The Bells* at the Scala, and two weeks later Bella's rehearsals started at the Irish Club in Chelsea. This simple fact transformed Donald's existence: almost at once they settled back into their old routine. House-hunting, even at the weekends, lost its charm and now, instead of being subjected to a gruelling inquisition when he came home, he found Bella absorbed in her studying. If he had had a performance and she had not already eaten, a sandwich or an egg on toast, she was quite happy now for him to preside over the preparation of an omelette, or steak, or kippers – anything quick. To be sure of delighting her he had only to stop off for a couple of portions of fish and chips on the way home. They would eat straight out of the paper at the kitchen table, adding lashings of vinegar and salt.

Now Bella positively shunned the kitchen. She no longer interrogated him about his day. More often she confined herself absently to 'How did it go?' or 'Good day, darling?' They sat down to supper together and he watched her across the table, quite oblivious to him. Her spoon arrested over the tomato soup, she gazed into a corner of the room. Expression followed expression across her face. Eyes narrowed, then opened; for a second she looked defenceless and sad, then dismissed the sadness; her chin went up, the eyes narrowed again, the corners of her mouth turned down very slightly. If they had been working together he would have played his favourite game with himself, trying to guess which particular scene she was running through her head, but even if he had studied it closely he suspected that the new play would have made this a tall order.

Catalan spanned six centuries and more than one country, from thirteenth-century France to twentieth-century Britain. Bella started in Act I as Agathe, a Cathar peasant woman, betrayed to the Crusader flames by an unrequited suitor, and progressed through succeeding Acts as Agathe's descendants, moving down the centuries from the spiritual Cathar, through decadence to a final, contemporary question mark. As well as Agathe, the play called upon her to portray a venal abbess, a spoilt New England heiress and, in the final Act, a young aristocrat – a potential spy – torn between her love of her husband and her country, and her political conviction. So Donald, across the table, though he derived as much entertainment as ever from his private cabaret, observed her in vain. The most he could hope for was to guess which Act she was currently in, whether she was with the saint, the sinner, the snob or the spy. Whenever Bella caught him looking at her she would pull a face and shake her head: he had made her lose track; or laugh and stick out her tongue at him.

Both their productions were to open in the same week and the week was drawing nearer. They had their lines down, they allowed themselves a little leisure. They began to treat themselves to some evenings out, supper, and even the theatre. Bella said she had better remind herself what the inside of a theatre was like. It had come as a shock to realize that they were about to be separated for the first time. Soon, with Bella on tour and Donald rehearsing as well as performing, they would be for ever just missing each other; at most there would be snatched hours in distant restaurants and hotels, with trains to catch and timetables to observe, unsatisfactory phone calls. The thought would waylay Bella and fill her with anxiety. She had to remind herself that the tour would not last for ever.

How they might spend their last weekend became a favourite topic of discussion. They toyed with the idea of going away for the precious time that would remain after their final Saturday morning run-throughs. They talked about escaping, even for such a short time, to the sea, to Norfolk perhaps, for light and ozone. Scotland, alas, was too far. Donald was all for getting away. He wanted to see more colour in Bella's cheeks, still too wan for his liking, but Bella was nervous as well as restless. One of her spells of pre-production agoraphobia had set in, which made her incapable of straying too far from base. Walking was her preferred method for going over her lines, once she was off the book, muttering and pondering to herself as she strode along, but she argued that she could just as well take long walks in Hyde Park. Or they could be really adventurous and go north to Hampstead Heath, have a picnic, go to the pictures. It was a long time since they had had a weekend on the loose in London. Spurs would be playing at home. Donald could take himself off to White Hart Lane for once, Bella keep her promise to catch a matinée of Nancy's *Major Barbara* which was on in the West End. The prospect of two quiet uncommitted evenings at home began to acquire an almost exotic allure.

When Bella got back from *Major Barbara* she found Donald in the kitchen making her favourite fish pie. He held his face out to be kissed, gripping her lightly between his wrists so as not to get flour and cheese sauce all over her.

'I suppose I must say goodbye to my favourite hat,' he observed. She had borrowed a trilby of Irish tweed that she had given him for his birthday, blue and green and flecked with yellow, and wore it now with the brim at a slant, shadowing her eyes.

'It did meet with huge acclaim,' she grinned.

He shook his head and sighed reprovingly. 'Next time I see something I want I'll give it to you for your birthday and see how you like that!'

She laughed at him.

'You may borrow it,' he added, 'but only for the duration of your tour. And only if you're good. Now out of my way, angel. Do something useful until I've got this in the oven.'

By the time he came into the sitting room half an hour later, Bella had changed into jeans and an old shirt which he had also lost to her and, having first carpeted the floor with old newspapers, was sitting encircled by a small heap of broken crocks, numerous red pots and sprinklings of feathery peat that had spilled out of a large plastic bag of compost beside her. She was busily potting up her geranium cuttings – her last chance. Otherwise, by the time she got back from touring, the geraniums – her pride and joy, some grown from seed – would be beyond rescue. He opened a bottle of red wine and picked his way past her to the sofa, depositing a glass by her side on his way, then settled down with his newspaper. A review caught his eye, of the latest production at the Royal, and he began to read with increasing irritation, pretending to himself that he was not reading it, reading while still in the act of turning on to the next page. After a moment Bella squatted up on her heels and brushed her forehead with the back of her rubber glove. 'By the way! Wonderful news. Guess who I saw.'

The reviewer's tone irritated him: he presumed to know so much; but reading between the lines Donald doubted whether this critic had the remotest conception of what was an actor's work and what was the director's. The review was full of bitterness against the director for pushing Norman Lyon too far, but Donald had worked with Norman Lyon. The poor director had probably done all in his power to restrain the man, short of putting a snaffle on him.

'What?' he said. 'Who?'

'Guess. Go on.'

Bella was fonder of this particular game than Donald and better at it: guessing by description or elimination some person they had met during the day.

'Male or female?'

'Female.'

'An actress?'

'No.'

'But you saw her at the theatre?'

'Yes.'

Next week the review would very likely be about his own performance. To read or not to read? Donald had no hard and fast rule. Reviews could be dispiriting, they were rarely uplifting. Just occasionally you could learn something, but sometimes it was worth letting a little blood flow under the bridge before you dived in. He sighed.

'All right. Give me some clues.'

'All right. Young – well, about twenty-seven; quite tall, sort of willowy; huge brown eyes, raggedy hair (just now – it used to be long though, she may have had it cut since you knew her). A real heart-shaped face, wonderful skin. Sort of self-contained. She looks rather like a Modigliani.'

'Sounds delicious. Are you sure this is someone I know?'

'Yes. She's probably dressed you.'

'Ah! A dresser?'

'Alice!'

'Alice?' Donald drew a complete blank.

'Alice. And she's going to solve all my problems.' Bella looked pleased with herself.

'How rude,' Donald said. 'I thought I'd already done that.'

Alice was leaving the Royal and had popped in to say goodbye while Bella was visiting Nancy after the play. Bella and Alice knew each other of old. Alice had dressed her on *The Three Sisters* and *The Changeling* and several other productions during Bella's first two seasons at the Royal. Then, when she had earned enough, she had taken off: a trip to India to find out what all the fuss was about, the hippies and the gurus. Dressing, for Alice, was a means to an end, something to keep the body together until the soul told her what to do. She did the job well, as she did everything, total immersion, as if this, now, was all she ever wanted to do.

'Alice is just about the best dresser there is.'

'Yes . . .' Donald inclined his head, his mind still half on the newspaper. ' "Wasted"! Norman Lyon wasted! "This sensitive actor" . . . She sounds sensational. How could I have missed her?'

Bella laughed and eased compost around the root ball of a geranium. 'I can't imagine! She's definitely your type.' She took a sip of wine. 'You'll know her when you see her.'

Though she swore that he must know Alice from the old days Donald was none the wiser.

'She knows you, even if you have forgotten her.'

'Ah well,' Donald fluttered his eyelashes. 'Nuff said.'

The piece of news that afforded Bella such pleasure was that it seemed possible, even likely, that Alice would come on tour with her. 'It is the most amazing coincidence. Alice gave in her notice because she was planning to go to Canada, to spend a year with her sister, and she's got some terrific job there, and then that all fell through. So she just happens to be free. For at least the next six weeks. Maybe longer. They'd take her back like a shot at the Royal, but they've got nothing now for the next month. With any luck she may even come into the West End with me.'

Donald knew that Bella had been worrying about the number of quick changes she had in *Catalan*; a dozen at least at the last count. Now instead of relying on uncertain quantities, hired at each date, she could feel confident that expert help would be always at hand.

Donald's fish pie was perfection. They had baked apples and cream for dessert and went to bed early.

chapter 24

Six previews reduced the cast of *The Bells* to a state of nervous disintegration, for no two audiences responded alike. The laughter on some evenings took them completely by surprise; on others, friends and spouses who came back were still reeling, moved by the unexpected power of the piece and most of all by Donald's performance, spiralling into guilty madness, as Mathias the burgomaster, haunted by a murder committed fifteen years before. Donald informed Bella that he had decided it must, after all, be his performance and not his beard – he was now trying out his third – that was causing the problem.

'We simply don't know any more whether we're in a tragedy or a complete farce.'

Catalan was also having a rough passage. Despite the seriousness of its themes the play had a determined lightness of tone and some of the scenes, especially in the second and third Acts, concerning the abbess and the heiress, were intended to be funny. But so far it seemed there were no laughs at all, and a great deal of work to be done. Bella's tour was turning out harder and more hectic than either of them had anticipated. The playwright attended every performance. Rehearsals continued daily to incorporate his assiduous deletions and additions, and at this rate looked like continuing right through the tour.

Miles apart, she and Donald settled down severally each night, glass in one hand, telephone in the other, to issue detailed bulletins. Bella's curtain came down well before Donald's, even on the first night. Throughout her own performance that evening her mind had kept straying to London, wondering how *The Bells* was going. After the curtain calls she rushed to her hotel without taking off her make-up, called room service to order a light supper (which then she could not touch), and waited for Donald's call. His voice told her at once that all was well. The wished-for miracle had happened – a mutual electricity that ignited the show, fusing audience and cast.

Next day the critics were unanimous, even those who expressed surprise that 'this hoary old chestnut could pack such an emotional punch'. The same reviewer who had got up Donald's nose the week before raved about his performance over three and a half columns the following Saturday and compared him favourably to Henry Irving, though neither he nor Donald nor anybody else around was quite old enough to have seen Irving.

Weeks later, that seemed to both of them like months, *Catalan* came into Shaftesbury Avenue. The critics hailed it as a triumph. The playwright's triumph, the director's and the designer's triumph; most of all Bella's triumph. A *tour de force* to equal her husband's. Even the supporting cast carried off accolades by the armful. Printed banners, slapped aslant every poster, proclaimed it; the long queues at the box office caused the curtain to be held every night by several minutes, which irritated Bella – though it was no worse than the house manager's alternative, which obliged her to suffer the clatter of rows of people rising in the stalls for latecomers during her opening soliloquy.

At the first opportunity Donald came to a matinée, turning Bella, so she claimed, into a jelly. He gave her notes afterwards, just a few, but stern enough to convince her, almost more than his praise and encouragement, of how pleased he was with her. He thought what she had done with the piece uncommon and exhilarating.

'The end of Act I – incredible. Your laugh when she's being taken away, and they are all so frightened because she laughs –

it's marvellously natural and simple. It could be so dicey but it's an extraordinary moment. I was weeping. And Mother Sebastian's drunkenness is hilarious – the gradualness. You don't see it coming at all. If I didn't know you better I'd have thought you were a confirmed boozer.'

Donald kept thinking of more things to praise in her performance. 'But everything you do is so clear and, best of all, so completely unsentimental. You mustn't let that go, whatever. It's a breathtaking performance – performances!'

He was not so complimentary about the production, which he found heavy-handed and in need of pruning, the sets too dominating, the costumes unhelpful. He suggested one or two places to circumvent some of what he considered to be directorial excesses, to help speed up the moments where the play was in danger of dragging; but Bella defended the designers, and Ben Strick, whom she had really enjoyed working with. Donald had been prejudiced against him from the start, she maintained. Besides, she said, audience reaction did not bear Donald out. 'Everyone else loves the production!'

Bella's exuberance invigorated Donald in the thick of his own strenuous season, and vindicated all his hard decisions. Bella had more than withstood the rigours of being on the road, and though she was tired and relieved to be properly home at last, she was buoyed up by the clamour of success and had energy to spare.

She insisted, however, that nothing – forget triumph – not even survival would have been possible without Alice. Nothing could have been accomplished without her: the original tower of strength.

'Thank God for Alice!' Bella declared. 'She watched over me like a mother. Not to mention secretary. She can actually type!'

The old routine, the return to normality that Donald had welcomed, did not outlive the duration of Bella's tour. It was not only the entrance of Alice that made all the difference, but their growing need of her in their lives. With the double success of *The Bells* and *Catalan*, once it came into the West End, their existence had sneaked on to another plane, up another rung. Now they had to have someone to keep them in order, and that was Alice. New success brought new demands and changed their lives, which became busier and at the same time diverged more and more. The bustle and chaos of the first years together had ceased to be a temporary accidental condition and turned into a continuous fact. They had become fashionable.

Love Catches Cold, the film they had made in Switzerland, came out (having been through as many titles as edits) and was a popular hit, with Donald and Bella held to be the best things in it. More and more, together and singly, they were newsworthy items. Their coupledom, its joys and difficulties, comforts and complications, offered a welcome angle for the press. The tragic loss of the baby became like a Greek talisman, which proved their humanity: that the fates do not spare even the most golden lives. Their public duality grew monolithic. They were in constant demand, often filming during the day as well as performing at night. The tour had separated them for five weeks, to all intents and purposes, but even now they were spending little enough time together. Busyness spawned busyness, and publicity trailed the trappings of celebrity.

Alice had emerged as the unexpected bonus of their success story, resourceful and invaluable. She saw to things. She dealt with visitors, welcoming or fending them off as necessary – her judgement was always accurate. She kept both Bella and her bouquets in good heart. 'She is my mender and my minder,' Bella said. Alice had first become essential to Bella's performance, then to Bella's life, her steadying presence even more precious because Bella knew it would not be there for ever. Bella did not delude herself into believing that rootless Alice would rest content for long in this one place. In time she could and must, inevitably, be replaced as a dresser, but by now she also filled innumerable other roles: secretary, co-ordinator, caretaker, potter-on and general life-enhancer. She turned estate agent too.

'Alice has found us a house, believe it or not!'

Alice had been forced to leave the flat she shared in Stoke Newington, in a row of houses due for demolition. A cousin had come to her rescue, with the offer of a basement lodging in Islington, plus the run of the little garden there. While exploring her new unfamiliar neighbourhood she saw a house she thought might suit her employers. Bella had no time any more to devote to house-hunting.

'She passes it on the way to the bus. It wasn't even for sale. She just went and put a note through the door on the off-chance. They phoned back that night.'

Donald loved the house as much as Bella, a tall terraced house in yellow London brick, overlooking a small square with trees and flowers; a little large for just two of them, on five floors, but Donald had no doubt that they would put the space to good use – a room each for a studio, a spare room or two for the occasional guest, the occasional baby perhaps. Bella had other ideas.

Bella had told Donald of Alice's magic way with plants, as with so many things. She thought Alice should set up some day with her own flower shop.

'You sound like Professor Higgins,' Donald remarked.

'But it's true, Donald. You've seen what she can do. Give her half a twig and a tulip and it's a thousand times superior to all those dreary dressing-room bouquets you get from florists. As long as she doesn't go off and do it just yet! Why shouldn't Alice have a flat in the basement, with the garden at the back so she can dig away and experiment to her heart's content?'

With the whole basement to herself, and the garden to play with, Alice would have loads more space and be totally self-contained. Bella thought the idea of having Alice on the spot was ideal.

'Ideal for whom?' Donald asked.

He hated the idea. He was grateful to Alice. He had bought her a rare and extravagant plant to thank her for looking after Bella so faithfully, but he had no wish to see it or Alice or any other stranger housed under his roof. Bella argued that everyone gained from her plan, but here Donald's blue pencil, poised to draw a thick line through this latest moonshine, was taken from his hand by Alice herself, who simply said no. She was happy to fall in with Bella's plans up to a point – she would go on dressing Bella for the time being, until she could be sure she had found a good replacement; she would come in three mornings a week to do secretarial chores and see to things for Bella, and for Donald if need be. But, she insisted, three mornings would be ample. And she was right.

The move from Fulham to Islington was accomplished one Saturday in June with the greatest of ease. Alice saw to everything. For the sake of their art, and to keep them out of her way, she booked Donald and Bella into the Savoy after their performances on Friday night. They could have late and leisurely breakfasts and a nice rest before their respective matinées. She entrusted Bella's quick changes to a young drama student for the day, having first drilled her and taken her twice through the show, with the help of exhaustive lists.

On the Sunday morning, after two stolen nights at the Savoy, in a suite overlooking the Thames – feeling a little like children playing at being grown-ups – Donald and Bella arrived full of beans in a taxi at their new home on the sunny side of the square, to find a picnic lunch awaiting them in their new kitchen. In each room, on each floor, an orderly series of labelled boxes awaited them, ready for unpacking. Most of the furniture (looking very lonely, dispersed over its new surroundings) had already found its best position. Alice joined them for lunch, then made her excuses. She had someone to go and see.

'What about this evening?' Bella said. 'Donald and I want to take you to the Brasserie.'

Alice smiled and shook her head.

'But we've been lolling at the Savoy while you've been slaving away here.'

Alice demurred. 'Hardly slaving. I enjoyed it.'

'Leave the girl alone,' put in Donald. 'She's had her fill of us for one weekend. She's got a heavy date for tonight. There you are – she's blushing.'

Alice laughed, 'I never blush!'

'If you did it wouldn't show under that famous golden skin.'

She dismissed their reiterated thanks and blessings with a raised hand. 'Enough!' she said. 'But I will let you do the dishes.'

She left them to it, washing up for the first time in their new quarters – or at least learning how to get the washing-machine to do it for them. The new regime had begun.

Donald and Bella each had small studios at the top of the house, that doubled as guest rooms. They had separate telephones installed and amused themselves at first by calling each other for no reason at all.

On Tuesday, Wednesday and Thursday mornings a large shaded front room on the ground floor alongside the hall, connecting with the sitting room, became Alice's office. There she answered letters, filed answers, made appointments and held in her head an overview of their daily timetables – what was within the bounds of the possible and what was not. Most of her work was done for Bella, but gradually, being on the spot, she began to look after Donald's diary too. On Tuesdays, which was Bella's matinée day, she and Bella (joined by Donald if he were not at rehearsal) would have a light early lunch downstairs in the kitchen before setting off for the theatre. On Mondays and Fridays and on some Saturdays, she had another job, helping a friend with an interior-design business in Camden Town.

Alice had started out helping with the planting but her eye was as good indoors as out and she was practical and calm and attractive. More than one client had proposed installing Alice herself on some permanent basis. But she was not planning to settle. She was in transition, on a floating bridge that had yet to link up to the further shore. Bella, at least in theory, was as keen for Alice to find the perfect landing-stage as she was herself, but it would be a blow when she did.

They had been in Islington nearly three months when Alice

alarmed Bella by finding her another dresser. With the show well run in and every change charted to the split second, she said that she felt she could be more useful doing other things. Was this the start of the end, of Alice's process of detaching herself and making ready to take off again? Bella found the idea of change threatening. Corinne, the new dresser, was small-boned, pale and ageless, with watchful grey eyes.

'She's so thin. She hardly looks as if she can stand up!'

'Oh, don't be fooled. She's very experienced and quite tough,' Alice said. 'Honestly. There's no need to worry – it's not as if I'm not still around. But it is as well to have someone who knows the ropes, in case something happens to me!'

'Oh you! You're as strong as an ox. I bet you've never been ill in your life.'

Alice was amused. 'Well, I suppose there are other things besides being ill . . .'

Bella accused her of being coy, but Alice resisted Bella's string of questions, denying that her remark held any hidden meaning. She promised faithfully that she was not running off to get married or paddle a canoe up the Amazon. From working so closely together, in conditions that could swing from urgency and tearful exhaustion to hilarity, plus some wilder combinations, Alice and Bella had an easy and intimate knowlege of each other. But they did not confide. Bella knew nothing of Alice's private life. Alice knew a lot about Bella's, but that was from her own observation, none of Bella's telling.

chapter 25

Bella called up the stairs to Donald for the third time to come down if he wanted lunch.

'I think he's on the phone,' Alice said. 'I won't put his soup out yet.' She filled a giant cup with soup for Bella and ladled some into another for herself.

'He'll be late,' Bella said. 'Then he'll get into one of his fusses.'

'There is time,' Alice said. Donald's matinée days shifted and today coincided with Bella's.

A door banged at the top of the house, and they heard Donald bounding down the stairs to join them.

'Sorry,' he said, scooping up his napkin and throwing himself into his place at the table. 'Morris Askey is in town. Can we get him seats tonight, for either show? Can we, Alice? I suspect it's *Catalan* he really wants to see. I don't think Shakespeare is up his street. Plus he's got some producer in tow from New York.'

Alice set his soup in front of him.

'Thank you, Alice. Mmm . . . delicious smell. I mean you of course.' He cut himself a large crust of bread.

'Jacques and Monique de Santis are going to see *Catalan* tonight and you're all having dinner afterwards,' Alice said.

Donald groaned. 'Completely forgotten that. Isn't Jacques coming to see *Coriolanus* this afternoon as well? A bloody marathon.'

'Yes,' Bella said. 'We're going to eat here afterwards. Tony's coming too. Alice has booked those two debs to come again, who you took such a fancy to, to do the cooking, so you won't be able to complain about the noise, or the service.'

'Who me?' Donald looked aggrieved. 'I never complain.'

Alice and Bella laughed aloud at that and he looked more aggrieved. He got up. 'Hey! Do I get any more soup? How am I supposed to do a show on one bowl of soup?'

Alice took his bowl away from him and went to fill it. Bella pointed out that at least that night he could go to bed whenever he felt like it.

'Like right now.' Donald sighed. 'I do not feel like doing two shows today.'

Tony had standing orders from Donald and Bella to turn nothing down and as a result they fitted in whatever could be fitted in and saw each other less and less. Simple fear drove Bella. As soon as she settled into the routine of *Catalan*, security itself began to make her feel insecure. She seized on anything that would take her mind away from the performance during the day, so that she might find something fresh to bring to it each evening. She dreaded getting stale.

Donald had only sheer greed to blame. His appetite for work had always been and remained gigantic. In the current season he was involved in four of the five plays. *The Bells*, which should have fallen out of the schedule, had been kept on because of public response, so that his workload did not diminish. Even Sundays were taken up, quite often, with poetry readings for charities or a good cause – rare chances for him and Bella to appear together on the same stage. (Both of them got very nervous.) Even so, he hated having to turn down the odd television or radio play, when it arose, or any other work. He loved a heavy workload, work sustained him. He claimed that it kept him fit because it forced him to get up early and go to a gym to work out every morning before he went to the theatre. But he was tired. They both were. They were like addicts. In many ways they thrived on it – it got their juices going; in other ways it acted like a blotter, soaking all their juices up. They enjoyed working hard, they were on top of it, they coped. When they began to flag they promised themselves the rich rewards of time together – a long holiday, as soon as their contracts freed them.

Bella had only a month to go now before her replacement took over in *Catalan*. Donald's season with the New ended in two weeks, but had a six-week European tour tacked on to the end of it, finishing in Paris. Alice planted the idea, which blossomed, that Bella might join Donald for part of the tour – perhaps spend ten days in Geneva with Helena and then join Donald for his two weeks in Paris. Then they would go south, or in any direction they pleased, for as long as they liked. They had at last instructed Tony to clear a space and he had half taken them at their word. Bella had a film in prospect. Donald had had offers from the Royal but nothing that had grabbed him as yet. Tony wanted a film or two for him too, after such a long stint in the theatre, but the possibility that the New Company might reconvene for another season and that they might work together was the prospect that tempted them most of all.

'Why don't I drop you off at the theatre when I take Bella, Donald?' Alice offered. 'At least you'll be on the spot. You can have a kip in your dressing room if you want before the show. And you can take a cab back tonight.'

Donald welcomed this plan and all three set off together. Before Alice started the car she handed both of them a large envelope.

'Here you are,' she said. 'A little light literature for you – to read in your break. You can choose to cruise or you can choose to crash on a beach, or on safari or trekking – which I can personally recommend, but I do think, though it's not my place to say so, that you need a holiday.'

During the matinée that afternoon the degree of Donald's fatigue became only too apparent, when he lost concentration in the fight along the ramparts with Tullus Aufidius. (At the first sight of the set there had been murmurings about safety from some of the actors, though not from Denny Baxter, playing Aufidius, nor from Donald.) It was Donald's idea and not the director's original intention for Coriolanus to beat the Volscians off from the narrow stairway before he and Aufidius were discovered grappling on the battlements silhouetted against the cyc. The walkway at the top was widened to allow a wider margin for manoeuvre. It looked effective from out front and quite a bit more dangerous than it actually was. Still, you needed to be alert.

Watching the rather fuzzy grey monitor on the prompt side of the stage and about to call the actors for Act II, Tim Beaulieu the stage manager thought he saw Donald stumble, lurching back and then swaying forward. The narrow rail at the back, invisible from the auditorium, was strong, but probably not strong enough to bear Donald's uncontrolled weight. It had enough give in it, too, to catapult him back towards the audience. Aufidius, quite out of character, thrust out his hand and Donald grasped it. They stood swaying back and forth together and for a moment it looked as if they were both going over; then they steadied, drew breath and, perhaps a little more gently than usual, took the fight to its now ironic conclusion.

There was a burst of applause from the audience, which Tim Beaulieu duly logged in the report, with further details of the incident – alongside the timings of each Act and the misplacing of Cominius' sword, and a continuing regrettable tendency among the citizens to corpse throughout the first half of the first scene, after the entrance of Menenius Agrippa. Now some of the actors, clustering in the wings after the event, applauded too, in dumb show, and threw an arm round Donald and Denny as they came off.

'I think we should keep it in, don't you?' Donald exclaimed to Denny in a whisper, coming straight round for his next entrance, and added, 'Sorry, Tim. Hope I didn't give you a heart attack.'

He stood still to let his dresser throw over him the cloak he had hurled down at the start of the scene, and which she had retrieved and was hurriedly fastening again at the neck. He thrust his chin in the air to make it easier for her, breathing hard. A group of actors and stagehands paused to watch, with sympathetic grins.

'You all right, Don?'

'I'm fine, fine.' He turned to Denny. 'I owe you a drink, friend, that's for sure.'

'Not very Method of me, I'm afraid!' Denny whispered. 'Made a bit of a nonsense of the scene.'

Tim Beaulieu heard Donald's lowered voice disagreeing as he started back on stage, urging that this interpretation, the chivalrous helping hand, added another layer to the complexity of the relationship.

Donald arrived back in Islington that night to a full house: Jacques de Santis and his wife Monique; Tony with a pretty young actress, a new client; Morris Askey and his business associate, a producer from New York.

Bella ran into the hall as soon as she heard the front door. She threw her arms around Donald. 'Darling! Are you all right? How was tonight? Why didn't you telephone me?'

Jacques' dramatic rendering of the afternoon's events had preceded Donald. The fact that the danger was past and that Donald was fine did nothing to diminish Bella's horror as she heard the story. She relived the scene that had happened and the scene that might have happened. In her imagination she saw Donald plunging to death or crippling injury. She held him tight. She was trembling.

'Hey! It's all right, little one. I'm okay. Sssh. Nothing happened.'

Her emotion was infectious. Somehow it brought the near-disaster nearer and shook him almost more than the thing itself.

At last she could let him go. She kissed him lightly and led him into the sitting room to loud cheers and applause. Morris Askey gave him a great hug. Monique took hold of his chin, pressing in his cheeks, and stared hard into his eyes before kissing him brusquely on the mouth. 'What a big fright you give everyone.'

Over dinner it was Monique who demanded to hear the whole story again from the horse's mouth, and Donald obliged by retelling the afternoon's events with harrowing embellishments. His story led to others, of near or actual disasters on stage: death, maiming and miraculous escape. Only Tony withheld his sympathy and administered instead his usual large dose of cynicism.

'Don't pander to him!' he cried. 'He'll begin to believe he's a hero. Actors get what's coming to them.'

'He is a hero to me.' Tony's young doll-like companion had up till then said very little, and this quiet observation, ventured out of the blue in Donald's defence, made everyone laugh.

'More fool you!' exclaimed Tony in disgust, while Donald rose from his seat and came round the table to reward her with a kiss.

'Some more champagne for my champion!' he called. '*Some*one has her priorities right.'

'Jacques tells me you will be for two weeks in Paris,' Monique said. 'I certainly hope he has insisted you stay with us.'

'Monique! What a delightful invitation!'

Bella watched as Donald leaned across to top up Monique's glass and at the same time plant a kiss on her cheek.

'I imagine the company may already have made their usual dire and unalterable arrangements for us – but it's a wonderful offer.'

Monique had placed her hand over Donald's and was looking prettily up at him, but it was her beautifully manicured hand that captured Bella's eye. The long lacquered nail of one finger had disappeared under the cuff of Donald's shirtsleeve, and Monique was absently caressing his wrist.

'You will be comfortable and quiet, I assure you,' she crooned.

'Yes, indeed, my friend,' Jacques agreed. 'You won't even have me around to cramp your style. I shall be starting to shoot my movie in three weeks' time.'

'You trust me in Paris with your wife!' Donald exclaimed. 'Well, I don't know whether that is a compliment to me or an insult to Monique.' He glanced at Bella, who seemed absorbed in sending a platter of cheeses on its way round the table. 'What do you think, darling? I don't know if I'd be so sanguine about offering Jacques the run of my house while I'm on tour.'

Bella smiled a little but continued to concentrate on naming the cheeses on the platter for the benefit of Morris Askey's friend and making sure that he helped himself freely to cheese and celery. Donald passed along the table and found another glass to fill.

'No, actually, Monique, Bella is planning to join me on the tour once we hit Paris. I think the two of us together might get under your feet.'

The protests of the de Santises were diverted by the passing cheese platter and the matter was left to be resolved. Jacques waved away the cheese but accepted another cognac from Donald, who continued to circle behind his guests with several bottles and a handful of cigars. Jacques passed a flame several times in front of his cigar and then took a considered suck at it, breathing in with satisfaction. He narrowed his eyes to look through the screen of smoke he puffed out.

'Tony,' he said, 'tell me, what is it that you have got against actors? Tell me.'

'Used to be an actor himself, didn't you, Tony?' said Morris Askey.

'That's what he's got against them,' said Bella. 'He knows them too well to have any respect for them.'

Bella's relationship with Tony had followed a contrary pattern. Not the common route, starting out as a business deal and turning into friendship, but the opposite. The original awkwardness of their relations had been considerably eased by being placed on a formal footing. Bella felt more comfortable with Tony since he had become her agent, as if the business element accounted for the lack of any spark between them. Tony lit a cigarette and inhaled deeply.

'Right, Bella, my dear!' He blew out a cloud of grey smoke. 'Absolutely right. Being an actor is a kind of greed, after all. A craze to cram more than one life into your life – dozens of lives –

sample more than you're entitled to, ask for more praise and affection than you, or anyone, deserve.'

There was a brief pause.

'And more money . . .' said Morris Askey's friend, with a mock-mournful intonation that brought the conversation to a neat close.

When everyone had gone Bella ordered Donald to bed, refusing to let him help her clear up. She loaded the dishwasher and removed enough glasses and ashtrays and general clutter to make the kitchen respectable for the cleaner in the morning, and followed him upstairs. He was already in bed, staring up at the ceiling. As usual he had forgotten to take off the bedspread, or even turn it down. She folded it back and sat down on the edge of the bed. He took her hand.

'You all right, really? I was so worried when Jacques told me. It sounded really frightening. Why didn't you phone?'

Donald reassured her. He was fine. It was just one of those things. He had lost concentration. 'I think I was thinking that a cruise might be rather fun. Though it might be ghastly.'

Bella laughed and got up from the bed. She folded the bedspread back some more and laid it on the long stool at the foot of the bed. Then she took the pins out of her hair and put them on the dressing-table.

'We don't have to decide yet, of course,' Donald went on musing drowsily. 'Alice said there are always places, even at the last minute. We'll have fun in Paris, anyway. Even if I'm working. It'll be a bit like Budapest, but we'll have the days free mostly. We can get used to each other gradually so that when we do get away it won't come as too much of a shock.'

On her way to the bathroom Bella said, 'Jacques still wants me to play that part. His money has come through for the film. He asked me again this evening after the show. But it would mean that I couldn't come to Paris.'

'What did you say?' Donald called. By this time Bella had disappeared into the bathroom. She shouted something that he couldn't catch. 'I do wish you wouldn't do that,' he shouted back.

She came to the door of the bathroom. 'What?'

'Wait until you're out of the room before you speak. Brushing your teeth at the same time doesn't exactly help either.'

'I was just saying, would it be very awful if I didn't manage Paris? It's not a huge part but it is very good. I don't like to turn him down again.'

'I think Jacques is sweet on you.'

Bella snorted. 'Oh don't be ridiculous. He adores Monique, you can see that.'

'Doesn't make any difference.'

Bella shook her head and went back into the bathroom.

'What does Tony think?' Donald shouted.

'That I should do it,' came the reply.

'Then you must do it.'

Bella came back in and went to turn out Donald's light. He caught hold of her other hand and kissed it.

'Of course you must do it, sweetheart. It's a wonderful part. We'll go away as soon as you finish. Or I can come to the location when I'm through, until you do.' She turned out his light. 'Come to bed,' he said.

She walked round the bed to her side, turned out her own light and got into bed, wondering what had happened. Between the bathroom and the bedroom her mind had changed. For in the bathroom, in answer to Donald's question, she had called out at first that she intended to refuse Jacques' offer – which she had until the weekend to do. She would not dream of giving up their days together in Paris for anything. But by the time she reached the bathroom door – why? – her answer had reversed itself. Some other Bella had taken possession of her and spoken for her. In bed Donald curled up to her and put his arm over her, his hand on her stomach, and fell fast asleep. Bella, lying beside him, thought on, wondering why she had taken one decision and announced another. She knew that she would not go back on what she had said the second time. Monique could have him. He should have heard her the first time.

part three

YELENA: (*she takes a pencil from his table and quickly hides it*)
I'm taking this pencil as a keepsake . . .

(Tchekov, *Uncle Vanya*, Act IV)

chapter 26

Donald sat at a café table on the Boulevard St Germain, in front of him a *grand crème* and a *pain-beurre*. The day was cloudy, though not at all cold, and the *terrasse* was not crowded. Most people had chosen to sit inside, in the glass-covered area of the café in front of the restaurant. Outside, in the first row of tables to Donald's right, next to the dust-laden barrier of artificial dwarf hedges, sat two young men reading newspapers, passing occasional comments as they read; in the row behind him, a few tables to his left, a sleek-headed young woman sat with a glass and a small jug of water, watching the street, and now and again looking at her watch.

Two nights before, *Coriolanus* had opened the New Company's brief season at the Odéon. Afterwards the actors had been fêted at a lavish party, thrown by the French impresario, full of scented sophisticated folk, and for once the food on the long buffet tables had not already run out by the time the actors got there. Donald had gone because he must, and had not stayed late, to Monique de Santis' disappointment. He had left her there, glittering among a group of admiring actors.

Now he allowed himself to revel in the luxury of not being expected anywhere. Except at the theatre, hours on, and only a short walk away. From time to time he dipped one end of his baguette into the cup and watched the butter melt and form transparent circles that floated on the surface, while the bread soaked up milky coffee. Then he chewed away at the soggy mass, taking pleasure in the ceremony rather than the taste, and in the general corniness of the situation. He had forgotten how many delights touring had to offer. No rehearsals, free mornings, free afternoons very often; new views, new tastes, new smells. Very little responsibility and a minimal timetable. Working became like a holiday. He had begun to relax; sleeping better, able to ease up a little, especially in the few nights he had been in Paris. He had begun to realize how worn down he had become, over a long time, how unlike himself he felt. The incident in *Coriolanus* had shaken him.

He had taken himself in hand and acknowledged that he must conserve his energies more scrupulously and keep his head clear for the night's work. It was a reasonable enough discipline, but as the tour progressed it had left him a little stranded. He began to find himself, after the height of the performance, with nowhere to go. Scuttling home to relax with a cup of tea and a book, or a TV supper, had never been his style. BB – before Bella – he had been far more used to follow the pattern of clamorous glamorous nights of the sort that are written up in gossip columns. Not always in expensive night-clubs or discos (which could be few and far between on tour in Scunthorpe), and not wild always, sometimes very quiet and cosy indeed. He recalled one particular disastrous tour, years ago, with Tony in tow, giving his Mercutio to Donald's Romeo. Evenings in Sheffield with Tony, Jack Weaver, Monica Grant, who had gone on to become a television mogul, little Tracy Simpson, others, names forgotten, roaming the streets looking for a meal, a drink, coffee – anything rather than return to the dreary digs, the jaundiced candlewick and the single overhead light (until Tony managed to wangle a flat, which simplified things). At least in San Francisco, on the same tour, there had been no shortage of places to eat, chopped steaks, hot-dogs, coleslaw, french fries, pickles, doughnuts, so-called English muffins, far into the night.

The sheer pleasure of the present moment took Donald by surprise: just sitting there enjoying the time-honoured Continental habit of staring at strangers as if they were zoological specimens; enjoying being out of England; enjoying being alone, on his own, being free.

Free from what, he wondered? Because he would have enjoyed Bella's company too and her enjoyment, and sharing the scene – and, no doubt, this baguette with her as well. Of course she would have refused it out of hand at first, and said she wasn't hungry. She would have stolen a nibble of it when he wasn't looking, as if she were not doing it at all, and then she would have asked for a little spot of jam; at which point he would have ordered not only the jam but another baguette for himself.

He did not dwell for long on this sense of pleasant lightness but simply noted it and went on watching the passing Parisians – although really he supposed that, even this early in the year, an awful lot of them were not natives but visitors like himself. Clearly the three girls in tight jeans and T-shirts, with heavier sweatshirts tied around their hips, whom he had seen approaching at a distance, were tourists and not office-workers, chattering, laughing, arguing and looking about them. They made an abrupt choice of Donald's *terrasse*, and as they negotiated their way to a table behind him, a little to one side, he noticed that their T-shirts were emblazoned with portraits of themselves, and this produced a curious effect – a built-in double take. One of them had a slight limp. They went on laughing and disagreeing as they settled into their woven cane chairs, speaking a language he had no clue to. They were pale blondes, blue-eyed goddess types, perhaps Scandinavian or Dutch. The waiter presented himself and stood unmoved before them looking into the middle distance, one hand on the back of a chair, head tipped back and a look of complete disdain on his face. They tried their French on him, overlapping and contradicting one another with increasing hilarity, but he clearly did not recognize an opportunity for chivalry when he saw one. He was not amused. '*Je vous apporte le menu,*' he said and went away. The girls fell silent for a moment, eyed each other and then fell about in mock remorse.

Donald laughed out loud, and went on watching and enjoying them. Which one did he find most attractive? He could hear Bella's voice, insisting that he turn god and award to one of them the chancey apple of excellence. Her own choice would have been different from his, but she would have guessed his all the same. She knew his taste. She could pick girls out as they walked along, or in idle moments in a restaurant, like this. Sometimes he protested that her choice was ludicrous, but in fact she was always spot on. Left to himself he preferred not to choose, but just to look. To choose was to exclude. Not to choose offered one way to have the éclair and the rum-baba too.

An elderly couple stopped on the pavement just in front of him, on the other side of the hedge, to study a map. They frowned together at the collapsing document they held out between them, paying no heed to more urgent pedestrians who stepped around them, pursing their mouths and cocking their heads, appealing – like the waiter – to a higher authority, with the little French sigh of exasperation.

Donald smiled at the scene as he took out his cigarettes, and felt in his jacket for his lighter, a present from Bella. He tried his trouser pockets. He must have left it in the hotel, on the pink marbled top of the dressing-table. In spite of the slow Americanizing of Paris with little supermarkets opening here and there and – *quelle horreur!* – bottled mayonnaise on the shelves, the café did not as yet promote itself with book-matches. He twisted round to see if he could catch the eye of the waiter, but that sour soul, having dumped a menu on the table in front of Venus, Juno and Minerva, was disappearing once more into the dark recesses of the restaurant.

He turned back and felt again in his jacket pocket.

'*Monsieur?*'

The voice came from somewhere behind him. He looked round. A lovely face, very open and clear, eyes that slanted a little, dark reddish hair drawn clean back exposing forehead and temples and small ears. The woman had risen a little and was leaning across her table, her arm outstretched.

'Excusez-moi. Vous voulez du feu?' A box of matches.

'How awfully kind!' Donald leaped to his feet. *'Mais très gentil,'* he added, on his way to fetch them.

'Ce n'est peut-être pas gentil du tout. Not for the health.' Her English was tentative, offered as a joking courtesy.

'You're right,' he agreed. 'But for my comfort . . . for my peace of mind, my . . . *paix. Pour mon âme . . . c'est magnifique!'*

She laughed. *'Mais non, monsieur. C'est vous qui êtes magnifique. Je vous ai vu hier au soir.* Yesterday. In the evening. You are *superbe*! I recognize you from the *scène*.'

'Oh! *Merci. Beaucoup.*' He had lit his cigarette and now waved the spent match to and fro.

'Mais non. Tout au contraire. C'est moi qui vous remercie.'

She refused to take the matches back. It was a tiny way to thank him for such an evening. She had sat down again, while he remained standing at the side of her table and they went on chatting for a while about the production, the audience, the critics, waiting for the conversation to draw to a natural conclusion. On the other side of the *terrasse* the three Valkyries had reacted adversely to the menu, cast before them like a gauntlet, and were filing out now with giggled exclamations and exhortations to each other. One of them, as she passed, beamed at Donald and the young woman, and gave a quick shrug of her shoulders. Suddenly, again, even on this grey day, it seemed quite perfect that Paris should have been saved to the finish, the last lap – the final weeks of the tour, an end within sight and a rest beckoning. The sweetness of the prospect took him by surprise.

Donald said, 'Look, I was just about to order another coffee. May I offer you something, or is that beyond the bounds?'

The young lady's name was Véronique Duhamel. She accepted a small apéritif in the most natural way, without hesitation. Two apéritifs later, after a little prompting from the waiter, they drifted on to consume a light lunch. She answered his questions with a simplicity that struck him as highly sophisticated and left him wanting to ask many more. She took for granted a whole swathe of issues that an Englishwoman would have coyly shied from. She lived, she told him, a few blocks away on the Quai Voltaire, overlooking the Seine; she was separated from her husband, she was a psychologist, engaged at present in writing her *thèse* for a doctorate; she read and understood English but was not confident in speaking it; she was waiting for her friend, a doctor, to come, but he might not. He could not always manage to get away.

She questioned Donald in her turn. Did he have many friends in Paris? (It turned out that she knew Monique – their families were old friends.) She pulled a little indecipherable face when Donald told her he had declined Monique's invitation to stay, but equally she understood at once that he would not wish to be under obligation to anyone. She expected that he must be at the George V or the Crillon. At the discovery that he had preferred the more modest Scandinavie, her face lit up with surprise: '*Mais c'est tout à fait dans le quartier!*'

Véronique impressed and enchanted Donald. She completed some picture he had not been aware he had in his mind. It was refreshing to meet someone who assumed that his work was exhausting and that he needed time and space to replenish himself. Interviewers and members of the public who often affected a desire to understand the curious mechanisms of actors ended up, as often as not, simply perpetuating cherished myths. The same people would ask, 'What do you do during the day?' – as if the evening's work did not count – and 'How do you personally "wind down" after a show?', the words 'wind down' being placed in almost edible inverted commas.

In his younger days, depending on his mood and the circumstances (and on his opinion of his interlocutors and how speedily he wanted to be rid of them), Donald sometimes replied that he suspected that some of his co-thespians coped by having people come round after a performance to flatter them out of their minds. He couldn't answer for others, he said, but he himself always found that by far the pleasantest and most effective way to relax was to find himself a congenial companion or companions and go off somewhere for a good old-fashioned slap-up fuck.

The four-letter option, as opposed to some circumlocution or vivid hint, sometimes represented a deliberate offensive on Donald's part, sometimes a bonding gesture. His unpremeditated responses and what they had to tell him, in retrospect, about his reading of a situation always intrigued him. And this would raise a laugh, more or less sincere; and the point would be taken (it was imagined) in the spirit in which it had been made; but of course it was also the truth. For after a performance, after so many hours of containment and preparation, followed – please God – by fine-gauged, disciplined spontaneity released to order over a span of a hundred and twenty minutes, a hundred and eighty, sometimes more, there was nothing that could quite match up to the exultant release, the yielding of the strings of his entire being, as much as getting laid – there was no elegant word – some glorious rolling celebration in the sack, with a woman he liked, or just had a fancy or affection for. Followed by a cigarette. A good meal before or after was not amiss. Other times, other customs. Before Bella.

Véronique informed him that she had taken seats for all three plays in the repertoire. She would see him play again on Thursday night. Donald frowned at her down his nose and told her that she disappointed him very much. She thought she must have misunderstood him. She looked alarmed, and then smiled relief when he explained, 'If you loved last night as much as you say I'd have expected you to be there again tonight.'

'Oh,' she cried, 'but you imagine I have not tried! I have taken my place a long time! There are no more places. Nothing! Nothing! Nothing!'

'Nothing will come of nothing,' Donald said. 'Would it bore you terribly to see another play tonight?'

chapter 27

Was fidelity only fortuitous, Donald wondered two days later, sitting at the same table in the same café? He stirred his *grand crème* and pondered the word fortuitous. In spite of the memory of a Latin master who had once tried to take him down a peg or two for misuse of the word, he persisted in thinking that it meant 'lucky'.

'Fortuitous does *not* mean "lucky", Ballader. It means by chance. And chance, Ballader, is not necessarily lucky, as you may find out in your life. It can be very unlucky. A fortuitous meeting with the Latin master in the High Street, when you are minus your school cap, might well lead to your having to give up a free period.'

Four weeks of the present tour, on the move between Milan and Berlin and Barcelona, had given Donald the leisure to assess the different moods and stages of his life, but he had no idea what should be attributed to what – how to disentangle effect from cause. Was it age or fatigue, or marriage to Bella that had – what? – tamed him, soothed him, reformed him, rotted him? Fidelity had never been something he had given a great deal of thought to; not something he had ever 'gone in for' – as Tony would have said. (As Claire would have testified.) He had not thought about it since marrying Bella, for that matter, but with the opposite effect. And now? Now was he changing back, reverting? Was his relative reformation merely the result of circumstance and geography, distance from temptation? The absence of a full moon? The absence of Véronique Duhamel?

Touring, like being on location, is a notorious loosener of bonds and morals. Unfamiliar surroundings supply a new backdrop for over-familiar selves, a licence to try out another role (or at least to throw over tradition and improvise in the modern way, not to feel constrained as if the original blocking were gospel). No matter whether the location be far flung and lavish, or close at hand and seedy; any unaccustomed setting may turn exotic and generate its own glamour. People are so hard to please, and so frequently confused, with civilization urging them mercilessly beyond instinct towards something supposedly higher, towards constancy, so that finally two of their most urgent desires are brought into conflict. A longing for safety, not to be frightened, to be known and loved and understood for themselves, as they are by their families and friends and those whom they themselves know and love and think they understand; and at the same time, coexisting, a longing for the unknown, for that which they don't know and which does not know them, for eyes that see afresh, that can be dazzled all over again by the yellow hair. New eyes that promise new existence and bestow the illusion of rebirth; clever life-giving eyes that are never around long enough to acquire scales. Bella, firmly on the side of civilization (otherwise there was no point), would have pooh-poohed all this as feeble, self-indulgent stuff. Actors had less excuse than anyone, she would say. Actors got all they needed in the way of new eyes upon them each time they stepped on stage. Bella was not, on the whole, an addictive personality.

For the first weeks of the tour Donald had been plagued by restlessness. He slept badly. And in this matter, too, was it a question of attribution? Should he blame the beds, the different food, or the fact that for once on this tour he had not joined the group – of actors and occasional local friends and fans, willing guides – to explore the new nighttime cities? (He found himself, instead, unbelievably, going off with the likes of Aubrey Morris for a quiet supper in some discreetly starred restaurant.) More than once he caught the dark sad eyes upon him of Tess, the stage manager, staring out of her pale moon face. And Jonty, whom he called Jinxy, who was playing Catherine, Mathias's daughter in *The Bells* – more than competently – wheedled him for a while.

One night in Berlin, having at last persuaded both Donald and Aubrey to come out with them all for a meal, Jonty refused to let it go at that; Donald must come dancing too. 'Don't be such a spoilsport, Don. Come on!' She grabbed his hand, to pull him from his chair. Tough as she was, and pulling with all her tiny might, she could not literally unseat him; but the metaphorical outcome, had he gone along to the disco, would have been less predictable – some sort of dislodgement almost certainly. Now, in Paris of all places, with time hanging off him in great folds, like spare skin from a sudden weight loss, when he should have been with Bella, along came Véronique, whom Bella would have picked out in a moment.

Véronique drew Donald like a magnet. He suspected an equal attraction on her side. He did not know yet whether the magnetic field existed only within the confines of Paris, or whether it were capable of extending beyond its limits. Her coolness had nothing chilly about it; she simply avoided putting pressure on their friendship. He knew that she had reorganized her timetable so that she could be with him, though she pretended not to. She had her doctor friend, who could not always 'manage to get away'. She knew about Bella. She had seen and admired her in *Love Catches Cold*.

The truth was that he had not been tempted to stray because he had not been interested; no one had captured his attention. Véronique interested him. But what made Véronique interesting also placed her out of reach. There could be no question of a dalliance with Véronique; not on her side, he guessed and – a stronger guess – not on his. Véronique had to be either/or.

Donald and Véronique met almost every night and, occasionally, when Véronique could manage it, during the daytime. The sun began to shine. She became his guide and gave him her own exclusive tour of Paris. They had lunch at the Parc Montsouris and sat by the little lake afterwards watching the nannies with their charges; she took him to the Roman amphitheatre, the Arène de Lutèce, and he declaimed in a thunderous voice, 'Friends, Parisiennes, Véronique!'; she decided he should go shopping with her in the bustling Rue Mouffetard. She insisted on visiting the domed Panthéon, not to be inspired by the illustrious dead, but to follow after her favourite uniformed custodian, as he indicated points of interest with an artificial hand clad in black leather, and hear him declaim '*Par ici pour les tombeaux!*' in his sepulchral tones.

She took up the slack of his freedom, no longer just when they were together, increasingly when they were not, invading his mind. She cast a net of enchantment round him and he let it settle – to struggle would be to disturb and perhaps draw it in, until it entangled him totally. At first Donald was proud of Véronique; of Véronique in his life and of the fact that he had so far resisted the temptation of her, which was powerful. But resistance implies a steady, sustained movement or effort against or from, and at first he felt no sense of struggle at all, only a most pleasurable regret. Dining with her one night, in a big noisy brasserie near the Odéon, Donald reflected that perhaps this lucid regret was a first inkling of old age. His personal Ages of Man must be fewer than the usual seven, by-passing maturity and moving via a skimped infancy and prolonged adolescence directly to senescence.

The next day, early, they were to go to the flea market, the Musée Rodin . . . Véronique's list of things to do in Paris got no shorter. Over supper – when she took out her pen and the elegant little blue leather diary to write down the things she kept thinking of that he absolutely must not miss – 'while he was there' shifted suddenly to 'before he went home'. A week had already passed. It hit them both in the same moment. He – they – had only one week left. Neither of them spoke. The waiter brought the bill, and Donald paid. Véronique insisted that he had as usual left too big a tip and tried to cram one of the notes back into his hand so that he would not spoil the waiters. The awkward tussle misfired and she gave up quickly.

He walked her back to the Quai Voltaire as he had done several times. She said very little. Donald forced himself to keep up a flow of chat, commenting on the audience, complaining about a prop that had gone missing; he had forgotten to mention a dinner he might not be able to get out of on the following evening. That plunged them back into silence. They stopped outside the great black-painted coach doors.

At this point they usually repeated a little ritual whereby she asked if he would like a drink, and he refused. Tonight she did not ask, and there should have been nothing untoward in that; but tonight the absence of an invitation carried an unexpected weight. On the previous evening he had kissed her goodnight, lightly on the cheek; tonight he did not. They parted without words, as if they had had a quarrel; but that was far from the case. She pressed the side button and they heard the little buzz as the small door within the *porte-cochère* was released. She pushed it open and went in. Donald walked on slowly back to his hotel.

Because of the difference in schedules, with Bella up early filming, and Donald working at night, they had adopted a routine of speaking in the mornings. Bella would telephone before her car came to take her to the studio, chatter to Donald – still only half-awake – and he would go back to sleep. Or not. Tonight he telephoned Bella, waking her, 'just to say hallo'.

She cursed him blearily. 'Is everything okay? You sound a bit on edge.'

Again, for something to say, he repeated the complaints he had made to Véronique half an hour earlier, and apologized for the rude awakening. They promised a longer chat in the morning, before she left the house.

'Funnily enough, I was almost going to wait up tonight and ring you. It must be telepathy,' she said. She told him she was excited. She had something to discuss with him, but not now, tomorrow morning. 'What time is it?' she asked, as she was about to hang up.

He told her, and found himself continuing, 'I've only just got in from supper.' He knew that she would want to know who with. Until now he had not mentioned Véronique.

'Is she a friend of Monique's? Who is she?'

He described Véronique, leaving the manner of their meeting vague.

Bella said, 'She sounds very nice,' and went quiet.

'She is,' he said, and went on talking about her, without being at all sure why, prompted by some inexplicable compulsion. He found himself using Véronique's name as if he could use it up, rob it of its charm, make Véronique ordinary. Or was he warning himself? Or Bella? Did he hope by telling Bella that Véronique existed to enlist her aid, even at long distance? Or had he devised this curiously devious way of testing Bella's powers – invoking Bella as you might wield a crucifix before the vampire, to conjure the deity?

(At supper, come to think of it, he had in fact chosen *soupe à l'ail à la Provençale*, chock full of garlic. 'I'm a desperate man,' he had joked to Véronique, but he could not be sure that she knew what he meant.)

Certainly in spelling out the danger, he made it more difficult for himself to lie. Claire, who to this day believed she had known about most of his infidelities, had really known about very few; and yet if the name of the current lady in question had ever cropped up between them she had always known at once – something in his voice, was it? – and her face would go so sad that he would put his arms around her, sweating to persuade her that he loved her as much as ever.

'Let's talk in the morning,' Bella said. 'Okay? I'm half-asleep. Good night, darling.'

'Good night, sweet. Sleep tight.'

Lately he had often fallen asleep wondering about Tess, or Jonty, one or two others. If they had been outside the company, strangers, how quickly might he have succumbed? It struck him now that, discounting all her other qualities, Véronique had the one thing they lacked. Even if she had not possessed the quickness and the beautiful smile, her way of laying her head to one side, almost on to her own shoulder, catching her lower lip with her teeth, frustrated on the brink of finding the word she had been hunting for – Véronique should have been the perfect, the irresistible stranger: a woman without repercussion. It should have been easy. What troubled him tonight (and had troubled Véronique also, he felt sure) was the very fact that he did resist, unreasonably. The more he resisted the more it mattered; the more faithful to Bella, the more dangerous, the more powerful, Véronique.

chapter 28

What Bella had to put to Donald the next morning was the prospect of being in a play together again at last. Bob Rayner had done it again – he had promised her he would. He had bought the rights to the first stage play by a well-known novelist. It was, she said, fabulous; tremendous parts, not like anything either of them had done before, a sort of farce that was not a farce. Morris Askey's producer friend had offered to put money into a co-production with Bob, with a view to taking the production to Broadway. A small cast, her favourite management – who would really do them proud – good money. The run had yet to be negotiated. At the moment they were stipulating a year, but Tony was confident that he could make them come down on that. One or two directors' names had been suggested but of course Bella and Donald would have their say there. The only snag seemed to be time. Rayner had a theatre coming free middle to end of June. Rehearsals would have to start in just over a month, to allow for a short pre-London tour. Donald might be robbed of a few weeks' break but they would still be able to fit in a proper holiday. They could go up to Scotland or take up the de Santises' offer of their house in the South of France and then come back and start rehearsing the new play.

The line crackled and made Bella's voice come and go. Donald turned over to face the long windows of his room as if the gentle gloomy light that came from the courtyard would help him to hear more clearly. He pressed the telephone hard to his ear. His thoughts were still coloured by fatigue, and this abrupt retint of his entire horizon threw him at first. He felt he needed a holiday just to be able to make so large a decision. Bella's enthusiasm carried her away and she poured persuasions at him down the wires. It would be almost like a holiday to work together again. A holiday followed by a holiday. With days free to spend together once the show was on – what luxury! He laughed. He could imagine her face at the other end. He missed Bella. What's more, he thought, he owed it to her – he remembered his earlier decision, when he had thrown her to the wolves. He had one of life's rare chances: he could reverse that decision now and make it up to her. He forgot that the decision he had taken had proved the right one.

'Send me the play,' he called down the phone. The line was getting worse.

'It may be already there. Ask at the desk. I told Bob to send it direct to the hotel. If not it'll be there tomorrow. I can't wait to hear what you think.'

Bob Rayner's office told Bella, when she called them from the studio, that they had not yet despatched the play to Paris.

'Don't!' she cried at once. 'I'll come and get it!' And Bella, after she finished filming on Saturday night, took the sleeper from Victoria to Paris.

The hotel receptionist woke Donald on Sunday morning to tell him that a script was on its way upstairs. He got up grumpily to open the door and found Bella cock-a-hoop on the other side. She was transported by the simple brilliance of her plan and its evident success. The amazement and delight on Donald's face when he set eyes on her exhilarated them both. She would be happy to join in any plans he had for the day – she did not have to leave for the airport until four – but Donald insisted on cancelling the one 'rather boring and vaguish' appointment he had, so that they should have the entire day to themselves, starting with breakfast. (When Bella suggested that Donald might like a little apricot jam with his baguette, she could not understand why he roared with laughter and got up from the table to kiss her.) Their intoxication lasted without interruption from breakfast time to train time. Why had they not done this more often? He took a taxi back to the hotel from the Gare du Nord and settled down to read.

The play concerned itself with a man and a woman who, each needing grounds for divorce, decide to save money on hiring professionals by spending a weekend together at a Brighton hotel. It was good – well written. The farcical setting had more to offer than its subject suggested at first – nothing profound, but with an intriguing slant, switches of sympathy, surprises and, as Bella had said, tremendous and unlikely parts for both of them. Donald became as enthusiastic as Bella; if they could find the right director he was on.

The second week in Paris vanished almost before it began. After his hasty telephone call to her on the Sunday it did not surprise Donald that Véronique should remove herself. She had many things to do, she said, to do with her thesis. He missed her, but he had not the right to pursue her. He had to accept her refusals at face value. They had one dinner together but both of them were subdued. Their usual table had been given to a rowdy group of tourists and they could hardly hear one another. An air of disturbance and melancholy hung over the restaurant. Then a number of semi-official functions which Donald was bound to attend began to swallow up the week – a company farewell; a party given in their honour by the British Ambassador. Having managed to persuade Véronique to have a final supper with him Donald had to cancel it; Tony seized the need to talk over details of the play deal as an excuse to come over and spend a few days in Paris. He took up the offer to stay at the de Santises' flat, came to the Odéon and insisted that Donald and Monique dine with him afterwards. Donald, although pressed by Tony to find himself 'a date', declined. He had to say goodbye to Véronique on the telephone and did not see her again before he left Paris.

In London things moved quickly. Rayner came up with an inspired suggestion for a director. Carola Fry, a girl who had worked for a time as Victor's assistant and whom they both knew and liked, happened to be free and keen. Everyone was happy. They had almost a clear month for their holiday, with one or two obstacles to be circumnavigated. They toyed with the idea of going up to Scotland, which they loved so much, but rejected it. What was wanted was a proper holiday with sun, or at least warmth, and luxury; they accepted Jacques and Monique's offer of the house at Cap d'Antibes, complete with domestics. Three weeks of unaccustomed lazing, sleeping, swimming and sunshine set them up. A month away from work had been almost too long. They arrived home full of beans, full of themselves and of one another, raring to go, and launched into rehearsals with a will.

The prospect of seeing Bella and Donald on stage together again generated enormous excitement and the PR people made the most of it. They rehearsed for four weeks, played two weeks in Brighton and opened on Shaftesbury Avenue at the end of June. Everyone's expectations were fulfilled.

But the path to paradise was not without potholes. An early heatwave made the first weeks hard going, though it did not affect the houses. Even at the height of summer the theatre was full.

'Don't say I didn't warn you,' Donald would declare to friends visiting from the States. 'It is, literally, the hottest ticket in town!', and he pleaded periodically with the theatre management to put in air-conditioning.

The heat got to Donald less than the monotony. Hard work did not trouble him, but he was used to variety. He had reckoned without the tedium of playing the same show eight times a week; sometimes, it seemed, to the same audience. Bella buoyed him up: he would get used to it. It would be easier once they got into the swing of it; and indeed, quite quickly, Donald did get on top of the routine, but then it was not long before the routine began to get on top of him.

Working at such close quarters it became essential that they lay down some sort of ground rules. They would drive one another mad otherwise. They made a pact that once they had passed out of the stage-door they would not discuss the performance. It was a sensible arrangement, but after a time it seemed to leave them with very little to say. Problems were left unresolved for the sake of peace – a line mistimed, a prop repeatedly forgotten – which then blew up out of proportion. Rayner had wanted them to sign for a year. Thank God Donald had held out. Six months and not a second longer. Thank God, thank God.

For, instead of becoming smoother as their journey's end drew near, the passage grew choppier and tempers shorter. Time wobbled and stretched the more tired they became. Performances grew, but literally – in length rather than stature. One Saturday after the second performance the stage manager knocked on Donald's door. She hated to have to do this but it was her job to point out that they were putting a couple of minutes on each act.

'A couple of minutes? I don't believe it!' Donald replied, and then, as the girl started reeling off documentary proof, cut her short with: 'It feels more like a couple of hours.'

The next time it was the company manager, whose 'old boy' approach irked Donald, so that he became surly: 'What are you complaining about? They should be overjoyed. Getting their money's worth.' When the man tried sweet reason Donald dismissed him: 'I'm not the only person involved. Why don't you discuss it with Miss Provan?'

In spite of all their good intentions to spend more time together they quickly fell back into old habits. Little by little they both started to take on other work at various times during the run; radio, tele, even a few days' filming if the schedule could be fitted round them. They justified themselves: it was one way of keeping staleness at bay, but it was an exhausting one.

They ached to get away, to Scotland or back to the South of France. They promised themselves another, even longer break 'when it was all over'. They needed to get away: they needed to get away from each other, they exclaimed. They made a joke of it. But, though Bella could acknowledge the need and laugh about it, the reality was not a joke. Bella had enjoyed working with Jacques, and his obvious admiration and enthusiasm had helped to give her a confidence that she had not yet found in filming. Jacques assured her that her performance would bring the whole of Hollywood knocking at her door. In spite of this there had been moments when she had bitterly regretted deciding to do the film. Donald's absence had shaken her. Her dash to Paris had been the culmination of weeks of nervous torment. The trip had reassured her; but reassurance had not obliterated the effect of his being away, which had left poisons in her that it would take a long time to throw off. The West End run was going to solve everything.

Except that now, in spite of having Donald always under her eye, she found herself more unnerved than ever, constantly on edge. It was easy to put this down to simple fatigue, but it amounted almost to a sickness. She thought that it was destroying them. If she had been working on a part she would have nagged away to get to the truth of it, but just now she did not examine her feelings, afraid of what she might find. She remembered a young actor moaning to her once that the director had said nothing to him and he did not dare ask for help.

'Speak out,' she had told him. 'Ask. Don't be afraid.'

'I can't,' he had replied. 'What if he tells me what to do and I can't do it?'

The heat and the summer wore on. One performance bled into another and both of them began to lose focus. Coming offstage one afternoon Donald rounded on Bella.

'Darling, you're milking that scene. It's getting slower and slower.'

Bella gaped at Donald. It was an all too familiar accusation, which she resented. '*I* am? *I* was trying to pick it up off the floor. What was all that business with the chrysanthemums for Pete's sake?'

Donald covered his face and moaned. 'Oh. Yes. Oh God. I couldn't for the life of me remember if it was Act II or Act III!'

At one time Donald had declared that he could tell what day of the week it was by the way the audience laughed, or held its breath. Now both, at different times, found themselves moving across the stage or halfway through a speech like somnambulists, scarcely knowing how they got there, or whether it was the matinée or the evening, let alone what day of the week. They coped in different ways. Donald set himself to try out new things, to keep things fresh, he said.

'To keep up your own spirits!' said Bella. 'Never mind about the audience or the play. You're totally irresponsible.'

Irritation built up. It disconcerted Bella to find herself floundering, unable to respond when Donald tried something new, a false exit, a new pause. One evening he simply stood regarding her with what she called afterwards 'an extremely sinister expression' and she could not tell whether this signified some new experiment or whether he had dried yet again. She, who tended to be the greater risk-taker and in performance was usually quick to sniff and explore any new possibility, found herself thrown by his inventions; and thrown by being thrown. Now, where Donald launched forth, inclined a little to wildness, she lingered on terra firma and resorted to low tricks which Donald could not abide: playing the audience for sympathy or laughter, milking her effects and either killing or diluting them.

'If you get any broader in that scene, darling, you won't be able to make it back offstage,' he said to her in disbelief one night, after counting to fourteen during what had once been a delicious two-second U-turn. Bella asserted that Donald himself was nowhere near so lily-white as he imagined.

'What were you *doing*?' they would ask of each other, undermined, exasperated, as the curtain finally came down. But it was worse if they said nothing at all. And better when they had friends out front, both for the performance and for the aftermath.

Fortunately, as the end of the run began at last to be

measured in the number of performances rather than in weeks and days, more friends came, some for the second or third time, bringing their friends. It lifted their performances to play to a few faces they knew; and a meal afterwards offered the prospect of something to look forward to, though not invariably.

One evening Bob Rayner put on a small dinner party for them at which one or other of them, or both, disgraced themselves, depending on your point of view. Bob Rayner liked to hold to old traditions, so, in spite of the lateness of the hour, when the time came for coffee the ladies filed upstairs to the drawing room of his elegant Georgian house. Bella found herself cast as hostess, handing the tray of golden coffee cups round. This she accomplished with her usual grace, until she came to Donald's neighbour at table, a bleached-blonde Zsa Zsa type, who had punctuated the meal with piercing giggles uttered after sly whisperings in Donald's ear. She had declined coffee, with a light laugh, because it made her too hot and interfered with her beauty sleep; and Bella, smiling a sweet understanding smile, had picked up a large jug of cream from the tray.

'What you need is something to cool you down,' she said, and poured the contents of the jug into the woman's lap.

Moments later Donald met Bella coming downstairs carrying their coats and announcing that they really had to get home. After this episode they cried off supper engagements, pleading a matinée next day, an excess of fatigue. But early nights did not always solve things; their own company left them weary. Tony had been making noises for the last two months about what they should be doing next, but they could not see beyond this present stifling life. The only believable solution was to finish, get the run over with. To this they raised their eyes.

They opted for Scotland – log fires and wilderness. They imagined the little house surrounded by a thicket of overgrown brambles, like Sleeping Beauty's castle. It would need reawakening, restocking, airing, dusting. With deliverance in sight they began to talk to each other again, full of plans and pleasantness, of things that had nothing to do with today. The prospect of Christmas in Scotland extended their vision, like new lenses; they could see another future. Four weeks' essential bliss. They were within sight of paradise.

chapter 29

It had been settled that Alice would accompany Bella and Donald north of the border, chiefly to act as chauffeuse. Once there her employment with them was to end. She had decided finally to move on. (Deep regrets all round, but she pointed out that she had already stayed four times as long as she had meant to.)

The initial plan had been for Alice to drive Bella, who in her present state of bone-tiredness would find the long drive beyond her. They would take their time over it. Alice would help get Bella settled, spend a few days with them, then take advantage of the opportunity to see one of her married sisters, who lived in Stornoway. Donald had several days' work to complete a film, and then he would fly up to Scotland or take the sleeper and they would bid Alice a fond and reluctant farewell. They had presented her with a handsome parting gift – an air-ticket to Canada for the long-postponed visit to her sister in Ontario.

At this point everything went out of kilter. The TV company, for whom Donald had to do his few days' filming, shifted to accommodate him; Jacques' production company shifted to accommodate Bella for her post-synching, with the happy result that in exchange for a slight delay she would be rewarded by not having to dash back halfway through their holiday. They might even grab an extra week before returning to whatever particular form of grind Tony had set up for them.

It meant that Bella rather than Donald would have to stay behind in London for a few days. Plans had to be relaid. Donald was for driving up on his own to get the place straight at his leisure, and letting the 'girls' follow on by plane or train as the fancy took them. To Bella that seemed pointless. Obviously he would need the car, but it would be exhausting to drive alone and too dreary to arrive all by himself. Why not stick to the original plan, she suggested, except that Alice would drive Donald instead of Bella, or at least share the driving?

In one of those misplaced, mistimed conversations that overtake the protagonists, matters that Donald thought should have been settled between him and Bella alone had to be aired in Alice's presence. How could you be honest? He could hardly say in front of Alice, or to Bella for that matter, that he had been craving those four days on his own like a man doing cold turkey. Four days of unimpinged solitude, without voices. No doubt they had acted with the best of intentions, to spare him boring trivialities, but from Donald's point of view the feeling that Bella and Alice had as good as sorted everything beforehand, without consulting him, only aggravated the whole business.

Unfortunately, although they had agreed never to talk at home about the evening's performance, Donald and Bella had sworn no counter-oath about discussing domestic arrangements at the theatre. In her dressing room between the matinée and the evening show – her precious nap-time – Donald let fly at Bella. What the hell did she think she was doing? How dare she, and Alice for that matter, set about organizing his life out of all recognition?

'Since when do you ever deign to do your own organizing? You are happy enough to let us do everything for you when it suits you.'

The stage manager knocked at the door, hoping to collect some props for the evening performance before Bella took her nap. Having heard their voices outside the door she apologized in a low voice for interrupting them and slunk out again quickly, bearing a bunch of chrysanthemums, a toothbrush, a man's bowler hat, a suitcase and a season-ticket wallet.

They calmed down a little. Donald took a deep breath. 'The

thing is,' Donald resumed, 'I don't want to be driving about with Alice for eight hours at a stretch!'

'But you won't *be* driving – that's the whole idea! She'll do most of the driving.'

'Oh, that's hardly the point, is it? I'd rather be on my own.'

'But you like Alice.'

'She's all right.'

'She's lovely, darling. You're always saying how terrific she is, and efficient. She's lovely.'

'So she's lovely! She's a very nice girl. Frightfully efficient. That's not the point. I don't know her.'

'You'll get to know her.'

'I don't want to get to know her. Why should I? Especially as she's just about to leave us.'

'You'd like her if you did. I think you're being very unfair. She adores you.'

'I don't care if she sweeps my toe-nail clippings off the bathroom floor and sleeps with them under her pillow. I'm tired. I don't want to spend four days making chit-chat with a total stranger.'

'But whose fault is it then if she is a stranger, Donald? You've never made the slightest effort to get to know her.'

'Well, it's a bit too bloody late to start now.'

Bella persisted. She could not help herself, though she could not have said why. The more Donald resisted the more something drove her to push back. 'Think of all the things she's done for you. It's a bit mean to do her out of her holiday. It's only a few days.'

He pointed out that Alice would still have her holiday, that in fact the first few days in the cottage might be quite hard work. Really they were taking advantage of her – not for the first time. But his protests were in vain, too late. The die was cast. The show that night was very good – tight and focused.

Alice and Donald set out while it was still dark, to beat the rush; but it was raining, which was bound to complicate things. Bella stood out on the pavement, a raincoat thrown over her red dressing-gown. She was holding an umbrella up high, trying to shelter both herself and Donald, in the end protecting neither. Rain dripped on to both of them off the wooden ends of the spokes.

'You look like Volumnia,' he said. '*Droop not, adieu* ... Go back to bed!'

'Nonsense. The car's coming for me in three-quarters of an hour. You get on. Go on, get in. Alice is waiting, darling.'

Donald leaned under the umbrella and kissed her, to the staccato accompaniment of raindrops battering the stretched nylon over their heads. His hand, cradling her skull, was buried deep in her hair. When she drew away she pulled a face at him of mock exasperation. He pulled a face back. She gave him another quick kiss.

'Get on!' she said.

'Bye-bye, baby,' he replied, and walked round to the passenger seat. Alice had offered to take the wheel so that Donald would be spared the tedium of the exit from London. Now he sought Bella's eyes across the car roof and mouthed a kiss. 'Bye, darling.'

She called back, 'Be good!' and bent down to wave goodbye at Alice through the window.

The car was loaded up with a variety of Christmas essentials, a big cardboard box with fairy lights and ends and shreds of red and green and furry tinsel hanging out and two points of a large silver star. Donald threw his coat and a small bag into the back, on top of some bulky and mysterious bundles – 'Careful!' from Bella – got in beside Alice and slammed the door.

They moved off almost at once, slowly, along the narrow thoroughfare between parked cars.

Alice said, 'Well, I hope we haven't left anything behind.'

Donald sighed. 'It doesn't look like it.' He was twisted round in his seat to wave to Bella, though it was doubtful whether she could make them out inside the car. Before they reached the corner of the square he saw her turn away and jump across a puddle to regain the low front step, letting down the umbrella. He turned to face the road ahead. 'Too bloody bad if we have. I'm not going back now.'

His own vehemence surprised him. He glanced across at Alice. Her pale profile glided unperturbed in and out of shadow, as they drove along in the light of occasional street lamps before finally turning into the glare of the High Street. He would have felt far more comfortable driving himself, but he had not bothered putting up a fight. If it had been Bella to drive, he would have been less acquiescent, though she drove well enough – a little fast, and keeping up a stream of nervous commentary as she went along: on the road, on driving, on her driving, on other drivers. Alice drove like a chauffeur, with a certain steadiness, as if driving were incidental. She could talk or not, gauging the mood of her passenger. Now they were both silent. Though it was so early, the rush-hour traffic was already building up, tentative because of the rain, saloons mingling with vans and lorries returning from early deliveries.

Alice turned off the High Street and proceeded down a back lane, a commercial service street, then into residential streets. If it had been Bella, Donald would have queried this route at once, but Alice always gave an impression that hers was the best and only, the inescapable route. Besides Alice was not family; she still called forth party manners – one reason for his objecting to this interminable journey with her alongside – and frankly he was feeling too fed up to give a damn. The whole enterprise was cock-eyed. Planned with care to be one thing, it had been titivated, manipulated and designed almost out of existence by the women: transformed from elegant rhomboid into plonking square, from cruise to assault course, sauna to cross-channel marathon – could you have a cross-channel marathon? – from chocolate that melts in the mouth to peanut brittle that locks the jaws . . . Donald found himself resorting to a childhood stratagem, trying to fend off boredom.

He gazed out of the window, drawing a kind of comfort from the comfortless gleam of pavement and road. 'What do I care?'

he asked himself. '*Rest of his bones, and soulle's deliverie . . .*' He could still have that, in theory. Bella's theory. But in practice it was not so. Alice was neither fish nor fowl, she was an employee, a familiar: an intimate stranger. She soothed, yet could not be taken for granted – so that to some extent she was a disturbance. She could not, politely, be ignored. Yet now she was ignoring him, concentrating on the back of the orange mini ahead. He scrutinized her profile; her eyelashes were a ludicrous length even for a girl. He returned to his morose schoolboy game.

He awoke to the sound of birdsong. The car was stationary. Alice had rolled her window down and was smoking a cigarette. They were in a lay-by, parked behind two lorries, an empty coach and a giant removal van. The skies were still grey but lightening. The rain had all but stopped.

'You really should give that disgusting habit up, Alice.'

'You can talk! Good morning, sir.' She turned her head to nod to him, and back again, to blow smoke out of the window. 'Do you want some breakfast, Donald? There's a little caff.'

'Where are we?'

'Somewhere between Grantham and Newark.'

'How ridiculous. What time is it?'

'Quarter past ten.'

'Is it really?'

He had been asleep for three hours. Alice had been driving for three hours.

'Why didn't you stop, for heaven's sake?'

'I just have.'

They walked towards the cabin, a grounded trailer, peeling white paint. The door of the serving-hatch had been propped up to form a rudimentary shelter for queuing customers.

'I wanted to get shot of London while the going was good. You went out like a light.'

'Sorry. I'll take over for the next stretch. What do you want to eat?'

Four or five drivers stood round chatting, drinking from great white mugs. From time to time the proprietor would lift his head from his morning paper to chip in. Donald nodded at the group, who shifted a little to make way for him and Alice, and continued with their teasing cross-talk while the two were being served with tea and bacon rolls. One of the drivers, a tall blond-haired young man, fixed Donald as he was handing up money for their food, and remarked: 'I know you, mate, from somewhere, don't I?'

'From the box, maybe,' Donald said, pocketing his change and reaching up for the mugs of tea.

'That's it! Right! You're an actor, aren't you? What was that in, then?'

Alice relieved Donald of the tea and he reached back for the bacon rolls. He named two recent series.

'*That's* right! You're that snotty copper, aren't you?'

Donald nodded.

'*That's* right,' the man repeated, glad to have pinned it down.

'But he always gets his man!' another driver put in, and the first added, to some laughter, 'And the bird and all!'

'No, but it's a good series, that is,' another one said. They were curious to know how the scenes were shot, the car chases, and did Donald have a stunt man?

'Notice you let the wife do the driving when you're in civvies, mate!' someone said.

'*I* wouldn't let my wife anywhere near a blooming wagon,' asserted the blond. 'Blooming lethal!' Then he looked at Alice. 'Sorry, missis. No offence.'

Alice, with her mouth full of bread and bacon, shook her head at him: none taken.

When they had finished Donald handed their mugs back up through the hatch and they moved through the group towards the car. One or two of the men raised their mugs: 'Cheers, mate!'

'All the best!'

Donald took the wheel. He felt better for sleep and food. 'Almost awake.'

They made good progress. Alice suggested stopping at

Harrogate for lunch, as they passed so near, and then they could drive on through Ripon to get back to the A1; but Donald wanted to get on. 'We've only just had breakfast!'

By the time he was prepared to acknowledge that his stomach might welcome attention again, it was well past one. Each place they passed not only looked unpromising but fulfilled its lack of promise. By half-past one, even in pubs, they were greeted with reluctance and disbelief, in-drawn breaths and expressions of doubt as to the whereabouts of the chef.

'I'm quite happy with a sandwich,' Alice said.

Donald shook his head. He murmured something about a proper lunch, and having a long drive ahead of them still – and drove on.

At two, Alice said with more force, 'I would *like* a sandwich, Donald. Please. Something.'

She insisted at last that he turn off at a sign to Richmond and there, by a small miracle, they found the very thing – a tea shoppe within sight of the castle, which owed its entire existence to not making rigid divisions in the day, sliding with ease from early breakfast to luncheon to high tea and back again. It even had oak beams.

Here Christmas signalled its approach in twisting tinsel strands that snaked around the beams and criss-crossed the ceiling, with sprigs of holly tucked into the frames of pictures where coaches and four streamed across old-English landscapes of hedge and down. A large bunch of mistletoe hung strategically near the door. They ate home-made soup, lamb chops with two veg, mince tart and custard. The shoppe was not licensed but they were at liberty to bring their own bottle. Donald raided the boot for a bottle of claret and got through most of it. Alice was next to drive, he could sleep it off. The shoppe was crowded when they arrived. There were one or two businessmen, but mostly women with children and parcels, high chatter. It emptied a little as they ate. But by the time they left, with darkness about to fall, it had filled up again with more women and children and more parcels and prams.

They did not reach Glasgow until well after eight and both were ravenous again. Last orders in the hotel restaurant were at nine, but neither of them felt like venturing out into the town.

'I have to have a bath,' Alice insisted. 'Why don't you go on in?'

'No rush,' Donald said. 'I'll have a wash and brush-up and meet you in the bar.' She found him there at ten to nine, seated on a high stool chatting to the barman. He downed the remains of his whisky and got up, putting a couple of notes down beside the glass, and they went in to dinner.

The dining room was almost deserted. One couple, outlined against the black window, and one man on his own near the door. The opaque, apricot-coloured glass fittings on the walls spread more shadow than light, throwing semi-circular pockets of dinginess on to the fleur-de-lys wallpaper. An elderly waiter had led them to a table close to the swing-doors that led to the kitchen, presumably to save his aching feet: his steps were uncertain, and when he burst into the dining room bearing their bottle of wine, followed very soon after by steaming plates of soup, his look of alarmed concentration did not promote confidence. In a distant gloomy corner a bus-boy went about the business of laying up the breakfast tables. They ate to the sound of the swing-doors banging to and fro, and of occasional defiant yelps that echoed from within the fluorescent recesses of the kitchen.

'At least the service is damn good,' Donald commented. He took some bread, and offered the silver basket to Alice.

'Only because they want to get us out of here as quick as they can.' Alice lifted her spoon, ignoring the proffered bread, and said, 'Look, I know you would rather have come up on your own. Frankly so would I.'

Donald, still holding out the bread, said, 'What?'

They stared at each other.

'Oh. God!' He was almost shouting. The couple by the window turned their heads, startled. Was there going to be a row? But, instead, a roar of laughter resounded through the room. Alice joined Donald. 'I am being an absolute bloody pig, am I not?'

'You are that!'

'And it's none of your fault at all!'

'It is not.'

Donald sighed and then burst out laughing again. 'Alice, I am so sorry. Forgive me if you can. I shouldn't take it out on you.' He smiled, feeling foolish. 'I don't even know what "it" is, come to think of it.'

'You would rather be on your own, that's all. Or with Bella.'

He shook his head.

'Of course you would,' said Alice. 'Perfectly natural.'

He denied it. 'No, no, no.'

'Yes, yes, yes,' Alice insisted.

'No, no, no!'

If it had been true it no longer was.

The waiter appeared at their side again, proffering a second bottle. He held it away from his body at arm's length as if it might go off. Donald waved it away. 'No, no, no!' he cried. 'The lady deserves something better after what she's been through! What do you have in the way of champagne? If at all?'

The man raised his shaggy brows and took himself off. He came back with the most expensive bottle he could find, waved the label at them, then fetched a bucket and stand.

After eleven p.m. the hotel lights were dimmed, leaving the public rooms and the corridors murky. Donald and Alice had adjacent rooms. Outside number 429 Donald took hold of Alice's shoulders and gazed down at her for a moment, his expression severe.

'I am forgiven? Sure?'

'You are. Yes, *sir*!'

'Thank you!'

He laughed and kissed her cheek, then held her from him for a moment as if she were a large book he wanted to read. Then he turned to go to his room. 'You *are* lovely,' he said, and leaned to kiss her other cheek. But – how do such things happen? – Alice was just turning away, there was confusion. She turned back, not to be rude, their lips brushed before his found her cheek – the same one it so happened – they held the pause a split second too long. He found her mouth again and experienced a profound relief and sweetness. He drank.

chapter 30

Donald had not seen Tony since before Christmas. It looked as if the office had been given a face-lift in between, a lot of chrome and thirties kitsch. Even the girl at reception was new, he noted. Trust Tony – gleaming wall-to-wall parquet and matching personnel. Except that on closer inspection, as he pushed through the glazed double doors, the figure behind the desk did not suggest either polish or grandeur. As he approached she seemed still less in keeping with her surroundings. Her skin was tanned, without make-up, her hair was too curly to be kempt – if it had been any longer it would have been quite wild. She stood up as he came through the second set of doors – she was actually wearing jeans – and now she leaned forward on both arms over the shiny black desk, and gave him a crazy grin.

'Good morning,' Donald said, peering at her. 'Er – afternoon in fact! Mr Tell's expecting me.'

'I'm so sorry, Mr Ballader. Mr Tell's been a little delayed' – and she burst out laughing. She sat down. 'Mr Ballader, sir!'

Donald stared. Then bellowed, 'You've cut your hair!'

'So have you!'

Naomi Richard jumped up, giving her chair a shove which sent it gliding backwards on its wheels until it collided with a black and silver trolley. She and Donald met at the side of the desk and Donald encircled her in a great hug and lifted her high off her feet until she pummelled his chest.

'Put me down, you great brute. You'll lose me my job.'

'What on earth are you doing here? And come to think of it, what on earth are you doing *here?*'

Donald had not seen Naomi since she and Gerd had taken off for Israel from Oldham to start a new life. How many years was it?

'You said you'd write,' he admonished her. 'Not so much as a postcard of the Holy Land!'

'Would you like a cup of coffee while you're waiting? Mr Tell's just been on to say he's been unavoidably detained with a client. He's in a filthy mood.'

Naomi retreated to her post behind the desk and lifted the phone to order some coffee.

Donald said, 'I think I need something stronger, in view of the turn of events. Tell me what you are doing here, of all places to wind up. I thought you were in Jaffa.'

'Jerusalem.'

'In the army.'

'On and off.'

'I want to hear all about it.'

Naomi laughed and told him to sit down, shut up and tell her what he wanted to drink. Drinks were in a lacquered black cabinet behind her desk. She poured him a vodka and tonic. The phone rang and she answered it, making notes and ignoring the faces he pulled at her, then she tore the message from her pad and placed it with a pile in a black plastic tray, underneath a small silver paperweight in the shape of an Oscar.

'Very efficient,' Donald said.

'I am,' Naomi returned.

'How long are you here?'

'In England? Or here?'

'In England.'

'Indefinite.'

'Not for good?'

'No, no.'

'Working for Tony?'

'Oh Lordy! As short a time as possible.'

'What about Gerd?'

'Still over there.'

Tony's regular receptionist was on holiday and Naomi had agreed to stand in for a lark, for money. Waiting to start a job. Over for a few months to see her family. Her mother was ill. She needed to stay around, she needed work. Tony had found her the perfect job, location manager on a film about to begin shooting in the Wye Valley. The phone rang, she took another message.

'You're coming to lunch with us?'

'Not likely. I have to mind the shop!'

'What about dinner? We must have a good long session, to catch up. You must meet Bella. What about dinner?' Then he remembered that he and Bella were going out that evening.

'Of course, you're a married man. Not to Claire, though.'

'Not any more.'

'Tony says she's great. I hope I'll get to see her.'

'Bella? Does he?'

'Claire.'

'Oh, Claire. Yes, I think so. I haven't seen much of her lately.'

They looked at each other for a moment.

'And how is life with the lovely Miss Provan?'

'Well – ups and downs. You know.'

'I do indeed.'

'But just at the moment, I am here to tell you, very much up. We had the most marvellous Christmas up in Scotland.'

They planned a lunch, to be confirmed. Naomi's unit would be based in Hereford, right near all his old stamping grounds. Donald was seized with a desire to revisit childhood haunts, bring Bella, introduce Naomi to Bella and both of them to his favourite country pub, high up high, looking down over the winding river.

The sight that greeted Tony Tell on his return from a prolonged and unsatisfactory negotiating session arrested him where he stood, between the two sets of double doors: Donald and Naomi, behind the desk, hunched close studying a map of

Herefordshire in an AA gazetteer, Donald's arm wrapped around Naomi. Something Naomi said made Donald throw back his head, and the doors muffled the sound, so that the laughter seemed to come from a long way away and did not fit the image. Then Donald put both arms round Naomi, kissed her and gave her a big hug.

When Tony bustled in at last the two of them had resumed their huddle over the map.

'Good grief, what's this? Don't tell me – you're playing "The Game"? This has to be from *Uncle Vanya*, the map scene. You don't waste much time, do you, Ballader?'

'You're bloody late, Tell. But I forgive you, in view of the floor show.'

'Naomi, did Gilman's office call?' Tony had on his dour expression. He was abrupt and bullish. He hated being late or being wrong and his meeting had not gone well. 'Arthur Tidwell is a buffoon,' he said.

'Why didn't you tell me, Tony, you sly bastard?'

'Tell you what, Donald?'

Tony had grabbed up his messages from the tray and was glancing through them, scowling. He began to bark out instructions to Naomi, who made notes on her pad, playing as cast; but from time to time she rolled her eyes at Donald in mock terror, which was not lost on Tony.

'Come on,' Tony said finally. 'We'll lose our table.' He grabbed Donald by the elbow and called over his shoulder, 'Did you phone the restaurant and tell them we were going to be late?'

'Not yet,' Naomi said. 'I didn't know how late you'd be.'

'Well, do it now.'

Naomi lifted the phone.

'Why isn't she coming with us?' Donald asked, as they reached the double doors. 'Can't take the competition, eh, Tell, is that the problem?'

'That's not what I pay her for,' and Tony ushered him out of the office.

*

'What are you trying to say? What are you saying?' Tony put his coffee cup down with emphasis and stared at Donald open-mouthed, his head thrust forward, his eyes goggling. Donald leaned back, away from him, unsettled by his tone. 'What are you saying, man?' Tony repeated. But when Donald resumed his story, suggesting that not even a saint could have emerged unscathed, Tony broke in with such an urgent 'Did you have her then?' that Donald laughed out loud, and Tony himself gave a little self-conscious titter.

'You are a crude bastard, Tone,' Donald said. 'Yes, I did "have her", as you so roundly phrase it. But it wasn't, as they also say, I believe, "like that".'

'What do you mean?'

'What?'

'What do you mean it wasn't "like that"?'

'What I say.'

'What was it like then?'

'Oh come on, Tone!'

'Well, you come on. Tell me.'

'Tell you what?'

Tony signalled to the waiter for more coffee. 'Are you in love with her?'

'Are you out of your mind?' Donald said, and added, 'She's gone to Canada.'

Tony ignored him. 'I'm sorry, Donald, I don't understand.'

Donald sighed. 'What don't you understand?'

Tony leaned a little to one side to make room for the waiter and paused while his cup was refilled. Donald waved the man away.

Tony continued. 'You slept with this girl, right? What's her name?'

Donald looked down, lowering his voice to encourage Tony to lower his. 'Alice. You know Alice.'

'Alice. You slept with her.'

'Would you mind taking it down a bit, Tony?'

Tony complied, putting his question a second time, lower and slower. 'You slept with her?'

'Yes. Right.'

'How old is she?'

'How old? I don't know. You've met her. Over sixteen!'

'Is she in love with you?'

'Good God, no. I doubt it. What is this?'

'I see. You mean she is. You were doing her a favour, is that it?'

'What are you going on about?'

'Putting her out of her misery? And what about you?'

'What *about* me, Tony?' Tony's battery of questions was beginning to seem less and less quaint now and not at all amusing. But still bewildering.

'What about you? Are you in love with her?'

'You've already asked me that once. You're losing your grip.'

'You haven't answered. Are you in love with her?'

'No.'

'Do you love her?'

Donald smiled a little at Tony's pedantry. 'No.'

'But you slept with her?'

Donald could only stare at Tony in total bewilderment. And still he went on.

'Once, twice?' Donald continued to regard him in silence. 'A dozen times? A score? And now that you're back?'

'Now that I'm back, what?'

'Is it going to go on? Are you going to go on sleeping with this—'

'Of course not, you bloody madman. Apart from anything else she's in Canada.'

She had always been going to be in Canada. Donald did not know why he kept drawing this fact in, as if it had some kind of relevance.

'Oh? Really? That's a bit unkind, isn't it? If she's so potty about you. Why not?'

'You know why not.'

'No. Why?'

'What's eating you, Tony?'

'It was just one of those things, was it? A casual fling. One of those bells, was that it?'

'She knew it couldn't be anything else. She didn't want it to be. She's devoted to Bella, as a matter of fact.'

'Oh that's nice! How cosy. That makes two of you then.'

'It just happened.'

' "It just came apart in me hands, ma'am . . ."?'

'Oh shut up, Tony. I'm sorry I mentioned it.'

He was beginning to wonder why on earth he had. Things were good, prospects were rosy. Since the month in Scotland he and Bella had been enjoying a state of harmony and pleasure in being together that he had thought they might never discover again. The out-of-the-blue delight of seeing Naomi, added to everything else, had somehow pushed him to share the joys of life with his oldest friend. He looked over his shoulder to see if he could catch the waiter's eye for the bill, but their man was nowhere to be seen.

'How is she, the girl? Alice?'

'She's okay about it. She's fine. She's gone away. To Kingston. Kingston, Ontario.'

'She's away and she's fine?'

'She was going away anyway. She's okay.'

'Okay is she? It was all worth it. One night of bliss. And you're "okay" about it too, are you? Easy come, easy go.'

At last Donald spotted their waiter adrift between the tables and beckoned to him. He turned back to Tony. 'You're a fine one to talk, Tony. You run a mile from any woman if you think there's any likelihood that you might like her, let alone fall in love with her.'

Tony bounced to his feet and bent forward. He swung his face low in front of Donald's for a moment, and hissed, '*You* are a married man, mate! A married man!' He sat down again with a thump. '*That's* the difference!'

Donald had long been haunted by an image that recurred

from time to time and flooded his mind: of confrontation with a lion or a tiger. The majestic creature of the jungle would return Donald's gaze, but the lazy eyes looked without seeing. Then the lips curled back in a snarl that released breath that stank of sheer heat. (It was the nostrils that saw, they smelled meat and sent the message to the great cat brain to uncoil the crouched hind muscles and catapult the animal forward, roaring, to seize its prey.) Donald had a name for the image. He called it 'the futility of reason' or 'no quarrel with the tiger'. It represented for him the coincidence of instinct and the force of unreason, ever present but so often denied. Donald was aware of it all around him. He acknowledged it in himself and used it, when he needed to, on stage: a dangerous actor. He did not confound this force with violence, which it might lead to; it was closer to Unheed. It was reckless, it did not acknowledge, or even know, consequences; it could not be swerved. If Donald put up such pitiful resistance to Tony's request it was because he recognized the blankness in Tony's eye. Unheed. No quarrel with the tiger.

Tony's decrees were royal. That is to say they did not brook denial. The one he now issued was simple: Donald was to go home, now, to Bella, and make full confession of his affair – Tony referred to it as his 'misdemeanour' – with Alice.

'Why?' Donald had asked.

'It's only fair, old chap.'

'She'll throw me out.'

'Nonsense!'

'You don't know her.'

'Only fair.'

'It will destroy her.'

'Don't be melodramatic.'

'It will. She'll go to pieces.'

'Should have thought of that before, old chap.'

Donald was stupefied. 'Don't be ridiculous.'

'No choice, my friend.'

No use wriggling. No use arguing. 'I can't do it, Tony.' Donald was quite clear about the effect all this would have on Bella, and his pressing thought was to protect her. Just now he gave no thought to the effect on himself.

'You should have thought of that before.' Tony's mouth twisted upward in a thin curve, and he added, 'If you don't tell her, I will.'

'What's the point?' Donald asked. He spoke softly, but he was aware that he was having to make an effort to keep it from rising in pitch.

'What are you after? What can it possibly matter to you?' Something clicked. 'Is this about Naomi? Is it? It is! You bloody fool. I'm not interested in her. No more are you. She's still with Gerd, you know.'

Tony's look was withering. 'Isn't that a rather petty attitude to take up?'

'Petty? Me! What?' Donald was almost speechless. 'What about you?'

'Oh Lordy! Far from it, old boy, far from it.'

'I just wish I understood what you're playing at.'

'Well, Donald, *I* think you should be bloody grateful to me, you know. You don't want to go on living a lie, do you? Think of Ibsen, all those ghosts coming home to roost. Sooner or later they tumble out of the cupboard and bring you and cupboard and all crashing down with them. Better to be the one who opens the cupboard door, make a clean breast of it, a fresh start, turn over a new page.'

This piling on of platitude after platitude, laying a palpable brick wall, caused Donald to desist at last, and he sat dumb, contemplating Tony, whose face beamed a ferocious patronizing smile at him. He contemplated it still, later on, as he trudged across the park. Tony's grinning disembodied countenance replaced the image of the tiger.

Donald left the restaurant at a quarter to three. Early. Usually their lunches stretched out in a pleasant and sometimes drunken haze until at least four o'clock. This time, if there were any haze, it had been a one-way haze and Tony had been the only one peering through it. Donald discounted the exceptional celebratory – and very light – vodka with Naomi. He was, relatively speaking, on the wagon. A New Year's resolution, with Bella as witness, had kept him to his reduced quota, no spirits, his share of the wine, nothing after; whereas Tony had started on gin and followed up the white wine with several *marcs de champagne.*

To acquiesce in all that was said – to seem to acquiesce – had seemed the only solution. Humour Tony until Tony tired of his own abysmal joke, and hope to prevent the whole thing from turning into a nightmare. In any case the idea was too ludicrous to stand up. By the morning Tony would have come to his senses and ceased his crazed insistence, the motive so obscure, buried somewhere deep in the convolutions of an unconscious that probably was not very often disturbed. Perhaps too many fallow years had produced a richer mix than anyone could conceive. Such determination, such certainty, wore an authority that seemed to issue from a higher source. No. Malevolence on this scale did not come from above. There was something diabolic about it.

Donald had recovered his raincoat and then stood waiting by the cash desk while Tony, having settled the bill, took his time, chatting up the waitress. Perhaps Donald should have paid, though it was not the order of things. From early times, unless one or the other was in major crisis, or glut, each took his turn paying in strict rotation. Perhaps having a drink would have helped – dispelled something or other. Allowed Tony to come out with whatever he was really getting at; allowed Donald to see the joke. But even taken as a joke the business had left Donald sour and shaken, and he was not inclined to be seen indulging his friend's latest lunacy nor, if he admitted it, to weaken his position by looking as if he imagined the lunacy were meant to be taken seriously.

Donald had stood staring out of the window at the rain, his back turned to the room still humming with customers. There would be people there he knew, though it was not a special haunt of actors. There was always someone. He was not in the mood. He recognized the foolishness of this, as if he were actually giving weight to the absurdity. Behind him, above the hum, he heard Tony greet someone and be greeted in return. Donald continued staring out through the thick lace curtains into the street. The noise of the traffic was drowned by the hubbub behind him. Tony was taking his time. Donald put up his hand and took a mint from the dish by the cash register. Tony came up.

'Didn't you hear me?'

Donald looked up, frowning.

'I was calling you. Micky's back there. Wanted to say hallo.'

'Didn't hear you over the noise,' Donald said.

Where in wonder should they go? He go? Tony opened the door.

'Pissing down.' He turned to the girl at the cash desk. 'Any chance of a cab, sweetheart?'

'You'll be lucky in this,' she said.

'Try, won't you? Just for me?' He smiled into her eyes.

Donald said, 'You could be here all night. I'm going to walk.' He took a step past Tony, whose body was propping open the door.

'Okay, mate.' He could feel Tony's eyes on him. 'I'll ring you tomorrow, Donald, what? About eleven. You can tell me how she took it.'

This parting pleasantry administered a sharper shock than the whole of the previous hour and a half. Donald continued on out through the doorway, turning up his collar, not looking back or saying goodbye or thanking Tony for lunch. He turned left, went as far as the corner, to the traffic lights, straight ahead across the main road, and then kept heading north. He crossed the park, passing the Zoo with its lions and tigers, vultures and penguins, on towards Camden Town, dodging endless traffic that threw up a greasy spray. He cut east. He was intent on walking, heading for home through the streaming grey streets. Part of him was awash with bitter rage against Tony for being able and willing to play such a bad joke on him (why?); part of him bobbed on the surface of this same rage, light with the relief that comes when danger is simultaneously exposed and removed. He tried to tell himself that when he got home he would wake up and all would become clear, his own foolishness. He would laugh. They would both laugh. He and Bella. There was an obvious flaw in this cosy thought but he did not examine it. In his imagination he was laughing with Bella, but if there were any laughs going the only person they could be shared with was Tony, and really there was no joke. It was Bella whose advice he needed, but she was the one whose advice he could not ask. Who else could he turn to? Claire? No. Naomi? Perhaps Naomi. He craved her sweet impartial sanity.

The thought of Naomi was one brightness in the thickening gloom, though she would laugh a good deal. Perhaps he would call her tomorrow morning to find out what was up with Tony. Tony had hustled him out of the office before he had had a chance to get her home number. But in reality, Donald reflected, he hardly knew her. Tony? He was the only other. He did not dwell on the possibility that he had only two friends in the world or on the fact that he might be about to hurt one and cut himself off for all time from the other. His thoughts kept pace with his shoes, which were by now saturated: expensive buckskin shoes with little leather tassels, Bella's present last birthday, ruined. Could they recover? Was it better or worse if the leather were of superior quality?

chapter 31

It was dark as well as wet by the time Donald reached Islington. Did he remember once again, as he turned into the glistening street that led into their square, that he and Bella were going out to dinner that evening? The pavement was shining under the street lamps, and the gentle rain dropped upon the milky patches of pavement beneath the lamp-posts and formed endless random patterns in the reflected light. Halfway down the street, outside number 15, the Mackenzies' house, Donald stopped to breathe and saw his breath steam out in front of him. He had not felt the cold. Everything but cold.

A cigarette. He had been trying to give up. The New Year's resolution had included tobacco as well as booze. A bit ambitious. He put his hand in his pocket and encountered a packet of Gitanes. He took one out and felt in his pocket for matches. A memory of Véronique flashed in on him. No matches. Cigarettes without matches – like golf-clubs without balls, the old joke, a definition of hell. His fingers closed over his keys.

Bella heard the front door and called down from somewhere upstairs, the bedroom or the bathroom. He was late, she was beginning to worry. (What time was it then? How long had he been walking?) Habit interpreted Bella's shouted calls for him. He did not need to distinguish her actual words. He threw his dripping coat over the bannister and went downstairs into the kitchen, took two tumblers from the shelf, poured whisky, added water, carried them upstairs two floors, into the bedroom. The white crochet bedspread was rumpled where Bella had been sitting to talk on the phone.

Apart from that the room, as usual, radiated a kind of order – preparation and intention. Bella's blouse with three layers of deep ruffles that needed no ironing was suspended from a hanger over the mirror on the back of the open door of her clothes-cupboard, with the long velvet skirt, midnight blue, slashed halfway up one side. The chenille shawl he had given her on the first night of *Catalan* was laid across the seat of the low pink nursing chair. Her marcasite earrings lay in front of the dressing-table mirror. One of his great pleasures was to watch her at her mirror, intent on it and ignoring it at the same time, talking at him through it, making up, brushing on fine lines and shadows, exaggerating, obliterating, focusing: and, better still, later on undoing it all, chattering, dissecting the evening, dissolving the contents of one jar with another, sweeping tissues across her skin, exploring the bones of her face, inspecting flaws. It was like being at the pictures, an intimate domestic melodrama.

Moist scents of sandalwood drifted from the open door of the bathroom. Bella always hated turning on the ventilator because of the noise, so that she generally ended up having a Turkish bath as well. He bore the glasses to the bathroom to begin the scene. A large steamy bathroom, with wicker fittings, chair, laundry basket, mirror; cork floor. Bella in the bath, her hair pinned up. Donald carried the glasses over to the bath.

'Darling! Thank goodness! I was getting worried – oh, thank you!' Bella reached out a hand braceleted with bath foam for the glass and took a quick sip. 'Just what I needed.' She held up her mouth to be kissed. 'That too! I shan't be long, if you want to shave. Do you? You don't need to. Where have you been? Tony said you left him at about half-past two.'

'Tony?' Donald said. 'Did you speak to him? It was much later than that actually.'

'He rang up about an hour ago. "To see how you are getting on," he said.'

'Did he?'

'He sounded awfully mysterious. He said you'd got something to tell me. He absolutely wouldn't tell me himself, he said.'

'Did he?'

'Well, I hope it's something nice. I'm sure it is. Is it a job? Be an angel and throw me the towel, darling.'

He brought her a fluffy pink bath sheet as she stood up in the bath. He draped it round her shoulders. He held her to him for a moment and kissed the damp nape of her neck, under her swept-up hair. She twisted her head round to give him a proper kiss, then broke away to step out of the bath, drying herself. She picked up a tin of talcum powder.

'Now then,' she laughed, 'no time for that, we're going to be late. You should have thought of that before! Are you going to shave?'

'Do I need to?'

'Not really, no. You'll do – I think! You'd better get changed, though.' Standing up now she caught sight of his feet. 'Oh darling, look at your shoes! You must have got soaked! I suppose you couldn't find a cab?' She patted her body with the towel. 'I won't be long.'

The scene moved to the kitchen. Donald carrying his damp coat and his whisky glass. He put his coat over a rail in front of the Aga and crossed to the shelf to pour himself another whisky. As he stood for a moment thinking about adding some water, the telephone rang. He hesitated, decided to ignore it, changed his mind again and lifted the phone; but by this time the answering machine had cut in, so that a moment of confusion ensued until the machine stopped bleating over the voices.

Donald recognized Tony's voice.

'Donald?'

'Hallo.'

'Have you told her?'

'You're out of your mind, Tony, you know that.'

'I meant what I said. If you don't tell her, I will.'

Then Bella's voice cut in on the upstairs phone. 'Tony, it's all right. I've told him he's got to tell me whatever it is. It all sounds very mysterious. But we've got to rush just now or we'll be late. We're going out.'

'Good,' Tony said. 'Okay. Bye, Bella. Donald. Take care.'

A strange reversal: as he plunged in the knife he seemed to see not his own but Bella's life flashing etc. and in the same split second he knew with precision that it was not just any knife but a devilish, historical knife, a device from the East, known as a kris. Its handle was ornate, crusted with jewels, aquamarine, amethyst and topaz, her favourite stones; its blade was cunning, formed like the waves of the sea; it was designed to remain embedded wherever it entered, to be removed only at the cost of pain worse than the initial wound and terrible mutilation.

She had refused to wait until they came back from dinner because she could not bear to see him so miserable. 'Christ, Donald, you'd better tell me, whatever it is.' They were in the kitchen.

In the moment before he spoke she had looked at him with such sympathy and concern, her fear and her pain were all for him. Afterwards she was like a dead person, with eyes fast open as if she had lost the power to close them. She never doubted for one instant what he told her. She asked no question, she made no protest, she erected no fantasy that he might be joking, teasing her. She stared. At the place where he was rather than at him. Through him. He had become a ghost. They were both dead. They had ceased to exist. Then came a shudder that convulsed her entire body and she twisted to one side, leaned over the sink and vomited.

He was afraid to go near her, as if she had become sacred – he was defiled. He found himself apologizing, pathetic. She turned the tap full on and scooped up handfuls of water, trying to hold it against her burnt mouth, then, gazing into the sink, turned on the waste-disposal unit. She put her hand under the tap and directed little streams of water around the sink, chasing the little yellow lumps of sick, swilling them into the black rubber mouth of the waste disposer. She was panting a little, and kept sniffing.

She turned off the tap and switched off the unit, reached for a piece of kitchen paper and held its scatter of printed blue flowers across her nose, blotting and sniffing, between little staccato breaths. At last she took one big gulp of air and forced herself to breathe more easily. She straightened up, pushing back her shoulders. She didn't look at him, just said, 'We'd better go. I'll just go upstairs a minute and do my face.' When she came down she checked her face and hair at the hall mirror and held out her arm towards her green silk coat on the back of the hall chair where she had laid it fifteen minutes before for him to help her into, their ritual of departure. Tonight their eyes did not meet in the mirror, nor did he complete the circle of his arms around her. They walked for some time in the rain before they found a taxi.

chapter 32

Hours later another taxi left them once again on the pavement outside their house. Bella stood back while Donald put his keys to the front door. The simple action took eternity. He did not fumble but felt as if he fumbled. The noise of the key entering the lock, the turning twice, the withdrawal, the Yale key after the Chubb, a second double turn, every grain of the action was felt. He pushed the door, Bella moved past him along the hall and turned across in front of the stairs into the living room. He followed, pausing to hang his coat and put the umbrella into the rack – art deco, bought for a song at a local auction.

At the front of the living room one small lamp was alight, the rest was in shadow. He could not see her. When he bent to switch on another lamp she said, 'No!' He switched it off again quickly. He had had a glimpse of her, seated in the high armchair, her long green coat over the blue velvet of her skirt. He resisted an impulse to go and put his coat back on again, as if he had come on in the wrong costume.

At dinner she had dazzled him by behaving absolutely as she always did; she had laughed and joked, provoked laughter. Only she ate almost nothing. She must have made some excuse to the hostess, explained their lateness by saying that she had not been feeling well, for no protest was made at the succession of dishes that left her place almost untouched. She had taken a little bread, a mouthful of soup, but avoided the elaborate pastry-clad centrepiece of the meal, apart from a few tiny sculpted potatoes.

She had refused her favourite pudding and taken no wine or coffee, drinking only water. Yet she might as well have been drinking – she was far from subdued. She scintillated, to the delight of the company.

Donald had been obliged to force himself to eat, by way of compensation; and also to try to hold off from the booze. He did all right with the wine, which in any case did not exactly flow in this household, but the consequent strain of making, unbolstered, any suitable contribution to the conversation drove him to make up for his restraint later, in after-dinner whiskys. His mind was not elsewhere but he could not have described where it was. Floating somewhere above the bright table, the place names, the candles and crumbs, the individual flower arrangements. Several times Bella had turned to him from her place further along the table, on a point of information.

'Oh when *was* that, darling, was it last year or the year before? . . . Oh what's his name, Donald darling, you know – Paul's factotum?' Or nudged him into an anecdote: 'Oh darling, you know – that time when Nancy, of all people, mistook the pass door and ended up in the auditorium . . .'

'In her nightdress . . .'

'Yes – that's it!', and she rounded the story off with a juicy extra that he had never heard. His performance was lacklustre beside her helter-skelter narration. 'Bella's on good form!' their host had complimented him. They had stayed long enough. Not the first to leave nor the last.

Now she sat stiffly in the dimness which gradually became all too sufficient as their eyes adjusted, and waited for him to speak; to save her, if he could, a second time. To save himself, also, but Bella did not think of that yet.

Something about the way he was standing there, as if his body had been draped over his skeleton by some designer to see how it would hang, and a fixed mournfulness in his face, made her think of James Stewart in *Vertigo*. For a treat they had been to see *Vertigo* two Sundays before. She had been struck by the moment when Stewart has just fished Kim Novak out of the bay.

'If you save someone's life you are responsible for them for ever after,' he says. But later in the film it is Stewart who brings about Novak's death. Had Donald saved her only to send her crashing down from the tower? Bella shivered. She was cold and frightened. She looked up at Donald where he stood looking down at her.

As a film critic she overlooked what she wanted to overlook – whatever did not fit in with her thesis – or she might have reflected a little further on Stewart's passionate obsession and been struck by the fact that, in causing Novak's death, his character to all intents and purposes destroys his own life. She might have given more weight to Novak's part in the plot, a murder plot – Novak's complicity, how she got more than she bargained for, if worse than she deserved. Vertigo is a dizziness associated with heights, but which may take other forms. Some people are afflicted by a social vertigo – garrulous Helena in Geneva always maintained that she endured agonies because of it – which leads them to speak the very word, utter the very name, they should most avoid. Others suffer from moral vertigo, which drives them willy-nilly to seek out the inimical force and confront it: to hunt down (in the castle from which every needle, tack, pin, brooch, hypodermic syringe, every perforating pricking wicked thing has been banished long ago) the one remaining spinning-wheel.

Though he badly wanted a drink, Donald did not go to the drinks cupboard. He went on standing near the door, on the edge of the big pink and green kelim rug. His impulse was towards her, his entire consciousness was with her, but he was immobilized. He was angry. His mind took in the irony of his being literally on the carpet and savoured it.

They looked at each other for too long. She began to feel at fault. There was something wrong with the blocking, the wrong choices had been made. Her chair for instance was wrong, too rigid, forbidding, judgmental. For the scene to work he needed to be able to sweep her up, off her feet, to envelop her, forgive her. Actors in rehearsal notoriously expend great energy trying to make things easier for themselves – to cut the line they have difficulty saying, to put the prop on a more convenient table; real life is full of obstacles. Bella ought not to have sat down so early – but she could scarcely have stayed on her feet a moment longer.

She began to freeze – the heating had turned itself off at one o'clock – but that was not it. She thought: I could die here from cold. She thought: am I the one to speak? Why should I have to speak?

The longer the silence, the greater, the colder her anger, sitting in the wrong chair. She forced herself to speak a word, 'Well,' which came out at the same time as Donald too spoke: 'I'm sorry' – and then she screamed at him, 'Don't say you're sorry!', which was all he had to say. And now Donald came forward, to her, because of her pain, but too late, and she pushed him with might and main so that he staggered, almost fell, and almost laughed in the half-darkness, at the fact that he could see no way out, nothing but disaster.

Now he went to the corner cupboard, opened it, switching on the lamp on the table beside it because really he could see nothing – it was absurd – which added an odd eery emphasis to the room, light at either end, as he poured himself a whisky.

'Do you want a drink?'

She snorted, 'Don't be ridiculous!'

He found himself wishing that she would remind him of his resolution, tell him not to have another drink, but she had checked an impulse to do just that. Nagging was too fond a thing. She would not engage with him so far.

He closed the cupboard, went and sat down: not opposite her in the other chair but at the end of the sofa, on the arm, facing the empty grate.

She said again, 'Well?', and waited. He looked at her. She waited. It was so hard not to supply that vacuum between them with an ice-cold emotion.

'I want you to tell me . . . Go on.'

'I've told you.'

She shook her head. 'There's more.'

'That's all.'

'Tell me again!' she commanded. 'Tell me again! I don't believe you!' And she cried out, 'Alice!'

Donald, on the brink of hatred, said, 'It wasn't what you think. It didn't mean anything.' He winced to hear himself say such lines. They were both shocked by the banality of the script.

'How ridiculous! . . . Good . . . Thank you . . . I'm so glad.'

She forced him then by question and weary answer to tell her how it had happened, when, where. Not why. And he saw the sordid reflection of every detail in the grim set stare of her face. She did not cry. They fell into silence again.

The senses are not immune, and mock the mind. At one point Bella had got up without warning and moved towards him, her limbs awkward with the cold. For a moment he believed that she had relented, that she wanted to huddle to him on the sofa, and he opened his arms wide to hold her; but she was coming for the rug. When he saw what she was after he stumbled to his feet to help her, but too late – just as she realized too late that he had thought to comfort her. She wrapped the rug around her body and returned, cocooned, to the hard chair. The words continued, disjointed and insufficient. At about five o'clock, she heaved herself up from the chair and left the room. He heard her go downstairs, heard her fill the kettle – she was making herself a hot-water bottle. Then her footsteps mounted the stairs to the bedroom.

After a time he filled his glass and followed upstairs, past their bedroom and on up a third flight of stairs to one of the two guest rooms. But that was where she had gone. A shape in the spare bed, her face to the wall. Her hair had spread out behind her over her shoulder and almost hid the pillow. At the sound of the door she turned her head, hoping for something, a miracle, blinking at the light from the hall. He shut the door at once. He went into his own study, emptied his glass and lay down on the leather sofa, pulling the sheepskin throw over himself. He fell into a deep sleep.

Next door to him, Bella did not sleep, though she drifted into a half-sleep not shielded by dreams. She bumped along a rocky river-bed, chased by monsters. Being in a strange room was part of the dream's landscape. She did not sleep but kept half waking, needing to find him, at once. She had terrible news to tell him. He was the terrible news. She stared into the darkness. She had remembered to close the curtains. A thread of light around them grew firmer and brighter. She slept for an hour.

At half-past seven she opened her eyes and her surroundings no longer surprised her. Already it would have seemed stranger still to have woken in her own room beside Donald. The sword had fallen. Not steel but lead had entered her soul. It was over. She was free but she had never wanted to be free. It was an exchange of pains. All her worst fears. People don't do such things. How was it possible to feel like this? Her anger was like ice; but her forehead was smooth, her eyes were open. No more forebodings. No more spinning-wheels. Deadly relief. She got up, put on the cosy brushed-wool dressing-gown and turned back the bedclothes, picked up the hot-water bottle from the floor, not yet cold. She found as she left the room that she was hugging it to herself like Masha's cushion in the third act of *Three Sisters*.

Downstairs their bedroom door was open as she had left it, and the bathroom door was open too. She could see that Donald was not there, but his presence would not have troubled her. She had no idea whether he was even in the house. She showered quickly and dressed. From the kitchen she telephoned for a taxi. She made herself some tea and forced herself to drink it while she waited.

When the doorbell rang she picked up her script from the table, tucked it under her arm, rinsed her mug under the tap and put it on the wooden rack. She noticed traces of sick round the edge of the sink. She didn't have time. A long ago sickness. Just as well she knew most of her words for Episode 2.

chapter 33

About three months later a letter arrived at the Royal for Donald with a Canadian postmark. He stared at it for a long time, wondering who could be writing to him from Vancouver. Then he realized that it must be from Alice.

By this time he had rented a small service flat. Bella had never come back to the house after her rehearsal. She had rejected Donald's offer to be the one to leave. She could not bear to be there; she could not enter the house, she said. She had telephoned from rehearsals and instructed Corinne to find her a service hotel or a furnished flat; she instructed her also to inform Tony Tell Agents that Bella no longer wished to employ their services. (Bill Forster welcomed her back with undiminished affection, and the news that his daughter had been accepted at RADA.)

Corinne had been recruited to dress Bella and, initiated by Alice, had also taken over Alice's secretarial duties. Like Alice before her, she came three times a week and was a model of efficiency. She had booked Bella into a small hotel in George Street, packed a case, following a list dictated by Bella, and delivered it to the hotel by taxi on her way home.

Corinne's occasional presence in the house maintained Donald's slim sense of being in touch with Bella. At this stage they did not speak directly but only through Corinne. The hotel screened Bella's calls.

In the days that followed Donald had become obsessed with the need to reach Alice and let her know. His obsession had nothing to do with Alice herself or with what had happened between them. He did not need or want to see her, nor did he suppose she had any wish to see him. But she must be told. It was the one action he felt capable of pursuing. He had a horror that she might send some cheery postcard that would reach Bella and in some way, Medusa-like, turn everything irrevocably to stone. It surprised him to discover they had no address for her. In the office he found her old London address and wrote to her there, hoping that her letters would be forwarded to Canada; but she had left Ontario for the west coast and did not receive it for several months. By the time she answered, Donald had moved out of the house. She wrote that his letter had only just reached her.

By that time Alice had already read with some surprise – weeks before in some showbiz gossip column – that Bella and Donald had broken up. She had meant to write and say how sorry she was; but her new life kept her busy and she had never got round to it. When Donald's letter arrived she had not known what to make of it at first.

It had crossed her mind that she might have misread Donald; that the whole, almost imperceptible fling – hardly even that – had been something more than that on his side. But the idea was absurd. She wrote back telling Donald the news had shocked her. She assured him she had never breathed a word – she hoped he didn't think it was any of her doing; if he wanted to talk to her, which he might well not, here was a telephone number, in case there were anything she could do. (Alice imagined more than this – that he must be devastated, and that she might well be one of the few people he would be able to talk to, but the last thing she wanted to do was to give the impression that she hoped for something more from their relationship.) Of course Bella would not wish to hear from her, she continued. She would do whatever he thought was for the best.

Donald telephoned, he reassured her – there was no question of the story having come from her. Who did it come from then? Who knew? Who had told Bella? Donald pretended not to hear

Alice's questions; she did not press him. Bella had gone to Ireland, he told her, six months' location on a big Hollywood film. Donald had signed up for another season at the Royal. The house was up for sale. Its fate was running in parallel to theirs, in balance at first, but not for long. Bella had insisted on letting it. Already there had been offers from two buyers. The tenants would be out and new owners in within another couple of months. The divorce might take a little longer.

Alice asked how he was managing.

'So-so,' he said.

'Donald, I am awfully sorry.'

'It's hardly your fault, love.' His voice sounded slurred.

'Well, fault aside, I'm sorry it's happened – or rather, I'm sorry about what's happened to you and Bella. It seems absurd.' Though now she knew it wasn't.

He agreed. There was a pause.

'Would it help to meet? I mean just . . . you know . . . to talk?'

'Yes, I know. No. I think not. Thanks all the same. It might just compound things. Although, on the other hand . . .' It would be nice to see her calm eyes again. But.

'There's no remedy, Alice,' he concluded.

She said, 'I know.'

Alice was the one person, apart from Naomi, who had not come back with iterations of hope, glib faith in the passage of time, expressions of certainty that Bella would 'come round' like a swooning heroine, or like spring. But by this time spring was almost a year away and he didn't know if he could last so long.

'Donald?'

'Yes?'

Alice hesitated. 'No . . . It doesn't matter.'

'What?'

'No. Nothing. It will keep.'

'Is there anything I can do for *you*? Are *you* all right?' For a moment he sounded like his old self.

She laughed. 'Yes. Fine. Terrific!'

'You will keep in touch. Please. Let me know what happens to you.'

'Oh yes. You too.'

When she hung up she realized that in London it was four o'clock in the morning.

He could not sleep at nights. Trickling down the back of his neck sweat ran on in rivulets along his spine, then slid across his back and soaked into the dampness of the sheet. Nightmares crawled slow-motion in his brain, one image merged with another. The dark dreamlight prevented him from seeing properly. There was no violence, nothing so distinct – but the horror overwhelmed him. He drank to avoid going to bed and put off the sweating turbulent slumber; but eventually the drink would lay him out and then the nightmares had their way, sometimes as dawn began to break. Time drifted on now towards full-blown summer.

All this while, miraculously, he had gone on working. Not working well – it cost him an inhuman effort to get himself to rehearsal, let alone on to a stage. But he was grateful to himself for doing it. The whole of his mind bent to the task of turning up, making up, speaking up – agony and relief combined in one foul medicine.

'Oh Caesonia, I knew it was possible to be in despair, but I did not know the meaning of the word. I thought, like everyone else, that it was a sickness of the soul. It isn't . . . It's the body that suffers . . . My skin hurts, my chest, my very limbs . . .'

A speech, from the Camus play that had first brought Donald to the public attention, returned to haunt him. His portrayal of Caligula's despair had bowled over the critics; but it was only now that he understood the meaning of the words he had repeated night after night, for months: '*And the worst thing of all is this taste in my mouth. It's not the taste of blood, or of death, or of fever – it's all three together. If I simply move my tongue, everything goes black again and every single being fills me with disgust.*' Like Caligula, Donald discovered the reality of despair to be a thousand times removed from his pale imaginings. And although he knew that he would never heal from his self-inflicted wound, which was the wound that he had inflicted on Bella, yet for him, as for the Emperor Caligula, the same paradox held true: the very idea that it was possible to heal held a fresh horror.

He kept pushing through so that he gave himself no time to think. Time became the element in which he must somehow keep afloat. 'It's only a question of time,' everyone said. Shakespeare said that it was a question of time. (He must have done, but where?) There could be only one cure, by miracle: Bella's hand held out, and not just her hand, but her whole being once again turned to him.

Bella had tried, he thought so. He believed in her sincere effort to forgive him. Bella herself, on occasion, on the phone, had said that he must give her time, the most costly gift: 'Then, perhaps . . .'

Naturally Bella needed more time. She suffered the complication of being the injured party. Donald's role could hardly be simpler. Bella trailed always one step behind. The telephone offered the only gleam of hope, their one remaining link. They spoke quite often. She could bear it all better on the phone, disembodied; things seemed more possible.

'I know I'm being foolish. I can't help it.' She had just admitted that she still loved him. She thought she did.

His voice lifted. 'Well then,' he said, 'can't we, somehow – why can't we try again?' When she did not answer, he said, 'Please?' like a boy remembering he'd left out the grown-up password.

She said again she knew she was being foolish. She said it, she felt it, but that did no good. She did not understand why. She kept saying things she meant but did not understand. She said she forgave him, that she bore him no grudge; but she hated him, she could not bear to see him. (For years afterwards her body would set up a shudder at the thought of being in the same room with him. Her revulsion frightened her. How specific and horrifying the images were, which ran over and over inside her head, like a sequence on a dubbing loop. Like watching other people's rushes. Donald inside some other woman. Donald and Alice. Take after take.)

'You mustn't blame Alice,' Donald said one night and Bella lost her temper and shouted at him down the phone.

'What do you mean? What are you saying? How can I not blame Alice?' He was asking her to come limping back to him, and knocking away her crutches at the very same time. Who else should she blame? Blaming Alice had to be a condition of her return, and here was Donald defending Alice. Why should she not blame Alice? Better, for Donald's sake, that she blame Alice, otherwise who else should she blame but him? Only him.

He defended himself, too – Bella could hardly believe it. 'God, Bella, it was you insisted on sending me up there with Alice. I wanted to go on my own. I told you. I kept telling you. I wanted four days' peace and quiet. You insisted.'

He was blaming her. 'It was my fault then?'

He stopped. 'No, of course not. Of course not. Can't we meet? I hate these calls.'

But their meetings, only three, had been unendurable.

'What's the point?'

Bella put down the phone, and sat beside it, trembling, for half an hour.

She had never had any foolish trust in Alice, or any feeling that Alice ought to owe her something like loyalty; nor had familiarity caused her to underestimate Alice's charms. She and Bella had seen each other almost every day for well over a year. Yet even if Alice's unending efficiency had robbed her a little of her mystery in Bella's eyes, she could not have ruled her out as an object of romance, or lust – she was a woman; and, in Bella's sweeping and unflattering assumption, no woman could resist Donald and every woman was fair game. What did it matter who it was – Alice or Hilary or Monique or Daphne Brent? For wasn't it clear that sooner or later it would have come to the same thing: Donald would have strayed and strayed again. And if, at first, she might have remained sweetly ignorant, sooner or later suspicion and other pollutants would have begun to seep into the system. (Though weren't the pipes bursting already with noxious substances? Bella recalled the hours spent hanging about outside cafés, desperate to discover what woman Donald was meeting.)

Work, for them, entailed separation – one away on location, the other way on tour; all sorts. Loneliness, lust, melancholy, vanity, variety, impulse, exhilaration, all the thousand disintegrators of wedlock would have worked on them as on others. Just like everyone said, it could never have lasted. She took a whisky to bed and sat upright half the night in the dark, shivering or trembling. She got up and found a shawl to cover her shoulders. As she reached for the shawl it struck her, suddenly, that he might be right; perhaps there had been a choice after all.

Only when the windows were beginning to show the first light was Bella exhausted enough to sleep for a few hours, and by then she had almost lost track of the shocking thought, or at least managed to blur and soften it, just so that she could live with it: that she herself might be in some way at fault.

All the same, before the dawn broke Bella had remembered herself, standing in her red dressing-gown watching the car drive away down the rainy street; remembered leaping over a puddle to get back into the warm. She should never have sent Donald off like that, alone with Alice. What was she up to? At the time she had said to herself brightly, 'I trust him. I have to trust him. Life would make no sense if I couldn't trust him.'

'Then why put it to the test?' she enquired of herself. 'Do you have to ask every question?'

And retaliated, 'I have no choice! It's only a few days, for heaven's sake. Someone's got to go.' Silence. 'She's not even his type.'

'Everyone's his type,' came the reply.

Such had been Bella's fancies, and still she had pursued her course. It did not matter whether Alice were Donald's type or no. She, Bella, was the captain of her ship, and she had chosen not only to steer a passage close to the rocky shoreline, but, at the same time, to put the pilot off and give up the watch.

At last she came so far that once, in the middle of the night, startled out of sleep and hearing his voice at the other end of the telephone, she took it all freely upon herself. 'You were right. Donald, I was to blame.' Three years had gone by. This was the night before she was to be married again. After months of silence what instinct had made him telephone? Should she tell him?

For some moments after she opened her eyes there was no light, it was as if she were blind; but it was not the darkness that had alarmed her – the darkness was a soft thing, gentle and timeless. She picked up the phone. As she took the receiver in her hand, in the split second before he spoke, she knew that it was Donald. His voice sent a shock through her, spreading doom to every cell in her body, invading her with the absolute knowledge that she was to blame more than him.

That same night she had finished recording *Hedda Gabler* for television and her mind was still full of that machinery of destruction, of self and others, which lays waste everything around it. But Hedda, holding out the glass of punch to Eilert Lovberg, had been brimming with self-disgust and unfulfilment, goaded by jealousy. What had possessed Bella, except the idlest curiosity, Pandora's sickness: the need to know more – was her world perfect or wasn't it? – the overweening need to know everything? She could curse her thoughtlessness, but thinking would not have helped her. For even if it had crossed her mind that she was taking a risk, had she ever been capable of understanding what the risk was? Not that she would indeed find out the truth but that, having found it out, she would be unable to live with the consequences? Donald had saved her once, galloped up and released her from her corset of principles; but not for all time. Before Donald, she had not known herself; he had allowed her to glimpse herself from afar, through his fond, liberating eyes. Now for the first time she looked through her own eyes and sampled her own nature, her rigidness, in the fullest way – passion as disgust.

He had said that 'it hadn't meant anything', and she had been shocked and insulted at the time, as if saying such a thing had made it worse. What if it had 'meant something'? Would she have wanted to fight for him then, to win him back at all costs? It had been 'one of those things', he said, such things were possible (especially for men!). No one but her in the world meant anything to him, she must know that. She knew it, and she believed him. She loved him. But not enough. Or she loved only a bowdlerized edition of him. He asked her to forgive him and she forgave him. He asked her to take him back but she could not bear the thought of him crossing the threshold.

Bella's friends rallied to support her. She viewed them with an odd detachment at first, watching as they floundered, not knowing whether to plead for Donald or revile him, trying to gauge whether she wanted them to take sides or not. In the end she took sides herself and kept in touch with very few of their circle – Helena, Nancy, Sir Paul and his wife, the Todmordens. That side of their life seemed now to have been a gaudy fluttering thing, like a piece of coloured card on a child's toy: you push it off the end of a stick and send it spinning and twirling, blending its colours into pretty patterns until it dives down to earth.

Bella's mother telephoned from Buenos Aires. (They had not spoken for ten years, though every year Bella received a card on her birthday and a package containing a large bottle of 'Joy' perfume: 'With love to you my darling Bella.' Bella duly returned a note of brief thanks. Otherwise they did not communicate. Though Bella and Walter never discussed it, she blamed her mother for years of hurt inflicted on him. Once or twice he had tried to raise the subject and begun to attempt a defence of his ex-wife's flight, but Bella had cut him short. What mitigation could there be?)

'How did you hear, Mother?'

'Your father, dear. We keep in touch.'

'He's never said.'

'Perhaps he saw no reason to mention it.' Through the maddening echo on the wire, her mother sounded tired or sad. She asked what Bella was going to do.

'Divorce,' Bella said.

After a short silence her mother said, 'Must you? Have you stopped loving each other?' Then, 'Is that what he wants?'

'What about what I want?' Bella said, irritated. She constructed a neat, scathing précis of Donald's behaviour and her mother fell silent again.

'Come to BA, Bella. Won't you? Can't you get away? Don't act too quickly, darling.' Her mother spoke as if they talked every day. It incensed Bella. She resented the woman's ability to stir her up, but her anger sprang equally from a longing to listen to her, which she could not bring herself to indulge. A part of her could imagine nothing better than to fly away and leave so much turmoil behind her, to somewhere where she could think.

'I'm about to go on location. I can't get away.'

'Perhaps when it's finished. Or would you like me to . . . ? I could . . .' Her mother's voice tailed away. Then she said, 'I'm so glad that your work is going so well, what you wanted to do.'

'Thank you,' Bella said.

'Don't be too hard on people, Bella. Yourself most of all in the long run,' her mother said. 'God bless. I'm here if you need me.'

Black heart without pity untouched by time. Bella remembered a poem that called into doubt time's reputation as a healer: 'the patient is already dead'. Every seven years all our cells have been renewed, we are no longer the same person. Is that it? Or is it that with the backward glance the perspective is different and we just look like someone else; everyone does: those who have chosen to continue the same path and those who have turned off. Time confers even on our former selves an air of completeness that usually belongs only to other people. It is not the same river. And even if it were, how could it ever look the same, knowing what we know now?

Bella's GP reinforced her mistrust of psychiatry. She expressed her fear that somehow the process would blunt her creative abilities. He thought this view of shrinks did their discipline, such as it was, too much honour, in conceding it such great influence. He was more cynical. 'Most people recover, or cure themselves, within a few years anyway. It's an expensive pastime. But by all means . . .' He offered her tranquillizers instead, to tide her over. She took the prescription but she did not take the pills. Those too, she thought, might blur her vision.

Donald, on the other hand, Donald tried every remedy, for well over a year: doctors – including a therapist – pills, drink, but he found little relief. His mind worked a treadmill, over and over it all he went, again and again. His arguments, however he reworked them, became predictable after a short time, and monotonous. He would return to the subject after only a very few drinks – people lost interest, even if he was buying. His good friends humoured him, but after a time even their eyes would glaze over. Life is too short. They could not help feeling that he had mourned long enough. It was sad, but they had problems of their own. He ought to try to pull himself together. Life had to go on.

But Donald persisted, trying to make sense. So many ironies struck him: for instance, that the marriage had survived its resurrection (for the holiday in the cottage had truly restored it to life) by only a few months; that it was Donald's own recovered exuberance that had blasted him into disaster. With one bound Jack was free – to leap forward and spring the trap that was to lame him for life.

In the end time and circumstance nudged him at last from his doldrum, which was threatening to go on too long. Jacques de Santis telephoned to offer him a part in his new film, shooting in the States. Donald liked Jacques and admired his work and, though at that moment he could not have cared less, he saw no reason not to go. He had a green card. Perhaps change and distance would do the trick.

All the same he had to wrench himself away. It frightened him to go. His friends encouraged him, saying that his removal from the scene was the best thing that could have happened for him just now. They were thrilled for him; and relieved for themselves. Through good fortune and the prevailing economic climate the filming was all on location in New York, the latest thing. And there time passed quite pleasantly, imperceptibly, almost without pain, hanging about on Manhattan sidewalks drinking coffee in between shots, and watching the action when he wasn't in it, alongside a crowd of curious and chatty bystanders. If the shoot had been on the lot in LA he would no doubt have gone along just the same. But a studio in LA, nursing a bottle between the commissary, the sound-stage and the trailer, would have done for him.

The film was a runaway hit, Donald too; but even before it was released he had met another director and been offered another part in another film, also on location, but up in Maine. Another film followed that. Time seeped on. By the time the Long Wharf Theater in New Haven called him, his courage had begun to trickle back, enough to let him think of learning an entire script, giving the theatre another go. He agreed to go up to Connecticut to do *Man and Superman*.

chapter 34

It was one of those rare crystal days of New York spring, when the sky is clear and the air comes to itself, shaking free from the grip of winter, and not yet clotted with summer dust, and heat that bounces back and forth between the canyon walls. Donald was headed east, walking across downtown Manhattan for the sheer pleasure of it, noting the newly minted leaves that the occasional trees were pushing out, ribbed and milky on one side, a darker green on the other. He was pushing out again himself, from a state of mental convalescence, memories of health and confidence stirring in him; contemplating the possibility of venturing once again into perilous, familiar territory: the corners of his mind.

He took heart from the trees, grateful that their leaves had not been nipped in the bud, that rebirth was possible even after crippling cold; that frost in its right time makes rebirth possible, and is even a prerequisite of good crops, killing off pests and diseases; that they were going on, though he doubted whether they could ever enjoy a full unstunted span of glory here. He came to Washington Square and started across the huge unaccustomed space. A play park, mothers and children, swings and slides and see-saws.

He saw Alice before she saw him, in the play park, her hand – for mutual reassurance – touched to the small of a little girl's back, though the little girl on the see-saw still held on fast to the bar in front of her, her face a study of concentrated experiencing. A child's delight, on credit: an instalment of terror. Once the experiment had been safely lived through it would be converted into total repeatable rapture.

The arc described by the girl was balanced by a bold little boy at the further end and by another mother, who called out to Alice some comment on the relative bravery of their offspring.

'How old is she? – what's her name?'

'Laurel. She'll be three in September.'

'Virgo! Teddy's Aquarius.'

Then Alice saw Donald. She had not seen or spoken to him for several years; the sight of him shocked her. It was the first time he had seen her at a loss. Her arm continued to follow her daughter up and down with the see-saw. She could not detach herself without alarming her. She raised her other arm in greeting. He too.

Donald had always put up a vociferous defence of Alice (and of himself, for that matter. He was not shameless, but grief and remorse cohabited in him with some sense that his guilt was not the only issue). Alice had no more been disloyal to Bella than he had been unfaithful. On the contrary, he maintained, if it had not been for Alice, for that episode, he would in all likelihood have left Bella. (It was so long ago. Donald could not clearly identify at this distance why they had been at such a low pass, he and Bella suspended over a chasm.)

He did not go across to Alice yet, but stood waiting. (If she had not seen him would he have stayed? Now he must.) Can you will things to be, because they happen? Now he wanted this encounter which he would never have sought or imagined, to talk with Alice. He was not sure what he wanted, but he knew that he did not want chat, cluttered with bits of social business, chatter of infant introductions, lifting little babies off see-saws and gathering belongings. He walked over the asphalt trying to indicate to Alice that he would sit on a bench and wait for her to be free. But that was too hard to achieve. Alice mistook his meaning and, thinking he was going off, made a move to interrupt him, both arms outstretched, one towards him, the other straining fingertips to keep reaching to the child's back; so that he had after all, to release her, to come to her and say that he would go and wait, though now the point of waiting was lost. He kissed her cheek as her arm rose and fell, and they exchanged a few absurd commonplaces, Alice a fulcrum between him and his daughter, seen fully for the first time, materializing above Alice's shoulder and dropping back out of vision.

Even this slight drift of attention, the brushing of cheeks, gnawed at the children, and they became fractious. Little Teddy witnessed the encounter in front of his eyes, Laurel absorbed it by osmosis from the altering pressure at her back. It was Teddy who cried out that the see-saw was bumping. His mother decided it was time to call a halt. 'Okay, Teddy. That's enough now.'

The see-saw was brought level. Donald held it steady while the two mothers lifted their children from the shiny plank and planted them on the ground. Teddy and his mother straightened each other up neat and tidy and waved goodbye. Alice inclined her head to Laurel in the deferential pose of a parent who hopes by good example to coax forth charming behaviour.

So circumstance contrived that they have their conversation in the cut version after all – which consisted almost entirely of subtext – even though the child could hardly have understood. It was a kind of superstition. Etiquette demanded that Donald be introduced to the little girl and not the other way round. And so he was. 'Laurel darling, this is Donald. Donald – Laurel.'

Laurel got as much of a look at Donald as it was possible to do with her face half-buried in her mother's coat and Alice's hand cupped round the back of her dark head. Hazel eyes. She had inherited her mother's eyelashes.

'Hallo, Laurel.'

Laurel squirmed out from under her mother's sheltering hand and clutched hold of it, tugging, turning her back on Donald.

'Come on, Laurel, don't be silly. Let's go and pick up your tammy and your wheeler.' Laurel was reluctant and hung back, eyeing Donald, so that she had to be half pulled along. 'How long are you here for, Donald?'

A simple question. He didn't know what to answer. He said, 'I had no idea you were in New York.'

There was no reason why he should have had. It was more likely that she would have known he was there. Had she known? Why had she not tried to reach him? (Was there any reason why she should?)

'I've been here two years. Since Canada.'

Alice's reticence silenced Donald. It was certainly not from idleness, or any social need to fill the air with chat, that he wanted to know; but still he could not ask about the child. Alice seemed to be indicating that he must not intrude. This was not the place or time. But Alice did not suggest a place or time.

'Are you working, on a film or anything?'

'I've just finished a film. I'm off up to New Haven. To the Long Wharf.'

Back to theatre, to see if he could sustain it again, if it could sustain him. He had got through that last season in London, but barely. It had all but done for him. He had thought he would never be able to step on to a stage again. Seeing Alice did not (at first) bring back the fear, but it reminded him that fear was a possibility. The lizard that 'lieth lurking in the grass'.

'The Long Wharf? That's marvellous! They do terrific things. Is it a new play?' She was pulling a red tammy on to Laurel's head, tucking the matching scarf in under the coat collar. 'When are you going?'

Would there be time for a meeting, or any point? Three and a half years since they met. Was there or not an important conversation to have?

'Almost at once.'

'Are you taking the train?'

'No. I'm going to drive. I've got a lot of clobber.' Not all that much. A load of books and LPS mostly. Aeroplanes were claustrophic.

'I have a sister in New Haven.'

Donald laughed out loud and she laughed too.

'Of course – a sister in every town!'

'I've only got four! I'll give you her number. Danielle. In case you want a break from "theatre folk". She's nice.'

'Of course she is.'

'How long are you going to be there? Perhaps when you get back . . .' Perhaps then, but not now. 'How are things . . . ?' also left in the air but clear enough.

'With Bella? She's fine. I think. We communicate. Barely.' And with such difficulty. Recrimination and remorse, on both sides. 'Through our lawyers mostly. Funnily enough I spoke to her last night.' The first time in six months. Some ancient tenderness.

Alice offered a sympathetic face, trying at the same time to placate Laurel: 'In a minute, sweetheart, we'll go home . . . Sorry, Donald.'

Now it was time to ask her, his turn. 'How about you?'

'I'm really terrific. Surprisingly.'

'Do you need anything?'

Why could he not make himself say, is that my daughter? That is my daughter. Do you want help – money? A woman alone. Anything short of marriage.

'I never thought I'd do it, Donald, but, do you know, I'm actually going to be married.' This was the moment when she made up her mind to be married.

And why should either of them feel the least bit awkward about that? Of all people she was not a person to do something she did not believe in, to marry for convenience.

'Someone I met here. He's from Hungary.'

There had never been any question of attachment between them. On the contrary, what had been had been almost pure in its detachment, in the absence of untruth. But for the lie to Bella. They remembered three nights together.

In the jumble of the moment in Washington Square, Alice gave him her sister's telephone number rather than her own, playing for time: in this way she conveyed to him that she did not expect – did not want – anything from him; but nor did she want a total severance, to cut him off from his daughter.

Alice's sister might, in time, have got in touch with Donald. Her instructions were to keep tabs on him. Alice had been concerned about him as well as concerned for herself, and confused. He had looked so drawn, lost, somehow absent. That was not surprising. He must have had friends in New York, but it could be lonely, she knew, even with friends.

Why had she said nothing about Laurel? That was so silly. It had been the wrong moment, unprepared. The idea had struck her that he might want to establish some sort of claim in Laurel's life, and fear had overtaken her, out of the blue. Foolish of her not to have anticipated a meeting. It was foreseeable. She had known Donald was in New York.

As well as fear she felt guilt, which she was unused to. She promised herself to write to Donald to tell him. As soon as he got back from New Haven, only a few months, they would meet. She would introduce him to Rudy, he would meet Laurel. He would get to know his daughter.

On the way to the airport after their wedding, approaching the Hogarth Roundabout, Bella and Guy had seen something bizarre. Their driver, trying to beat some sluggish traffic, had moved into the outer lane and they found themselves drawing up behind a small pick-up truck which carried a strange cargo. From a distance they had been intrigued to see a man apparently standing upright in the truck, head and bare shoulders outlined against the blue cab, arms thrust aloft in protest. The sight agitated Bella.

'What *is* it?' she said.

Drawing nearer, they could make out that it was a statue, not a man; and then they saw that it was not a man but a centaur, with a man's torso and the strong hind quarters of a horse. An angry centaur, secured with ropes and lifting up his arms to rage against the curbing of his powers, against the indignity of his transportation. It was an extraordinary sight, exhilarating, surreal.

'*I* know what it is.'

Guy had read about the statue in a newspaper, only a few days before. It was quite a famous piece, and was *en route* to or from some gallery in Ireland, on loan. He could not remember the details.

'I'm surprised that's how they shift him. You'd have thought they'd crate him up.'

'Perhaps they did and he smashed his way out,' Bella had suggested.

Donald's sister Sukey telephoned to New Haven from Lincoln so that he should not have the shock of learning about Bella's remarriage for the first time from a newspaper – it was in all the British papers and on the TV news. She had not phoned at once. She had worried about it; but then she reckoned, if it were her she would want to know. It was one thing knowing about somebody's plans – if he did – and another thing hearing that they had done what they said they'd do.

It had given Donald a bit of a shock, hearing his sister's voice (it must have been well after midnight in Lincoln), and dreading to hear, since long-distance calls were not her style, that his sister Janet, or one of her boys or Alex, her husband, had died. A marriage was not so grave, compared with death – nowhere near as final. And he was grateful to Sukey that he could hear the news in the privacy of his rented house and did not have to wait to shed his terrible tears, calling out and staggering about the place, crashing against the walls and falling into the furniture and his suitcase, still unpacked.

On the way back to his digs after the next day's rehearsal Donald's car drove off the road and into a small pond. He had been on a minor road for some reason, deserted at that time of night; for some reason; perhaps to escape the near-blizzard, which the light snow flurries of the early evening had turned into; perhaps thinking to escape the monotony of the parkway. Late at night the long straight roads had a way of staring back at him through the windscreen, running footage that he did not want to see.

chapter 35

The task of telephoning someone to bereave them on their honeymoon was hideous. Jacques de Santis had first met Bella and Donald in the early happy days, around the time of the celebrated *Macbeth*. For that very reason, if he tried to put himself in Bella's place, he would wish to hear the bad news in a voice from the past rather than learn it from a stranger. Bella and her husband were staying on one of the Balearic Islands. Jacques knew the hotel, one of those which offer serviced bungalows instead of suites, for famous and fabulously wealthy folk, who want to be alone but not to have to cook. Add on an extra hour – six hours' difference. It would be just around dinner-time in Spain. What a bloody deed. He decided he must wait another hour, and in the meantime called Tim back at the Long Wharf for a fuller briefing, in case Bella were collected enough to want details. In his experience there was a terrible hunger to know everything. Information became an analgesic to keep understanding at a bearable distance.

At last Jacques dialled and got straight through to the hotel. He hoped he would get the new husband. Bella and Guy had been drinking champagne cocktails on their balcony, watching the sea. Bella had just come indoors to fetch a shawl. They were not expecting calls.

'Bella? It's Jacques here.'

'Who?' She had heard the name all right, but it took her by surprise.

'Jacques. Jacques de Santis.'

She put her hand over the mouthpiece. 'It's Jacques de Santis, darling,' she said, across the room. 'He must be at the hotel. Do you mind seeing him? . . . Jacques! How amazing! Are you on the island? How did you know I was here?'

But as she finished asking the question her mouth dried up, her heart began pounding.

'Bella, I'm in New York.'

She sat down on the bed. 'Yes.'

She listened to Jacques, whom she loved. He made a mess of it.

'I thought I better call you, Bella. I don't know whether you'll be seeing the papers, since you're on your honeymoon . . .' His voice was breaking up.

'No. I haven't seen any papers, Jacques . . .'

There was a long pause.

'Jacques . . . Tell me . . .'

It took a long time for him to speak. All his preparation went for nothing. It was on himself that the weight fell as he tried to say the words and could not. Bella, suspended, beginning to break without knowing the reason, held on to the phone. Guy came towards her, but she lifted up her hand. He understood and withdrew.

'I'm sorry, Bella.'

She heard sniffing. She had a vivid picture of Jacques wiping his nose with one of his big plaid handkerchiefs.

'It's all right, Jacques. It's all right.'

So Bella was forced to be Jacques' therapy, a band of steel around her ribs so that she did not breathe too deep, and could hang on to calm. He got control of himself until he could speak at last. 'Donald . . .'

'Yes.'

'Last night. He was in a smash.'

'A car?'

'Yes.'

She waited; foolishly asked, 'Is he all right?'

'No.'

Ease me with death . . .

'He's dead.'

Except it be too late . . .

He told her what had happened. The play in New Haven. The car. The snow. The pond. She said, 'Will you let us know where – what is going to happen?' She meant the funeral. 'Here is Guy.'

Now she handed over the phone to Guy and he wrote down Jacques' number on the pad by the bedside lamp, spoke a little longer, in a low voice, thanked Jacques for his considerateness and made an arrangement to speak with him again soon.

Alice's sister Danielle was one of nature's eavesdroppers. She worked in a coffee shop in New Haven, which allowed her to exercise her flair. Any number of reasons for Donald's death were found and offered, and of course drink was one, and that was pretty much substantiated.

The guy had one too many and fell asleep at the wheel. He was not used to driving on the right side of the road.

Ah, but why was he drunk?

He had a lot to drink about, if you believed what people said. He had a problem. Hadn't he just been divorced?

His wife, ex-wife, was that pretty British actress – she was in *Harpers* – hadn't she just remarried?

How good an actor was he?

Damn good. In films anyhow. He was going to open in a play at the Long Wharf.

Maybe he didn't like his role. Maybe he wasn't happy with his performance. Maybe that's why he was drinking.

He'd only just gotten there.

Lucky he didn't smash into someone else.

Lucky he chose a good spot for it. Seems the car had failed to follow the bend in the road, simply went right on into the pond. The pond was not that deep, but deep enough.

Sounds like he knew what he was doing.

Sounds like he was too drunk to know what he was doing.

That's the story!

*

Bella had married Guy, a business man, a man of some grace. His success in business, which was immense, came not from any ruthlessness, but from his unusual sensitivity to the people he did his deals with. As a child he had had to learn to mediate between two warring parents, and to understand and to supply their needs – a painful education that had stood him in good stead. He understood Bella. He thought she should go to the funeral.

'Think about it, darling. Very carefully. Please. I know how you feel just now, but I think it might actually be quite a good thing for you to go. If you're trying to spare me, don't. Don't think about me.'

He voiced only the suggestion that it might be a good thing – he was careful to put it no more strongly. In fact he thought it essential that she go, for himself as well as for her.

Guy's generosity and support had already been so great that, listening to his uncluttered argument against going on with their honeymoon, Bella thought him truly heroic and told him so. This was the most generous of all his beautiful wedding gifts, and she decided the only way she could express her gratitude was to return the gift. She too talked straight, or thought she did. Her counter-arguments directly reflected his own dazzling simplicity.

She was matter-of-fact.

'If we go back to England – and you would have to come too, I know that, I know I couldn't face the journey alone. Well – don't you see – we couldn't come back. Could we? If we go away now, we simply could not come back, after the funeral and everything. And then this place, which is so magical, would be destroyed for us for good. We would never be able to come back here. Even in these few days it's come to mean so much to me. I can't describe it . . .' She had nowhere to put her distress.

They considered other possibilities: abandoning the honeymoon, starting all over again, later; but that threw up too many difficulties. Later when? Given their crazy schedules, could they be sure of finding any time later? Even if they did, it would be a nonsense, unreal. 'Macabre,' she thought, but did not say it.

Yet there was something almost macabre in the real reason that prevented her from leaving. It was a risible, irrational logic which she felt in her bones, which disturbed her: she did not want to go to Donald's funeral because Donald would be there. Besides, even if it were the best thing for her, as Guy implied, what right had she to go to Donald's funeral? If there were rights in these matters. Sukey and Janet, Donald's sisters, and their families had rights – and Claire. Bella's presence could only add to the pool of pain. And she was not sure she could face them. The sacrifice that Guy proposed, of giving up the honeymoon, was wise, but it was beyond Bella's reach. She could not accept it.

They stayed where they were. They continued to swim, to be lazy, to enjoy the island. To the outward eye the honeymoon continued; but the magic, as they say, was gone.

chapter 36

Two wrongs do not make a right, they say that too. Bella's sense of failing Guy had a clarity that was almost therapeutic. It seemed sometimes all that she could be sure of.

After ten days they returned from Mallorca to Guy's house in Chester Terrace, and soon afterwards Bella received an unexpected visit – one which, left to herself, she might have attempted to avoid. She had gone for her usual walk round the perimeter of the park, an afternoon ritual that calmed her, at a time when not many people were about: mothers with young children, old men sitting on benches gazing across the empty playing fields, foreign students at a loss between English lessons and the English. She liked seeing life going on at a distance, had no wish to see it close up. She could not bring herself to work again yet. A little more time, she told herself.

She let herself in at the front door, not wishing to disturb Mrs Rennie; but, hearing her, the housekeeper hurried out of the kitchen to tell her that Mr Guy was in the drawing room upstairs with – someone whose name Bella could not catch. She guessed that Mrs Rennie had grasped only some of its elements. In the downstairs cloakroom hung a smart bright coat woven in a broad checked pattern with a gold brooch pinned to it, in the shape of a leaf with a drop of diamond dew. A soft pull-on hat in white chenille. Who wore a hat?

Guy had heard her come in too. He met her at the foot of the stairs.

'Darling. Your mother's here. Do you want to see her? It's perfectly all right if not, I promise.' (If he said it, this must be so, Bella thought.) 'She telephoned while you were out. I persuaded her to come, but only on the understanding that she can go away at once if you'd rather not see her. In some ways, you know, it may be better, for both of you, to be thrown in like this. That was my thinking, anyhow. Take your time.'

Bella nodded, dazed, but she had learned to trust Guy. She followed him up the curving staircase and he opened the door for her. 'I'll see to some tea,' he said, and closed the door gently behind her.

A woman of about her own height with sandy gold hair restrained in a low bun stood looking out at the trees. She wore a pale jacket and trousers, with a cowl-necked jumper of duck-egg blue silk. She turned as the door closed, and at the sight of Bella her hands came up across her breast. The two women stood looking at each other.

'I'm sorry, my darling. Tell me to go away. Guy insisted I come. He said you needed someone – not him. It's true, Walter's no use in these situations.' Irene Navarro hesitated; then she held out her arms and Bella gave up, covered her face and sobbed.

Mrs Rennie, discretion itself, wheeled in tea twenty minutes later, and said that Mr Guy had some urgent business and would join them in a while. Bella went upstairs and washed her face, came back and sat down facing her mother on the long striped sofa and they had tea, another sustaining ritual. She offered her mother one of Mrs Rennie's perfect fruit scones. She took one herself. She handed raspberry jam and butter. A feeling incongruously mixed of calm and absurdity possessed Bella; but, for the first time since she had heard of Donald's death, she had a sense that she might one day be able to breathe again, and she did not question it.

'How long have you been in London? How long are you here for?' She asked the immediate, social questions.

'Not long. It depends.' Bella had to get used to her mother's

Boston accent. 'I came to see you. I came when I heard about Donald. So hard for you. And I'm afraid it will get harder.'

Bella, looking at her mother's suntanned face, and into eyes that were very like her own, bowed once again to Guy's wisdom. He was trying whatever means he could, in the hope that they might still pass out of danger and not themselves fall foul of all the wreckage of the past. He understood that – however great his understanding – thoughts she could not express to him went on stifling her.

For the moment she did not try to measure the strange contrary comforts of this woman's presence. Her mother, yet a total stranger; a woman to whom she was linked but not bonded; a woman who had hurt instead of protecting her and to whom therefore she owed nothing; so that all the unreasoning resentment and anger Bella had directed against Donald, for inflicting the unforgivable final hurt of dying, no longer felt out of place.

Curiously, though her mother's presence released her to speak – so much confusion and grief – it also made speech less necessary. Bella felt that there would be time. Too much had been wasted.

They spent the next days together, walking, explaining. Bella talked about Donald – how well he and her mother would have got on.

'I'm sure of it. I already loved him on stage.'

'Did you see him on stage?'

'Oh of course! I saw you both, dear. Not often. A couple of times. You're not so bad yourself!'

'Why did you never come to see me?' Bella asked. They both knew that Bella did not mean backstage visiting. Her mother sighed.

It surprised Bella to learn that her mother did see Walter Provan, and a passing reference of her mother's to Marion Hunter surprised her still more. When Bella asked Irene, 'Have you seen Pa this time?' Irene replied that Walter had come straight up to town when he heard that she was there. 'He told me about this woman Marion, who sounds very nice and all that. I told him he ought to marry her. She'll leave him if he's not careful. He doesn't learn. He's too old for such goings-on. I sometimes think he still imagines I'll divorce Federico and come back to him.'

'What do you mean?'

'Oh, you know as well as I do what an incorrigible flirt your father is. Well – it's not even that. He gets himself into these situations.'

Bella's expression checked Irene for a moment. 'Pa does?'

'Well, you know that! You do know that's why I left him? It's so silly.'

'I thought you left him for Federico.'

'Oh I did! Federico was the most marvellous opportunity – too marvellous. But really, it all started out with me trying to get even with your father. I'd had just about enough. It was a mistake – a benign mistake as it's turned out, but still a mistake. But at that time I do believe that whatever I did would have been a mistake. There was no right decision . . . I was terribly in love with your father.'

Irene, seeing Bella's look of bewilderment, went on.

'Once we were embarked the whole thing developed a momentum of its own – the divorce just went on through. I let Walter divorce me, so that it wouldn't hurt his career – but of course it never occurred to me that he would ask for custody – sole custody. Or that he would get it! I was devastated. I realize now the thought of losing you as well terrified him. But you know all this?' Irene sounded less sure. She too had begun to look puzzled.

'All I know is that you left Pa for someone else and that it broke his heart. But of course,' Bella reflected, 'I don't really know that. He never talks about it.'

'Oh! I see.' Irene gave a wry laugh. 'He told you about my one "someone else", not about his dozen "someone elses"?' She paused and regarded Bella sadly. 'My darling child. All these years – how afraid poor Walter must have been that he would lose you too. How you must have been hating me.'

In the evenings Bella and Irene and Guy would go to a concert or the opera, have supper together at home or out – quiet times, like three old friends. Irene wanted to go riding in Rotten Row. It horrified her that Bella had never learned to ride but she insisted that it was never too late, and took her for her first riding lesson.

'When you come to visit, Federico will teach you. He is the best teacher in the world!'

One afternoon Irene told Bella that she had seen Walter that morning. 'I've told him that you know my side of the story now.'

'What did he say?' Bella asked.

'Poor Walter, he looked quite frightened. I told him that you might be angry with him for a while. He's very anxious. Perhaps you'll call him.'

Bella did not answer. Once, she used to imagine that the past stayed where it was and became history, complete and unalterable. Now she saw it seething and shifting and cracking open and resettling, no longer the same reassuring solid ground to tread on.

'He loves you very much,' her mother said. 'Don't be too hard on him.'

It made Guy happy to know, when Irene begged them to come and visit her in Buenos Aires, that Bella would certainly, at long last, make that journey. He made it himself and valued his new friendship with Federico and Irene; but he went alone. After being married only ten months Guy and Bella parted. They remained regretful friends, meeting from time to time, keeping in touch, watching out for each other. He still would never admit that the failure was hers, but Bella seemed to need to feel it to be so, and he allowed her the strength of her feeling. That was a fact that they could face. Bella could face Guy. It was a relief to be dealing with one situation that she could understand. They parted, and she felt it a relief to be on her own. She would not allow Guy to keep her; and besides he saw that she needed to work and needed the excuse of necessity. From time to time she would emerge from her solitude, and she worked hard and well, mostly in television and the theatre.

chapter 37

Bella had found fault with quite a few film scripts, good parts, and turned them down, before she realized that she had become allergic to films, to filming, the whole process. She did not want to see herself.

'Theatre, radio – circus if you like – but no film, no television,' she instructed Bill Forster, and Bill sighed. Bella had not changed. Occasionally he would try to entice her out once again in front of the camera, infuriated by the waste of her and a good part and good money; but nothing, not money or ten weeks in Tahiti, or the prospect of working with old friends could move her. He had to grit his teeth and watch the work go to lesser talents.

One of the big drama schools asked her to take some workshops and she discovered she had another gift. She joined the staff, as an illustrious practitioner, and took workshops when she was not in the theatre, and sometimes even when she was, rehearsals permitting. Lindon Grant was also on the staff, another practitioner. Bella liked to tease him by introducing him to people as her 'old singing coach'. They rediscovered one another with relief and pleasure. It was a leap back in time to go with him for meals, to resume their odd symbiosis. He seemed the same as ever, except that he was as bruised now as she had been then – chastened by the breaking up of his marriage. They treated each other gently. After a year, a little to their surprise, they married, and it worked. Occasionally they looked at each other and wondered why.

'Perhaps we don't expect too much of each other,' Bella ventured.

'Perhaps we know each other too well to expect anything at all. So everything is a bonus!' suggested Lindon.

They had each observed the other's struggles from a distance, and perhaps that had endowed their dealings with a necessary compassion. They pursued their careers, following separate courses, keeping an eye on one another and an ear open. They were glad to meet at the end of the day.

One afternoon Bella emerged from the tube at Goodge Street on her way to take a class. The warm rush of air from the Underground gave way to an intermittent wind that was shifting the low clouds, even pushing them apart to allow glimpses of blue. As she rounded the corner of Tottenham Court Road and Tiverton Street a man came out of a newsagent's shop and swung down the street a little way in front of her. She noticed his coat, which she liked, a dark raincoat, large and loose, made of a fine silky fabric with a sheen to it. It moved beautifully, floating behind and around him, caught up by strong gusts of wind that chased down the street. It was a confident coat. The man carried himself with a matching, billowing arrogance. He was tall and had thick white hair, cut short at the sides, longer on top, up to the minute; the back of his neck was tanned. It was the white hair that prevented Bella from understanding at first that this was Tony Tell. She knew that he had moved to the States and spent most of his time in Los Angeles. It must be almost fifteen years since she had seen him.

He stopped at the traffic lights and she was forced to catch up with him; but she took care to stand behind, a little to his right – he was watching the traffic coming from the left along Gower Street. Then, for no reason, he turned 180 degrees and she was looking into his eyes – light, polite lion's eyes. This time it was Tony who looked away, and beneath his tan she witnessed a blush that spread from the top of his shirt collar to the roots of his white hair. The lights changed. Bella crossed the road and left Tony still standing on the pavement.

In an effort to wean them away from relying too much on props and elaborate business, Bella had set her class to study Racine's *Andromaque*. They had resisted the play at first. They found the story dull and they presumed the characters to be antique and dusty ciphers. The lack of action floored them. They had no idea how to tackle the duologues, scenes of extended speeches following one after another.

'Nothing happens,' they complained. 'It's not dramatic.'

She played them a recording of Sarah Bernhardt speaking Phèdre, and though only a few of them knew French they were dazzled. They could not believe the speed and the intensity of it.

'It sort of pins you to the wall,' one of them said.

'Through the neck!' added another. They began to enjoy the combination of discipline and extremes of passion, the swoops from ecstasy to despair, 'like stepping on a rollercoaster'.

Today they had prepared scenes from the last Act, where Pyrrhus, the King of Epirus, announces to his betrothed, Hermione, his intention to marry the captive Trojan queen, Andromaque, instead of her. Left to herself Hermione, distracted with grief and frustration, veers between loathing and panic. Her confidante hurries in with the news that the wedding is about to take place, and that the temple has been entered by Orestes, whom Hermione has promised to marry, but only if he kills Pyrrhus. The student caught some of Hermione's anger, but Bella encouraged her to go further, to feel her humiliation and her hurt so that she could hate more. The girl listened, her head cocked to one side.

'I know.' She sighed. 'I know what you mean. The trouble is she is such a bitch, isn't she. She's so unreasonable. She doesn't know what she wants.'

'Hasn't anyone ever done anything awful to you, that made you want to get your own back? Think. Be spiteful. Cut off your nose,' Bella suggested.

The girl must have thought of something. The second time round she hit some ferocious exulting notes, but still she shrank from Hermione's full horror.

Scene 3 had been prepared by a second pair of students. The Orestes had an attractive broad-cheeked eager face; the girl who took over Hermione had a pale face and short black hair. Bella had noticed her early in the term and had followed her progress with interest. Though the work was not yet fully achieved she held the eye. It was her Bella watched, as Hermione listened mesmerized to Orestes' long account of the murder of Pyrrhus. She had the courage to do nothing, to show nothing, and her apparent indifference paid off. She intrigued and compelled the spectator.

'What have they done?' she murmured, very low, as if she genuinely did not understand; and then, as Orestes continued, her comprehension seemed to expand like a sponge immersed in water, or in blood, as if she were still, only now, taking in Orestes' first speech. When finally she spoke, interrupting Orestes in mid-speech, her coldness froze the audience as well as her co-actor, challenging him to answer her terrible accusations. Orestes groped for his reply – did you not yourself, here, one short hour ago, ordain his death? The last three words sent a shudder through Hermione, and as she snapped and flew into a terrifying frenzy of grief and rage, pain drenched Bella suddenly, as if a splinter of the Snow Queen's ice had melted in her heart. She bowed her head, hardly able to hear the words of Orestes' speech, which carried them to the end of the prepared scenes. It did not need a glimpse of Tony Tell to make Bella's thoughts turn to Donald. Still, after all these years since Donald's death, Bella would find herself wondering at the violence of her response to his unfaithfulness, the strength of it. Her reasons seemed so remote now. She understood them well enough, but the memory of the emotion, so far beyond reason, could still shake her.

Now, watching Hermione, it was a long time before she could

speak. She bent over her papers as if studying the text. At last she spoke, frowning, so that she could better control her face.

'Good,' she said. 'Now there's something you should always bear in mind . . .'

The warning that Bella issued to the class concerned the perils of hindsight: it was as dangerous to introduce hindsight into the moment as foreknowledge.

'A good director will always pull you up if you start anticipating the end of a scene. That's something we all tend to do, and if one person does it all the others are likely to follow. We've read the play, we know what's going to happen, and it's infectious. It can turn into a collective bad habit.'

They were, as she had said, familiar with the idea of anticipation, but they found the principle of hindsight harder to grasp. How did the effects of hindsight differ from those of anticipation?

'What is the difference?' Bella thought for a moment. 'In terms of a whole play anticipation is . . . Well, for instance – knowing that the cherry orchard is going to be chopped down. In terms of the scene, it's knowing that never in a million years is Lopahin going to manage to propose to Varya. Knowing all that in advance can cast a pall over the entire proceedings and you undercut the play.'

'Then what's hindsight?'

'Hindsight's a bit harder to define. It's got to do with character rather than plot. Obviously it's looking back after the event.' She thought about it for a moment. 'I suppose, of itself, it's too forgiving. To understand all is to forgive all – hindsight implies forgiveness. Whereas with anticipation you're leaning in towards the action – knowing the end – and you deform it. The effect of hindsight is to make you lean away. You stand back, make allowances. Jenny had trouble with Hermione earlier because she couldn't bring herself to believe anyone could be as beastly as that. That's another way of avoiding the issue. Sometimes in life we judge our own behaviour in the same way, and rationalize and find excuses, otherwise it becomes too difficult to live with ourselves – or we go mad. If you do that in performance it blurs the edges, it robs you of immediacy. It allows you to know too much too soon about why your character behaved that way *and* – which can be worse – why other characters did. You start to have too much sympathy, not enough energy. Your batteries lose charge. You start leaking.'

The class laughed.

'But you do,' Bella insisted. Blood and tears. 'You start diluting everything. Leave pity to the audience, that's up to them. You have to stay right inside that moment where the future doesn't exist, where looking back you can't believe you could ever have said or done that. *You* could never have been that person.'

It was time to end the class. They started to gather up their books and sweatshirts, chattering to each other and to her. Two or three were discussing an autobiography they had just read.

'Have you ever had that feeling, Bella? She says that she always realizes exactly how to play a part on the last night, at the curtain call!'

'Oh yes,' Bella smiled. 'Alas! I do feel that only too often.'

'*I* get that feeling in real life,' said the boy who had played Orestes, 'especially in scenes with my father.'

'How awful! To find out the secret of everything just when it's too late.'

'It's hindsight again, Bella, isn't it? Do you get that in real life as well?'

Some of the students raised their eyebrows at such a personal question, but Bella said, 'Less often now. I suppose these days I forgive myself more. That makes life a lot easier. Well – it makes it possible!' She smiled. 'But never on stage,' Bella admonished them. 'No pity there!' The class laughed again. She got up. 'I must be on my way,' she said. 'I have a rehearsal to get to. You'll all have to manage without me for the next five weeks.'

The first read-through, unusually, was not happening until the afternoon, to allow the young director, Tom Todmorden, to travel down from Glasgow after an opening night. As soon as

Bella learned that she had the morning free, she had reinstated her class at once. It would be good to keep her mind occupied during the morning, and in any case she always learned from the students.

Now they wanted to know more about her play, Shaw's *Heartbreak House* – when was it opening? They promised her they would be there. When would she be coming back to take some more workshops? Was she nervous, they asked her?

'Of course I'm nervous! The first day is always terrifying. Even if you know lots of the cast.'

But there would be more to it than nerves. Today would occasion more than the usual bumpings of the heart. The cast assembled for *Heartbreak House* was a publicist's dream: a Bob Rayner production, including Bella Provan as Hesione Hushabye, Claire Ballader as Lady Utterword, Sir Paul Stern as Captain Shotover, Sir Norman Lyon as Hector Hushabye, Aubrey Morris as Alfred Mangan, Nancy Bailey as Nurse Guinness, Michael Brodie as the Burglar, and a newcomer, Laurel Danzig, as Ellie Dunn.

In life it was not so easy to anticipate. Impossible things happen one by one, hurdle by hurdle, unforeseeable. Bella had already worked with Claire, in a production at Manchester, and had liked and admired her as she had once guessed she might. Laurel, whose existence and whose likeness to Donald was still in every way a marvel to her, she had met only briefly, reading in at the auditions for Ellie Dunn. They would get to know each other in the months to come.

The wind had grown sharper by the time Bella left the building. It thrust the clouds past the sun, and the pavements in and out of light. Bella decided against taking a taxi. She would go on foot some of the way, to get her bearings and breathe a little, and then get the bus, over on Charing Cross Road. She walked down past the University and Bedford Square, and paused for a moment to admire the umbrellas and shooting sticks in James Smith's at the corner of Bloomsbury Street, then continued along Shaftesbury Avenue and off towards St Giles to cut through Denmark Street. As she rounded the corner she saw a line of buses turning into Charing Cross Road headed by a 176, and ran to meet it as it drew up at the stop.

It was one of the new buses, which had doors where her favourite seat used to be, and no conductor – the driver collected the fares as the passengers got on. Bella climbed upstairs. To her delight, both front seats were free. From here she would still have the view of London that she loved best, crossing the river over Waterloo Bridge. The bus, which had set off again, hesitated for a moment as the traffic lights changed, and then moved forward.